Demetrius Charles Boulger

The Life of Yakoob Beg; Athalik Ghazi, and Badaulet; Ameer of Kashgar

Demetrius Charles Boulger

The Life of Yakoob Beg; Athalik Ghazi, and Badaulet; Ameer of Kashgar

ISBN/EAN: 9783337411770

Printed in Europe, USA, Canada, Australia, Japan

Cover: Foto ©Raphael Reischuk / pixelio.de

More available books at **www.hansebooks.com**

THE LIFE

OF

YAKOOB BEG;

ATHALIK GHAZI, AND BADAULET;

AMEER OF KASHGAR.

BY

DEMETRIUS CHARLES BOULGER,

MEMBER OF THE ROYAL ASIATIC SOCIETY.

WITH MAP AND APPENDIX.

LONDON:

W^M H. ALLEN & CO., 13, WATERLOO PLACE, S.W.

1878.

THE LIFE

OF

YAKOOB BEG.

TO MY FATHER,

BRIAN AUSTEN BOULGER,

I Dedicate

THE FOLLOWING PAGES, AS SOME FAINT TOKEN OF FILIAL AFFECTION

AND GRATITUDE.

PREFACE.

THE following account of the life of Yakoob Beg was written with a twofold intention. In the first place, it attempts to trace the career of a soldier of fortune, who, without birth, power, or even any great amount of genius, constructed an independent rule in Central Asia, and maintained it against many adversaries during the space of twelve years. The name of the Athalik Ghazi became so well known in this country, and his person was so exaggerated by popular report, that those who come to these pages with a belief that their hero will be lauded to the skies must be disappointed. Yakoob Beg was a very able and courageous man, and the task he did accomplish in Kashgaria was in the highest degree creditable; but he was no Timour or Babur. His internal policy was marred by his severity, and the system of terrorism that he principally adopted; and his external policy, bold and audacious as it often was, was enfeebled by periods of vacillation and doubt. Yet his career was truly remarkable. He was not the arbiter of the destinies of Central Asia, nor was he even the consistent opponent of Russian claims to supremacy therein. He was essentially of the common mould of human nature, sharing the weaknesses and the fears of ordinary men. The Badaulet, or " the fortunate one," as he was called, was essentially indebted to good fortune in many crises of his career. He cannot, in any sense, be compared to the giants produced by Central Asia in days of old; and among moderns Dost Mahomed of Afghanistan probably should rank as high as he does. Yet he gives an individuality to the history of Kashgar that it would otherwise lack. The recent triumphs of the Chinese received all their attraction to Englishmen from the decline and fall of Yakoob Beg, the hero they had erected in the country north of Cashmere.

In the second place, the following pages strive to bring before the English reader the great merits of China as a governing power; and this object is really the more important of the two. It is absolutely necessary for this country to remember that there are only three Great Powers in Asia, and of these China is in many respects the foremost. Whereas both England and Russia are simply conquering Governments, China is a mighty and self-governing country. China's rule in Eastern Turkestan and Jungaria is one of the most instructive pages in the history of modern Asia, yet it may freely be admitted that the brief career of Yakoob Beg gave an interest to the consideration of the Chinese in Central Asia that that theme might otherwise have failed to supply. The authorities used in the compilation of the facts upon which the following pages have been erected are principally and above all the official Report of Sir Douglas Forsyth, and the files of the *Tashkent* and *Pekin Gazettes* since the beginning of 1874. Mr. Shaw's most interesting work on "High Tartary," Dr. Bellew's "Kashgar," and Gregorieff's work on "Eastern Turkestan," have also been consulted in various portions of the narrative. A vast mass of newspaper articles have likewise been laid under contribution for details which have not been noticed anywhere else.

In conclusion, the author would ask the English reader to consider very carefully what the true lesson of Chinese valour and statesmanship may be for us, because those qualities have now become the guiding power in every Indian border question, from Siam and Birma to Cashmere. Mr. Schuyler's " Turkestan," which still maintains its place as the leading work on Central Asia, although not treating on the affairs of Kashgar, has been frequently referred to for the course of affairs in Khokand; but, in the main, Dr. Bellew's historical narrative in Sir D. Forsyth's Report has been followed.

CONTENTS.

CHAPTER VIII.

CHAPTER IX.

CHAPTER X.

CHAPTER XI.

CHAPTER XII.

CHAPTER XIII.

CHAPTER XIV.

APPENDIX.

YAKOOB BEG.

CHAPTER I.

GEOGRAPHICAL DESCRIPTION OF KASHGAR.

THE state of Kashgar, which comprises the western portion of Eastern or Chinese Turkestan, has been defined as being bounded on the north by Siberia, on the south by the mountains of Cashmere, on the east by the Great Desert of Gobi, and on the west by the steppe of "High Pamere." This description, while sufficiently correct for general speaking, admits of more detail in a work dealing at some length with that country. Strictly, the name Kashgar or Cashgar applies only to the city, and it was not until after the time of Marco Polo, when it was the most populous and opulent town in the whole region, that it became used for the neighbouring country. The correct name is either Little Bokhara or Eastern Turkestan, and the Chinese call it Sule. Recent writers have styled the territory of the Athalik Ghazi Kashgaria. It certainly extended through a larger portion of Chinese Turkestan than did any past native rule in Kashgar, the Chinese of course excepted. The definition given above of the limits of Kashgar states that on the north it is bounded by Siberia, but this is erroneous, for the extensive territory of Jungaria or Mugholistan intervenes. Jungaria under the Chinese was known as Ili from its capital, and now under the Russians is spoken of as

Kuldja, another name for the same city. This very
extensive and important district was included in the
same government with Kashgar when the Chinese
dominated in all this region from their head-quarters
at Ili; but in the final settlement after the disruption
of the Chinese power in 1863, while Kashgar fell to
the Khoja Buzurg Khan, and the eastern portion of
Jungaria, together with the cities of Kucha, Karashar,
and Turfan south of the Tian Shan range, to the
Tungani; Kuldja or Ili was occupied by the Russians.
The frontier line between Kuldja and Kashgar is very
clearly marked by the Tian Shan, and the same effectual
barrier divides the continent into two well-defined
divisions from Aksu to Turfan and beyond. Eastern
Turkestan is, therefore, bounded on the north by the
Tian Shan, and on the south the Karakoram Mountains
form a no less satisfactory bulwark between it and
Kohistan and Cashmerian Tibet. As has been said, on
the west the steppe of Pamir and on the east the desert
of Gobi present distinct and secure defences against
aggression from without in those directions. There are
few states in Asia with a more clearly marked position
than that of which we have been speaking. Nature
seems to have formed it to lead an isolated and independent existence, happy and prosperous in its own resources
and careless of the outer world; but its history has been
of a more troubled character, and at only brief intervals
has its natural wealth been so fostered as to make it that
which it has been called, "the Garden of Asia." This
condition of almost continual warfare and disturbance
during centuries, has left many visible marks on the
external features of the country, and in nothing is this
more strikingly evident than in the small population.
A region which contains at the most moderate estimate
250,000 square miles, is believed by the highest
authorities to contain less than 1,000,000 inhabitants.
In breadth Kashgaria may be said to extend from
longitude E. 73° to 89°, and in width from latitude N.

36° to 43°; but the ancient kingdom of Kashgar has been always considered to have reached only to Aksu, a town about 300 miles north-east of Kashgar. When the Chinese about fifty years ago conceded certain trade privileges to Khokand, they were not to have effect east of Aksu; this fact seems conclusive as to the recognized limits of the ancient dynasty of Kashgar. The capital of this district, which at one time has been a flourishing kingdom under a native ruler, at another a tributary of some Tartar conqueror, and then distracted by the struggles of his effete successors, and at a third time a subject province of the Chinese, has fluctuated as much as the fortunes of the state itself. Now it has been Yarkand, now Kashgar, and yet again, on several occasions, Aksu. The claims of Kashgar seem to have prevailed in the long run, for, although Yarkand is still the larger city, Yakoob Beg established his capital at Kashgar, and made that town known throughout the whole of Asia by the means of his government.

Kashgar is situated in a plain in the north of the province, and the small river on which it is built is known as the Kizil Su. Immediately beyond it the country becomes hilly and mountainous, until in the far distance may be seen the snow-clad peaks of the Tian Shan, and the Aksai Plateau. Although the population is barely 30,000, there is now an air of brisker activity in the bazaars and caravanserais of this capital than in any other city in the country. The trade carried on with Russia in recent years has given some life to the place; but few, if any, merchants proceed more inland than this, whether they come from Khokand or from Kuldja. The town stretches on both sides of the river, which is crossed by a wooden bridge; but there are no buildings of any pretensions for external beauty or internal comfort. The *orda* or palace of the Ameer, which is in Yangy Shahr, five miles from the city, is a large gloomy barrack of a place with several buildings within each other; the outer ones are occupied by the household troops and by the court officials, and the inner one of all is set apart for the family and *serai* of the ruler himself. In connection with this is a hall of audience, in which he receives in solemn state such foreigners as it seems politic for him to honour. In the old days, Kashgar used to be a strongly fortified position, but the only remains of its former strength are the ruins which are strewn freely all around. Kashgar is, therefore, an open and quite defenceless town, and lies completely at the mercy of any invader who might come along the high road from Aksu or Bartchuk, or across the mountains from Khokand or Kuldja; but at Yangy Shahr, about five miles south of Kashgar, Yakoob Beg constructed a strong fort, where he deposited all his treasure, and this may be taken to be the citadel of Kashgar as well as the residence of the ruler. Yangy Shahr means new city, and as a fortification erected by a Central Asian potentate with very limited means, it must be considered to be a very creditable piece of military workmanship. The Andijanis or Khokandian merchants who have at various times settled here, form a very important class in this town in particular, and it was they who more than any one else contributed to the success of the invasion of Buzurg Khan and Mahomed Yakoob. It is, however, said that these merchant classes had become to some extent dissatisfied with the late state of things, whether because Yakoob Beg did not fulfil all his promises, or for some other reason, is not clear. If Kashgar under its late rule was not restored to that prosperous condition which excited the admiration of Marco Polo, and the Chinese traveller, Hwang Tsang, before him, it may be considered to have been as fairly well-doing as any other city in either Turkestan, while life and property were a great deal more secure than in some we could mention.

Situated about half-way on the road to Yarkand is Yangy Hissar, a town which has always been of importance both as a military position and as a place of trade. It has greatly fallen into decay, however, but still possesses a certain amount of its former influence from being a military post, and from the exceptional fertility of the neighbouring country.

Yarkand, about eighty miles as the crow flies, and 120 by road, to the south-east of Kashgar, is still the most populous of all the cities of Eastern Turkestan. It lies in the open plain on the Yarkand river, and its walls, four miles in circuit, testify to its former greatness. Under the Chinese it was quite the most flourishing town in the region, and even now Sir Douglas Forsyth estimates that it contains 40,000 people, while the surrounding country has nearly 200,000 more. The fruit gardens and orchards, which extend in a wide belt round it, give an air of peculiar prosperity to the country, and quite possibly induce travellers to take a too sanguine view of the resources of the country. In addition to the abundance of fruit and grain produce that is brought into the city for sale, there is a large and profitable business carried on in leather. Yarkand has almost a monopoly of this article, and the consumption of it is very great indeed. The Ameer himself took large quantities yearly for his army, for, in addition to that required for boots and saddles, many of his regiments wore uniforms of that substance.

But, although Yarkand is the chief market-place of the richest province, and although its population is thriving and energetic, there is a general *consensus* of opinion that it has become much less prosperous and much more of a rural town since the transference of the seat of government to Kashgar, and the disappearance of Chinese merchants with the Chinese ruler. A very intelligent merchant of the town replied as follows to questions put to him, as to the Chinese and native rulers, and it will be seen that it was especially favourable to the claims of the Chinese as the better masters.

" What you see on market-day now, is nothing to the life and activity there was in the time of the Khitay.

To-day the peasantry come in with their fowls and eggs, with their cotton and yarn, or with their sheep and cattle and horses for sale, and they go back with printed cotton, a fur cap, or city made boots, or whatever domestic necessaries they may require, and always with a good dinner inside them; and then we shut up our shops and stow away our goods till next week's market-day brings back our customers. Some of us, indeed, go out with a small venture in the interim to the rural markets around, but our great day is market-day in town. It was very different in the Khitay time. People then bought and sold every day, and market-day was a much jollier time. There was no Kazi Rais, with his six Muhtasib, armed with the *dira* to flog people off to prayer, and drive the women out of the streets, and nobody was bastinadoed for drinking spirits and eating forbidden meats. There were mimics and acrobats, and fortune-tellers and story-tellers, who moved about amongst the crowd and diverted the people. There were flags and banners and all sorts of pictures floating at the shop fronts; and there was the *jallab*, who painted her face and decked herself in silks and laces to please her customers." And then, replying to a question whether the morals were not more depraved under this system than under the strict Mahomedan rule of the Athalik Ghazi, the same witness went on to say—"Yes, perhaps so. There were many rogues and gamblers too, and people did get drunk and have their pockets picked. But so they do now, though not so publicly, because we are under Islam, and the shariàt is strictly enforced."

This very graphic piece of evidence gives a clearer picture of the two systems of government, than perhaps paragraphs of explanatory writing; and, to return to the immediate subject before us, it shows that Yarkand has deteriorated in wealth and population since the Chinese were expelled from it fifteen years ago.

Khoten is situated 150 miles south-east of Yarkand,

and about ninety miles due east of Sanju. It lies on the northern base of the Kuen Lun Mountains, and is the most southern city of any importance in Kashgaria. Under the Chinese, it was one of the most flourishing centres of industry, and as the *entrepôt* of all trade with Tibet it held a bustling active community. The Chinese called it Houtan, and even now it is locally called Ilchi. In addition to the wool and gold imported from Tibet, it possessed gold mines of its own in the Kuen Lun range, and was widely celebrated for its musk, silk, and jade. It likewise has suffered from the departure of the Chinese; and the energy and wealth of that extraordinary people have found, in the case of this city also, a very inadequate substitute in the strict military order and security introduced by Yakoob Beg.

Ush Turfan, New Turfan, is a small town on the road from Kashgar to Aksu, and is not to be confounded with the better known Turfan which is situated in the far east on the highway to Kansuh. This latter town is called Kuhna Turfan, or Old Turfan, to distinguish it from the other. Ush Turfan, without ever having been a place of the first importance, derived very considerable advantage from its position on the road followed by the Chinese caravans, and Yakoob Beg converted it into a strong military position by constructing several forts there.

Aksu, one of the old capitals of Kashgar, may fairly be called the third city of the state, although it has, perhaps, more than any other declined since the expulsion of the Khitay. Before that event took place there was a road across the mountains to Ili, by the Muzart glacier, and relays of men were kept continually employed in maintaining this delicately constructed road in a state fit for passage both on foot and mounted. But all this has been discontinued for many years now, and not only is the road quite impassable, but it would require much labour and more outlay to restore it to its former utility. In the neighbourhood of this town there are rich mines of lead, copper, and sulphur. These have, practically speaking, been untouched in recent years. Coal is also the ordinary fuel among the inhabitants; and both in intelligence as well as in worldly prosperity, the good people of Aksu used to be entitled to a foremost position among the Kashgari. As a consequence of the blocking up of the Muzart Pass, the old trade with Kuldja has completely disappeared, and all communications with this Russian province are now carried on by the Narym Pass to Vernoe. This change benefits the city of Kashgar, but is a decided loss to Aksu. Aksu may still justly rank as an important place, and under very probable contingencies may regain all the ground it has lost. In conclusion, we may say that Yakoob Beg has converted its old walls and castles into fortifications, which are said to be capable of resisting the fire of modern artillery.

We have enumerated six cities—Kashgar, Yangy Hissar, Yarkand, Khoten, Ush Turfan, and Aksu—and these constitute the territory of Kashgar proper. At one time, indeed, it was called Alty Shahr, or six cities, from this fact. In addition to these may be mentioned, in modern Kashgaria, Sirikul, or Tashkurgan, in the extreme south-west, which is principally of importance as the chief post on the frontier of Afghanistan. Near Sirikul are Badakshan and Wakhan, and it has been asserted that Shere Ali, of Afghanistan, viewed with a suspicious eye the presence of Kashgar in this quarter. It is quite certain that he would not have tolerated that further advance along the Pamir, which Yakoob Beg seemed on several occasions inclined to make. Sirikul commands the northern entrance of the Baroghil Pass, and has consequently been often mentioned in recent accounts of this road to India.

Maralbashi, or Bartchuk, a military post of some strength, is strategically important, as being placed at the junction of the roads from Kashgar and Yarkand, which lead by the bed of the Yarkand river to Kucha.

But it possesses greater interest for us, as being the chief town of the district inhabited by the extraordinary tribe of the Dolans. These people are in the most backward state of intelligence that it is possible to imagine human beings to be capable of. In physical strength and stature they are, perhaps, the most miserable objects on the face of the earth, but their social position is still more deplorable. Some of their customs are of the most disgusting character, and their dwellings, such as they are, are of the rudest kind and subterranean. Travellers who have seen them in the larger cities, say that all the rumours that have been circulated about them do not exaggerate the true facts of the case; and the most pitiable part of the matter is, that they have become so resigned to their degraded position, that they are averse to any measure calculated to improve their existence. They have been compared to the Bhots of Tibet, but these latter are quite superior beings in comparison with them. They are treated with contempt and derision by all the neighbouring peoples.

Kucha is, or rather was, another very flourishing city which has never recovered the loss of Chinese wealth, and the subsequent disturbances during the Tungan wars. At one time Kucha had at the least 50,000 people, and it was not less famed than Aksu for the resources and ingenuity of its people. But now it is almost a deserted city. The greater part of the old town is a mass of ruins, and during the nine years that have elapsed since the Tungani were crushed by the Athalik Ghazi, scarcely anything has been done to repair the damage caused in those very destructive wars.

Korla, Kouralia, or Kouroungli, as it has been named, and Karashar, two towns which lie to the east of Kucha, have likewise never revived from the period of anarchy and bloodshed, through which the whole of this district has passed; but even the state of these places contrasts favourably with the far worse ruin wrought at Turfan. Turfan, perhaps more than any other, profited by the trade with China, for, although it may not itself have been as rich as either Aksu or Kucha, it derived a certain source of income as the rendezvous of all the caravans proceeding either east or west, or north to Urumtsi and Chuguchak. Very often a delay of several weeks took place, before merchants had arranged all the details for crossing the Tian Shan to Guchen, or for proceeding on to Hamil through the desert, and Turfan flourished greatly thereby. Now its streets are desolate, the whole country round it is represented to be a desert, and all its former activity and brightness have completely disappeared. Yakoob Beg had extended his rule a short distance east of Turfan, to a place called Chightam, but Turfan may be styled his most eastern possession.

We have now given a somewhat detailed description of the chief cities of Kashgaria, and in doing so we have distinctly intended thereby to convey the impression to the reader that it is only these and their suburbs that were at all productive under the late *régime*. To those who have been to Kashgar, nothing has remained more vividly impressed on their mind, than the exceedingly prosperous appearance of the farms in the belt of country from Yarkand to Kashgar; but at the same time this wealth of foliage and of blossom has only made the barrenness of the intervening and surrounding country more palpable. The farms are certainly not small in extent, but rather isolated from each other, and surrounded by orchards of plums, apples, and other fruit trees, in which they are completely embowered. A Kashgarian village is not a main street with a line of cottages and a few large farms; but it is a conglomeration of farmsteads covering a very extensive area of country, and presenting to the eye of a stranger rather a thinly peopled district than a community of villagers. Again, although the soil is naturally fertile, the system of agriculture is of an exhaustive character, and it seems probable that only a small portion of the land on each farm is at all productive. But these settlements, which present an exterior of rural happiness and simplicity, are but oases in an enormous extent of barren country. If each proprietor seems to possess more land than he can require, and if the fertile soil produces bountifully that which is unskilfully sown therein, the total amount of land under cultivation is still very limited indeed. Worse still, the soil is gradually exhausted, and as the system of sowing but one kind of grain seems to have taken deep root among the people, it is to be feared that it may be perpetuated without hope of recovery. There is a constant difficulty to be overcome, too, on account of the meagre supply of water. The general aspect of the region is barren, a bleak expanse stretches in all directions, and in the distance on three sides the outlines of lofty ranges complete the panorama. The scarcely marked bridle track that supplies the place of a highway in every direction except where the Chinese have left permanent tokens of their presence, offers little inducement to travellers to come thither; nor must these when they do come expect anything but the most imperfect modes of communication and of supply that a backward Asiatic district can furnish. If we wish to imagine the scene along the road from Sanju to Yarkand, we have only to visit some of the wilder of the Sussex Wealds to have it before us in miniature. The spare dried-up herbage may be still more spare, and the limestone may be more protruding on the Central Asian plain; and the wind will certainly remind you that it comes either from the desert or from the mountain regions; but you have the same undulating, dreary expanse that you have above Crowborough. The miserable sheep watched by some nomad Kirghiz will alone forcibly remind you that you are far away from the heights of the South Downs. In the far distance you will see the cloud-crested pinnacles of the Sanju Devan or of the Guoharbrum, and then the traveller cannot but remember that he is in one of the

most inaccessible regions in the world. But if these
southern roads are scarcely worthy of the name, the
great high road from Kashgar to Aksu, Kucha, Korla,
Karashar, and Turfan is a masterpiece of engineering
construction. It need not fear to brave comparison with
those of imperial Rome herself, and remains an enduring
monument to Chinese perseverance, skill, and capacity
for government. In China itself there are many great
and important highways, but there the task was facilitated by the possession of great and navigable rivers.
In Eastern Turkestan no such assistance was to be found,
and consequently this road, along which was conducted all
the traffic that passed from China to Jungaria, Kashgar,
Khokand, and Bokhara, had to be maintained in the
highest state of efficiency. To do this we cannot doubt
was a most expensive undertaking, and, not mentioning
such an exceptional work as the Muzart Pass, one that
required a very perfect organization to accomplish with
the success that for more than a century marked it.

The great drawback in the geographical position of
Kashgar, is the want of a cheap and convenient outlet
by water. The country itself suffers in a less degree
from the same cause, but with a more perfect system of
irrigation, the rivers, such as the Artosh, &c., which in
spring carry down the mountain snows, might be made
to give a more extended supply throughout western
Kashgar at all events. The climate is equable, and the
people suffer from no very prevalent disease, except in
the more mountainous parts, and in Yarkand, where
goitre is of frequent occurrence. The people themselves
seem to be frugal and honest, but indeed there are so
many races to be met with in this " middle land," that
no general description can be given of them all. The
Andijanis, or Khokandian merchants, are the most prosperous class in the community, and they appear to be,
from all accounts, possessed of more than an average
amount of business capacity in the arts of buying and
selling. The Tarantchis are the descendants of Kash-

garian labourers imported by the Chinese into Kuldja in 1762, and there is still both in the army and in the state a large number of Khitay remaining, who were permitted to pursue in secret the observances of their religion.   The other races are ill disposed towards them, and attribute all the vices they can think of to their doors.   But these Khitay managed to efface themselves in the country, and although they formed a very important minority among the males, they never appear to have been regarded in the light of a possible danger when their brethren from China should draw near. In addition to the native Kashgari, and these two important elements just mentioned, there are numerous immigrants from the border states, particularly from Khokand, to the people of whom Yakoob Beg naturally manifested especial favour.   We have now given at some length a description of the geographical features of Kashgar, and are about to follow it up with an ethnological description as well as a historical statement of the past features of the same region.   It is hoped that these preliminary chapters will clear the way from some obscurity for a correct appreciation of the career of the late Athalik Ghazi.

Kashgaria may be said to be a portion of Asia which possesses some great advantages of position and very considerable resources, but by a singularly hard fortune, except for the brief period of Chinese rule in modern times, it has been so distracted by intestine disturbances that it has retrograded further and further with each year. It is quite possible that its natural wealth has been too hastily taken for granted, and that it does not possess the necessary means of restoring itself in some degree to its former position.   This is quite possible, but the best authorities at our disposal seem to point to a more promising conclusion, and to justify us in assuming that the position, natural resources, and general condition of Kashgar will enable a strong and settled rule to raise it into a really important and flourishing confederacy.

CHAPTER II.

ETHNOGRAPHICAL DESCRIPTION OF KASHGAR.

IN the extensive region stretching from the Caspian and Black Seas to the Kizil Yart and Pamir plateaus, and from the Persian Gulf to Siberia, the two great families, the Aryan and the Turanian, have in past centuries striven for supremacy. The latter, embracing in its bosom in this part of the world the more turbulent and warlike tribes, succeeded in subjecting those who claimed the same parent stock as European nations. The Tajik or Persian is the chief representative in this region of the Aryan family, and he has now for many centuries been the subject of the Turk rulers of the various divisions of Western Turkestan. These latter are the personifiers of Turanian traditions. The Tajik appears to have been subdued, not so much by the superiority of his conqueror in the art of war, as by his own inclination to lead a peaceful and harmless life. The pure Tajik, hardly to be met with now anywhere in Asia, except in the mountainous districts of the Hindoo Koosh, is represented to us to have been of an imposing presence, with a long flowing beard, aquiline nose, and large eyes. He is generally tall and graceful; yet in Khokand and Bokhara the Tajik is at present viewed much as the Saxons were by the Normans. In those states, too, a man is spoken of by his race. He is an Usbeg, a Kipchak, a Kirghiz, or a Tajik, as the case may be, and by this means the rivalry of past ages is to some extent preserved down to the present time. It is the dissension spread, or rather the destruction of any sympathy between the various races caused, by these outward tokens of diversity in origin, that has made Western Turkestan the familiar home of intestine disturbance, which has in its turn led up to the easy dismemberment of the various Khanates by Russian intrigue and by Russian force. In Eastern Turkestan the rivalry of races has become less bitter, and in nothing is this better manifested than in the fact that there a man is described by his native town. He may be a Tajik, or an Usbeg, or a Kirghiz, or a Kipchak, too, but he is only known as a Yarkandi, or a Kashgari. And while we are at once struck by this broad and salient difference in popular custom, and consequently in popular sentiment also, between the Western and Eastern divisions of Turkestan, a slight inquiry is sufficient to show that the antipathies of the various races towards each other have become much more a thing of the past in Kashgaria than they have in the Khanates of Khokand and its neighbours. At all events, the antipathies that still prevail in that state are clearly traceable to other causes than Aryan-Turanian hostility, and are undoubtedly produced either by religious fanaticism, motives of personal ambition, or the hatred roused by Chinese pretensions on the one hand, and Khokandian on the other, to the supreme control of Kashgaria. Bearing these facts clearly in mind, it is evident that ethnographical descriptions will not make the political relations of the peoples of the state more easily intelligible ; yet, as matter of historical import, these cannot be altogether passed over in silence.

The inhabitants of the little known regions now variously known as Jungaria and Eastern Turkestan were, until recent years, considered to be of pure Tartar origin, and consequently members of the Turanian family. There are some still who believe that this definition is the most accurate. Others dispute it on various grounds, and with much plausibility. There is no question that the original inhabitants, historically speaking, were the Oigurs, or Uigurs, and these people were certainly Tartars. But frequently the Tajik merchants who traded with Kashgar in the earlier centuries of the Middle Ages, took up their abode in the country, and by degrees a large colony of Tajik immigrants was formed on the foundation of the original Oigur stock. These Tajiks gradually became Tartarised, but they still retained the unmistakable characteristics of the Aryan family. The two brothers Schlagintweit, and Mr. Shaw following in their footsteps, were the first to maintain this view, which is becoming generally accepted. We have, therefore, in Kashgar the strange spectacle of a Tajik people becoming not only unidentifiable from the Turanian stock with which it has been intermingled; but we have also a race tolerance that is unknown in any other portion of Asia. Undoubtedly the hostility of the settled and peaceful Andijani immigrant and Kashgari resident to the irreclaimable Kirghiz is deep-rooted, and, so long as the latter continues a source of danger to all peaceful communities, abiding; but even this sentiment, and the religious hatred that has at various epochs marked the political intercourse of Buddhist and Mahomedan, are probably less durable, and susceptible of greater improvement in the future, than the race antipathies that seem perennially vital among the tribes of Western Asia. The vast majority of the inhabitants of Alty Shahr are of Tajik descent. In the course of centuries the purity of their lineage has been leavened by much intermingling with Tartar blood, both at the time of the Mongol subjection and of the Chinese. In addition to these two great divisions, there are many Afghan and Badakshi settlers, who have flocked to Kashgar whenever the progress of events seemed to justify the expectation that military service in that state would prove a remunerative engagement. Many of these remained, and they have also left a clear impression on the features of the inhabitants. It is, however, to prehistoric times, or certainly to a period lost in the mist of history, that we must refer for that general exodus of the Aryan family from the Hindoo Koosh and the plains of Western Asia into the more secluded prairies of Kashgar, which took place when the Turanian nations first spread like destroying locusts over the face of that continent. It was at this period that Khoten, which in its name shows its Aryan origin, was founded.

The great nomadic tribe of the Kirghiz, or Kara Kirghiz, as the Russians call them, to distinguish them from the Kirghiz of the various hordes who, by the way, are not true Kirghiz at all, has at all times played a fitful, yet important part in the histories of Khokand, Jungaria, and Eastern Turkestan. Preserving their independence in the inaccessible region lying west of Lake Issik Kul, and along the Kizil Yart plateau and range, this tribe has always been a source of trouble to its neighbours, whosoever they might be. On various occasions, too, they have joined the career of conquest to their usual avocation of plunder, and under the few great leaders that have arisen amongst them they have appeared as conquerors, both of Eastern and Western Turkestan. But their achievements have never been of a permanent nature. Like the irregular undisciplined mass of horsemen which constitute their fighting force, their chief strength lay in a sharp and decisive attack. They had not the organization or the resources necessary for the accomplishment of any conquest of a permanent kind. Their incursions, even when most formidable and most sweeping, were essentially mere marauding onslaughts. Their object was plunder, not empire; and having secured the former, they recked little of the value of the latter. At one time they were able to carry their raids in almost any direction with perfect impunity; but as settled governments arose around their fastnesses, and curtailed their field of operations, what had been a life of adventure through simple love of excitement, became a struggle for sheer

existence. The region where they dwelt was far too
barren to support throughout the year even the limited
numbers of the Kirghiz, and yearly they had to issue
forth against prepared and disciplined enemies in search
of the sustenance that, to preserve their existence, had
to be obtained. But for the intestine quarrels that were
sapping the life strength of the Asiatic states slowly
away, there is no doubt that the Kirghiz would have
been gradually exterminated. Soon, however, they had
the skill to avail themselves of these disagreements to
sell their services as soldiers to the highest bidders ; and
although they were not equal to the Kipchak tribes in
valour, their alliance was considered of importance, and
on many a dubious occasion sufficed to turn the fortune
of the day. By such measures of policy their existence
has been preserved, and at the present time they perform
much the same functions, and are regarded in much the
same manner by their neighbours, as in the past.

The Kipchaks, another great tribe, who however are
scarcely represented at all in Kashgaria, pride themselves on being the most select of all the Usbegs, but
their day of power has passed by, for the present at all
events. Thirty years ago they were at the height of
their success, but they incurred the jealousy of other
Usbeg tribes and of the Kirghiz. Owing to the abilities
of their great chief, Mussulman Kuli, they succeeded in
erecting in Khokand a powerful state, which was able
to restrain the encroachments of Bokhara, at that time
the great enemy of the former Khanate. But the plots
that broke out against them in 1853, in conjunction with
the advance of Russia on the Syr Darya, were crowned
with success, and with the execution of Mussulman
Kuli the Kipchak power was completely broken. Since
that date, however, several of the more distinguished
leaders who have appeared on the scene, such as Alim
Kuli and Abdurrahman Aftobatcha, have been members of this clan. The eastern portion of the dominion of Yakoob Beg is almost exclusively inhabited by

Calmucks, or tribes of Calmuck descent. The great majority of the inhabitants of Manchuria and Jungaria are of Calmuck descent, and even in Russia in Europe there are many settlements of this tribe along the Volga and the Don. None of these, however, possess any political importance except those who inhabit the country north of Gobi and between Eastern Turkestan and China, and the chief of these are the Khalkas. The Calmucks are attached by old associations to the Government of Pekin; and, although they have sometimes revolted against, and often caused trouble to, the Central Government, they have generally acknowledged their culpability and submitted to the Chinese authorities. In the revolt of the Tungani the Calmucks remained true to China, and performed very opportune service on various occasions. The Chinese army in Eastern Turkestan was mainly recruited from among these tribes, who became distinguished from the Tungani by their religion and fidelity.

The origin of the Tungani, or Dungans, as the Russians call them, is much in dispute; and as they played so important a part in the loss of Kashgar and Ili by China, as well as in the history of the rule of Yakoob Beg, it may be as well to put the facts as they stand at some length before the reader. There is no question, we believe, that the Chinese in applying the term Tungani attach the meaning thereto of Mahomedan. There is equal reason for supposing that the term Khitay, literally meaning simply Chinese, has been applied to the Buddhists by general usage. If we acknowledge the validity of these two assumptions —and, so far as we have been able to ascertain, the best authorities have adopted them—there would be little difficulty in explaining who the Tungani were. Granting these, they would simply be the Mahomedan subjects in the eastern portions of China. But others believe that the Tungani are a distinct race, presenting peculiar ethnological features. According to this version, the tribe of the Tungani can be traced back as a distinct community to the fifth and sixth centuries, when they were seated along the Tian Shan range, with their capital at Karashar. The most recent investigations, under Colonel Prjevalsky, are believed to show no signs of there having been any important cities in this quarter. It may be convenient to mention here, that at that time they were Buddhists; but when Islamism broke over Asia in the eighth century, they were among the first to adopt the new tenets. This defection from the religion of China brought them into collision with the Emperors of Pekin, and many of these Tungani were deported into Kansuh and Shensi, where we are to suppose they continued a race apart, with their own religion and their own code of morality, for more than ten centuries. Even granting the possibility of such a consistency to a new religion, which history informs us was thrust upon them at the point of the sword, it seems scarcely credible that we should not hear more of this troublesome tribe in Chinese history. Frequent allusions are made in imperial edicts and other official proclamations to the Tungani, but always in reference to their religion, and not in any way as if they were any other but heretic Chinamen. Besides, even in this way little is heard of the Tungani until the sixteenth and seventeenth centuries, when very sharp measures were taken against them by the emperors, solely because religious propagandists from their ranks were appearing as enemies of a Buddhist Government. The theory that the Tungani were a people and not a sect is new, but it is possible that it may be a true discovery. On the other hand, it is far more probable that it is only an ingenious attempt at elucidating what appears on the face of it to be a simple matter enough. The reader must decide for himself between the two versions. If the Tungani are to be considered a distinct race, then the majority of the inhabitants of Eastern Turkestan are not Calmucks, but Tungani; if the view taken here

is adopted, then they are Calmucks who have at various
times adopted Mahomedanism.   These are the chief
tribes of this portion of Central Asia; and in the following pages it may be as well to bear in mind that
Khitay is applied exclusively to the Buddhist or governing class, and Tungani to the Mahomedan or subject
race in Kansuh and its outlying dependencies.   As race
antipathies have not entered during recent times so
much into the contests of the people of the regions
immediately under consideration as religions, the difference as to the true significance of the term Tungani
does not materially affect one's view of the general
question.

CHAPTER III.

HISTORY OF KASHGAR.

THE great difficulty encountered in giving a description of the past history of Kashgar is to evolve, out of the series of successive conquests and subjections that have marked the existence of that state for almost two thousand years, a narrative which shall, without confusing the reader with a mere repetition of names that convey little meaning, place the chief features of its history before us in a light that may make its more recent condition intelligible to us. We may say in commencement, that those who desire a historical account in all its fulness of Kashgar must turn to that contributed by Dr. Bellew to the Official Report of Sir Douglas Forsyth on his embassy to Yarkand. They will there find ample details of the events that took place in this region of Central Asia from the commencement of our era; but a mere reiteration of the various calamities, with brief and intermittent periods of prosperity, each wave of which bore so striking a similarity to its predecessor, would not serve the purpose we have at present in view—viz., of considering its own history, for the purpose of better understanding its relations with its neighbours and with China, and how the state consolidated by the Athalik Ghazi was constructed on ruins handed down by an almost indistinguishable antiquity.

For a considerable number of years anterior to the ninth century, the Chinese Empire extended to the borders of Khokand and Cashmere. But the dissensions that marked the latter years of the Tang dynasty were not long in producing such weakness at the extremity of this vast empire that the subject races and their proper ruling families were enabled to obtain either their personal liberty or their lost positions once more, unhappily without in any case achieving with the severance of their connection with China any perceptible amelioration in their lot—indeed, on almost every occasion only binding themselves with harder fetters, and sinking into a deeper state of servitude. When the petty princelets of Kashgar, Yarkand, Turfan, and the rest broke away from their allegiance to Pekin, and when the imperial resources were unable to coerce their rebellious subjects, the whole country passed under the hands of their feudatories, who split up into innumerable factions, waged continuous war, and sacrificed the happiness and welfare of the subject people to a desire to promote their own individual interests. As the barons and counts of Italy in the Middle Ages devastated some of the fairest provinces of Europe, so these Oigur princes fought for their own hand in the valleys of the Artosh and the Ili. It is very possible that this state of things would have continued until China became sufficiently strong and settled to reassert once more her dormant rights over her lost provinces, but that a new force appeared on the western frontiers of Kashgar. As early as 676 the Arabs, under Abdulla Zizad, had crossed over from Persia, and were carrying destruction and terror in their course along the banks of the Oxus. At that moment a beautiful and gifted queen, named Khaton, ruled for her son in Bokhara. She had not long been left a widow when her country was threatened by this unexpected and terrible invasion. Although assistance came to the queen from all the neighbouring States, including Kashgar, she was defeated twice in the open field, and compelled to seek safety within the walls of her capital. But the Arab leader was unable to take the city by storm, and slowly retired, with a large

number of captives and an immense quantity of booty,
back to Persia.   Some years later the Arabs again
returned, but withdrew on the payment of a heavy
indemnity.   Another chief, Kutaiba, was still more
successful, for on one occasion he carried fire and sword
through Kashgar to beyond Kucha.   This was the first
occasion on which the doctrines of Mahomed had been
carried into the realms of China, and with so cogent
an argument as the sword it is not wonderful that some
hold was secured on the country.   Subsequent expeditions in the next few centuries strengthened this
beginning, and it was not long before the ruling classes
of Kashgar became infected with the new doctrine.

In the tenth century, Satuk Bughra Khan, the ruling
prince of Kashgar, who had been converted to Islam,
forced his people to adopt that religion, although it is
tolerably clear that up to this time there had been no
acknowledgment of supremacy to the representative of
Mahomed on earth.   A disunited state, which had on
several occasions felt the heavy hand of the authority of
its generals, and at whose very gates its power was consolidated, could not but be in some sort of dependence
to the stronger power, as there was no ally to be found
sufficiently powerful to protect it, now that the Chinese had retrogressed into Kansuh.   Towards the end of
the tenth century the Mahomedans met with a series of
reverses from the Manchoo and Khoten troops, who still
preserved their relations, political and commercial, with
China.   It was in the neighbourhood of Yangy Hissar
that their general, Khalkhalu, inflicted the most serious
defeat on the Mahomedan rulers of Kashgar, but within
the next twenty years, assistance having come from
Khokand, these defeats were retrieved, and Khoten
itself for the first time passed under the rule of Islam.
The family of Bughra Khan was now firmly established
as rulers of Eastern Turkestan, and their limits were
almost identical with those of the late Yakoob Beg.

The Kara Khitay, who had migrated from the country

bordering on the Amoor and the north of China, after long wanderings, had settled in the western parts of Jungaria, and, having founded the city of Ili, in course of time formed, in union with some Turkish tribes, a powerful and cohesive administration. Their chief was styled Gorkhan, Lord of Lords, and their religion was Buddhism. It was of this tribe, according to some, that the celebrated Prester John, or King John, was supposed to be the chief in the Middle Ages. Some neighbours who had been harassed by predatory tribes came to Gorkhan for assistance, which was willingly conceded; but, having successfully repulsed the Kipchaks and other tribes, this leader did not withdraw from the country he had occupied as a friend and ally. Not only did he then annex Kashgar and Khoten, but he crossed the Pamir into the province of Ferghana, and in a short period brought Bokhara, Samarcand, and Tashkent under his dominion. This extensive empire was of very brief duration however, and civil war was waged for more than half a century after the first successes of Gorkhan, in which Khiva, or Khwaresm, and the Kara Khitay fought for supremacy. A chief of the Naiman tribe of Christians, Koshluk by name, then entered the lists against the aged Gorkhan, who was, after some hard fighting, defeated and captured. This was in the year 1214. Koshluk's triumph was also, however, of very brief duration, for he now came into contact with one of the most formidable antagonists that the soil of Asia has ever produced, Genghis Khan.

The Mongols or Mughols began to appear as a distinct tribe about the same time that the Kara Khitay migrated to Jungaria, and as early as the commencement of the twelfth century they had carried destruction into the Chinese provinces of Shensi and Kansuh. When Genghis Khan appeared upon the scene he found the tribe which he was destined to lead to such great triumphs in a state of singular strength, and its neighbours either at discord among themselves or only just recovering from a long period of anarchy. The Chinese were particularly divided at that moment, and Genghis Khan, who had family connections in that empire, soon found it an easy task to lead successful inroads into the heart of his rich but defenceless neighbour. Genghis Khan was born at Dylon Yulduc, in the year 1154. His father, Mysoka Bahadur, was a great warrior, and waged several successful wars with the Tartars. The earlier years of Genghis Khan were occupied exclusively in overcoming the difficulties of his own position. His tribe, divided into several distinct bodies, formed only one confederacy when a foe had to be encountered in the field. It required years to remove the dislike they experienced at submission to a distinct authority; and it was only when the renown of his military achievements threw a halo over his name that these tribes could be induced to acknowledge a supremacy which they had become powerless to resist. But during these years, when he led a life unknown and insignificant as the chief of a small nomad clan, he was all the time preparing for a wider career, and for a more extended authority. It was while he was residing in the remote district round the salt springs of Baljuna that he drew up the code on which his administrative system was founded. It was based on the fundamental principle of obedience to the head, on the maintenance of order and sobriety in the ranks of the warriors, and on the equal participation in the spoils of battle by all; but its regulations were so strict on the former points, and the gain of the individual had to be so completely sacrificed for the advantage of the many, that at first the establishment of this code of order had rather the effect of driving his followers from him, than of attracting to his standard zealots capable of the conquest of a world. It was not until the year 1203, when he was nearly forty-nine years of age, that Genghis Khan succeeded in bringing all the Mongol tribes under his leadership. No sooner had he accomplished this much than he embarked on military enterprises, which, in the course of a very few years, placed the greater part of Asia at his disposal. Having subjugated various Tartar and Tangut tribes, he included them in his military organization, and by making them embrace his system of compulsory service in the army, he found himself in the possession of an enormous following. Genghis Khan therefore ruled at the time we have specified over Kashgar, including Khoten, Jungaria, and the Tangut country; and there was no force capable of opposing his except, in the east China, and in the west the government of Khiva, at this period omnipotent in Western Turkestan. The rumours which reached the Shah of Khwaresm of the formation of this new confederacy in Mugholistan induced him to send an embassy to discover the true facts of the case, and accordingly, while Genghis Khan was prosecuting a war against the Chinese, there arrived in his camp the emissaries of Western Asia. Haughty and imperious as this conqueror undoubtedly was, he received the embassy affably, and with expressions of the deepest friendship. He sent them back with rich presents and the following characteristic message :—" I am King of the East. Thou art King of the West. Let merchants come and go between us and exchange the products of our countries." In furtherance of this wish he sent a mission composed of merchants and officials to represent the advantages that would be derived from mutual intercourse. But the Shah of Khiva, either incredulous of the formidableness of the adversary with whom he had to deal, or mistaking his own strength, did not reciprocate the amicable expressions of Genghis Khan, nor, when the merchants who had been despatched to his country were murdered, did he make any offer of reparation. Such treatment would not be tolerated by any civilized ruler of the nineteenth century, much less was it brooked by an irresponsible conqueror, whose will was his sole law, in the thirteenth. As soon as his campaign with China had closed with success, Genghis Khan made every preparation for the punishment of this act of treachery. It was then that Genghis Khan, with an armed horde of many hundred thousands, burst upon the astonished peoples of Western Asia like a meteor from the east. It was then that some of the fairest regions of the earth were given over to a soldiery to devastate, a soldiery who had raised the work of destruction to the level of one of the fine arts; and whose handiwork in Bokhara, Balkh, Samarcand, Khiva and the lost cities of the desert, is to be seen clearly imprinted in the ruins which mark the site of ancient capitals, even at the present moment, 700 years after the Tartar conqueror swept all resistance from his path. Afghanistan, and the mountain ranges which are now considered to be impassable by Russians, did not retard the progress of this "Scourge of God." Cabul, Candahar, Ghizni fell to the warriors of far distant Mongolia, as they fell not forty years ago to British valour, and as they must again fall when the onset shall be made with equal intrepidity and with equal discipline. And not content with having defaced the map of Asia, with having converted rich and populous cities into masses of ruins, and with having depopulated regions once prolific in all that makes life enjoyable, Genghis Khan carried the terror of his name into the most remote recesses of the Hindoo Koosh. He wintered in the district of Swat on our north-west frontier, a territory which is quite unknown to us except by hearsay, and which has only been occupied by the Mongol and Macedonian conquerors. From his headquarters on the banks of the Panjkora he sent messengers to Delhi; and it is uncertain whether he did not meditate the addition of an Indian triumph to those already obtained.

A rebellion in the far eastern portion of his dominions distracted his attention from the Indus, and he was compelled to hasten with all speed to quell in person the rising that was jeopardising his position in the seat of his power. He hastily broke up from his quarters in Swat, and, by the valley of the Kunar and Chitral, he entered Kashgar, through the Baroghil Pass. Although he suffered much loss from a journey across mountain roads, which were scarcely practicable in the early spring, he succeeded in reaching Yarkand, with his main body, and hastening across Turkestan arrived at Karakoram, his capital, in time to quell the disturbance. After this his life was spent in conquering China, a feat which he never accomplished. But in several campaigns, extending over a period of about twenty years, he worsted the Imperial troops so continually, that before his death, in 1227, he had occupied all the northern provinces of that empire, with Pekin, and left to his son and successor, Ogdai Khan, the task of completing the work which he had commenced. On the death of Genghis Khan, his vast possessions were divided amongst his children, and Kashgar, including Jungaria, Khwaresm, and Afghanistan, fell to the lot of Chaghtai Khan. This ruler was able to hold during his life the extensive territory he had succeeded to ; but on his death dissensions broke out in all quarters of the country, and produced a fresh distribution of the various provinces. It may be mentioned that, although Chaghtai was a fanatical Buddhist and a confirmed debauchee, he was a prudent and sagacious ruler, and no unworthy successor to his distinguished father. The dissensions that broke out on his decease continued, with more or less violence, for a period of almost 100 years after that event took place, and they finally only received a momentary solution in the formation of a new kingdom of Mugholistan, or Jattah Ulus, as it was more specifically called, under one of Chaghtai's descendants.

As briefly and as clearly as possible, we will endeavour to lay before the reader the chief events of this troubled epoch, when the numerous progeny of Genghis Khan warred throughout the whole extent of Central Asia, and a term was only at last placed to their restlessness by their disappearance. In the first place, it may be as well to mention, that the religions of Christ, Buddha, and Mahomed, were equally tolerated in Eastern Turkestan during the greater part of this period. The Arab invasion and the advance of Islam, had been hurled back beyond Bokhara "the Holy," by the victorious arms of the great Buddhist conqueror, Genghis Khan; and for a long period after the Mongol conquests, little was heard of attempts at conversion to the tenets of the "true Prophet." But it must not be supposed that, although Genghis Khan, in the sack of Bokhara, had almost exterminated the race of Mahomedan priests, he was disposed to stamp out the new heresy from his realms. Having crushed its power in the field, he was quite content to let it live on or die out, so long as his imperial or personal interests were not affected. So we have the strange picture before us, of the three great doctrines of the earth flourishing side by side in Eastern Turkestan in the fourteenth century. The Nestorian Christians of Kashgar, who in the time of Marco Polo were rich and flourishing, were obliged later on to succumb to the violent measures of the other members of the community, and have entirely disappeared for many centuries.

Shortly after the death of Chaghtai Khan, Kaidu, a great-grandson of Genghis, obtained the throne of Kashgar and Yarkand; and a few years later on, by a skilful piece of diplomacy, backed up by force, added thereto the greater part of Khokand and Bokhara. His triumph was, however, of brief duration, and he was displaced by other competitors. Dava Khan, the son of Burac, the great-grandson of Chaghtai, had been appointed governor of Khoten, but his ambition was not satisfied with less than the throne of Western Turkestan also. He eventually obtained his desire; but in a rash moment he threw himself in the path of the Chinese Emperor, Timour Khan, who was returning from a raid carried almost to the gates of Lahore. He was defeated somewhere in the neighbourhood of Maralbashi, and was compelled to acknowledge the supremacy of China. He is of some note to us, as having been the father of Azmill Khoja, who was selected as ruler by the people themselves, about the year 1310, and from whom descend that line of Khoja kings of Kashgar, who have clung to their hereditary claims for a longer time than any other royal Central Asian house. The last of the Chaghtai Khans who held the sceptre with any effective purpose, was Kazan Ameer. On his death another period of trouble broke out, and military governors and rival princelets of dubious titles advanced their pretensions to the vacant seat. Up to this all the rulers had, however, been Buddhists. Toghluc Timour, one of the few remaining representatives of the Genghis families, had only been saved by the pity of a leading man in Kashgar, from one of the most extensive massacres of his kinsmen, and for years he was obliged to lead an uncertain existence in the mountains or deserts bordering on the state. His associations were all Buddhist; but one day he was so struck by the definition of the " true faith " given by the descendant of a Mahomedan priest, spared by Genghis Khan at the destruction of Bokhara, that he made a vow to become a Mussulman when he had regained his rights. Not long after this the turn of events in Kashgar made people seek for some person with recognized claims to be their ruler, and none in this respect surpassed Toghluc Timour. He, on succeeding to the throne, openly owned his conversion to Islam, and in a few years he was gradually imitated by all the leading chiefs of Turkestan. From this time downwards to the present day, the religion of the majority in this state has been Mahomedanism, except perhaps during the Chinese rule, when the number of Chinese merchants, officials, and soldiers, put the minority of the followers of Buddha on a par with those of the rival religion. Toghluc died in 1362.

It was about this time that the second great conqueror of Asia appeared upon the scene. Timour was born in 1333 in the Shahrisebz suburb of Kish. He was the son of Turghay, governor of that district and chief of the Birlas tribe, and on the death of his father he himself became governor of Kish also. During his earlier years he was hospitably received at the Court of Kazan Ameer, and that ruler, in addition to giving him several high and distinguished appointments, married him to his beautiful granddaughter Olja Turkan Khaton. Timour did not continue long in favour at Court. His restless spirit impelled him to fields of greater activity than any the Ameer could, or indeed felt disposed to, place at his disposal. He openly mutinied against the central authority in his government of Kish, and on being overthrown by the troops of the state, he sought safety with his wife among the Turcomans of the Khivan desert. Among these uncertain nomads he felt scarcely secure, and collecting round him a small band of desperadoes, he entered upon a more ambitious enterprise by undertaking a marauding expedition into the Persian province of Seistan. This was attended with considerable success, but he himself was wounded in the foot by an arrow. From the effects of this wound he never completely recovered, and was known henceforth as Timour Lang, Timour the Lame, whence the well-known name of Tamerlane. The *éclat* obtained by this marauding expedition stood him in good stead, for shortly afterwards he was able to raise a sufficient force to invade Tashkent. He occupied the whole of what is now Russian Khokand including Ferghana, and he placed a fresh occupant on the throne, Kabil Shah, in 1363. In the following years he contended for supremacy with another chief named Husen, and in 1369 had so far been victorious that he threw off the mask, and declared himself king. He made Samarcand his capital, and converted that once populous city into the wonder and admiration of Western Asia. Having settled his internal affairs, he commenced operations against the states lying beyond his border. The mountaineers of Badakshan were the first to incur his wrath, and after several stubborn battles they were obliged to acknowledge his supremacy. He then turned his attention to his northern frontiers, beyond which the Jattah princes reigned in Jungaria. He overcame their prince, Kamaruddin, in several encounters, but not with complete success until his final campaign against him in 1390. As he advanced they retired to the fastnesses east of Lake Issik Kul, and only reissued from their hiding-places when the invader had withdrawn.

To return to Kashgar, on the death of Toghluc, his son Khize Khoja was displaced and did not regain possession of his kingdom till 1383, when he was thirty years of age. He was a stanch Mussulman, and was on terms of as much amity and as close alliance with Timour as it was possible for any neighbour, wishing to preserve his independence, to be. Allied as he was with, yet not participating in the wars of Timour, against the Jattahs, he suffered in common with those people from the expedition of 1389-90, when both sides of the Tian Shan were ravaged by the armies of that ruler. Although for the next fifteen years they maintained friendly relations, it can easily be imagined that Khize Khoja was not very comfortable with so formidable a suzerain just over his frontiers. The irksomeness of the position is well illustrated by the orders transmitted to Khize Khoja by Timour, to have corn planted and cattle collected at certain places for the immense army which he was levying for the invasion of China. It was while engaged in fulfilling these commands, that news reached the ruler of Kashgar that this "Scourge of God" had died suddenly on the 5th of February, 1405. Khize Khoja himself survived but a short time afterwards.

For the second time within the short space of 150 years had the possessions of a great conqueror to undergo the process of redistribution. In Timour's case it was simpler than it had been in that of Genghis Khan, for the former ruler left no worthy representative of his cause as the Mongol conqueror had in Ogdai and Chaghtai. The branches of the great family of Genghis struck root so deeply, that down to modern times he has had descendants who perpetuate his name, but Timour left none such. With the death of his favourite son Jehangir, his hopes of having a worthy successor expired.

Kashgar was in particular the scene of confusion and trouble, and it was not until about 1445 that any settled government was attained, when Seyyid Ali, grandson of the aged and patriotic minister Khudadar, restored some order and cohesion to the distracted country for a short period. He died in 1457. During these years Yunus, king of Jungaria, played a very prominent part in all the disturbances that were occurring on his borders. He is represented to have been a very enlightened prince, and emissaries from foreign nations returned from his court relating with surprise how they had found a courteous and refined man where they expected to have seen a coarse and savage Mongol. While Yunus ruled in Jungaria another striking individual was predominant in Kashgar. Ababakar, son of Saniz, who was the son of Seyyid Ali, ruler of Kashgar, was one of the few sovereigns of that state whose acts entitle them to consideration. During a long and troubled tenure of power he had the good fortune to overcome many difficulties, and although his career was to become clouded before his death, the brilliant years that preceded the catastrophe justify us in considering his career for a little while. He was a great athlete, hunter and soldier, and was so favoured by his mother on that account that he distanced his brethren in the race for supremacy. As governor of Khoten he soon absorbed

Yarkand, and long and furious were the wars he waged with Hydar, the ruler of Kashgar, who was assisted by Yunus of Jungaria. Nor, although successful on several occasions in the field against the allied forces, could Ababakar hope to overcome the huge armies at the disposal of Yunus; and it was not until Hydar himself foolishly broke off from Yunus, that Ababakar succeeded in asserting his claim to all Eastern Turkestan. War then broke out between Hydar and Yunus, and the latter with the assistance of large reinforcements from Jungaria overthrew and captured his former ally. But these dissensions favoured the cause of Ababakar, and on the death of Yunus in 1486, his possession of Kashgar became undisputed. The first serious danger with which he was menaced after his complete possession of Kashgar, was in 1499, when Ahmad, the son of Yunus, or Alaja the "slayer," as he was generally called, invaded his territory at the head of the Jattah Mongols. The campaign was in the commencement indecisive, but Ababakar before long triumphed over his northern invader.

During the next fifteen years Ababakar ruled in peace and prosperity in Kashgar, accumulating great riches and presenting an object of attraction to his covetous neighbours. During these years the country, although ruled in an arbitrary way, flourished, and, as one of the native chronicles put it, " A traveller could go from Andijan to Hamil on the borders of China without fear of molestation, and without having to make an extra long march in order to find a place wherein to rest and obtain refreshment." But in 1513 a storm broke upon his country that resulted in his complete overthrow. Said, son of Ahmad and brother of Mansur, who was ruling in Jungaria, undertook the invasion of Kashgar in that year, and it was not long before he occupied Kashgar, which, however, Ababakar left but a heap of ruins. His advance on Yangy Hissar was opposed, but, having defeated the army of Kashgar before that city, he occu-

pied it without any further opposition, and thus secured
what has been called the key of Yarkand as well as of
Kashgar. For some months Ababakar remained shut
up in Yarkand, but on the approach of Said's army he
abandoned that position and fled to Khoten. But not
long afterwards he retired still further into the mountainous country south-east of Kashgar, and halted some
time at Karanghotagh. But being first plundered and
then deserted by his attendants, he withdrew into the
valleys and deserts of the Tibetan table-land. For many
months he wandered, half-starved and solitary, in this
deserted region, and at last it was reported that he had
been found murdered by some of the mountaineers.
Such was the end of the once magnificent Ababakar, a
prince who in his fortunes reminds us very much of the
great Darius. That he was avaricious is clear to those
who read of the great treasures he had stored away;
that he was bloodthirsty and cruel is impossible of
denial; but that he possessed in his earlier years many
of the virtues, with some of the vices, of a great ruler
is equally incontestable. His son Jehangir, whom he
had left in command at Yarkand, on the approach of the
army of Said fled to Sanju, and was in a few months
captured and executed. About this epoch the third
great Asiatic conqueror was appearing on the scene.
Babur was born in 1481, and was chosen to succeed
his father Uman Sheikh on the throne of Khokand,
by the nobles of that state, when he was only twelve
years of age. This conqueror of India influenced but
indirectly the fortunes of Kashgar. His career was in
another sphere, and it is not necessary here to enter
into any description of his life, such as has been given
of his predecessors Genghis Khan and Timour.

Said, having overcome Ababakar, employed himself
in extending his rule over the neighbouring states.
He was seized with the desire of occupying that mountainous region, which is divided into almost as many
petty states as it contains mountain chains, lying be-

tween our Indian frontier and the Pamir and Badakshan. But although he employed all his resources in endeavouring to subject the Kafirs of Bolor, or Kafiristan as it is now called, he was unable to make any permanent additions in this direction. In other years he carried fire and sword into Tibet and Cashmere; and it was when returning from one of these expeditions, in the year 1532, that he expired from the effects of the rarefied atmosphere, near the Karakoram pass. His death was the signal for the outbreak of fresh disturbances. His legitimate sons were ousted by Rashid, the son of Said by a slave, who had already distinguished himself as a general in the wars against Kafiristan and Tibet, and on the death of Rashid after a brief reign, the confusion became, if possible, worse confounded. It would be tedious in the extreme to follow the variations that now took place. Benedict Goes, a Portuguese missionary and traveller, found a ruler named Mahomed Khan on the throne in 1603, by whom he was hospitably received; but as he had placed the sister of the Khan, when returning from a pilgrimage to Mecca, under an obligation to him, this is scarcely a fair criterion either of the personal merits of this ruler, or of the state of civilization to which the country had attained.

It was now that the Khoja family appeared prominently upon the scene. Two factions were playing the parts of Montagu and Capulet in Eastern Turkestan in the earlier years of the seventeenth century. They were known as the Aktaghluc and Karataghluc, and in the course of their strife the leader of the former called in to his aid the Khoja Kalar of Khodjent, a descendant of Azmill before mentioned. It was in the year 1618 that this Khoja first came to Kashgar, and his grandson, Hadayatulla, was the chief means of attracting the affections of the people to this family. That veneration has not disappeared to-day, and the Hazrat Afak, as he is generally spoken of, is scarcely inferior in

the eyes of the people to Mahomed himself. The
great miracles he is reported to have wrought, and the
peculiar sanctity which attached to him during his life,
gave him complete ascendancy throughout the country,
and before his death he was entrusted with the supreme
authority. His son, Yahya or Khan Khoja, succeeded
him during his lifetime,. but was murdered in a riot
a few months after the death of Hadayatulla. Then
recommenced with fresh vigour the old series of disturbances. Aspirant after aspirant appeared in the political
arena, but, as each had little claim to lead on account
of original merit, a successful rival always was forthcoming, and so this wearying cycle continued until
1720.

The course of the history of Kashgar has now been
brought down to the commencement of the eighteenth
century, during which a fresh change occurred in the
history of the country by the Chinese conquest. It may
be well, therefore, before narrating that event and the
causes which immediately produced it, to consider the
chief lessons taught us by the history of Eastern
Turkestan, as revealed in the preceding pages. The
most cursory reader must have been struck by the fact,
that only twice in the course of eight centuries did the
country secure a firm and settled government, and they
were when two conquerors, Genghis Khan and
Tamerlane, reduced every semblance of authority to
one bare level of subjection. At fitful moments there
arose, indeed, some leader, Yunus, Ababakar, or the
first Khojas, capable of preserving for a few years his
frontiers against the inroads of hostile neighbours, and
of maintaining an outward show of prosperity and
tranquillity to foreign travellers; but even such gleams
of sunshine as these were transitory on the dark horizon
of the condition of mankind in Central Asia. With
the fall of each pretender, too, hopes of an improvement
became fainter in the breasts of the people; and when
the successors of the Khoja saint showed themselves

not less amenable to the errors and frailties of their predecessors than any past ruler had been, it was to some extraneous circumstance, we may feel sure, that the people looked for aid. There is an old saying in this part of the world, that when "the people's tithe of bricks is full, then comes a Moses in the land;" and it cannot be doubted that in the year 1720 the people of Kashgar had suffered much and for so long, that relief, so that it came effectually from some quarter or another, could not be otherwise than welcome. But the Moses who had been, for centuries almost, expected, had as yet not proved forthcoming, and as " hope deferred maketh the heart sick," so had the Kashgari lost the courage even to look forward to a period when their life of misery, under oppressive tyrants and exorbitant taxation, aggravated by every form of peculation in its levy, might be changed for a more favourable state of being. There can be no doubt that if the chaos which reigned throughout Jungaria and Kashgar had continued much longer those vast regions would have been completely exhausted. As it was the population decreased in alarming proportions, and the wealth and general resources of the country disappeared with no apparent means of supplying the gap. What is, perhaps, most surprising of all is that all these later rulers seem to have lived in a sort of fools' paradise with regard to the resources of their state. The thought never seems to have occurred to them that there must be an end some day or other to a realm distracted by continual wars and sedition, and that subjects who have been tyrannised over for centuries will at last rise up in arms and teach their tyrants, in the words of the poet, " how much the wretched dare." These Khans or Ameers of Central Asia are not worthy of one moment's consideration for their own sake; but, as some account of them is a proper preparation for the modern history of Kashgar, they have been described in this chapter. From the disappearance of Chinese authority in Central

and Western Asia in the eighth and ninth centuries,
down to the commencement of the eighteenth century,
the history of Kashgar, in common with that of its
neighbours, was a series of misfortunes. There is
nothing to attract our sympathies in any of the rulers,
with the exception perhaps of Yunus; and all our commiseration is monopolised for the unhappy races who
peopled that region. We therefore have arrived at this
crisis in a fit state to appreciate the feelings of the
Kashgari at the changes that occurred in the eighteenth
century; and before we consider, in a fresh chapter,
those alterations we may close this without regret at
the disappearance of a long line of Central Asian
Khans, who possessed scarcely one redeeming quality
among many vices.

CHAPTER IV.

THE CONQUEST OF KASHGAR BY CHINA.

BEFORE continuing the narrative of the events that took place in Kashgar after the year 1720, until it fell into the hands of the Chinese in 1760, it may be as well to consider briefly the history of China, in order that it may be intelligible to us how that power was induced to undertake such far distant enterprises, and how, moreover, it was able to accomplish them successfully. In the earlier years of the seventeenth century the dynasty of Ming was seated on the throne of Pekin, but its power had been shaken to its foundations by repeated disasters in wars with the Mantchoo Tartars, who had wrested the province of Leaou Tung from the Emperor Wan-leh, before his death in 1620. The Mantchoos are said to have been the descendants of the Mongol conquerors of the thirteenth century, who had been forced to take refuge in the wilds north of China when the native Chinese rose up and destroyed their power. Whether this very plausible suggestion be true or not, or whether, as some affirm, these were a new race issuing from the frozen regions of Kamschatka and driven south by the necessity for obtaining sustenance for their increasing numbers, matters little for our present purpose. It is certain that they were a warlike people at this time, and that they could bring considerable numbers into the field, and it is very probable that, when they had obtained some success, their ranks were swollen by recruits from their Tartar kinsmen of Eastern Jungaria. On the death of the Chinese Emperor Wan-leh, dissensions broke out in China as to his successor, and in the struggle that ensued the Mantchoos were invited in to support the cause of one of the claimants. Their aid turned the scale in his favour; but when the fortunes of war had been clearly manifested, the Mantchoos showed no disposition to take their departure as had been stipulated. As the Saxons in our own history, and the Mongols in the Chinese had acted, so now did the Mantchoos, and in 1644 their first Emperor Chuntche was installed in the imperial dignities, as the first of the present ruling dynasty of Tatsing, or "sublimely pure." When Chuntche was crowned by his victorious soldiery, it must not be supposed that he had conquered the whole of China. During the seventeen years of his reign he was constantly engaged in warring with the native Chinese forces; but always with invariable success. In 1661 Kanghi, his son, ascended the throne, and by a series of judicious measures and successful enterprises, firmly maintained the position won in China by his father. It was during this brilliant reign that Tibet was annexed to the Chinese Empire, and from Cochin-China and the frontiers of Birma to the River Amoor there was none to question the power of the Mantchoo Government. It cannot be doubted that the conquest of Tibet opened up fresh ideas in the minds of the Chinese as to their right to rule in Eastern Turkestan; and with the re-assertion of their old suzerainty over the Tibetan table-land, the remembrance of a similar claim, at a far distant epoch, over Jungaria and Turkestan would be forced on the minds of the Chinese people, until some ambitious ruler or viceroy might avail himself of the opportunity of distinction by acquiescing in, and giving effect to, the popular desire. Kanghi was too prudent to jeopardize his recently consolidated state by expeditions either into Jungaria or Turkestan; and was quite satisfied with the respect shown to his empire by the Eleuthian princes of those regions. On Kanghi's death, in 1721, his son, Yung-Ching, came to the throne, and during his short reign, the example of his two predecessors not to interfere in the troubles of the states lying beyond Kansuh, was closely followed. Yung-Ching died in 1735, and thus made way for his ambitious and war-like son, Keen-Lung. When Keen-Lung first commenced to reign for himself he found that he was irresponsible ruler of a most powerful empire, at peace within itself, and satisfied to all outward seeming with its *de facto* government. His treasury was full; the country was, perhaps, at its very highest point of prosperity, and the sovereign had only to maintain in this wealth and vigour the nation which had been brought to such a pitch by the wisdom of his predecessors. To a warlike monarch, however, the career of ruler of a thriving, peace-loving, and domestic people, has never been a palatable one, and Keen-Lung thought, as have many other great sovereigns of our own age, that the only use of a wealthy and numerous subject race was to enable the ruler to undertake high-sounding enterprises, and to spread the terror of his name through distant regions. The reputation and the real strength of the Chinese Empire were so great at this time in Asia, that no single power, or even any possible confederacy, would have thought of entering the lists against it. Keen-Lung had, therefore, no just cause for hostilities with the neighbouring states, as they were always too willing to offer the amplest reparation for any cause of offence to the Imperial dignity. The conquest of Turkestan was therefore an object with which he would heartily sympathise; and when we remember his warlike disposition, and the exact condition of China at the time, possessing a superabundance of wealth, and of numbers sufficient to achieve far more difficult enterprises than the one in question, it is easier to understand the eagerness with which Keen-Lung intervened in the affairs of Jungaria, when the following opportunity, which we are about to narrate, offered for so doing.

It is now time to return to Kashgar and narrate the events that were happening in that troubled district. The feud between the Aktaghluc and Karataghluc factions reached its height when Afak, who had been placed on the throne of Yarkand by the Calmucks, under Galdan, the chief representative of the Aktaghluc, succeeded in expelling all the prominent supporters of the rival clan. Afak ruled for some years, but with difficulty maintained himself in some parts of Kashgar, against the Calmucks, Kirghiz, and Kipchak. His sons had no better fortune, and the state was finally divided between a Kipchak and a Kirghiz leader. These quarrelled between themselves, but happily they each expired in the first encounter. Acbash, one of the sons of Afak, was executed at Yangy Hissar in the course of this contention; but he had previously called in to his assistance from Khodjent, in Khokand, a Khoja, Danyal, of the rival Karataghluc faction. This roused the enmity of the more bitter among the Aktaghluc, and, on this, Khoja Ahmad was brought in to represent their interests. Danyal was besieged in Yarkand, but, with the assistance of a contingent of Kirghiz, he was able to repulse his assailants. But, although successful in the field, Danyal was compelled shortly afterwards to flee, and leave his rival in possession of the state. He fled to the Calmucks, in Jungaria, and pleaded so well, that an army was lent him to regain Kashgar. Victory attended this expedition, but the Calmuck leader, who had captured Ahmad at the siege of Kashgar, instead of placing Danyal in power, took both him and his rival as prisoners to his capital of Ili. With so forcible a settlement of the question, little room was left for useless complaining to the ambitious Danyal, and from this time down to the Chinese conquest, the Calmuck rulers of Ili asserted their right to supremacy over Eastern Turkestan. Danyal, himself, was appointed, some years later on, governor of Kashgar, now called Alty Shahr, or six cities ; but, under him, there was a local governor for each town, appointed by the Calmucks themselves. His power was more apparent than real. His eldest son was kept at Ili as a hostage for the good behaviour of his father, and Danyal, himself, had frequently to proceed to Ili to make his report on the state of affairs in Kashgar. Such was the condition of Kashgar, as a subject province of the Calmuck rulers of Ili, governed by Danyal, a member of the Karataghluc party, in the year 1740. On the death of Galdan, the son of Arabdan Khan of Jungaria, in 1745, two chiefs, Amursana and Davatsi, or Tawats, seized the governing power, and for a time they divided the authority fairly between them ; but it was not long before they fell out, and resolved to advance their own interests at the expense of each other. Amursana was unable to cope with the armies of his rival, Davatsi, and, having been defeated in several encounters, fled from Jungaria to China. On his arrival at Lanchefoo he demanded permission to proceed to Pekin to lay his grievances at the feet of the Emperor, and to offer in his name, and in that of many of his compatriots, the districts of Ili and of Kashgar to his omnipotent majesty.

The request was granted, and Keen-Lung received him with favour, promised to consider what he had stated, and, in the meanwhile, gave him titles and revenues within the Chinese Empire. Amursana's address was so insinuating, and he played so skilfully on the king's ambition and love for military renown, that at last Keen-Lung consented to lend him the forces, which he had been so lavish of promises to secure. In 1753, the Chinese army, under Amursana, appeared in Jungaria, and, after several desperate encounters, Davatsi was driven out of that state, and, according to one account, was delivered up to the Chinese by Khojam Beg, the governor of Ush Turfan. According to another version, he was captured in the field ; but both agree that he was taken to Pekin and there executed. Amursana, having regained his position in Jungaria, now turned his attention to the conquest of its dependency, Kashgar. He was now supreme in Jungaria, with his capital at Ili; but his army, which maintained him in his position, was a Khitay force, owing allegiance solely to the Emperor of Pekin, and only obeying the instructions issued by his general accompanying the Eleuth prince Amursana. At this epoch Yusuf, a son of Galdan, had seized the chief authority in Kashgar, and, raising a cry that the true religion of Islam was in danger from the advance of the Khitay, endeavoured to rally to his cause in the struggle that he saw was approaching the Mahomedan governments of Khokand and Bokhara. Amursana, on the northern frontiers of Kashgar, was eagerly watching for the opportunity to arise for an active interference in that state, and Yusuf was prudent in seeking beyond his frontiers for allies that were able to assist him against the machinations of his foes. Yusuf had made himself the leader and representative of the Karataghluc party in the state, and Amursana accordingly resolved to put forward the pretensions of the rival Aktaghluc faction. In this design the Chinese general acquiesced, and, with the assistance of the Calmuck governors of Ush Turfan, and Aksu, no delay interfered with its prompt realization. The descendants of the ancient Khojas were consequently sought out, and Barhanuddin, son of Ahmad, was selected for the purpose. He, at the head of a mixed following, promptly seized Ush Turfan, and was there received with acclamation, and several of the minor tribes joined him at once. Yusuf was, however, hurrying up with a large force from Yarkand, and Barhanuddin's chances seemed to be more than doubtful, when Yusuf died on the way. His son Abdulla, who took the name of Khoja Padshah, hastened on, however, and besieged Barhanuddin in Ush Turfan. Abdulla then endeavoured to come to terms with Barhanuddin, and made overtures for the reconciliation of the Karataghluc and Aktaghluc parties to be cemented in a crusade against the invading Khitay. Barhanuddin, a true Mussulman, was personally inclined to accept the arrangement offered, but, as he was surrounded by Chinese officials and their allies, he was constrained to give instead the advice that Abdulla should surrender to the Chinese and acknowledge their supremacy. Abdulla was not at all willing to forfeit his independence without some struggle, and the siege of Ush Turfan was pressed on. In the camp of the besieging forces there were some who favoured the pretensions of Barhanuddin, and these deserting from the Karataghluc cause, the remaining forces of Abdulla were compelled to retreat with precipitation. Barhanuddin immediately advanced on Kashgar, where he was received with open arms. Yarkand soon afterwards fell into his possession, and the conquest of Kashgar by the descendant of the Khojas and the triumph of the Aktaghluc party were complete.

So far the Chinese had been merely spectators of the progress of events in Kashgar. Amursana had induced them to approve of this enterprise of Barhanuddin, and they had given general support in the war with Yusuf and his son; and it was not until Barhanuddin, elated with his success, set their wishes at defiance, that they resolved to occupy the country. But before that, Amursana's career had been cut short. Although escorted by a large force of native Chinese troops, he had aspired, in 1757, to establish himself as an independent prince in Jungaria, and had broken loose from Chinese control. The forces he raised were, however, defeated with remarkable ease by the Chinese, and Amursana was compelled to flee once more from his home—this time with no certain refuge, as he had before in Pekin. The Russians were then in possession of Siberia, but their influence for good or for ill beyond their desert and almost impenetrable stations was practically *nil;* but, such as it was, it seemed to Amursana the only place affording any prospect of security. He died at Tobolsk, in 1757, soon after he arrived there; but the implacable Chinese haughtily demanded from the Russians his body as a proof of his decease, and the Russian government sent it to Kiachta for surrender to them. Such was the career of the ill-fated, but ambitious, Amursana, who was the immediate cause of the introduction of Chinese power into Eastern Turkestan.

With so unmistakable a proof before his eyes of the power of the Chinese, it is strange to find Barhanuddin also proving contumacious in Kashgar, but so it was. In 1758, the very next year after the death of Amursana, this ruler and his brother Khan Khoja broke out in open mutiny to the Chinese. At Ili some Khitay officers were maltreated, and outspoken contempt was shown for Chinese commands. Such attitude could not be brooked by any established rule, and, to do the Chinese simple justice, never had been tolerated by them on any occasion; and accordingly a Chinese army was despatched from Ili to chastise this recalcitrant ruler, and to remind him that the arm of Chinese power was terribly long. Barhanuddin and his brother were defeated in several pitched battles, city after city opened its gates to the dreaded invader, and the last representatives of the Khojas were compelled to seek refuge in the isolated region of Badakshan. But even here they were not safe. The terror of the Chinese name had gone before them, and the sovereign of Badakshan, eager to propitiate the conqueror, sent the heads of the two brothers to the Chinese general, who was advancing from Yarkand. Only one of the numerous sons of Barhanuddin escaped the destruction wrought in the family of the Khojas by the victorious Chinese: his name was Khoja Sarimsak. The Chinese had now completely annexed all the territory north of the Karakoram and east of the Pamir and Khokand, and it does not appear that in doing so they had suffered any great loss. By availing themselves of Amursana's claims in Jungaria they had obtained a firm foothold in that state, and then by an equally skilful manipulation of the rival parties of Aktaghluc and Karataghluc, they had extended their authority over Kashgar as well. When their puppets, Amursana and Barhanuddin, became restive as Chinese vassals, and strove for independence, the Chinese forces were called into action and swept all opposition from their path. All this may seem the most unjustifiable ambition, nor do we wish to palliate in any way the terribly harsh repressive measures adopted by the Chinese. There is no doubt that, so long as there remained the shadow of any opposition to their rule, they did not temper their power with any exhibition of mercy. It is computed that almost half a million of people were slain during the wars of these two or three years, and that the great majority of these were the innocent inhabitants, who had been massacred. Nor, although we should be disposed to think that this is a greatly exaggerated number, have we any reason to doubt that the sword of the Chinese was called into use whenever any resistance was offered to their advance, and that the feelings of the soldiers were embittered to a great extent by religious fervour, in their encounters with the Mussulmans. The Chinese, having conquered Kashgar, turned their arms against Khokand, and entered Tashkent and the city of Khokand in triumph. As the year 1760 was drawing to a close, quite a panic was spreading through Western Asia at the advance of the Chinese. Afghanistan, then as now the only formidable Mahomedan territory left intact from foreign conquest, was implored by the suffering Islamites to check the Chinese advance. Then, as recently on a somewhat similar occasion, Afghanistan thought prudence the better part of valour, and confined her action to the invasion of Badakshan, which she coveted, in order to punish its ruler for the murder of the fugitive

Khojas. But, having terrified Khokand, the Chinese wisely retired to the proper frontier of Kashgar, and then set about consolidating their rule there by an energy and administrative capacity which must excite the admiration of every governing nation.

It was some years, however, before the conquest of Kashgar, which had been so rapidly accomplished, could be considered to have been altogether completed. Fresh troops had to be summoned from Kansuh, and military settlers imported in large numbers from Shensi and other Chinese provinces, to supply the place of the massacred Kashgari. Settlers were also brought from the neighbourhood of Urumtsi and Hamil; and with these and imperial troops sent from Pekin, the Chinese felt complete masters of the situation. It was only then that the Chinese viceroy considered himself sufficiently strong to place his army in detachments in the various cities. Up to that time it had been kept mobilised in one, or at most two or three stations, ready for instant action. When the Chinese withdrew from Khokand they imposed a tribute on that state, and then they turned their arms against the nomad tribes on the north of the Jungarian frontier. The various hordes of the Kirghiz nomads sent in their submission one after the other, and the Chinese invariably accepted their fealty, and as a rule rewarded their duteous behaviour with Chinese titles and rank. Thus Ablai, Chief of the Middle Horde, was made Prince in 1766, and Nur Ali, of the Little Horde, went so far as to send special emissaries to Pekin, where they were favourably received, and returned with recompenses for the fidelity of their master. The Chinese had thus secured their position in Jungaria and Kashgar before the close of 1765, and by their possession of Khoten, they had opened up communications with their province of Tibet. On the south they possessed an admirable frontier, and it was only in the south-west that any check seemed to be put upon their advance. As already mentioned, the Ameer of Afghanistan had overrun Badakshan, in chastisement for the murders of Barhanuddin and his brother; and he was continually receiving applications to declare an open war against the Chinese. His own troubles with the rulers of Scinde and Persia were sufficient to keep his religious sympathies within due bounds. But he sent an embassy to Pekin, to point out that his fellow-religionists were suffering under the conquering sway of the Chinese forces in Central Asia; and on its return with an unsatisfactory reply, he appears to have stationed a large body of troops in Badakshan. The proud Durani monarch was probably eager to oppose the Chinese, but, wiser than his contemporaries in Turkestan and Jungaria, he accurately reckoned up the risks of the enterprise, and contented himself with the maintenance of the powerful empire he had erected on the ruins of the conquests of Nadir Shah. When the Afghans had done so much, and given promises of aid in the defence of Samarcand, it is not to be wondered at if the people of Kashgar thought they would do more, and risings took place in several parts of the state, notably at Ush Turfan. The Chinese measures were prompt and effectual; the rebellion was suppressed, the inhabitants massacred, and the town destroyed. This failure struck so complete a panic into the hearts of the people, that no inducements, for more than half a century, could encourage them to rise against the Chinese. The Chinese conquest of Kashgar gave an effectual solution to the rivalries of the numerous claimants to its sovereignty, and among other competitors to the Khojas, that is, to the descendants of that Sarimsak who alone survived the massacre of his family in 1760. While very possibly the people may have suffered that mental depression which must accompany the installation of a foreign rule, and despite the very harsh and unmistakable evidences given by the Chinese of their intolerance of opposition, there was some prospect, notwithstanding these, that the Chinese would prove permanent masters, and that their rule would consequently become milder and milder every year. It was this feeling, that things could not become much worse, that rendered the Kashgari apathetic in their resistance to the Chinese. They did not dare to expect much improvement in their lot; but at all events they might suppose that Chinese massacres would cease with the disappearance of resistance, whereas massacres by their own countrymen and tyrants had been for centuries an every-day occurrence.

Before considering the Chinese occupation of Kashgar, it may be useful to give some description of the Aktaghluc and Karataghluc parties, of whose rivalry the history of Kashgar in the sixteenth, seventeenth, and eighteenth centuries is so full. It may be remembered that in 1533, Reshid, the younger son of Said, who had distinguished himself in his father's wars, seized the state from his brothers, to whom he was inferior both in age and in birth on his mother's side. In effecting this he availed himself of the alliance of the Usbeg rulers west of Pamir, and during the negotiations that were transacted between them, the distinguished divine, Maulana Khoja Kasani, of Samarcand, visited him. He was greeted with the most striking marks of Reshid's affection, and granted a large estate in Kashgar. He married and left two sons in that state to represent his interests and share his possessions. The elder son, whose mother was a Samarcand lady, was averse to the younger, whose mother was a native of Kashgar. In the course of time they each rose prominently in the service of the state, but they transmitted their antipathy to their descendants. Khoja Kalan, the elder, whose influence was greatest in Yarkand and Karatagh, was the founder of the Karataghluc, or "Black Mountaineers." Khoja Ishac, the younger, whose influence was greatest

in Kashgar and Actagh, another form of Altai, was the
founder of the Aktaghluc, or "White Mountaineers."
The descendants of either of these Khojas, or priests,
the sons of the great divine of Samarcand, claim the
title of Khoja, but that must not be confounded with
the more exclusive signification it possesses as representing the once ruling family.

CHAPTER V.

THE CHINESE RULE IN KASHGAR.

THE Chinese conquest of Jungaria and Eastern Turkestan having become an accomplished fact, what did the new rulers do to justify their forcible interference in Central Asia? What measures did they adopt to conciliate the subject peoples, and what to increase the prosperity of a vast region, naturally fertile, but impoverished by centuries of improvident government and of civil anarchy and war? Did they follow the precedent that had been set them by every past ruler of those countries, and leave the people to their own devices, to starve or to exist as best they might, so long as the tribute money was forthcoming? Did the Chinese Viceroys of Ili, or their lieutenants in Kashgar, Yarkand, Aksu, or Kucha adopt a policy of inaction, and pursue a line of conduct of unprincipled selfishness in advancing their own personal fortunes, and thus prove that they were of the same stamp as all other Asiatic despots, careless of the day and utterly regardless of the morrow? The best way to see how they acted, what they did, and what they did not that was possible, is to follow their rule in Kashgar with some attention. In itself this may be found to be no uninstructive lesson for us, who are also a great governing people; and from the perusal of what the Chinese administrators did in Central Asia we may arise willing to accord them high praise, because we are better able than other nations to appreciate the difficulties of their task.

After the fall of Amursana, the Chinese, in the first

place, organized their administrative system upon the following basis :—The supreme authority was vested in the hands of the Viceroy of Ili. Under him an amban, or lieutenant-governor, administered affairs in Kashgar. His place of abode was Yarkand. In internal matters the Yarkand Amban was without a superior south of the Tian Shan, but in external affairs he only acted in subordination to the Viceroy of Ili, who alone was in communication with Pekin. Under each of these potentates there were the usual deputy-ambans and Tay Dalays, or military commanders. All the cities had Gulbaghs constructed outside of them, and these forts were held by Chinese troops—that is, by a mixture of Khitay and Tungani. It is computed that 20,000 troops used to garrison Kashgar and the neighbourhood alone. The military posts were restricted to Chinamen, and the higher judicial and administrative offices were also withheld from the subjected race. But these were the only privileges retained by the Chinese.

The Khan, or chief Amban, who resided in Yarkand, made all the appointments to the minor offices, which were filled almost exclusively by Mahomedans. The only precaution the Chinese seem to have taken was to refuse employment to a Kashgari in his native town, so that a Yarkandi would have to go to Aksu, or some other place away from his home, if he desired to participate in the government of his country. But beyond this there was no restriction, and nominally the Hakim Beg, the highest Mussulman officer, ranked on an equality with the Chinese amban. His subordinates were all Mahomedans, with the exception of his personal guard of Khitay troops. In the hands of these natives of the country lay all the administration of justice among their co-religionists, the collection of the revenue, and the levying of customs dues on the frontier and of trade taxes in the cities. It was only when cause for litigation arose between a Buddhist and a Mussulman that the amban interfered. We have therefore the instructive spectacle before us of a Buddhist conquest becoming harmonized with Mussulman institutions, and Chinese arrogance not content with tolerating, but absolutely fostering, a régime to which its hostility was scarcely concealed. This is the only instance of the Chinese exhibiting such more than Asiatic restraint towards Mahomedans; for their dealings with Tibet, a country of peculiar sanctity and Buddhist as well, is not a case in point. The scheme worked well, however. Chinese strength was husbanded by being employed only when absolutely necessary to be called into play, and the people, to a great degree their own masters, did not realise the fact of their being a subjected nation. Their first anxiety was the payment of their taxes—far from exorbitant, as it had been under their own rulers; but that task accomplished, they could free their minds from care.

Very often their own countryman, the Hakim Beg, was a greater tyrant than the Chinese amban in the fort outside their gates; but against his exactions they could obtain speedy redress. When their Hakims, or Wangs as the Chinese called them, became unpopular in a district, the amban promptly removed them; even if he considered they were not much to blame, he always transferred them to some other district. The first object in the eyes of the amban was the maintenance of order, and he knew well enough that order could not be maintained, unless he resorted to force, which he studiously avoided, if the people were discontented. The people therefore could repose implicit trust in the Chinese amban securing a fair hearing and justice for them in their disagreements with their own leaders; and the Mussulman Wangs, who were the old ruling class, saw the unfortunate tax-payer at last secure from their tyranny through the clemency of a Buddhist conqueror. We are justified in assuming that the population saw the force of these patent facts, and that, if not perfectly to be relied on in any emergency, the Chinese had no danger to expect from the tax-producing and patient Kashgari.

So long as the Chinese rule remained vigorous—that is, for about the first fifty years—the Ambans worked in perfect concord with the Wangs, and through them with the people. But the internal relations between these various personages became more complicated and less cordial through the importation, about the beginning of this century, of a fresh factor into the question. The Chinese had granted the cities west of, and including, Aksu very considerable privileges in carrying on trade with Khokand; and in the course of commercial intercourse a Khokandian element was slowly imported into these cities, when it became a people within a people, enjoying the prosperity to be derived from the Chinese Empire, but not experiencing any sentiment of gratitude towards those by whom the favours were conferred. After some years, when these Khokandian immigrants had become numerous, the Chinese acquiesced in their selecting a responsible head for each community, and this head, or Aksakal, was nominated by the Khan of Khokand, the only temporal sovereign these people recognized. The creation of this third power in the state, which was first sanctioned as a matter of convenience, was to be fraught with the direst consequences for the Chinese. The Khitay would be justified in saying that the Aksakals were "the cause of all their woe," in Kashgar at all events. The Aksakals were far too prudent to challenge the supremacy of the Chinese officials, and their first object was rather to make themselves independent of the Wangs than to compete with the Ambans. In this they were successful, for the Chinese neglected to take into account the dangers that might arise from these same bustling, intriguing, and alien Aksakals. The Wangs had always been obedient vassals, but the plausibility of the Aksakals put them on a par with their rivals. The Chinese washed their hands of the quarrel, and may have imagined that their rule was made more assured by divisions among the Mussulmans. In this they were mistaken. The Aksakals, who after a time repudiated their obligations to the Wangs, became the centre of all the intrigue that marked the last half-century of Chinese rule, and, puffed up by their triumph over the Wangs, did not hesitate to challenge the right of the Ambans to exercise jurisdiction over them. But of this more later on.

While the Chinese adopted these liberal measures in their dealings with the Mussulman population, they did not neglect those other duties which belong to the government by right. The greatest benefit they could confer was of course the preservation of order, and to maintain the balance impartially between the numerous litigants was the first article in the creed of the Chinese viceroys. As tranquillity settled down over these distracted regions, trade revived. The native industries, which had greatly fallen off, became once more active; and foreign enterprise was attracted to this quarter, which Chinese power soon made the most favoured region in Central Asia. But the rulers did not rest content with the mere preservation of good order. They did not leave it to the inclination of an indolent people to progress at as tortoise-like a speed as they would wish; but they themselves set the example which the rest felt bound to imitate. Not only did the enterprising Khitay merchant from Kansuh and Szchuen visit the marts of Hamil and Turfan, but many of this class penetrated into Kashgar proper, where they became permanent settlers. These invaluable agents supplied the deficiency that had never before been filled up in the life of the state, for they brought the highest qualities of enterprise and practical sagacity, together with capital, as their special characteristics. In the train of these Khitay merchants came wealth and increased prosperity. Yarkand, Kashgar, Aksu, and Khoten became cities of the first rank, and the population of the country in the year 1800 was greater than it had ever been before.

There was perfect equality too between all the various races in respect to trade. The Chinese did not demand special immunities for their own countrymen, as might have been expected. The Khitay, who came all the way from Lanchefoo in search of a fortune, must be prepared to compete in an equal race with the Khokandi, the Kashgari, or the Afghan. His nationality would obtain for him no immunity from being taxed, or could give him no advantage over the foreign or native traders. The main portion of the trade of the country remained in the old hands. Khokand benefited as much as Kashgar by the trade, and China, in a direct manner, least of the three.

The Chinese have at all times been justly famous for their admirable measures for irrigating their provinces. The wonderful canals which cut their way, where there are no great rivers, in China proper are reproduced even in this outlying dependency. Eastern Turkestan is one of the worst-watered regions in the world. In fact there is only a belt of fertile country round the Yarkand river, stretching away eastward along the slopes of the Tian Shan as far as Hamil. The few small rivers which are traced here and there across the map are during many months of the year dried up, and even the Yarkand then becomes an insignificant stream. To remedy this, and to husband the supply as much as possible, the Chinese sank dykes in all directions. By this means the cultivated country was slowly but surely spread over a greater extent of territory, and the vicinity of the three cities of Kashgar, Yangy Hissar, and Yarkand became known as the garden of Asia. Corn and fruit grew in abundance, and from Yarkand to the south of the Tian Shan the traveller could pass through one endless orchard. On all sides he saw nothing but plenty and content, peaceful hamlets and smiling inhabitants. These were the outcome of a Chinese domination.

The Chinese, besides possessing a dual line of communication with their own country, one north and the other south of the Tian Shan, had also a caravan route from Khoten to Lhasa, the capital of Tibet. There was also some intercourse with Cashmere by this way. The jade, for which Khoten was justly, and is still, famous, was exported in immense quantities, both to Tibet and to China, through Maralbashi. This mineral was held in high esteem by Chinese ladies, and alone sufficed to make the prosperity of Khoten assured. Gold, silk, and musk, were other articles included in the commerce of this flourishing city. There was also, in the Chinese time, a very extensive manufacture of carpets and cotton goods. The gold mines, which, with two exceptions, have not been worked since the same time, are believed to be scarcely touched, and only await a fostering hand to be put in working order once more.

The Chinese also devoted great attention to the coal mines in the vicinity of Aksu, and these were worked both by private enterprise and the Government. Coal was an article of common use in that city, but it does not appear to have been exported beyond the neighbourhood. It is known that the Chinese took greater interest in the development of the internal means of wealth of the country than in inducing foreigners to enter it. Thus, we see that mines, in a special degree, received state approval and support. The gold mines of Khoten, the coal of Aksu, and the zinc of Kucha, are all conspicuous instances of this ; as, under all past, and the recent Mahomedan, rule, they have been most foolishly, but consistently neglected.

Nor were those special trades for which Kashgar had in prosperous moments been renowned, neglected. The leather-dressers of Yarkand and Aksu, the silk-mercers of Kashgar and Khoten, were never so busy as in the warlike days of Keen-Lung, and the great mass of the people, the agricultural class in the villages, was equally prosperous and well governed. Trade was fostered on all sides, and the conquering power was content to stand aside and witness the steady progress of its subjects towards hitherto unattained and unattainable prosperity.

Lastly, the Chinese directed their attention to the improvement of the means of communication between one part of the province and another. It was absolutely necessary to the security of their rule that there should be an easy and always open road between Ili and Kashgar. Therefore, a way was cut, at great expense, through the Tian Shan, north of Aksu, and this pass was known as the Muzart, or Glacier. So difficult was the country through which it passed, and such the danger from ice-drifts and snow-storms, that relays of men had to be kept constantly at work in order to prevent it getting out of repair for a day. The construction of this road was, in the first place, most expensive, but, perhaps, the cost of repairing was much more. This, the most striking engineering achievement of the Chinese, has become practically useless, through fifteen years of neglect. If China is to regain Ili, it will, no doubt, be restored. The passes west of this, by the Narym River to Vernoe, and through Terek to Khokand, were those selected by Yakoob Beg to supply its place.

The next object to which the Chinese specially paid attention was the preservation of their road home to China. Thus the road in Tian Shan Pe Lu, and the other in Tian Shan Nan Lu, were kept in the most effective state possible. The former, north of the mountains, passed through Manas and Urumtsi to Hamil; the latter, south of them, through Aksu and Kucha to the same place. The alternative route from Kucha to Kashgar and Yarkand, through Maralbashi, was also much used, more especially, however, by those who desired to break off at that outpost in the desert to reach Khoten and Sanju. In each city there was appointed a committee to superintend the roads in the district, and this Road Board was a highly important and useful corporation. It was by such measures as these that the Chinese made their rule a blessing to Kashgar and Jungaria for more than fifty years. Of course, there was the fiscal side of these schemes of public utility. Roads could not be opened up and maintained in order, canals could not be dug, the state could not administer justice, promote trade, and make itself respected abroad, without an assured revenue, and this revenue, after the first ten years, was very productive.

The principal taxes were the tithe on the produce of the land, called "*ushr*," and the *zakat* (fortieth), on merchandise and cattle. Then, in the cities, there was a house tax, which was essentially, like our own income tax, a war tax, fluctuating in accordance with the military necessities, caused by foreign or civil war. From the mines, too, the state derived a large annual sum, which was generally devoted to some object of public utility. There was also the tribute money from the Kirghiz nomads, whose flocks and horses were numbered and taxed at a low rate, in return for which they were taken under the protection of China. In addition to these great taxes there were several smaller ones, such as a fee on fuel sold in the market, and another levy on milch-kine kept in cities. A writer on Kashgar has said that these " proved a ready means of oppression, and a prolific source of that discontent which left the rulers without a single helping hand, or sympathising heart, in the hour of their distress and destruction." But this assumption of cause and effect is scarcely just.

Of course, all taxes can be made a ready means of oppression by the tax-gatherer, who, in this case, was a Mussulman and fellow-countryman. But taxes are absolutely necessary to all good government, and when we consider what China did with her revenue, with what public spirit her representatives laid it out in plans for the advantage of the state, can we pronounce an opinion that she imposed unfair burdens on the subjected race? Moreover, no one denies the prosperity general throughout Kashgar in those days, a period looked back to with regret by the inhabitants during the most favoured years of Yakoob Beg's rule. It is not in accordance with facts, then, to imply that the Chinese ground Kashgar under them by severe taxation, and whatever petty tyranny there was, was carried on not by the Khitay Ambans, but by the Mahomedan Wangs.

In the hour of distress and destruction the people, indeed, proved traitorous to their best friends, or, more generally, apathetic; leaving to the energetic Andijani element within their gates the task of crossing swords with Buddhist rule, to which the hostility of these immigrants had always been declared.

The short-sightedness of the Kashgari played the game of the more fanatical and ambitious people of Khokand; but the rule of China did not pass out of Eastern Turkestan until the disturbances of forty years had generated ill-feeling that formerly was not, and had so embittered the relations of governing and governed, that what had come to be considered a lenient and impersonal government, assumed all the darker hues of a military and foreign despotism. Even then China did not fall until there was dissension within herself, when, split into three hostile camps, her sword dropped nerveless from her hand in Central Asia, 2,000 miles away from her natural border. To follow Chinese rule in Kashgar down to 1820, is to observe the monotonous course of never varying prosperity. From that year to 1860, the tale is of a different complexion, less monotonous but also less satisfactory.

In 1758 and 1760 Chinese armies entered Khokand. Tashkent fell in the former year, and the capital in the latter. The Chinese then withdrew, after imposing a tribute upon Khokand. During the long reign of Keen-Lung—that is, down to 1795—the tribute was regularly paid. After that year, however, the payment became irregular, and border warfare of frequent occurrence between the two neighbours. At last, in 1812, Khokand, then under an able prince, refused to pay tribute any longer, and the Chinese acquiesced in the repudiation. Nor did the change in the relations between China and Khokand stop here; for, a few years afterwards, the Chinese found it expedient to pay Khokand an annual sum to keep the Khoja family, whose representatives were residing in Khokand, from intriguing against them. The amount of the subsidy was £3,500 of our money. In addition to this, the Khan of Khokand was permitted to levy a tax on all Mahomedan merchandise sold in Kashgar through Andijan merchants. This tax was collected by the Aksakals before mentioned, and was a very profitable source of income for the impecunious khans. But even these concessions and perquisites did not satisfy the Mussulmans of Central Asia, who saw in Chinese moderation an evidence of weakness and decline. The Aksakals, in these years of Mahomedan revival, became political agents of the greatest importance. It was they who gave a point to all the discontent there might be in Kashgar; it was they who attributed to the Chinese the blame for whatever evils this world is never wholly free from; and it was they who agitated for the return of the old Khoja kings, who were always destined, in their eyes, to bring the most perfect happiness. With such causes at work both within and without their position, the Chinese had not to wait long before their authority was more openly challenged.

Sarimsak, the only member of the Khoja family surviving the massacre by the Chinese, had fled, as a child, into the impenetrable recesses of Wakhan. From thence, in later years, he had gone to settle in Khokand, where he married. This prince had three sons— Yusuf, Bahanuddin, and Jehangir, the youngest and best known. In 1816, the first outbreak against

Chinese authority occurred, when a small rising took place in Tash Balik, a town to the west of Kashgar. This was speedily put down, and its leaders executed. It was but the forerunner of the storm.

In 1822, Jehangir resolved to reassert his claims over Kashgar, and, while his eldest brother continued to reside in retirement at Bokhara, he joined the Kara Kirghiz. With a party of these, under the command of their chief, Suranchi Beg, Jehangir raided up to the city of Kashgar. He was there repulsed in the suburbs, and compelled to flee. He then joined the Kirghiz of Bolor round Narym, who were nominally feudatories of China, and, with their aid, commenced a petty sort of border war. A small Chinese force was despatched against him, and drove the Kirghiz up as far as Fort Kurtka. On their return from this successful attack, they were, however, surprised in one of the defiles, and almost all were destroyed. This was the first reverse the Chinese had ever met with in the field, and it was at once bruited about through all parts of Central Asia. It gave a life to the Khoja cause which it had hitherto lacked, and adventurers from all parts flocked to the standard Jehangir now raised on the borders of Kashgar. The Khan of Khokand so far assisted him as to send him a skilled general, Isa Dadkhwah, and extended over his cause that protection and sanction which Khokand has ever since thrown over the Khoja family.

In the spring of 1826, Jehangir advanced in force against Kashgar, and the Chinese, despising their assailant, left their fortifications to encounter him in the open. A battle then ensued, of which the particulars have not come down to us, but which resulted in the defeat of the Chinese. Jehangir entered Kashgar in triumph, was received with acclamations by the people, urged on by the Aksakals, and proclaimed himself sovereign of the country, under the style of Seyyid Jehangir Sultan. His first act—the most significant exposure of the true sentiment of the Kashgarian people there well could be—was to order the execution of the Mahomedan Wang of Kashgar, by name Mahomed Seyyid.

The fall of Kashgar was the signal to the Aksakals throughout Altyshahr to begin that work for which they had been long preparing. In Yangy Hissar, Yarkand, and Khoten risings at once took place. The Chinese, surprised and unarmed, were butchered in the streets, and the Gulbaghs, as the visible token of the foreign rule, were razed with the ground.

The Gulbagh of Kashgar itself alone held out, but it at last fell, after sustaining a long siege, into the hands of Jehangir. His triumph completed, he had to concern himself more with his relations with Khokand than about the Chinese, who were mysteriously quiet. Mahomed Ali Khan, of Khokand, who thought that Jehangir's success was solely due to him, laid claim to a certain historical superiority over his vassal of Kashgar, to which the Khoja prince was not willing to assent. A large Khokandian army which had been sent to Kashgar returned, after losing 1,000 men before the walls of the Gulbagh, and its withdrawal was the signal for plots and counterplots to break out in the palace of the new ruler. These he promptly repressed, reduced the intriguing general, Isa Dadkhwah, in rank, and had emancipated himself from his thraldom to Khokand, when the news came that the Chinese were at last returning.

Although the western portion of Altyshahr had fallen away from the Chinese, Aksu and Maralbashi remained true to their allegiance. The Chinese still possessed the military keys of the country. Moreover, their possession of Ili gave them an enormous strategical advantage, and in the Tungan population they possessed an almost inexhaustible supply for recruiting "revindicating" armies. It is apropos here to state that China retained both of these advantages down to the time of Buzurg Khan and Yakoob Beg, and that, so long as she possessed them, the utmost Mussulman fanaticism and Khokandian patronage of the Khojas could do was futile against the arrest of fate. During six months Jehangir ruled in Kashgar, and during six months the Chinese viceroy made his preparations at Ili for a thorough revenge. An army of more than 100,000 men, raised from the Tungani, the Calmucks, and the Khitay garrison, was despatched from Ili, and in January, 1827, entered Aksu. Here all the brigades were concentrated, and the Viceroy, in conjunction with the general under him, by name Chang-Lung, drew up the plan of campaign, which was as follows:—A small army of 12,000 men was sent against Khoten across the desert through Cày Yoli, while the remainder of the host advanced on Maralbashi. Here another detachment of 7,000 strong was directed against Yarkand, while the main body marched on Kashgar by the banks of the Kizil Su.

Their advance was unopposed until they reached Yangabad, or Yangiawat, where Jehangir had concentrated an army computed at 50,000 men, but probably considerably less. When the armies sighted each other they pitched their camps in preparation for the decisive contest that was at hand. In accordance with immemorial custom, each side put forward on the following day its champion. On the part of the Chinese a gigantic Calmuck archer opposed on the part of Jehangir an equally formidable Khokandi. The former was armed with his proper weapons, the latter with a gun of some clumsy and ancient design, and while the Khokandi was busily engaged with his intricate apparatus, the Chinese archer shot him dead with an arrow through the breast. Of course, neither army would have acquiesced in the decree of the God of Battles as shown by the fate of its champion, but, in this case, it was true that—

> "Who spills the foremost foeman's life,
> His party conquers in the strife."

After a sharp, but brief, skirmish, the Kashgarian army

withdrew in confusion, and the following day the Chinese surrounded Kashgar on three sides. During the night the heart of Jehangir misgave him, and he fled to the Karatakka mountains. But here the snow had rendered the passes impracticable, and, after hiding for a few days in that difficult region, he was captured by the Chinese. His fate was that usually met with by traitors to that empire, for, being sent to Pekin, he was executed after torture. In this war Ishac Wang, of Ush Turfan, played a great part against the Khoja prince, and was rewarded for his good service by being appointed Wang of Kashgar. The Chinese constructed a fresh fort, Yangyshahr, in the place of the destroyed Gulbagh, and left a large Khitay garrison under Jah Darin. But Ishac Wang, who was given some such title as Prince of Kashgar, was soon afterwards deposed and recalled to China.

The Chinese authority was re-established without difficulty in the three cities, and peace settled down over Eastern Turkestan. But the repressive and punitive measures that the Chinese felt compelled to adopt raised a bitterer sentiment in the minds of the people than had previously existed. The Chinese were, indeed, only employing the same weapons that had been used against themselves, but none the less did these reciprocal atrocities dissipate whatever friendship there had been. Among other acts the Chinese removed 12,000 Mahomedan families from Kashgar to Ili, and these, destined to play an important part in the history of that province, became known as Tarantchis, or Toilers.

The Chinese resolved to punish Khokand as well. They broke off all trade with that state, and happy would it have been for them if they could have continued to preserve a closed frontier. But the Khan of that time was Mahomed Ali Khan, the most ambitious, as he was the ablest, of the princes of that country. He had just annexed Karategin, and had acquired some of the outlying provinces of Badakshan, which Mourad Beg, of Kundus, had absorbed about the same time. It was not probable that he would put up with the Chinese defiance. He was prudent enough to delay his advance until the main body of their army had been withdrawn. But, as soon as he was informed that the Chinese had gone back to Ili, Mahomed Ali, calling Yusuf, Sarim-sak's eldest son, from his retirement in Bokhara, placed him at the head of an army, under the charge of his own brother-in-law, Hacc Kuli Beg. The Chinese were worsted at Mingyol, and all the cities west of Aksu turned against the Chinese, as before, and proclaimed for Yusuf Khoja. Then the massacres were repeated, and the invasion of Yusuf was that of Jehangir over again in exact detail. But Yusuf's triumph was still more brief. Whereas Jehangir had ruled for nine months, Yusuf only swayed the sceptre for three.

The Chinese movements were delayed by small Mussulman revolts in Barkul and Shensi until the spring of 1831, but then, when they returned, they found that Yusuf and the Khokandian army had retreated some months before. The facts were that the moment Khokand invaded Kashgar, Bokhara attacked Khokand, and Hacc Kuli Beg had to be recalled to cope with matters more pressing than Khoja rights. With the general had gone Yusuf, far from anxious to encounter the Chinese alone. The return of the Khokandian army sufficed to dispel all danger from Bokhara, and, a few months after, Mahomed Ali Khan recommenced operations—in the east this time—against the Kirghiz under Chinese protection. The Chinese were thoroughly sick of these petty disputes, and made a treaty with Khokand, by which that state acquired fresh commercial privileges, in addition to the old ones, and by which the importance of the Aksakals rather increased than waned. Mahomed Ali Khan had acquired all he wanted, and discouraged the Khoja party, as, indeed, the terms of this treaty compelled him to do. The risings under

Jehangir and Yusuf were undoubtedly a great blow to Chinese prestige. To all appearance each had nearly been successful, and the Chinese, whose prestige was enormous in Central Asia—quite as great as that of Russia is now—had been, on one or two occasions, openly defeated. But, after all, this was a little matter compared to the shock the sentiments, called into being by sixty happy years, had received. Between Buddhist and Mussulman, between Chinaman and Central Asiatic, all the old antipathy was revived in the butcheries of Yarkand and Kashgar. The Kashgari showed that they could not appreciate the benefits they had received from China, and the Chinese, enraged at the slaughter of their countrymen, and, perhaps, also at the ingratitude evinced towards them, retaliated in kind. They did not appreciate that moderation, which Europeans have not always shown under similar circumstances, and wrought out their revenge in their own ancient fashion. It is absolutely necessary that the reader should remember that the two rapidly succeeding invasions of Jehangir and Yusuf form a turning-point in the history of the Chinese rule in Kashgar. Up to that epoch it is difficult to find words sufficient to do justice to China's beneficent government there; after that year it would be absurd to employ the same language. For the change the chief blame must fall upon the fickle and ungrateful Kashgari themselves, and then on the intriguing Andijanis. The Chinese are justified, at least, in saying that, having for more than half a century ruled this people with justice, they only relaxed in their efforts to promote its well-being when their unarmed countrymen and soldiers had been surprised and butchered by thousands.

Strange, and almost contradictory, as it may appear, there was a brief respite during which things seemed to have got into their old groove of happy prosperity; and the chief credit for this must be given to a Mahomedan sub-governor of the Chinese viceroy. Zuhuruddin, such was his name, had raised himself to the high post of Amban in Kashgar, a post never before held by any other than a Khitay. By birth he was of Kashgar, but he always represented himself as having been born and brought up in Khokand, where he had been imprisoned for a political offence. For seven or eight years he governed Kashgar to the perfect satisfaction both of the people and of the Chinese, and among some of his public acts may be mentioned the reconstruction of new forts outside the cities, in the place of those destroyed in the recent revolts. These were known now as Yangyshahr instead of Gulbagh. But in 1846 Zuhuruddin's rule was disturbed by hostilities on the part of Khokand and the Khojas.

In 1845 Khudayar Khan had been called to the throne after the death of Mahomed Ali, but his authority was not without its rivals. In the state of confusion that then ensued, Khokandian adventurers urged the Khoja princes, who were now represented by the sons of Jehangir, to renew their old attacks against the Chinese. To these advisers the Khojas turned a willing ear, and preparations were accordingly made for the enterprise. At that time Khokand was full of adventurers to whom Mahomed Ali had been able to give constant employment, but who now under the more peaceful rule of Khudayar idled their time in the cities of that khanate. Among these and the ever willing Kirghiz, it was not difficult for the princes of Kashgar to raise an army, formidable in numbers, if not remarkable for cohesion. At that time there were seven prominent Khoja princes in Khokand, of whom we may here mention Eshan Khan, usually called Katti Torah, Buzurg Khan, and Wali Khan. This inroad did not take its name from any one of these, but from them all combined ; thus it was distinguished as Haft Khojagan, or that of the Seven Khojas.

With his brothers and relations and a considerable following, Katti Torah advanced upon Kashgar, always

the first object of these invaders, which fell after a siege
of thirteen days through treachery. This was the only
success they achieved; the other cities would have nothing to do with them; and after two months' indulgence
in unbridled licence the Chinese beat them in a fight at
Kok Robat, and drove them out of the country. For
the first time there was an air of ridicule thrown over
these Khoja invasions in the eyes of the Kashgari,
while the outrages they had committed during their
brief stay had raised bitterer feelings still. Zuhuruddin, who fell under the displeasure of the Chinese, was
removed from his post, and fresh Ambans, once more
Khitay, were appointed. For nine years the Khojas
remained passive, but in 1855 Wali Khan and his
brother Kichik Khan, began to bustle once more on the
Kashgarian frontier. It was not until 1857 that Wali
Khan succeeded in forcing the advanced guard of
pickets maintained in the passes by the Chinese, but
having accomplished that his triumph was rapid.
Kashgar fell into his possession by a *coup de main*, and
once more a Khoja prince was seated in the *orda* at
Kashgar. Artosh and Yangy Hissar fell into his possession, and he threatened Yarkand. But everywhere the
Chinese garrisons remained unconquered in the forts,
biding the exhaustion of their foe and the arrival of
reinforcements. After a rule of nearly four months the
armies of Wali Khan having been then defeated by
the Chinese, the Khoja fled to the remote state of
Darwas, where he was surrendered to Khokand by its
chief Ismail Shah. This ruler, the most tyrannical,
bloodthirsty, and licentious of all the Khojas, met the
fate which he deserved long afterwards at the hands of
Yakoob Beg. His temporary tenure of power is still
remembered with dread by the people, who consider
him to have been the most incarnate monster who ever
held the destinies of their country in his hand. The
Chinese were more severe in their punitive measures
after this campaign than they had been after any other,

but, notwithstanding the part Khudayar and his people had played in Wali Khan's affair, the old relations between "these incompatible people," as Dr. Bellew aptly calls them, were restored. After this event there was but one minor disturbance caused by an inroad of Kirghiz nomads, headed by the sons of one of the principal victims of Chinese vengeance, but this had no political importance.

The invasion of Wali Khan was the last of those Khoja expeditions which took place prior to the Tungan revolt. In the thirty-two years that elapsed from the date of Jehangir's attempt to that of his son, there had in all been four of them. That of Jehangir himself being the first; of his elder brother Yusuf, the second; of Yusuf's eldest son, Katti Torah, the third; and of Jehangir's second son, Wali, the fourth. Not one of these is in any sense noteworthy, except for the crimes with which it was attended, and none of them did more than inflict an untold amount of misery and suffering on their own followers, as well as on the people they claimed to represent by right divine. It may also be noticed that with each enterprise there was a decline in moral character. Thus Jehangir was infinitely the best of them in every sense, and ruled fairly according to his lights. His brother Yusuf was of a more timid mind, but evidently not less imbued with some notion as to the sanctity of his mission. But from these to Katti Torah is a long descent. That prince seemed to aspire to securing his personal comfort and enjoyment alone, and disregarded all his subjects' complaints at the arbitrary rule of his deputies. But Wali Khan, the next of these Khoja kings from "over the mountains," excelled his cousin in vice, and tyranny, and utter want of purpose, not to speak of honour, quite as much as Katti Torah surpassed their sires. Nor can there be much hesitation in saying, from what Buzurg Khan did during the few months he held power, that, had not Yakoob Beg clipped his flight, he would have surpassed Wali Khan in his own peculiar vices. The reader will scarcely be disposed to take much interest in this irredeemable family, mad with the insanity of wickedness. But in justice to the Chinese, and to Yakoob Beg, it is only right that the rivals of the former should be made to appear in their true colours. All the sanctity that a peculiarly venerable descent from Hazrat Afak could give; all the stories told of the good deeds of some of their ancestors; all the affection that naturally attaches to a native rule, and all the dislike that must undermine a foreign, be it never so beneficent; all these things were destroyed by the weakness and ill success that attended the first two Khojas, and by the cruelty, indifference, and licentiousness that marked the last two. When Buzurg Khan came he found loyalty to the Khoja the heirloom of a few families, not of a people.

Had the Chinese restrained their vindictive feelings after the war with Jehangir, and proclaimed a free pardon to every one save the Khokandis, and then devoted their attention with the old vigour to peaceful pursuits, we believe that the Chinese rule would have been permanently secured. At that moment the Chinese were strong enough to have defied Khokand, and to have broken off all intercourse with that state. By dismissing the Aksakals, and severing the connection between the two states, the Chinese would have dispelled a danger that was for forty years to be ever before them, and, in the end, when the Tungani also rose, was to overcome them. Even clemency after Yusuf's inroad, which was really caused by the Chinese repressions, might not have been wholly in vain, and would have consolidated their position, when reinvigorated by Zuhuruddin's tenure of power. But the Chinese did not appreciate the quality of mercy. They could be just and impartial in the ordinary avocations of life, but to those who revolted against their authority they showed no trace of human feeling. For a man to rebel against them was certain death ; for a people, history tells us, the fate was not far different. Nor in dealing with such did they hesitate to supplement their military strength by the most despicable of artifices. Garrisons, accorded honourable terms, ruthlessly butchered ; princes, who threw themselves on their mercy, deported to Pekin to be hanged or tortured out of life : these are frequent occurrences in the history of China, and of her career in Central Asia the tale is identical. Yet, while drawing a veil over these blots on an otherwise brilliant surface, should we not desire to conceal them wholly from the view. It is necessary that they should be stated to understand what Chinese domination means as a whole ; of its great benefits there can be no doubt, if the people will remain quiescent. For fifty years, or for five hundred, China will rule an unmurmuring people with justice, and lead them into the paths of prosperity and peace; but if they rebel, if they openly defy authority, if they invite a hostile stranger within their borders, the punishment will be as sweeping, as cruel, and, in one and a higher sense, as wrongfully foolish, whether the association of the races may have been for fifty years or five centuries, as it was in the case of Kashgar. There is not much reason for hoping that China will deviate from her ancient custom, on the occasion now transpiring, of demanding "an eye for an eye" and "a tooth for a tooth."

CHAPTER VI.

THE BIRTH OF YAKOOB BEG AND CAREER IN THE SERVICE OF KHOKAND.

WE have now traced the history of Kashgar and of the neighbouring states down to the year 1860, immediately before the last Khoja invasion under Buzurg Khan, and the Kooshbege, Mahomed Yakoob. Before giving an account of that enterprise it is necessary that the reader should know what the past career of the future Athalik Ghazi had been. The previous chapters have, it is hoped, thrown some light on the state of Central Asia, and will assist the student of the question in comprehending how it was that Yakoob Beg achieved success, and what claims he may have to be considered a great ruler, for having done a work that is unique in the annals of modern Asia.

Mahomed Yakoob was born in or about the year 1820, in the flourishing little town of Piskent, in the khanate of Khokand. His father, Pur Mahomed Mirza, had, at various periods of his life, filled positions of responsibility in the government of the towns in which he resided. Thus, a native of Dihbid, near Samarcand, he had migrated to Khodjent, in the reign of Mahomed Ali Khan, with the intention of entering the priestly order. There, although he enrolled himself as a student in a religious seminary, for some reason or other, he appears to have changed his mind, and, instead of entering the Church, turned his attention to secular affairs. He was soon made Kazi of Kurama, a district and town of Khokand, and married a lady of that place. By this marriage he had one son, Mahomed Arif, who has since filled several posts of trust in Kashgar, notably that of Governor of Sirikul ; but of late this half-brother of Yakoob Beg seems to have been, either for incompetence or some other reason, under a cloud. Pur Mahomed, or Mahomed Latif, as he was more usually called, changed his residence from Kurama to Piskent, about the year 1818, and he shortly after his settlement in his new abode married again, his second wife being the sister of Sheik Nizamuddin, the Kazi of Piskent. Yakoob Beg was the issue of this marriage. The family of Yakoob Beg's father seems originally to have come from Karategin, on the borders of Badakshan, but in the time of the Usbeg conquest of that district the father of Mahomed Latif, then an infant, took refuge in Khokand. It is uncertain whether Mahomed Latif was born before their arrival at Dihbid or afterwards ; and it is now asserted that he claimed descent from Tamerlane. Whether this was a claim brought forward when his son was advancing in the world or not, it is impossible to test its accuracy. The parents of Yakoob Beg were therefore not without some pretensions, and it would seem that the bad fortune, from which for some generations they had been suffering, was beginning to disappear before the ability of Yakoob Beg raised it to a higher point than ever. In addition to the claims of his father and grandfather as Kazis of an important community, a sister of Yakoob Beg married Nar Mahomed Khan, Governor of Tashkent ; and, as we shall see later on, this connection was very instrumental in promoting the interests of the youthful Yakoob.

Piskent, Pskent, or Bis-kent, as it is sometimes spelt, is still a flourishing little community, fifty miles south of Tashkent, on the road to Khodjent. Its inhabitants are a thrifty, good-tempered set of people, who take great pride in the fact that the great Athalik Ghazi, the supporter of Islam, and the reputed terror of the

Russians, was one of themselves. In this little settlement there are many Tajiks, and this, doubtless, with other reasons, induced Mahomed Latif, a Tajik himself, to take up his abode there. To the east of Piskent the mountains begin to rise, which stretch onward until they become the Tian Shan and the Kizilyart ranges, and in these elevated regions the Tajik descendants muster in strong numbers. The Tajiks are Persian in their origin, and consequently of the Aryan stock, in contradistinction to the Turk or Tartar ruling class in Western Turkestan. They have, however, for so many generations been restricted to a limited career in the organization of the state, that, quite unjustly as it is, they have come to be regarded as an inferior race. English writers have fallen into this mistake, and have accepted as correct the definition given by the Turks of this subject race. As a matter of fact the contrary holds true, and the Tajik is superior to any of his masters in point of mental capacity. They are represented to still retain the fine presence and long flowing beards which distinguish those of Aryan blood from their Tartar opposite; and in height and strength they quite eclipse every other race of Central Asia. It was of this race that Yakoob Beg was the representative, and, although the greater part of his life was passed in ruling nations almost exclusively Tartar, some of the more prominent among his supporters, as well as the flower of his army, boasted that they, too, represented that master race, whose birth-place was to be found in the Indian Caucasus. The Tajiks still speak a Persian dialect, and their Iranian origin is thereby rendered almost indisputable.

Mahomed Yakoob's early years were passed at his home at Piskent, and it is said that it was intended that he should follow the profession which his father had repudiated. As a youth he was too wayward to submit to any check on his impulses, and the design of educating him as a "mollah," if it was ever seriously entertained, was abandoned long before he arrived at man's estate. He appears to have passed the first twenty years of his life in an idle, uneventful manner at Piskent, and then suddenly to have resolved to seek his fortune as best he might in the troubled waters of Khokandian politics. In 1845, we find him in the train of the newly seated khan, Khudayar, as "mahram," or chamberlain, and shortly afterwards, by the influence of his brother-in-law, the Governor of Tashkent, nominated a Pansad Bashi, a commander of 500. This was in 1847, about which year he married a Kipchak lady of Zuelik, a village in the district of Ak Musjid. He had three sons, of whom we shall hear more hereafter, by this marriage— Kooda Kul Beg, Kuli Beg, and Hacc Kuli Beg. Later on, in the year 1847, he was raised to the rank of Koosh-Bege, or "lord of the family"—more intelligibly described as vizier—and entrusted with the charge of the important post on the Syr Darya, called Ak Musjid, " White Mosque." This post he held with credit for six years, until 1853, when the Russians commenced that forward movement, of which we have not yet seen the close. At that time, Russia had not acquired one of the numerous strategic points now in her possession. The Syr Darya then was as far off from her frontier as the Oxus is now. Ak Musjid, built in the lower reaches of the river, and representing a Khokandian outpost of exceptional importance, was the grand obstacle in the path of the Russians operating from Kazalinsk, at the mouth of the Syr Darya. It was resolved, therefore, that this post, which, doubtless, encouraged all the marauders in the neighbourhood to continue their depredations against the Russian caravans, should be wrested from the hands of its owners, and either razed to the ground or converted into a Russian stronghold. General Perovsky was entrusted with this undertaking. The distance from Kazalinsk, or Fort No. 1, to Ak Musjid is not much over 200 miles, along the banks of the Syr Darya. Not many commissariat arrangements were necessary, nor did the distance to march require much time to delay the Russian officer in beginning his operations against the fort. The army with which he appeared before the walls may not have been large in numbers when compared with the armies of modern times, but, in all that makes a disciplined force formidable, it was exceptionally well supplied. The artillery was in greater strength than is usually considered necessary, and the expedition was still more efficient in engineers and cavalry. The garrison of Ak Musjid was, on the other hand, ill supplied, both in provisions and in ammunition, and the fort itself presented, neither in its position nor in its construction, any feature that an engineer officer would have considered calculated to make it capable of sustaining the attack of artillery for twenty-four hours. The Russian lines were constructed in the most approved method; but twice were their approaches destroyed, and twice their mines countermined. During twenty-six days the Russian bombardment was fast and furious, and during all that time the Khokandian defence was stubborn and persistent. But all the efforts of the garrison to break through the beleaguering lines were unavailing, and after so long a cannonade little more resistance could be expected from ramparts which were pierced in several places by wide and gaping breaches. The resolute commandant, who had done everything required by the most exacting code of military honour, confessed that there was nothing to be gained by a continued defence, and as it was known that the Russians were making preparations for an early assault, a messenger was despatched without delay to the Russian commander, expressing the willingness of the garrison to capitulate on honourable terms. General Perovsky, who had expected an easy triumph here, and possibly some more extended triumph in farther regions, was indignant at the resistance opposed to him by a paltry place like Ak Musjid, and received the messenger from the fort with ill-concealed impatience. Scarcely bestowing any attention on the letter, couched in humble terms as it was, of the commandant, General Perovsky petrified the astonished emissary with the declaration that on the morrow the fort would be taken by assault. This arbitrary assertion of his power, which was carried into practice, of course successfully, the next day, on an occasion when magnanimity ought to have been shown by the successful general, does not redound to the credit of the officer in question, and throws an instructive light on the latitude left to Russian generals in their instructions, and on the opinion felt for Central Asiatics by the civilizing representatives of the White Czar. To say that General Perovsky was urged to this act of gratuitous tyranny by a desire to obtain a cross of either St. Anne or St. George, is, after all, only to magnify the offence, and that Ak Musjid has taken the name of its conqueror, Fort Perovsky, is the means of perpetuating, not his fame, but his infamy, and the courageous conduct of the defenders. In the winter following its fall Yakoob Beg, with Sahib Khan, brother of the Khan of Khokand, attempted to retake the fort, but the *coup* proved abortive, and the Russians have never receded from their new acquisition.

Khudayar Khan had been elevated to the throne of Khokand in 1845, by the energy of Mussulman Kuli, a Kipchak chief, of singular astuteness, and aptitude for business. During his tenure of the post of Wazir, Khokand was peacefully and beneficently governed; but, as on every similar occasion in Central Asia, the ruler soon became jealous of the popularity acquired by his minister, although his own position was in reality confirmed by the wise measures of the very man to whom he had conceived a covert hostility. So with Khudayar Khan, the effeminate, and his minister, Mussulman Kuli, in the decade of which we are now speaking; as with Buzurg Khan, the debauchee, but correct representative of the Khojas, and his general and vizier, the

Kooshbege, Mahomed Yakoob, in the following. In 1858, Mussulman Kuli was seized by order of Khudayar Khan, and barbarously murdered; and from that occurrence the decadence of this unfortunate ruler of Khokand can be traced until, at last, he became a mere pensioner on the bounty of the Russians. Although Yakoob Beg became, to a certain extent, notorious for his gallant defence of Ak Musjid, it would appear, from his being styled after that event simply "Mir," or chief, that he had sunk in grade in his official status. It is probable that the chief cause of this was his failure to retake it, and not his ill success in defending it. He was, however, entrusted with the charge of the Kilaochi fort, a post which he held down to the murder of Mussulman Kuli.

Khudayar Khan had an elder brother, Mullah Khan, who had been passed over by Mussulman Kuli, when the state was put in order after the dissensions that arose on the death of the great ruler, Mahomed Ali. Now, on the death of Mussulman Kuli, who had given vitality to the régime of Khudayar, Mullah Khan and his partisans began to intrigue once more. Several Kipchak and Kirghiz leaders joined his cause, and Yakoob Beg at once became one of his most active supporters. Khudayar Khan was deposed, and retired into temporary seclusion. For his services to the new ruler Yakoob Beg was made Shahawal, an officer corresponding to a chamberlain or court intendant. He was soon restored to his old rank of Kooshbege, and appointed governor of the frontier fort of Kurama, the same place of which his father had been Kazi. And in 1860 he came still more to the front, when he was summoned to Tashkent to assist Kanaát Shah, the Nahib of Khokand, in making preparations in case the Russians, who had for some time seemed to be threatening Khokand, should cross the frontier. Mullah Khan was murdered at this time, having held the reins of power but for the brief space of two years, and Khudayar Khan emerged from his hiding place. He was welcomed both by Kanaát Shah and Yakoob Beg; and in return for their support he consented to forget the past. Yakoob Beg, as his reward, received the governorship of Kurama. It was during these troubles that Alim Kuli, a Kirghiz chieftain, appeared upon the scene. He possessed many of the attributes that distinguished his predecessor Mussulman Kuli, and his successor, in the eyes of the people, Yakoob Beg. He had undoubtedly a great capacity for intrigue, but was inferior to the former in administrative capacity, and to the latter in military skill. He now set Shah Murad, grandson of Shere Ali Khan, up as a claimant to the throne, and was speedily joined by Yakoob Beg, who once more abandoned the cause of Khudayar Khan, who, it must be remembered, had always treated Yakoob Beg in a friendly way, and who in their early days had been his boon companion. This conspiracy was unsuccessful, and Yakoob Beg, who had yielded up Khodjent, with the defence of which he had been entrusted by Alim Kuli, on the approach of the forces of Khudayar Khan, took refuge in Bokhara. Here he was favourably received, and resided as a noble attached to the court. In 1863 the Ameer of Bokhara, Muzaffur Eddin, marched a large army into Khokand for the purpose of restoring his brother-in-law, Khudayar, to the throne, for he had again been deposed by the intrigues of Alim Kuli; Yakoob Beg accompanied this force, and once more appears, for the last time, on the troubled arena of Khokandian politics. The Bokhariot army was soon recalled, and Khudayar Khan was left to face the difficulties of his position unaided. In a few months an arrangement was come to between Alim Kuli and Yakoob Beg and other leading nobles against Khudayar. Sultan Murad, who had first been supported and then murdered by Alim Kuli, having been thus effectually removed, this king-maker had set up Sultan Seyyid in his place. Yakoob Beg so far profited by this new confederacy that he was restored to his old offices and perquisites, and sent once more to hold his former post as governor of Kurama. He collected as many allies as he was able, and brought them with him to assist in the capture of Khodjent. On this important town being secured the regent Alim Kuli passed through Kurama on his way to seize and settle the capital, Tashkent. He appointed a connection of his own, Hydar Kuli, with the title of Hudaychi, as governor of Kurama, and took Yakoob Beg in his train to Tashkent. Shortly after their arrival at Tashkent, news came of the Russian occupation of Tchimkent, and the survivors of the force driven out by Tchernaief soon appeared with a confirmation of the intelligence. This was in April, 1864, and until October of that year, when the Russians appeared before the town, Yakoob Beg was engaged in strengthening the fortifications of the capital. When the army of General Tchernaief did appear in the neighbourhood, Yakoob Beg, with a rashness that cannot be too strongly condemned, went forth to encounter it in the open. As might have been expected, the Russians were victorious, and Yakoob Beg was compelled to seek refuge with his shattered forces within the walls of Tashkent. The Russians themselves had suffered some loss, and either awed by the bold demeanour of their old antagonist, or, as is more probable, encountering some difficulty in bringing up supplies, and being unprovided with a siege train, thought the more prudent policy would be to retire to Tchimkent until reinforcements and other necessaries should arrive. Alim Kuli, in the course of a few days after this reverse, arrived at Tashkent in person with a large body of troops, and employed all his energies in strengthening the defences before the return of the Russians. It is very certain that on this occasion, the first on which Yakoob Beg had a command of any consequence, he permitted his natural impetuosity to get the better of his discretion, and that it was the height of madness on his part to enter into an engagement in the open with the disciplined and formidable forces of Tchernaief, when, by leaving that general to undertake the siege of Tashkent, he might have had it in his power to inflict a serious, and for the time conclusive, blow against the Russians when the reinforcing army of Alim Kuli came up. With half his army discouraged by defeat, Alim Kuli found himself restricted to a policy of inaction, through the over-hastiness of his lieutenant. The Russians did not return until after the departure of Yakoob Beg for Kashgar, but when they did they found that Alim Kuli had made every preparation in his power to receive them. On the first occasion they were again forced to retreat after a skirmish which the Khokandians claim as a victory; but in 1865 they appeared before the walls in greater force. Alim Kuli, with a gathering vastly superior in numbers to the Russians, attacked them a few miles to the north of Tashkent, and the fortunes of the day hung in the balance, until the fall of Alim Kuli, who, whilst boldly leading a charge of Kirghiz cavalry, was pierced in the chest by a musket ball. He was carried from the field by a faithful officer, and expired that night in Tashkent. Alim Kuli appears to have been actuated to some extent by a disinterested patriotism, as much as by more personal motives. With his fall, and the departure of Yakoob Beg for another sphere of operations, all hope of a continued state of independence for Khokand was dissipated. After this severe defeat the Russians laid close siege to Tashkent. The Khokandians in their distress applied to Bokhara for aid, and the Russians hastened to occupy Chinaz to intercept it. The Bokhariot army was routed by the Russian army under General Romanoffski at the battle of Irjar, in May, 1866, eleven months after Tashkent had been occupied by Tchernaief. It was during this period of anarchy, with a hostile Russian and an allied Bokhariot force on his soil, that Khudayar Khan once more supplanted the nominee of

Alim Kuli, Sultan Seyyid, and at the close of the campaign Khudayar was left in possession of the southern portion of Khokand. This Khan appears to have been of an unambitious nature, for, during his various exiles, he devoted himself to private business with an energy he had never shown in the management of the public affairs, and when he at last sank into private life and became a pensioner of the Russian Court, on the complete annexation of his state, he is said to have acquired not only a happiness, but many virtues unknown to him in his more elevated lot. The unfortunate Sultan Seyyid, after wandering for some years out of Khokand, was, when he ventured to return in 1871, executed. Many of the partisans of Seyyid on the defeat by the Russians, and on the overthrow of his rivals by Khudayar, sought refuge in the mountains of the Kizilyart, whence they proceeded to join Yakoob Beg in Kashgar, where they arrived at a most opportune moment as will be seen.

To return to Yakoob Beg. After his defeat before Tashkent he was employed under Alim Kuli in repairing the defences of that town and collecting troops from the whole district, but his reputation had been lowered by that reverse. There was a certain jealousy between the Kirghiz chief and the Tajik soldier of fortune. Yakoob Beg saw in Alim Kuli an obstacle to his further promotion, and Alim Kuli recognized in the Kooshbege a possible rival and successor. Any excuse therefore to keep Yakoob Beg in the background, or indeed to get rid of him altogether, would be very welcome to Alim Kuli. We hear little more of the unsuccessful general until his departure for Kashgar a few months afterwards. He had to wipe out in other regions and against other foes the stain he had incurred in his encounters with the Russians.

While these events were in progress at Tashkent, an envoy arrived there from Sadic Beg, a Kirghiz prince on the frontiers of Ili and Kashgar. He brought intelligence that his master had availed himself of the dissensions among the Chinese, to seize the city of Kashgar, and he requested the Khan of Khokand to send him the heir of the Khojas, in order that he might place him on the throne. As the facts really stood, Sadic Beg had only laid siege to Kashgar, and, finding that he was met with a strenuous resistance, had recourse to the plan of setting up a Khoja king to strengthen his failing efforts, but of the true state of affairs in Kashgar it is evident that everybody in Tashkent was profoundly ignorant. The Khokandian policy had always been, however, to maintain their interests intact in Eastern Turkestan, and to weaken in every possible way the credit of the Chinese. An envoy bringing news of a fresh revolt in Kashgar was, therefore, sure of a friendly reception at Tashkent, even if he did not return with some more striking tokens of amity. But on this occasion the danger from Russian movements was so close at hand, and all the efforts of the state were so concentrated in preparations for defence, that Alim Kuli, whatever he may have thought of its prospects, and however much he may have sympathized with its object, was unable to give the Kirghiz emissary any aid in his enterprise. When, however, Buzurg Khan, the only surviving son of Jehangir Khan, either of his own free will, or instigated, as some say, by Yakoob Beg, offered to assert his claims on Kashgar, Alim Kuli expressed his approval of the design, and gave his moral assistance so far as was compatible with no active participation therein. He, however, gave Buzurg Khan the services of Kooshbege Mahomed Yakoob to act as his commander-in-chief, or Baturbashi. Thus did Alim Kuli free himself from his troublesome subordinate, and despatched on an errand which seemed likely to end in disgrace and defeat, but which really led to empire, the only native whom he dreaded as being capable of supplanting him.

Yakoob Beg had up to this point given little promise

of future distinction.   He had, indeed, earned the
reputation of being a gallant soldier, if a not very
prudent one ; and in the intrigues that had marked the
history of his state for twenty years, he had borne his
fair share.   But no one would have dreamt of prognos-
ticating that he possessed the ability necessary to win
campaigns against superior forces, and then to erect a
powerful state on the ruins that fell into his possession.
The most favourable opinion would have been, that he
would have died manfully as a soldier, and as a true
Mussulman.   When he embarked in the enterprise of
conquering Kashgar, he was no longer in the first flush
of youth, but was a man who covered his fiery spirit
and great ambition with a cloak of religious zeal and
diplomatic apathy.   Twenty years' experience in the
most intriguing court in Central Asia had placed every
muscle at his complete command, and even in the most
disastrous   moments   in   his   career,   he   is   always
represented as being calm and collected—calm in his
belief in Kismut, and collected in a persuasion of his
own resources.   One fact that will account for the
slowness with which he advanced into notoriety is that
he was entirely dependent on his own capacity for
promotion.   He had no wealth, no large following, and
in the two leaders, Kipchak and Kirghiz, Mussulman and
Alim Kuli, he had competitors of almost equal merit with
himself, while they each possessed personal power and
family connections that placed them far beyond the reach
of the hardy soldier and court chamberlain.   Some of his
detractors had availed themselves of his impecuniosity
to circulate stories of his having had dealings with
the Russians ; but these, although invested with circumstances originating in non-Russian quarters, are
probably without any truth.   The chief charge, to be
taken for what it is worth, is, that the weakness of his
defence of the Ak Musjid district, after the fall of the
fort, was owing to his having received a large bribe
from the Russians.   Another is, that in 1863, after his

return from Bokhara, he neglected to retard the Russian movements for a pecuniary consideration. In both cases the sum mentioned is very large; and besides the apparent falseness of these rumours, we have only to consider that he was not worth a bribe, and that his opposition to the Russians was marked by all the want of foresight of religious zeal. All these considerations make such rumours appear in their true light; and although we are aware that a follower of Yakoob Beg confirmed, if he did not originate, these charges, it seems to us that the Russians, if there had been truth in the report, would long ago have placed the fact before the peoples of Asia, and required Yakoob Beg when Ameer of Kashgar to have acted in a more friendly way towards his former employers. But the simple reason that Yakoob Beg could not have rendered any service to the Russians worth the thousands of pounds he is said to have received, ought to demolish the whole fabrication. If Yakoob Beg's life proves one thing more than another, it was that he was a most fanatical Mussulman, and as such hating the Russians, as the most formidable enemy of Islam, with the most intense hate his fiery nature was capable of. This man's whole life must have been the greatest hypocrisy if he was not genuine in his religious intolerance, and that intolerance rendered any connivance with Russian measures an impossibility. Owing to his early connection with the church, and his maternal grand-father's high position therein, Yakoob Beg was always distinguished for the strict orthodoxy of his views. Through all his life he seems to have made it his chief object to keep the church on his side. When he was reduced to the most desperate straits in his after life in Kashgar, when some of the most faithful of his followers fell off from him, and when even Buzurg Khan, the man whom he had placed upon a throne, declared him a rebel and a traitor, he never lost heart so long as the ministers of the church held by him; and, on the other hand, they, recognizing the fidelity of their champion, supported him through good and ill repute. Whilst residing at Bokhara " the holy " he had attached to his person several of the most distinguished preachers of Islam throughout Asia, and he had taken all the vows that give a peculiar sanctity to the relations that connect the layman with his priest. It was here that he publicly announced his intention of going on pilgrimage to Mecca; an intention which he repeated on several occasions during his rule of Kashgar, but was obliged, by the position and precarious existence of that state, always to perform by deputy. When he had established himself as ruler, his first measure was to re-enforce the Shariàt and to endow several shrines that had been erected to the memory of the chief Khoja saints. It was by such means that he at every crisis of his life had striven to make his interests identical with those of his religion, and when he became a responsible and successful prince his past life stood him in such good stead, that he easily came to be regarded throughout Asia as the most faithful and redoubtable supporter of Islam.

At this period of his life he is described by one who knew him as being of a short but stoutish build, with a keenly intelligent and handsome countenance. He had, during the vicissitudes of his career in Khokand, been so often near assassination, or execution, that the result of the morrow had, to all external appearance, become a matter of secondary consideration to him, and his features, schooled to immobility by a long career of court intrigue, appeared to the casual observer dull and uninteresting. When, however, the conversation turned on subjects that specially interested him, such as the advance of Russia, the future of Islam, or the policy of England, he threw aside his mask, and became at once a man whose views, with some merit in themselves, were rendered almost convincing by the singular charm of his voice and manner. He was honourably distinguished at all times by the simplicity of his dress, and his freedom from the pretension and love of show characteristic of most Asiatics; and at the very highest point of his power he was only a soldier, occupying a palace. As was well said of Timour, the Athalik Ghazi placed the " foot of courage in the stirrup of patience," and he evidently set himself to copy the great lessons of military success that might be learnt from the careers of Genghis Khan, Timour, and Baber. Such is some account of the commander-in-chief to the expedition of Buzurg Khan. The Khoja, himself, was a man about the same age as his lieutenant, but in every other respect as different as he well could be. Personally a coward, fond of show and every kind of luxury, and of the treacherous, fickle nature that marked his race, he had done nothing during his past life to compensate for the want of the most ordinary virtues. Although he participated in the expedition of Wali Khan, he showed no possession of merit, and in the subsequent occupation that the Khojas maintained in Kashgar during a few weeks, he, perhaps more than any other of his kinsmen, disgusted the people by his open and unbridled licentiousness. Such were the two men who, in the latter days of 1864, set out from Tashkent for the recovery of a kingdom. Of their chances of success few would have ventured then to predict a settlement in their favour; none, certainly, such as was obtained by Yakoob Beg. It is now time for us to relate how they fared in Eastern Turkestan.

CHAPTER VII.

THE INVASION OF KASHGAR BY BUZURG KHAN AND YAKOOB BEG.

THE Chinese were on several occasions, as we have seen, threatened in Eastern Turkestan by the pretensions of the Khojas, and the secret or open machinations of Khokand. But they had at all times triumphed over every combination of circumstances, so long as they themselves were united. The temporary success of Jehangir Khan was obliterated by the excesses which characterized his occupation of the country, and by the energy and large display of force with which the Chinese pacified the state on his flight; and the last, under Wali Khan, can scarcely be dignified by any other appellation than that of a marauding incursion. But a great and important change had occurred in the few years that had elapsed since 1859. The Chinese no longer presented a collected force to the onslaught of an assailant. In every quarter of their empire, victorious rebels had established themselves, and had detracted in an immeasurable degree from the effective strength of the Government. A Mahomedan ruler swayed over the Panthays, in Yunnan, from his capital at Ta-li-foo; the Taepings round Nankin were at the summit of their career, just before the appearance of Colonel Gordon, when, in 1862, a fresh danger broke out in the provinces of Kansuh and Shensi. From a remote period there had been extensive Mussulman settlements in these provinces, and so early as the seventeenth century they had been the cause of trouble to the great

Kanghi. The Emperor Keen-Lung, indeed, at one time attempted to settle the question for ever by ordering the massacre of every Mahomedan over fifteen years of age. Even this sweeping measure did not have the desired effect, and whether persecution was the means or not of giving vitality to the cause, it is certain that they had become more numerous, more resolute, and more confident in their own superiority to the other Chinese by the middle of the present century. These Mahomedans were known as Tungani, Dungani, or Dungans, while the Buddhist Chinese are spoken of as Khitay. Many writers are not satisfied with this simple explanation of the name Tungani, and will have it that they were a distinct race, who were either transported to China at some period of Chinese conquest, or were compelled to seek refuge there by some advancing barbarian horde. They even assert that they can trace the name and origin of this people to a tribe dwelling in the country of the lower waters of the Amoor; but while there is complete uncertainty on the subject it seems simpler to accept the signification that the word Tungani conveys to the Chinese, and that is Mahomedan. We know, for certain, that these people had resided in Kansuh and its neighbouring province for centuries—that they were remarkable for a superiority in strength and activity over the Khitay, and that they possessed the virtues of sobriety and honesty. They were also not infected by the disease of opium smoking, and we should imagine them to have been a quiet, contented, and agreeable people at their most prosperous period. Their physical superiority to the Khitay would probably be owing to their abstention from " bang " and opium, and we need not suppose that they were the descendants of a stronger race, who had issued from the frigid north, when we have an explanation so much simpler and more natural at hand. They were found by their Khitay rulers to form excellent soldiers, policemen, and other Government servants, such as carriers, &c. In this last employment many found their way to Hamil, thence to Turfan and Urumtsi, and their numbers were increased by discharged soldiers, who remained as military settlers sooner than return to Kansuh.   In the course of a few generations their numbers became much greater, until, at last, in the cities we have named, they formed the majority of the inhabitants.   In Kuldja, too, they were very numerous, but south of the Tian Shan they do not seem to have advanced westward of Kucha in any great force. At Aksu the Andijan influence, supreme in Western Kashgar, presented an impassable barrier to the Tungani, who, it must be remembered, had no sympathy with Khokand.   The Tungani were, therefore, Mahomedan subjects of China, originating in Kansuh, but who had also, in the course of time, spread westward into Chinese Turkestan and Jungaria.   They were employed in the service of the country without restriction, nor can we find that they were subjected to any unfair usage, after the measures taken against them in the earlier days of Keen-Lung.   They may not have been as highly favoured as the Sobo tribes, and they may have been subjected to some ridicule in Kansuh; but in Jungaria they were on an equality with all the other Chinese, and immeasurably better placed in the political scale than the Andijanis or Tarantchis.   The Chinese had just grounds for believing that no danger to their rule in Eastern Turkestan or Jungaria would ever be caused by the Tungani, and it is not easy to explain how their reasonable anticipations were falsified.   The Tungani were fervent, if not the most orthodox in form of, Mahomedans, and it would appear that they were not free from a belief in their own superiority to the Khitay.   This feeling was fostered by the "mollahs," or priests, who became very active within the Chinese dominions, when these had been extended by conquest into the heart of Asia. As if in retaliation for a Khitay conquest the Mahomedan religion was undermining the outworks of its rival's power slowly, but surely.   The impulse given to trade by the security and patronage that accompanied Chinese rule was, at least from a purely Chinese point of view, neutralized as an advantage by the admission into the empire of energetic and eloquent preachers of the superior merits of Mahomedanism. It required many generations before the effect of their efforts became perceptible, and it was not until the power of China fell into an extraordinary decline—a decline which many thought, with some show of reason, was to herald the fall, but which later events have seemed to make but the prelude to a more vigorous life than ever—that these Mahomedan missionaries among the Tungani knew that the time to reap what they had sown with patience and persistency was at hand. It is impossible not to connect this event in some degree with that unaccountable revival of fanaticism among Mahomedans, which has produced so many important events during the last thirty years, and of which we are now witnessing some of the most striking results.

In 1862, a riot occurred in a small village of Kansuh; it was suppressed with some loss of life, and people were beginning to suppose that it possessed no significance, when a disturbance broke out on a large scale at Houchow, or Salara. The Tungani had risen, and the unfortunate unarmed Khitay were massacred right and left. The rising soon assumed the proportions of a civil war, and the infection spread to the neighbouring province of Shensi. Then ensued scenes of the most atrocious barbarity. The Khitay, who all their lives had lived at peace and as neighbours with the Tungani, were butchered without mercy. The Mahomedan priests seized all the governing power into their own hands, and set their followers the example of unscrupulous ferocity. The movement, even if we make allowance for the difficulties besetting the government in other regions, must be considered to have been attended by unexpected success. It can only be accounted for by the supposition that the Khitay were taken completely by surprise, and realized neither the extent nor the nature of the danger to which they were exposed.   Before the end of 1862, a Tungan government was established in Kansuh, and its jurisdiction was for a time acknowledged in Shensi.   The priests formed an administration amongst themselves, and set themselves to the task of consolidating what they had won, and of preparing for the time when the Chinese should come for vengeance.   The events happening in Kansuh were naturally of interest to the Tungani in the country lying beyond it, and it was not long before the example set them was followed in Hamil, Turfan, Urumtsi, Manas, and other cities of that district.   The same success attended the movement here as in Kansuh.   The Chinese power was subverted, the Khitay massacred with greater circumstances of cruelty, if possible, and a new Tungan state was formed in those cities.   Each district retained a nominal independence, under the headship of a priest, or body of priests, or of one of the native Tungan princes, and then the movement spread with irresistible strides to Karashar, Kucha, and Aksu.   There it stopped, and south of the Tian Shan the Tungan revolt proper never extended west of Aksu.

In Altyshahr and Kuldja for some months longer the Chinese maintained the external show of power, but all their communications with China were cut off, and neither in numbers nor resources had they sufficient means to cope with the Tungani unaided.   They would have accomplished as much as could have been expected from them if they succeeded in keeping possession of that which they still occupied.   The Tungan element in Kucha and Aksu was not predominant. It had to share power with the Khojas, and, as we shall see later on, the Khojas of these two cities seized the governing power for themselves.   It was the appearance of the Tungan sedition in these cities, which occupy a middle relation to the purely Chinese cities of Hamil and Urumtsi, and the almost totally Khokandian cities of Yarkand and Kashgar, that roused the Kashgari to a full appreciation of the importance to themselves of this movement, and the Chinese garrisons and settlers to an equally just realization of their own danger. The Kashgari, not free from the fanaticism of all their co-religionists, and naturally elated at the successes of the Tungani, forgot, with their well proved fickleness, all the benefits they had received from the Chinese, and waited eagerly for a favourable opportunity to come for them to imitate the example set them by their eastern neighbours. Nor had they long to wait, although it was not from them that came the first spark that lighted the firebrand of civil war and anarchy throughout the length and breadth of Altyshahr.

It will be remembered that the Khokandian government had the right to nominate in each city, where they received dues on Mahomedan merchandise, an agent or tax-collector to look after the proper levy of the tax. In some of the larger cities this official would require a considerable staff of assistants, and thus a certain number of skilled Khokandian officials were permanently located on Kashgarian or Chinese territory. After the failure of the expedition of Wali Khan, in which these officials seem to have disappeared, either having become merged in the body of his partisans or sacrificed during the massacres of that time, a fresh batch of Khokandians was installed, and occupied, in a legal sense, the same position as their predecessors. It would appear, however, that the natural result of their aid to Wali Khan followed, and that the Chinese Ambans regarded their presence with scarcely concealed dislike, and proclaimed that these Khokandian tax-gatherers were devoting more of their attention to the propagation of heretical religious and political doctrines than to the collection of dues on silk and other articles of commerce. It would require but the slightest untoward circumstance to fan this ill-feeling into the most insatiate hatred and hostility. The danger was rendered the more serious when the Chinese Ambans perceived for the first time that the sympathies of a large portion of their Tungan soldiery were estranged from them. It was doubtful whether the Tungan regiments could be relied on against a fresh Khoja revolt, and it was certain that they would not combine in any repression of the Mahomedan religion, even though the sufferers should only be Andijanis. Such was the state of the public mind in Altyshahr in 1862, when the Tungani revolted and obtained success in Kansuh and Shensi.

As early as 1859 the hostility of the Chinese Ambans to the Andijani tax-collectors received a forcible illustration in the town of Yarkand. At that time Afridun Wang was governor, and, whether there was any personal enmity at the root of the action or not, he found little difficulty in convincing both himself and the other Chinese residents that the Andijani agent had been stirring up discontent against them in the town. Accordingly, as self-preservation is the first law of nature, this Khokandian official, with his attendant, was arrested and executed. There may have been some foundation for the accusations made by Afridun Wang against his rival: more probably there was none; but on referring the matter to the Viceroy of Ili for decision it was decided that the governor should be removed. The Khokandian government sent fresh agents, and it is not stated that any reparation was given to the families of the sufferers. From this it would appear that the post of tax-collector in Altyshahr for His Highness the Khan of Khokand was not a very desirable position. Afridun Wang retired to his native town of Turfan, where, three years later on, he contributed more than any one else to the success of the Tungan movement. His policy, if anti-Khokandian, was pro-Mahomedan or Tungan, and his case is very typical of the nature of this rising. In Turfan he continued to be one of the chief men, until, six years later on, it fell to the Athalik Ghazi.

His successor in the governorship of Yarkand did not interfere with the Khokandian officials, but for this moderation he made up by the exactions he committed on the residents, more particularly on the Mahomedan portion of them. His extortions and cruelties had the effect as much of disgusting his own followers as of rousing a spirit of opposition among the oppressed. It was while things were in this uncertain state at Yarkand that the governor received secret notice of the Tungan revolt in Kansuh, and he at once perceived that, when this important intelligence became known, not only would his own Tungan troops become more openly mutinous, but that the Khojas might seize the opportunity to assert their claim to the country once more. In this special case, in addition to the general apprehension that would be felt by any Chinese governor at the aspect of affairs, there was personal fear for the unjustifiable acts of his government, and the Amban, in his trepidation, resolved on the most strenuous precautions to avert the danger from himself. He summoned a council of war of his Buddhist lieutenants, and stated the exact position to them; how the Tungan portion of their forces could not be depended on; how the Tungan settlers would join them; and how the Andijani agents would do their utmost to unite in one cause against themselves all those who followed the teaching of Islam; and how all these events, which before were possible, had been rendered probable by the Tungan successes in the east. He dwelt on the fact that no time was to be lost in the execution of such precautions as they thought necessary; that at any moment the news might arrive, and then they would be in a minority; and he did not attempt to conceal the purport of his address—that he was in favour of sharp measures, of going to the root of the evil at once, and of massacring every Mussulman in the town. The council of war was not prepared to endorse such a violent proceeding without careful consideration. There were many dissentients, and the meeting was adjourned. It reassembled, and, on this occasion, although the supporters of more moderate measures had decreased, it adjourned once more before deciding. The danger evidently appeared more appalling to the governor than to his subordinates; perhaps also there was some personal dislike for their chief even among his Khitay following. At the second meeting they seemed, indeed, more willing to acquiesce in his proposed strong measures, and this may have been caused by their observation of the state of public opinion in the interval. But even then no final decision could be arrived at, and the Khitay never had a chance after that of making any defence in Yarkand. The Tungan troops were not long in hearing, through their chief officer, Mah Dalay, that there was a plot on foot among the Khitay to disarm, or, as others said, to massacre them, and they then learnt of the Mahomedan revolt in China and along the road thither. They immediately determined to be beforehand with the Amban and his lukewarm council, and no weak hesitation marred the execution of their plot, as it had that of the Chinese governor.

The Khitay troops, unarmed, were surprised during the night, and cut down without quarter, and the small body of survivors sought refuge in the Yangyshahr fort. This was in August, 1863, and no fewer than 7,000 Khitay soldiers are computed to have fallen on this single occasion. The Tungan troops were thereupon joined by the townspeople, and the question then to be decided was, who was to be supreme, the Tungani or the Andijan-Kashgari Mahomedans. The former were simply an unlettered and rather savage soldiery; the latter possessed keen intellects for manipulating a fanatical people, and for improvising an administration of a superficial character. The balance of power was evenly distributed until reinforcements arrived from Aksu and Kucha to the anti-Tungan party. Two Khojas who had been banished from Kucha, for endeavouring to promote their own interests in the name of Khokand, had fled to Aksu, where they met the same fate. In this latter flight many of similar principles joined them, so that when they reached Yarkand they had a numerous force at their back. The Khojas in the first place joined their forces to the Tungani, to storm the remaining Khitay in the Yangyshahr. The Khitay after a gallant resistance perceived that further opposition was impossible. Then occurred one of those deeds, which, if Europe instead of Asia had been the scene, would have been handed down to posterity as a rare example of military devotion and courage, but which, although not unique even in the annals of the campaign we are entering upon, having occurred in little-known Eastern Turkestan, is not realized as an event that has actually taken place. It is a myth of the myth-land to which it belongs. And yet, when we read how the Amban summoned all his officers to his chamber, where he sat in state surrounded by his wives, his family, and his servants; how all were silent, and yet sedate and prepared; how, at the given signal that all were present, and that the foe was at the gate, the aged warrior dropped his lighted pipe into the mine beneath; how the exulting foe won after all but a barren triumph; and how the Khitay taught the natives that if they had forgotten how to conquer they had not how to die, we feel that there is an under-current throughout the story, that, apart from the admiration it must command, has claims to our own special sympathy. The Chinese, as we did in India in the dark hours of 1857, asserted their superiority over the semi-barbarous races under their sway, even when all hopes of a recovery seemed to be abandoned. After the fall of the citadel the Khoja element was supreme in Yarkand, and a priest named Abderrahman was set up as king.

The other cities of Altyshahr promptly followed the example of Yarkand, and the Chinese power was completely subverted on all hands. The Khitay were massacred whenever they fell into the hands of the Mahomedans, and the only places that still held out were the citadels, notably the Yangyshahr of Kashgar. The inhabitants of this city appear to have been unable to keep their advantage over the Chinese, for they appealed to the Kirghiz to come in and assist them. These nomads, under their chief, Sadic Beg, were nothing loth to join in expelling the Chinese, as such a change could only increase their advantages by substituting an unsettled for a settled government. Siege was accordingly laid to the citadel of Kashgar, but the irregular troops of the new allies were unable to make any impression on the fort, defended as it was by a large Khitay garrison. If the Chinese commander had assumed a more active policy, he might have destroyed his opponents, but he was waiting for the arrival of reinforcements, which he expected before many months. In not relying solely on his own resources he proved himself unable to read the changed signs of the time; if, indeed, he was not already meditating that surrender, which he ultimately concluded with Yakoob Beg. Sadic Beg, finding himself unable to take the fort, and knowing that it was uncertain how long the Kashgari would remain friendly to himself, resolved to play the part of king-maker, and sent the embassy to Tashkent for a Khoja to come and rule Kashgar, only he omitted to say that Kashgar was not conquered.

We can now return to Buzurg Khan and his commander-in-chief. When they left Tashkent they had only a following of six, among whom were Abdulla, Pansad; Mahomed Kuli, Shahawal; and Khoja Kulan, Hudaychi. All of these played a very prominent part under Yakoob Beg. From Tashkent they went to

Khokand, where their numbers rose to sixty-eight. Here the final preparations were made, and during the first days of January, 1865, this band of adventurers crossed the Khokand frontier into Eastern Turkestan. The mountain forts seem to have been deserted, for no opposition was encountered in the passage of the Terek defile. Several small bodies of troops joined them, and they reached Mingyol in the neighbourhood of Kashgar with increased numbers and confidence. Sadic Beg had conceived a more sanguine view of his situation by this time, and half repented that he had invited the Khojas in at all, more particularly when he found that the Khoja had a following of his own, and a skilled commander and minister in Yakoob Beg. He then strove to dissuade Buzurg Khan from proceeding further with an enterprise fraught with great peril, for he represented the Chinese as sure to return, when summary vengeance would be exacted. But his arguments were unavailing. Either Buzurg Khan or his adviser, Yakoob Beg, was deaf to all entreaty. The enterprise they had embarked on must be continued to the bitter end. They could not think of returning to Khokand with nothing accomplished, with the stigma attaching to them of a retreat when there had been no foe. Sadic Beg could not but submit with the best grace possible; and Buzurg Khan was accordingly placed on the throne of his ancestors.

In his "*orda*" or palace he administered justice and received the congratulations of his own followers and of the Andijani townspeople. The court rules were drawn up on the model of those in use in Khokand, and while the expedition had but established itself, in an uncertain manner, in one city it was thought necessary that etiquette should be as strictly defined and enforced as if all this were taking place in a brilliant and luxurious capital. In a few days Sadic Beg, on finding that he played but a secondary part, revolted, and set himself up as ruler at Yangy Hissar. It was now that Yakoob Beg came to the front, and assumed the control of affairs until the fall of the contemptible Buzurg. With great difficulty after the desertion of their Kirghiz allies was a force of 3,000 men collected around the new Khoja in Kashgar. Sadic Beg advanced on the capital with a much larger army, and Yakoob Beg had for a time to remain on the defensive. Each day, however, brought in recruits to his camp, while, the army of the Kirghiz leader presenting no object of sympathy to the people, his rival's remained stationary, if it did not decrease. An encounter at last commenced between the two forces which was made general by the intrepidity of Abdulla. The Kirghiz levies of Sadic were unable to withstand the vigorous charges that were led against them, and broke after a short combat into headlong flight. In the mountains the Kirghiz gathered around their chieftain in force, and, hovering on the northern districts of Kashgar, presented a danger that must be removed by Yakoob Beg before he could advance farther. His troops were therefore directed to proceed against the Kirghiz in their fastnesses, and it was not long before the Kirghiz, driven into a corner, turned at bay on their pursuer. The forces on either side were about equal, some 5,000 men in either army. But, as is customary in the East, the Kirghiz army put forth a champion, Suranchi by name, who had obtained great renown for his extraordinary height and strength. The challenge did not remain unanswered, for Abdulla stepped forward to the encounter. The fight, though furious, was short, and the smaller Khokandian warrior was victorious over his more ponderous antagonist. The Kirghiz power after this reverse was broken up, and Sadic Beg took refuge with Alim Kuli at Tashkent. Yakoob Beg's first campaign against the Kirghiz, who had sworn alliance with him, and by whose invitation he was present in Kashgar, had thus ended victoriously, and he was now able to resume the main purpose of conquering

Kashgar. Having rendered Kashgar secure from surprise on the north, and leaving a force to maintain their hold on it, and to keep in check the Khitay garrison, Buzurg and Yakoob proceeded south to occupy Yangy Hissar. The town was occupied without difficulty, but an attempt to storm the citadel in which the Khitay had taken refuge was repulsed with loss. Sending Buzurg Khan back to Kashgar, Yakoob Beg resolved to go on to Yarkand and endeavour to bring that city under their immediate influence.

At this period he loudly proclaimed that there should be no differences among the Tungani, or Mahomedans, in their war with the Buddhists, and that Khojas and Tungani had but one interest in common. As we have seen, the Tungan disturbances broke out first in Yarkand of any city of Altyshahr, and accordingly an earlier settlement founded on a compromise had been attained there, than was the case in its northern neighbours, Kashgar and Yangy Hissar, where an ambitious Kirghiz chief had sought to carve a kingdom for himself. After Abderrahman Khoja had been made king or ruler in Yarkand, and after the Khitay had been destroyed with their citadel, a fresh arrangement was agreed upon between the Tungani and the Khoja party. By its terms the Tungani maintained possession of the citadel, and the Khojas held jurisdiction in the city. Neither of them would be disposed to view with any friendly eye the appearance of a claimant to supremacy in the person of a Khoja sovereign of the whole country, and it was as the representative of such a person that Yakoob Beg resolved to visit Yarkand. His march was delayed as much as possible, and it was not without some difficulty that he at last obtained admittance with his small following into the city. Yakoob Beg was naturally incensed at this inimical treatment from his fellow-religionists, and he soon set himself to the task of humbling the dominant Khojas of Yarkand. During a street riot that was probably instigated by the wily Khokandian, the leading Khojas were seized, and their followers expelled from the city. With a force of only a few hundred men, Yakoob Beg had established himself as master in the largest city of the country; his success on this occasion was very temporary. As ill fortune would have it for him, a fresh army of 2,000 men from Kucha had arrived at Tagharchi, and, there joined by the forces from Yarkand and the neighbourhood, presented a very formidable appearance. They marched on the city at once with complete confidence in their superior numbers, and Yakoob Beg, always in favour of the boldest course, marched out to meet them. In a skirmish, however, the detachment under Abdulla was badly cut up owing to the rashness of that officer, and Yakoob Beg at once recognized the necessity for a prompt retreat. During the following night he made a forced march and arrived the next day at Yangy Hissar with no very great loss in men, but without any baggage whatever. The enterprise to Yarkand then appeared in its true light as a rash venture.

The Khitay in the fort of Yangy Hissar still held out, and Yakoob Beg resolved to overcome them before he attempted any fresh enterprise. He called up reinforcements from Kashgar, and pressed the siege with renewed vigour, and after strictly environing it for forty days the garrison surrendered. Although Yakoob Beg himself seemed desirous of showing moderation to the prisoners, more than 2,000 Chinese were massacred. During all these petty events, which had not produced even the results of past Khoja enterprises, there had been discontent and division within, as well as opposition from without. At this time a fresh danger was appearing on the horizon. A Badakshi army was advancing with hostile intent on Sirikul, and although Yakoob Beg disregarded its approach while he pressed on the works against the citadel of Yangy Hissar, when that fort fell it attracted his attention once more. The

Khitay garrison in the Yangyshahr of Kashgar was also a source of danger to the newly founded dynasty, and, although its inactivity had continued for a long period, it was uncertain at what moment it might pass off. We can only account for the extraordinary lethargy of the Chinese commander by supposing that he was in complete ignorance of what was passing in the country. At many moments it must seem to an observer of the facts that the Chinese governor, who had under him 6,000 or 7,000 disciplined troops, could have crushed all the opposition of such heterogeneous crowds as those fighting under or against Yakoob Beg were up to this time. With the destruction of the Yangy Hissar garrison the prospects of Yakoob Beg greatly improved, and less opportunity was left to the Chinese governor for assuming the offensive, than when he possessed an ally in so close a position as Yangy Hissar. Yakoob Beg also resolved to press the Khitay still more in this their last stronghold, and before he encountered other opponents to crush the Khitay, as he already had the Kirghiz. At this point Sadic Beg reappears in Kashgar at the head of a Kirghiz force to oppose Yakoob Beg, and for a moment it seemed as if he were to have better fortune on this occasion. But Abdulla, the most trusted as well as the most courageous of Yakoob Beg's lieutenants, collected such forces as he could, boldly threw himself in his path, and, having routed Sadic in a sanguinary engagement, prepared to press that unfortunate chieftain into flight or ruin. Yakoob Beg, in want of allies and soldiers however, interfered and suggested an alliance instead of a war *à outrance*. The thwarted Sadic was only too glad to get off on such favourable terms, and joined his forces to those of his late enemy now besieging the Khitay with renewed vigour. This merciful termination of a difficulty, that might have become serious had it not been cured in time, was a performance very creditable in a diplomatic sense to Yakoob Beg. In a small way it may be compared with

Frederick the Great's action at Pirna, where he received the services of 40,000 Saxon troops. But, perhaps, still more remarkable was the manner in which Yakoob Beg averted the danger from the Badakshi army. The Badakshi, like their kinsmen the Afghans, may be considered, *cæteris paribus*, to be superior soldiers, on account of their larger build and more active habits, to other Asiatics, so that Yakoob Beg with his half-disciplined followers would have had some difficulty and must have incurred considerable loss in overcoming these new invaders. He made overtures to them, and the Badakshi, seeing that he was likely to give them exciting and profitable employment, entered into negotiations with him. The result was that they took service under him; and Yakoob Beg for the first time found himself at the head of a large army, composed of Khokand, Kashgar, Kirghiz, and Badakshan levies. It was fortunate for himself that he had been able to arrange his affairs so satisfactorily, for a fresh danger was approaching from the east.

The reader may have observed that we have said little of Buzurg Khan during the operations of the campaign up to this point. Indeed, there is little or nothing to say of the movements of that prince, for he had been mainly stationary at Kashgar, where he passed his time in his harem, or besotted under the use of drugs. Yakoob Beg had from the very commencement come to the front as responsible chief, and as events progressed the people and the army came to look upon him as their future ruler. But Yakoob Beg, it would seem, was really in earnest in supporting the Khoja prince, for on several occasions not only did he give Buzurg the most salutary advice, but he also compelled him to take an active part in the public business. Such fits of action were most distasteful to the effeminate prince, and he always returned with renewed zest to the illicit pleasures in which he indulged. One of the occasions on which Yakoob Beg endeavoured to instil into his sovereign some idea of the responsibilities of his office was this invasion by the Khoja-Tungani power of Altyshahr. Early in the summer a large force, estimated at 40,000 men, collected by the cities of Aksu, Kucha, and Turfan, appeared at Maralbashi, whence it equally threatened Kashgar or protected Yarkand. Yakoob Beg's utmost efforts, if we are to credit the native report, only availed to bring some 2,500 men into the field; but it is more reasonable to suppose, that, with his Kirghiz, Kipchak, and Badakshi auxiliaries, he had many more troops under him, perhaps 12,500 instead of 2,500 men. Be the exact numbers of the forces what they may, however, it is certain that he was greatly outnumbered by the invader, and that the diverse elements of his army detracted very much from its effective strength. The Tungan army advanced from Maralbashi on Yangy Hissar, where Yakoob Beg had concentrated his army. He had drawn Buzurg Khan and such of the court followers as he could from their ignominious inaction in the capital to encounter the dangers and risks of a field of battle. Both sides were eager for the encounter, which took place in the neighbourhood of Yangy Hissar. The tactical disposition made by Yakoob Beg of his forces was such as would command the approval of skilled officers, and, having done all that mortal man could do to insure the result, he commended himself and his cause to Allah. The battle was long and stoutly contested. During hours it was impossible to say to which side the balance of victory was inclining; at last the Kirghiz troops, half-hearted in their fighting, were driven from the field, and the Badakshi division, which had up to that moment stubbornly held its ground, immediately followed the shameful example thus set it. There now only remained the division under the immediate orders of Yakoob Beg to withstand the onset of a whole army victorious in two different quarters of the field. The situation, on which the fate of the whole enterprise depended, might have filled the boldest heart with momentary despair. Yakoob Beg had, however, so braced himself to the effort, that no more than ordinary emotion was permitted to betray the disturbed mind within, and with the exclamation that " Victory is the gift of God," he inspired his soldiery to continue the fight throughout the afternoon. The enemy, dismayed at the dauntless courage shown by this mere handful of men, and having incurred great loss in his effort to crush them, drew off his weakened forces towards evening; and Yakoob Beg, boldly seizing the opportunity for assuming the offensive, drove them from the field in disorder and with considerable loss. In addition to the loss in killed and wounded, more than 1,000 Tungan soldiers enlisted under the standard of Yakoob Beg, and that general found himself on the morrow of one of his greatest battles, with a greater force under his command than he had just before it commenced. This great triumph gave fresh lustre to the Khoja family, and redounded to the military renown of Yakoob Beg. Nor should it be forgotten that on this occasion he showed that he possessed, besides military genius of some merit, qualities of an estimable character. For the first time in the annals of these wars the prisoners were treated with some consideration. For some reason or other this victory was not followed up, and the defeated Kucha army retired on Maralbashi, which it continued to hold for some months longer. The indirect results of this victory were scarcely less important, however, than the immediate and direct consequences of it.

Buzurg Khan, who had been present at this battle, was among the first to seek refuge in flight; and when he received intelligence of the final success his satisfaction was almost eclipsed by his personal chagrin and mortification. Up to this event he had been content to let Yakoob Beg act the king so long as he could indulge undisturbed in his debaucheries; but from this date there became mingled with his wounded vanity a conviction that Yakoob Beg was becoming so powerful and so popular that he might prove a dangerous subject. The weak-minded prince then permitted himself to be made the tool of every rival that the success of Yakoob Beg had raised up for himself either in the court or in the camp, and listened to tales brought him of his lieutenant's plots, when the conspirators most to be feared by himself were the ambitious chieftains in whose power he was placing his person and his crown. After the defeat of the Kucha army, the ruling parties in Yarkand thought it would be wise to come to terms with their victorious and aggressive neighbour, and accordingly an embassy was despatched to Yangy Hissar by the Khojas of Yarkand to tender their submission to the sovereign of Kashgar, and to ask to be favoured by the nomination of a city governor, who would be agreeable to Buzurg Khan and his vizier, Yakoob Beg. It is suggestive to watch how the name of the vizier occupies almost as prominent place in all their addresses as that of his master. The Tungan governor in the Yarkand Yangyshahr, not to be behindhand in his worship of the rising sun, immediately sent a similar expression of obedience to Kashgar.

The course of events once more takes us back to Kashgar, where the Chinese still held the citadel against all comers. But with each fresh success of Yakoob Beg over his numerous opponents, and with the spread of the Tungan power into Jungaria, hope almost completely deserted the unfortunate Khitay, who, in this solitary fort, alone maintained the name of Chinese authority. Treason, within the walls, was now to aid the efforts from without. Kho Dalay, the superior officer in the citadel, although not the commandant, came to an arrangement with Yakoob Beg, by which honourable terms were conceded to the garrison; and 3,000 Khitay troops surrendered and settled in Kashgar. They were required to acknowledge formally the supremacy of the Khoja, and to make a profession of Islamism. But they were never really interfered with in the observance of their own rites among themselves, and had nothing to complain of in their duty. They were called after their recantation "Yangy Mussulmans," or "New Mussulmans." These were the last Khitay troops who surrendered to the new conquerors, and with them every vestige of Chinese authority disappeared from every part of Jungaria and Eastern Turkestan. Even among this garrison, reduced by a long siege and its attendant deprivations to despair, there was a small minority who preferred death to the dishonour involved in surrender. Chang Tay, the commandant, refused to be any party to the arrangement made between Kho Dalay and Yakoob Beg. When the day approached for the entry of the Kashgarian army, this resolute Amban withdrew to his palace, and having collected his family and dependents around him blew them all up with the explosion of a mine that he had constructed underneath. In the confusion that arose from this incident, the enemy broke into the fort, and it was not for some hours that Yakoob Beg succeeded in obtaining control over them once more. During that interval of insubordination many Khitay were murdered, but not without resistance. Kho Dalay and almost 3,000 men remained to take service in the conquering army, as already explained. The new alliance was cemented by the marriage of Yakoob Beg to the beautiful daughter of Kho Dalay, by whom he has had several children, too young as yet to take any part in public affairs. Perhaps Yakoob Beg's moderation to the Khitay is to be explained by this circumstance, and it is certain that down to the very end his Khitay wife exercised great influence over her husband.

This was in September, 1865, nine months after his first arrival in Altyshahr, and in that period he had worked, if not very rapidly, with considerable thoroughness. The Khitay destroyed, the Kirghiz subdued, and the Tungan influence checked in its aggression against Western Kashgar, such was the tale of his achievements. Several battles and sieges successfully brought to an issue, and a numerous army formed out of the diverse fragments of conquered and conquerors. Personally, too, Yakoob Beg had done much towards preparing the public mind for the assumption of power by himself, and the reigning chief had done still more by his neglect of duty and abandonment to pleasure. Buzurg Khan might stand for the typical *roi fainéant,* and Yakoob Beg was a more than ordinarily resolute and determined *maire du palais.*

The citadel of Kashgar had not long surrendered when messengers arrived, reporting the near approach of a large body of men from Khokand, but who they were, or with what intention they came, none knew. These were the unsuccessful conspirators against Khudayar Khan, who, after the death of Alim Kuli, had obtained his power once more; and these having been driven out of Khokand by his armies, were compelled to seek refuge in Kashgar. Yakoob Beg sent them the laconic message, while they were hovering on the frontier, that "if they came as friends, they were welcome; if as foes, he was ready to fight them." Until the arrival of this declaration there appears to have been some hesitation among the Khokandians what to do, as some were wishing to attempt the conquest of Kashgar in their own interests; but when so clear a statement was sent them by Yakoob Beg, and when they learnt more definitely of the permanence of his success, they threw off their reserve and joined the confederacy of Kashgar. In the meanwhile fresh disturbances were breaking out in Yarkand, and thither he proceeded in the later months of 1865 to quell them, taking Buzurg Khan with him. On his arrival before the town both the Khojas and the Tungani hastened to profess the greatest desire to fulfil his wishes, although they kept him outside their gates. It is probable that neither party could have offered any prolonged resistance to him, had they not been encouraged to do so by Buzurg Khan. That prince had for some time been fretting against the iron will of his lieutenant, and, now, in an ill humour at being carried from his amusements and idleness at Kashgar to suffer the deprivations of a camp life before Yarkand, broke loose from all control, and plotted in his own camp, and in the enemy's, to free himself from his troublesome general. The plot among the Tungan soldiery had assumed alarming proportions, and all was ready to put an end to the career of Yakoob, when it was fortunately discovered by his faithful friend Abdulla. Precautions were taken, and the plot in the camp was effectually thwarted; but Yakoob Beg was not strong enough then to show his resentment. This danger was only removed to give place to another. The Tungani soldiers in Yakoob's service now opened up communications with their kinsmen in the Yangy-Shahr, and they formed the following plan to destroy the remaining portion of the Kashgarian forces. The garrison was to simulate a desire to yield into the hands of Yakoob Beg both their own persons and the fort, and when he, unsuspecting any covert design, should be lulled into a false sense of security, the Tungani in his service could join the Tungani in the fort in making a night attack on the other forces. The plan promised well. Yakoob Beg was deceived by the friendly overtures of the Tungani, and relaxed his precautions, and, during the night that was to precede the surrender of the Tungani, the conspirators marched out of the fort, and being joined, as had been arranged, by the other confederates, surprised Yakoob Beg and his immediate followers. A desperate resistance was offered by the half-armed men, but the Tungani were victorious, and Yakoob Beg had much difficulty in collecting around him on the morrow a few hundred soldiers. Among those, however, was Abdulla and some of his more trusted companions. The Kirghiz under Sadic Beg could not be trusted, and it seemed that that chief was still inclined to play for his own hand. At this, the most critical period of his life, Yakoob Beg's tact and resolution were most conspicuous. When he was surrounded on every hand by hostile factions, and could count on the fidelity of scarce five hundred men, he triumphed over every obstacle, and rose omnipotent over the petty jealousies and dissensions of those who sought to crush him. Buzurg Khan seized the moment of this disaster to draw off into a separate camp with a large body of troops and all the Kirghiz, and it is very possible, as has been asserted, that he instigated the successful Tungan *coup*. There is no evidence that he did, and I am personally of opinion that it originated among the Tungani themselves, and that Buzurg Khan only rejoiced at its occurrence, as he would have done at any other reverse to Yakoob. The position now was as follows:— In the citadel were the victorious Tungani, and in the town they shared the distribution of power with the townspeople. Outside in one part was Buzurg Khan, with a force that was equivocal in its sympathies, and that might at any moment become hostile, to Yakoob Beg; and in another part was Yakoob Beg himself and his attenuated following. Affairs could not look less hopeful, and if the three parties could have accommodated their own differences for but the short space of twenty-four hours, Yakoob Beg must infallibly have been destroyed: as it was, they did nothing with an enemy like Yakoob Beg in their proximity, and permitted him to redeem all he had lost by his too great credulity in the good faith of his brother Mussulmans. Let us now see how he saved himself. The first point to do was to restore the courage and self-confidence of his own soldiers, and to do that, it was necessary to strike a sharp blow that was sure of success. The fort could not be taken by a *coup de main*, but the city, large and straggling, presented a more inviting aspect for such an attempt. Abdulla, the Murat of the army of Kashgar,

with the most determined intrepidity, carried it by
assault, although here again he attacked without awaiting
the arrival of the other contingents. Like Edward Bruce,

> " Such was his wonted reckless mood,
>   Yet desperate valour oft made good,
>   Even by its daring, venture rude,
>   Where prudence might have failed."

This achievement put an end to the rejoicings among
the Tungani, and compelled them to recognize what a terribly energetic and enterprising foe they had to deal with.
But, at this moment, a severe mishap occurred which
almost neutralized the advantage thus gained. Buzurg
Khan, unable either to crush Yakoob Beg or to enjoy
the indulgences to which he had enslaved himself, resolved to secure the latter, happen what might. He
accordingly fled from Yarkand with many followers,
and retired to his palace at Kashgar. There, not content
with pillaging the palace of Yakoob Beg, he proclaimed
him a traitor and rebel, and offered a reward to whom-
soever should bring him his head. Another general
was appointed to the command of the army, and preparations were made for defending Kashgar against any
attempt of Yakoob Beg to attack it. But fortunately
the Tungani in the citadel of Yarkand were not aware
of this dissension among the Kashgari, and as they were
struck with admiration for the valour of Yakoob Beg, they
surrendered to him soon after the flight of Buzurg. He
was then able to turn his undivided attention to his
refractory chief. Yakoob Beg had always, as we have said,
befriended the church ; he was now to experience some
benefit for that very commendable respect. Among the
first means of crushing Yakoob Beg that Buzurg Khan had
employed was an appeal to the Sheikh-ul-islam of Kashgar to proclaim his Baturbashi outside the pale of the
law. This the ecclesiastic refused to do, and asserted, on
the contrary, that Yakoob Beg had deserved well both
of his country and of the Mahomedan world. Foiled in
his effort to stir up a religious feeling against his general,

Buzurg Khan was reduced to the more cogent, but in his hands quite useless, argument of the sword. Nor was the field, limited as it must appear to us, free from other pretenders. Sadic Beg, instead of coalescing with Buzurg Khan, set up his own pretensions to rule the country; and the Kucha Khojas and Tungani began to collect troops in view of possible eventualities.

The army of Buzurg Khan, which had marched out to oppose the entry of Yakoob Beg, was outflanked and defeated by Abdulla in the country between Yangy Hissar and the capital; and Yakoob Beg, pressing on with irresistible strides, was received in Kashgar with the acclamations of the people and of his soldiers. He was then publicly proclaimed ruler, and his friend the Sheikh-ul-islam ratified the people's choice. Buzurg Khan, who had taken refuge in the Yangy-Shahr, was seized in his palace there, after a very slight resistance. Some of the more prominent of Yakoob Beg's rivals were executed, and Buzurg Khan himself was placed in a state of honourable confinement. He still persisted in futile intrigues, and so long as he remained in Kashgar was a source of endless trouble to the new government. For more than eighteen months he was permitted to remain however, and then, being detected in instigating the murder of Yakoob Beg, was banished to Tibet. After wandering for some years, he found his way to Khokand, where he is believed to be still residing with a large family. He may be considered to have been the last Khoja prince ruling Kashgar, for it is scarcely probable that, in any future settlement of that country, a restoration of the old reigning family will be supported by any one. He is no exaggerated type of the rule among Central Asian despots, who present to our gaze a long series of petty tyrants and debauchees, until for a few years they are displaced by a successful soldier such as the Athalik Ghazi, or by a skilful minister such as Mussulman Kuli was in Khokand.

The Kirghiz chief, Sadic Beg, did not long hold out

against the consolidated power of Yakoob Beg; and the
Kucha movements were suspended.   In a little more
than twelve months Yakoob Beg had occupied Kashgar, Yangy Hissar, and Yarkand.   Sirikul and Khoten
also acknowledged his rule; but his further operations
against them will be narrated by-and-by.   He felt now
so secure in his seat that he permitted the Badakshi
contingent to return home, presenting each soldier
with a large present.   Ever since that time Yakoob
Beg seems to have maintained some influence in Badakshan, and to have been inclined on several occasions
to compete with Shere Ali of Afghanistan for the possession of that province.   His ambition was never
fully revealed in this quarter; but it is certain that
Shere Ali regarded him with scarcely concealed suspicion and dislike.

With the assumption of personal power by Yakoob
Beg, on the deposition of the Khoja Buzurg Khan, the
first part of the enterprise undertaken in the later days
of 1864 was brought to a termination.   In the more
extended operations of Yakoob Beg against the Tungani and Khoten, may be perceived the effects of events
outside his immediate sphere upon this energetic ruler,
who, until his last years, never realized the strength
of the Russians, and who had, up to the year 1870
when Kuldja was occupied, convinced himself that he
could retard the progress of the great Northern power.
It was that idea, besides a thirst for military renown
and excitement, that urged him on to the construction
of what he fondly believed might prove a formidable
and extensive state.   As ruler of Kashgar, he could
not be anything but a kind of vassal of the Khan of
Khokand; as monarch of Eastern Turkestan, he might
treat on terms of equality with the Czar of Russia or
the Emperor of China.   It was no unworthy ambition,
and Yakoob Beg, created Athalik Ghazi, Champion
Father, in 1866 by the Ameer of Bokhara, accomplished so much of it as was possible.

CHAPTER VIII.

WARS WITH THE TUNGANI.

YAKOOB BEG, having deposed Buzurg Khan and suppressed all resistance on the part either of the Tungani or of the Chinese in Western Kashgar, had some leisure to make a careful survey of his exact position. The result of the desultory fighting of the previous twelve months had been eminently satisfactory to himself; but, to say the least, it was dubious how long this state of things might last. Former adventurers had accomplished as much as he had, but the Chinese had always returned with renewed vigour. How was Yakoob Beg to know that the rumours were well founded which asserted that that empire had been sore stricken in other fields than against the Tungani, and that even the victories over the Taepings were not considered a complete set-off to the disasters in every other quarter of the empire? European critics predicted that the last hour of the Chinese Empire was fast approaching; but Yakoob Beg, with far more imperfect means of intelligence at his disposal, feared still, even when the citadel of Kashgar surrendered, that the Khitay would return for revenge. His fears were not groundless, as we now know, but he anticipated events by more than ten years. Yakoob Beg was not so sanguine in his own resources or good fortune that he believed that he should not have to encounter the danger that had overwhelmed all his predecessors, and his first object accordingly was to gather all his strength together in a compact mass to resist the Chinese when they should come. But the dissensions

that had, during the conquest of Altyshahr, manifested
themselves so palpably in the ill-assorted conglomeration which had gathered round the standard of Buzurg
Khan brought home to the mind of Yakoob Beg the
disadvantages of a divided people. He accordingly
determined that, whatever else he might fail or succeed in achieving, his most resolute effort should be to
weld into one cohesive and effective whole Andijani
and Tungani, Kashgari and Khitay. It was no mean
ambition; but to cement such discordant elements
a policy of "blood and iron" was required. Yakoob
Beg did not shrink certainly in its application; but
when he had accomplished the task he had set himself to
bring about he discovered that the cost had been so great
that the state, both in population and in wealth, was
at a lower point than it had ever been before. But in
the earlier days of 1866 no doubt crossed his mind on
this latter point.   It must be remembered that, strange
to say, the great success of Yakoob Beg in Kashgar
had alienated the sympathy of the government of Khokand from his cause; and, although this may be explained by the antipathy of Khudayar Khan, now
firmly seated on the throne, who could not entertain
any amity for a subject who had on several occasions deserted his cause, it is impossible to attribute to that sentiment alone a fact which must have had some deeper and
less personal explanation. At all stages of the history
of these petty princes of Asia are we met by the spectacle of mutual jealousy and recrimination, whenever
any one of themselves seemed about to exalt himself
above his fellows, either by the success of his arms or
by the beneficence of his rule. Rarely, indeed, had
any of them shown that he possessed more than ordinary ability or courage; but, whenever the phenomenon
did appear, he was at once proclaimed by his neighbours to be a dangerous innovation, and as such to be
thwarted and opposed. The practice has come down
to our own day, and during the long wars that Russia

has waged in Asia we have never beheld two states, no matter how insignificant, combine to oppose the common foe. The Khokandians have never aided the Bokhariots or the Khivans, nor have the Afghans or the Kashgari the Khokandians. They have kept the ring, so to speak, as each of them has gone down singly before the prowess of the Muscovite, in a manner that ought to excite the admiration of all those who preserve the memories of the traditional honours of the prize ring; but, as their own existence has been the penalty, it is questionable whether their conduct, inspired by regard for no law of chivalry, but simply by mutual antipathy, has been very prudent. Over such petty jealousies had Yakoob Beg to triumph before he could hope to complete his dream of an united Kashgaria. His path was beset with difficulties. In satisfying himself with too little he might imperil what he had secured, but in attempting too much he might jeopardize everything he had won. Under such circumstances the boldest man might have stood uncertain, and the most resolute inactive until hurried into action by the progress of events. For some months Yakoob Beg seems to have remained uncertain what should be his next move.

In 1865, before his last advance on Yarkand, he had seized Maralbashi or Bartchuk, and by so doing not only had he secured communication between Aksu and Yarkand, but also between Aksu and Khoten. This position, lying 200 miles to the east of Yangy Hissar, has always been and is still very important, and Yakoob Beg is supposed to have fortified it very strongly. This success was the permanent result of his great victory over the Tungani from Aksu and Kucha in the neighbourhood of Yangy Hissar, and it effectually secured his flank during further operations. It was not, however, until he turned his attention to the southern city of Khoten, that the importance of this acquisition was made incontestable. Then it enabled him to devote his attention exclusively to the extension of his sway southward to

the mountains of Karakoram and Kuen Lun, beyond
which he might expect no enemy. In Khoten the Mufti
Habitulla had been invested with supreme control, after
the deposition of the Chinese authorities; and during
his government of the city and district, order appears
to have been maintained without unnecessary exactions.
When Yakoob Beg made his first appearance in Yarkand,
after his earlier successes round Kashgar, it will be remembered that the Yarkandi acknowledged the supremacy of the new Khoja king. Their example was
speedily followed by Habitulla of Khoten, and it is not
stated that, even during the progress of hostilities with
Yarkand, this ruler repudiated the arrangement into
which he had entered. It is true that he was far removed
from the immediate sphere of action, but that will not
alone account for an indifference to the progress of events
in Kashgar, which Khoten had never manifested on any
previous occasion. Khoten may, therefore, be considered
to have been exceptionally well behaved towards the new
Khoja dynasty located at Kashgar; and when Yakoob
Bég advanced to the south of Yarkand, Habitulla
hastened to send representatives to the camp of the
conqueror. They were received with consideration, but
deep down in the breast of Yakoob Beg there lurked
either an inveterate distrust of, or dislike to, the Mufti
Habitulla. Dissembling his true feelings, Yakoob Beg
sent a message requesting the presence of the Mufti in
his camp. The Mufti, deluded by the friendly treatment
bestowed on his emissaries, came with many of his
relations and followers into the camp of the Kashgarian
general. At first, we are told, they were treated with
every mark of respect and kindness; they were feasted
and clothed in precious garments, but all these honours
were but the preliminaries to the concluding ceremony.
During the progress of the evening meal they were
disarmed, and led out to execution, while an attack was
made from several quarters on the town. Even then
the resistance was prolonged, and the slaughter by the

infuriated soldiery of the Athalik Ghazi continued long after all serious opposition had ceased. It is impossible to exonerate Yakoob Beg from the chief blame on this occasion, and if he had been a civilized European general, we should have made use of the phrase, that "It must ever remain a blot on his career;" but it would be the height of irony to apply such a phrase to this unscrupulous Asiatic, who, if not worse than the school in which he was brought up, was certainly not much better in a moral sense. As the fact stands, the seizure of Khoten, and the massacre of the unarmed leaders of that city, appear to have been acts as unnecessary as they were unjustifiable. Khoten may have seemed to the Athalik Ghazi of exceptional importance for several reasons, and he may have felt doubtful of the fidelity of Habitulla and his followers; but, so far as we are aware, the reasons for this action are shadowy in the extreme, even regarded from the point of view of political expediency. Down to the present day, too, the memory of this massacre, needless even in the eyes of a people accustomed to the shortest cuts to power by wholesale slaughter, has rankled in the minds of the inhabitants of Khoten and Sanju, and the Athalik Ghazi was least popular in that part of his state in which, according to the traditions of his predecessors, his action had been most sweeping, and accordingly most safe. This was early in the year 1867, and the Athalik Ghazi had now an opportunity for settling his relationship with his eastern neighbours, the Tungani.

The Tungan movement proper originated, as explained in the last chapter, in the Chinese provinces of Kansuh and Shensi, and then extended with scarcely a check to Turfan south of the Tian Shan and to Urumtsi north of that range. The flame soon spread from Turfan to Karashar, Kucha, and Aksu, and at all of these towns it was fomented by the appearance of the new element of the Mahomedan Khokandian, and native settlers, acting in combination with the Chinese Tungani.

North of the Tian Shan the movement received a temporary repulse; and it is necessary to say something in explanation of the course of the Mahomedan revival in Ili before we proceed to discuss the earlier wars of Yakoob Beg with the Tungani. As early as 1860 serious complications had arisen in that province, although the Chinese had always been more firmly situated there than in Kashgar. In that year a plot was concocted to murder the Chinese viceroy and to upset the existing government. It was discovered, however, and fell through. There appear to have been more causes at work in Ili to produce discontent than in the southern state, and it was not so much a question here between Khitay and Tungani, as it was between a people clamouring for work, for less taxation, and for payment for what they had done, and an administration that was unable to satisfy the demands made upon it from all sides. That last resource of a government at its wits' ends for money, the depreciation of the current coin and the issue of fictitious paper, was adopted by the Viceroy of Ili. The measure, which it had been expected would lessen the difficulty, only added fuel to the flame. The situation of affairs was becoming desperate; the people were encouraged by the disasters of the Chinese in the neighbouring states to increase the number of their demands; and the Chinese officials appear to have lost their heads in the storm that was gathering from all sides around them. They were but the effete representatives of a system which in its vigorous days had claims to general admiration, and they are only saved from incurring our contempt by the possession of courage, the sole virtue left them. When the Chinese first conquered Eastern Turkestan they brought from Kashgar a large number of settlers, and placed them in the country round Ili. They became known as Tarantchis, and, in the course of two or three generations, had increased into a very numerous community. These were always at heart disaffected to the Chinese, but, as they occupied

a very subordinate position, would probably never have
thought of revolt had not a large division of the conquerors set them the example of insubordination. So
soon as the discontent among the working classes had
assumed formidable proportions by the pecuniary embarrassment of the Chinese, and the Tungan successes
in the east of Jungaria had raised a fanatical feeling to
swell the hatred against a declining and Buddhist rule,
the Tarantchis were not backward for their part in reviv-
ing their almost forgotten grievances, and in joining in a
defensive and offensive alliance with the Tungani. Each
party collected such forces as they could, but in the
encounter that ensued the disciplined soldiers of the
Viceroy overcame the far more numerous mob by which
they were opposed. The fortress of Bazandai, however,
within the next few days, fell into the power of the
insurgents, and that achievement more than compen-
sated for the disaster in the open field. Ili itself surrendered in January, 1866, and a Tungani-Tarantchi
government was formed. The Chinese viceroy had
in the meanwhile destroyed himself and many of his
followers and assailants by setting fire to a mine of
gunpowder under his palace. The Tungan element
gradually superseded the Tarantchi in the administration of the state, and the five years of independence,
which continued until the Russians came in 1871, were
chiefly marked by petty disagreements which had no
influence on the progress of events in this part of Asia.
The trade with Ili fell off, and many other valid reasons
for Russian intervention were accumulated during those
few years of national existence.

With the beginning of 1867, Yakoob Beg, secure
on the south and on the west from aggression, found
himself in a position to cope with the disjointed but
allied Tungan states on his north and east. The hostility of the Tungani and Khojas of Aksu and Kucha had
been already demonstrated, and it was to be surmised
that they were only waiting to recover from the disastrous

campaign of 1865 to renew their efforts to drive the Khokandian adventurers out of Kashgar. The facts that they acknowledged the same religious tenets, and that they had overcome, to some extent, a common enemy in the Chinese, and that they certainly had each to fear most from their return, seem to have weighed little with either the Tungani or the Athalik Ghazi. To do the latter simple justice, it must be remembered that the Tungani had been the aggressors, and that their attitude never ceased to be unfriendly towards himself. It is certain that he made some efforts to effect an amicable arrangement with the ruling party in Aksu, but his advances were received with coldness, and both the Khojas and the Tungani of that city held aloof from all intercourse with the new-comer. Both parties remained watching each other for some time, each waiting for the other to take the initiative. The Tungani had experienced the weight of the military power of Yakoob Beg, when they had taken the offensive in the earlier days of his appearance at Kashgar. It was, therefore, not very probable that they would repeat the experiment when he presented a far more formidable and united presence to their attack. Practically speaking, Yakoob Beg was safe from invasion from the east so long as he maintained order within his own frontier; and the Tungani in Ili on his north had manifested no special hostility against his state. Secure from any aggression on the part of the Tungani, Yakoob Beg might with some reason have declined to push to extremities his relations with them. It was certainly inconvenient that an antagonistic state should exist on his very borders, but, as he was in a very strong position for defence, the disadvantages of abandoning it to assume an offensive policy were all the more apparent. What necessity could be alleged to justify a scarcely excusable attack in a moral sense, and a quite unnecessary in a political? The proximity of Aksu was in a strategic sense more than neutralized by the possession of Maralbashi, and, with the lapse of time and the return of peace, the trade route from Kashgar to Aksu might be expected to revive once more. But such temporizing measures as these, involving the endurance of Tungan indifference, could not be brooked by the Athalik Ghazi. The orthodoxy of these Mahomedans was not above suspicion, and to so devout and energetic a Sunni as Yakoob Beg these differences were scarcely less offensive than if they had been believers in a rival religion. Dictatorial announcements were made to the Khoja-Tungan rulers of Aksu; and, on their persisting in defiance, Yakoob Beg collected his forces to chastise them. The doctrines of the Tungani were impeached as not being in strict accordance with the Shariàt, and the religious fervour of the Sunnis was appealed to, to bring these recalcitrant people to an acknowledgment of the error of their ways. In addition to the semi-religious element thus imported into the question, Yakoob Beg also laid claim to the country up to Kucha as part of the old territory of the Khoja kings.

In the spring of 1867 his army set out in two divisions for Aksu. The Tungani appear to have been paralyzed when the danger that had for many months appeared menacing came upon them. The resistance encountered at Aksu, naturally and artificially a very strong place, was not prolonged, and Yakoob Beg swept on against Kucha. Here the Tungani, having some-what recovered from their trepidation, made a desperate stand, and with the reinforcements that had arrived from Turfan presented a sufficiently formidable appearance. The ruling authorities in Kucha were Khojas, who in the time of the Chinese had the custody of a shrine sacred to the memory of a Mahomedan saint, but who at the outbreak of disturbances left the temple for the council chamber, and the offering up of prayers to the memory of the saint for the more difficult task of issuing edicts for the management of a people. Unhappily for their reputation in our eyes, they had specially distinguished

themselves in the massacres of the Khitay.   Their
brief tenure of power seems to have been fairly beneficent, and, in the lull that succeeded the deposition of
the Chinese and preceded the invasion of Yakoob Beg,
they obtained without doing anything very noteworthy
the approval and affection of their subjects.   At Kucha,
therefore, more than 500 miles distant from his own
capital, with a long line of hostile country in his
rear, Yakoob Beg found himself opposed by the full
power of the Tungani.   Previous to advancing beyond
Aksu he had sent back officers to Kashgar to bring up
fresh levies, and he had resorted to that doubtful
expedient of drafting into his army many of the
Tungani captured at Aksu.   Arrived in front of Kucha
he was unable to prosecute the siege with any vigour
until the arrival of his reinforcements.   The moment of
delay was attempted to be turned to account by Yakoob
Beg and some of the more prudent of his counsellors;
but the Tungani, whether unwilling to acknowledge
their inferiority or incredulous of the good faith of the
Athalik Ghazi, refused to enter into negotiations that
they asserted were unnecessary.   Yakoob Beg had invaded them in their possessions, and he had annexed
Aksu; the only condition in which they could acquiesce
was a withdrawal of his army.   All the efforts of the
more peaceful and the more prudent on either side were
unavailing, and each party used every exertion to bring
up fresh troops to decide the question of superiority between Tungani and Kashgari.   For several weeks the
two armies stood facing each other, the one stationed on
the hills to the north and west of the city, commanding
the main road from Aksu, the other in the environs and
the fortifications of the city itself.   The Tungani were far
the more numerous, but in the quality of his main body,
and in general efficiency both of weapons and of experience among the officers, the advantage was completely
on the side of Yakoob Beg.   The nucleus of his force
comprised Afghan, Khokandian, and Badakshi troops,

veterans in the wars of the two previous years. The Tungani were either the assassins of helpless Chinese, or the fugitives of Aksu or Yangy Hissar. They were imperfectly armed, without any organization, and without any competent leaders. Above all, the cause they were fighting for was vague, and many of them in their hearts sympathized more with Yakoob Beg than they did with their own chiefs. The Kashgarian army, on the other hand, was encouraged by a long series of brilliant achievements, and looked forward with eagerness to the fray as the means of exalting their own religion, and as affording them an opportunity for advancing their own personal interests by the plunder of so rich a city as Kucha. The reinforcements were consequently eagerly expected, and some of the more ardent spirits demanded that they should be led without delay against the enemy. Yakoob Beg was so far prudent that he refused to be urged into premature action by the impetuosity of his followers, and the arrival of reinforcements sooner than was anticipated enabled him not only to keep the excitement of his soldiery within due bounds, but also to commence active operations at an earlier date than had seemed possible. The Tungan leaders, deluded by the inaction of Yakoob Beg into a belief that he was unable to prosecute the enterprise he had undertaken, assumed the offensive, only to be worsted in several minor engagements. The Tungan troops were driven within the walls, and the siege was prosecuted with the closest rigour. The garrison of Kucha was not sufficiently numerous to guard in proper strength the wide-stretching suburbs and extensive fortifications of the existing Kucha, and the cities that had in olden days stood upon its site. Not many days elapsed before Yakoob Beg perceived that the defence was confined to a limited portion of the fortifications, and that several points were entirely neglected. He resolved, therefore, to put an end to the slow process of a siege by carrying the town by a general assault. With the whole of his available force he attacked the city on three sides; but the Tungani resisted strenuously, and all his direct attacks were repulsed with heavy loss. To his son Khooda Kul Beg he had entrusted an attack in the rear of the city, and on the success of that movement now entirely depended the result of the assault on Kucha. That division by great good fortune and the gallantry of its leader was victorious, and, although this promising son of Yakoob Beg, then only a little more than twenty years of age, was killed in the confusion that ensued on the entrance into the city, Kucha fell. The triumph was, perhaps, not too dearly purchased. The Tungan power had received a blow, which took the sting out of its menace, and effectually protected Kashgar from any possible confederacy among the Tungan cities. Yakoob Beg followed up the success of Kucha with all his usual promptitude, but his power was not yet sufficiently matured to justify him in carrying on extensive operations at such a distance from the base of his resources. But another reason at this time combined to recall his attention to another part of his dominions. The Russians were advancing both in Khokand and in the district of Vernoe to the west of Kuldja.

It was evident that prudence demanded a prompt return, and for the present all further triumph must be abandoned. However, before Yakoob Beg returned to regulate events in the western portion of his dominions, he had the satisfaction of receiving the submission humbly tendered by the ruling bodies of Karashar, Turfan, Hamil, and Urumtsi. After this brilliant campaign, he slowly retraced his steps through Kucha to Aksu. Then he turned into the mountains, and reduced Ush Turfan, which in his onward march he had passed by; and, after this acquisition, the Tungani of Ili expressed a desire to enter into terms of amity with one who had brought his empire into direct contact with their state. All these events occurred during the year 1867; and, although now and then uncertain

rumours reached England of these changes in Eastern
Turkestan, the world in general, even the Russian
world, remained indifferent to the progress of events of
which it is now difficult to trace the exact course. But,
with the close of this first Tungan campaign, and with
the extension of the new state up to the walls of Kucha,
the Russian Government, as will be seen in a later
chapter, endeavoured to arrive at some clear view on
the exact condition of the newly formed confederacy to
which they in their career of conquest were approaching
so rapidly.

This commencement of foreign interest in, nay,
almost supervision of, his actions in Eastern Turkestan,
imposed some restriction on the hitherto unrestrained
caprice of Yakoob Beg, and the country beyond Kucha
up to Turfan was saved for a short time from the
depredations from which in 1871–73 it suffered so
much. On his return to Kashgar after this triumphant
progress, and after having annexed the three important
cities, Aksu, Kucha, and Ush Turfan, the danger which
had seemed to threaten the state from Russia passed
off, and Yakoob Beg proceeded to consolidate his hold
on what he had secured. Aksu and Kucha were fortified, and various small forts were constructed in the
passes leading to Khokand and Kuldja. Every precaution was taken that he had it in his power to observe,
to ensure the safety of his little kingdom from without,
and for the moment all murmur within seemed to be
hushed by the loud acclamations at the victories of the
Athalik Ghazi. He had, indeed, accomplished no slight
task, and could afford to regard his handiwork with
some complacency. To erect a powerful state on the
ruins of the Chinese power, and to unite in some sort
of settled government turbulent races and antagonistic
sects, was no mean achievement; and to all the credit due
to such Yakoob Beg has indisputable claims. But for
him, confusion and disunion would have settled down
over Eastern Turkestan, until either the Russians or the

Chinese had come to establish a respectable government; but for him Kashgar would have lapsed into a state of almost hopeless disorder, and Russian triumphs would have been facilitated. But, when Yakoob Beg returned to find that he was not seriously threatened in Kashgar, he experienced deep regret and mortification that he had abstained from prosecuting his wars with the Tungani with a greater vigour. He eagerly looked forward to an excuse for resuming his discontinued operations against them. In the interval that elapsed, he waged a small war in the mountainous region of his territory extending into Badakshan and the Chitral. Sirikul had, ever since the appearance of the Badakshi army in the service of Kashgar, acknowledged a certain kind of obedience to Yakoob Beg; but in 1868, the governor hitherto supported by the Athalik Ghazi broke out into revolt, and committed several acts of depredation in the contiguous districts of Sanju and Yarkand. Yakoob Beg without delay despatched a small force against him, and, by the help of some mountain guns and the judicious employment of a small but select body of cavalry, was successful in overcoming all resistance with very slight loss. In February, 1869, Yakoob Beg, having tried several milder alternatives, formally annexed this district, and carried the inhabitants into Yarkand. He resettled the territory with Kirghiz nomads and Yarkandis. Once more, he was able to turn his attention to the east, and in 1869 commenced those final campaigns against the Tungani which only ceased with the reappearance of the Chinese. The great blot in the career of Yakoob Beg is the resumption of hostilities against the Tungani. In 1867, when he first engaged with any vigour the Tungani, some excuse may be found for that unforeseeing action, in the fact that the Tungani were unbroken, and might have proved formidable neighbours. But in 1869, they had been hurled back on Korla, and, although it may be true that they were inconvenient neighbours, robbing caravans and molesting travellers, it is difficult to justify the later campaigns of Yakoob Beg against them, especially as they were conducted by himself and his lieutenants with exceptional ferocity. But, however weak may have been the impulse, and however disastrous in the result may have been his crusade against the Tungani, it was not difficult to discover a plausible excuse for proceeding to extreme measures with his troublesome neighbours. In the autumn of 1869, Korla fell before his triumphant arms, and it would appear that he then turned north into the valleys of the Tekes and the Yuldus, two rivers rising in the Tian Shan, and flowing through Jungaria. This movement aroused the susceptibilities of the Russians, and afforded a very simple excuse for the acquisition of Kuldja. In that state, disturbances had arisen between the Tungani and the Tarantchis, and it must have fallen an easy prey to the Athalik Ghazi had he been permitted to advance. The Russians had, however, in 1871, entered Kuldja, and explained their action by asserting that they had only done so to restore order, and to prevent its falling into the hands of Yakoob Beg. They merely held it in trust for the Chinese, so they said, and would restore it to them, its rightful owners, so soon as they should be able to keep permanent possession of it. While Yakoob Beg despatched a large detachment into the country of the Tian Shan, his main body was prosecuting with vigour the war against Karashar and Turfan. Yakoob Beg did not always conduct the war in person, for his two sons, Kuli Beg and Hacc Kuli Beg, were now growing up, and they, assisted by some of the older lieutenants, triumphed in various actions over the Tungan rulers of Turfan and Hamil, while even the princes of Urumtsi and Manas over the Tian Shan were unable to oppose the valour and energy of their adversary. The glory of these military achievements was tarnished by the ruthless manner in which the district was laid waste,

and the inhabitants were massacred; and the senseless-
ness of these proceedings only required an hour of trial,
such as the Chinese invasion, to prove how fatal it would
be to the enacters of these atrocities. Without any
great cessation, their operations were carried on down
to the end of 1873, and it does not appear that Yakoob
Beg derived any benefit whatever from these costly and
remote undertakings. Although the Tungan chiefs of
Urumtsi and Hamil were on several occasions defeated
by the armies of the Athalik Ghazi, their cities were
never occupied, and they consequently escaped that
desolation which stretched from the walls of Kucha to
the regions north of Lake Lob. Chightam, a small town
lying half way between Turfan and Hamil, was the
extreme point to which the Kashgarian forces penetrated. The noble families of Urumtsi, Turfan, and
Hamil were almost totally destroyed in the fall of
Turfan; and their place in their own cities was seized
by Tungan generals and adventurers, who began to
retreat westward from Kansuh, on the rumours of
Chinese preparations for invading Jungaria.

The wars against the Tungani certainly served one
useful purpose in enabling Yakoob Beg to collect a
large and disciplined force round his standard; but the
attractions of service in his army lost much of their
value in the eyes of the hardier clans of Turkestan and
the neighbouring states, when it became known that
the prospect of loot and prize money in districts impoverished by several years of hostilities had dimin-
ished. The rigour of the discipline maintained, too,
was irksome to nomads and irregulars accustomed to
the easier service and freedom from restraint of the other
Asiatic princes; and during the later years of his rule
there were many desertions, and a difficulty was encountered in inducing recruits to enter his army. The
old practice, employed with such success in the earlier
years of his rule, of inducing the conquered to combine with the conqueror, was no longer possible, for

extermination had become the order of the day. The Usbegs, Kirghiz, and other tribes, could not supply in sufficient numbers the requirements of the state, and the Tungani, who should have comprised the largest portion of the subjects of the Athalik Ghazi, were coerced into subjection with an undiscriminating severity. The result was really a paralysis through sheer want of people, and it was not known until the hour of trial came how weakened his forces had become. Every inducement was held forth to Afghan, Badakshi, and, above all, to Indian soldiers to join, but these, although they formed a nucleus of trustworthy and efficient soldiers, were far too few to constitute a formidable army. We are justified in assuming from the facts that these Tungan wars, conducted in an unsparing manner, were the greatest mistake that marked the career of Yakoob Beg. So far as his occupation of Kucha goes, he could at least say that he had secured a valuable prize. He had acquired every part of what could be considered Kashgar, and his kingdom was effectually guarded, and his revenues prospectively increased, by the possession of the great cities of Aksu and Kucha. He might exclaim with justice that he had eclipsed all his predecessors in military prowess, and if he had been wise he would then have turned his attention to the well government of his state, and by so doing have demonstrated that he was of a higher capacity for ruling a people, as well as for commanding an army, than any Khoja prince of the past. Had he abstained from prosecuting with such unflagging persistency his inveterate dislike of the Tungani, he might easily have come to terms with his neighbours, and the harm they could have done him would have been infinitesimally small. But the chief advantage of that more prudent policy would have been visible when the Chinese advanced to chastise the Tungani. Not only would the Tungani have been more capable of resisting the Khitay, not only would

Manas and Urumtsi have been capable of offering a
more determined defence, but the Tungani could have
retired on Turfan, and held the country round that
town, as well as Karashar and Korla, for a protracted
period against General Kin Shun. The Athalik Ghazi
with untouched resources could have awaited with just
confidence the advance of the Chinese upon his strong
frontier city of Kucha, and, as the Chinese accomplished the difficult task of crushing the Tungani, he
would have had the satisfaction of knowing that in all
probability the Chinese effort would have been spent
before it reached his own borders.

It is impossible to judge men except by the results
of their actions, and the result of Yakoob Beg's inces-
sant and unnecessary interference with the Tungani
was that the Chinese army was able in a few months to
dissipate the remaining Tungan communities, and to
encounter in the full flush of their triumph the nume-
rically weaker forces of Yakoob Beg. It is, therefore,
impossible to exonerate the ruler from great blame in
hastily undertaking operations which a little consideration ought to have shown to be unwise. Having
traced Yakoob Beg's wars with the Chinese Mahomedans,
it is time to consider his rule of Kashgaria proper, and
the events that during these years were transpiring in
other quarters of the state.

CHAPTER IX.

YAKOOB BEG'S GOVERNMENT OF KASHGAR.

YAKOOB BEG'S chief claim to our consideration is that, for more than twelve years, he gave a settled government to a large portion of Central Asia, and that, however faulty his external policy may have been in critical moments, his internal management was founded on a practical and sufficiently just basis. As a warrior he had done much to justify admiration, and had proved on many a well-fought field, and in many a desperate encounter, his claims to be considered a fearless and resolute soldier; but in this quality he was equalled, if not excelled, by his own lieutenant, Abdulla Beg, the Murat of Kashgar, while some of the deeds of his son, Beg Bacha, will rank in daring and surpass in ferocity anything achieved by the Athalik Ghazi. But in capacity for administration Yakoob Beg far surpassed his contemporaries, and the merit of his success was enhanced, not so much by the originality of the method adopted, as by the unique vigour and perseverance with which it was put into force. The secret of his power can only be discovered by constantly bearing in mind the fact that he had constituted himself the champion of the Mahomedan religion in Central Asia. The Ameers of Bokhara and Afghanistan might trifle with the seductive promises of the Russians, and might consent to sacrifice the interests of their religion for a transitory advancement of their worldly possessions; but to such degradations the Athalik Ghazi—true "champion father" as he was—never stooped. With

whatever imaginary power the sympathy and good-will
of the Mahomedan peoples of Turkestan may have
clothed this ruler, there is no question that his attitude towards the Muscovite would have warranted the
assertion of greater power than was ever attributed to
him; and the secret of this delusion, an attitude of
defiant strength without any solid foundation for so
bold a course, can only be unravelled by remembering
that the Athalik Ghazi strove to represent, not so
much Kashgaria, as the whole Mahomedan world of
Central Asia.   The necessities of his own position,
when, having conquered Kashgar, he found that he
had aroused the susceptibilities of the Russians, compelled him to seek in every direction for aid, and to
have recourse to every artifice for increasing his
strength, or its semblance, in order to avoid the dis-
solution of his state and a subjection to the Czar.   So
well did he succeed in his efforts, and so prompt were
his movements and so fearless his attitude, that the
Russians were deluded into a belief—which was, as we
emphatically insist, unfounded—that Kashgar would
prove a more formidable antagonist than either Bokhara, or Khokand, or Khiva.

The interior management of a state, which, young
in years, yet seemed to tower among its fellows, might
be supposed to be a very interesting topic to dilate
upon; but on this subject there is less direct evidence
than could be wished.   Even Sir Douglas Forsyth, in
his official report, is not able to throw as much light as
is desired on the inner working of the administrative
system of Yakoob Beg.   Still, such as it is, with the
exception of the Russian writer, Gregorieff, he is the
only authority on the subject.

To commence with the court and the immediate
surroundings of Yakoob Beg, we are struck by two
inconsistencies.   In the first place, there were no great
nobles, or indeed adherents of his family; those chiefs
who, whether they were Khokandian nobles or Kirghiz

or Afghan adventurers, had proved their fidelity to his rule, and their capacity for service, were actively employed as governors of districts, or as commandants of fortresses in the wide-stretching dominions of their imperious master.   Periodically they came to pay their respects in the capital, and at frequent intervals Yakoob Beg, in his journeys to the frontier, visited them, and superintended their operations in person; but, in so active a community where there was a dearth of mankind, the intellectually gifted members of the society were too valuable to be permitted to devote their energies and their attention to the object of becoming palace ornaments.   Yakoob Beg had forced himself on a people who regarded him with indifference, and he had to maintain himself in his place by a never relaxing vigour.   To make this possible, he required a large staff of efficient and trustworthy subordinates, who may be divided into three classes of various capacities, viz., soldiers, administrators, and tax-gatherers.   Until the last few months of his reign there was no symptom that his system was declining in vigour, or that his supply of competent officials was limited and susceptible of being exhausted. Even in his most prosperous years, however, there was always a difficulty in obtaining a full supply; and in all inferior posts the disaffected Khitay had to be employed.   The Tungani of Kucha and Aksu were scarcely more to be trusted in an emergency than their Buddhist kinsmen.   Yet the extensive civil service of the state, which undertook the education, the religion, the civil order, the local administration of the people all into its own hands, had to be kept in working order, whatever else might happen. It can at once be perceived that, when a government which never obtained any deep hold on the affections of the people had only a limited population to draw upon, it was only a question of time to solve the difficulty by an exhaustion of the supply of suitable brain material, or by the uprising of an, at heart, dissatisfied people.   No one will ever understand the secret of Yakoob Beg's rule unless he constantly bears in mind that his strict orthodoxy as a Mussulman, and his still stricter enforcement of the laws of his religion within his borders, were elements of strength only in his external relations; in his internal affairs they placed him in the light of a tyrant, and prevented his people ever experiencing any enthusiasm for his person and rule. It is doubtful whether outside the priesthood and the more fanatical Andijanis there was any great religious zeal at all, and it is quite a delusion to speak of the Kashgari, as a whole, as being fanatical Mahomedans, in the same degree that it is true to say so of the Bokhariots or Afghans. In addition to there being no noble or wealthy official class in the city of Kashgar, there was also the strange inconsistency of an intensely strict etiquette being enforced side by side with extreme plainness in costume and ceremonial. It is rare indeed to hear any traveller to Kashgar speaking of the richness or finery of court functionaries. Even Hadji Torah, or the Seyyid Yakoob Khan, as he is now called, and Mahomed Yunus, the governor of Yarkand, two of the most trusted and prominent followers of the Athalik Ghazi, were not to be distinguished from a host of minor luminaries in the court circle by any external insignia of their elevated position. Some of the military, officers of the household troops, wore a device of a dragon's head worked in silk over their plain uniform of leather; and this seems to have been a custom surviving the disappearance of the Chinese. Hadji Torah—who recently visited this country, and who had on previous occasions travelled in Russia, Turkey, and India—however, alone among Kashgarian notables, had introduced into his household some of the comforts and luxuries of European life. His example was not imitated by many others, and, after a brief period of fashion, the improvements he had striven to make popular died out and were lost sight of. The ordinary dress of a person above the rank of gentleman is a large blanket-like cloak worn over a close-fitting tunic and breeches; and the dress of the peasant is similar, only his cloak is usually a sheepskin. The Ameer himself set the example of exceeding plainness in his costume, and his followers were far too skilled courtiers to vary their practice from that of their ruler. But what his court lacked in pomp it gained in impressiveness by the perfect system of etiquette enforced, and by the external show of reverence to the ruler and to his religion, manifested in every petty detail of the palace ceremonial. The Ameer received publicly in his audience-chamber every day, when all petitions and stringent punishments were submitted to him. His *shaghawals*, or foreign secretaries, made their report to him on whatever business might be most pressing, whether it was concerning his relations with India or Russia, with Afghanistan or the Tungani; and the local governors, who might happen to have arrived at the capital, were received in audience, either to present their personal respects to the ruler, or their reports of the government of their provinces. But with the exception of a few of his kinsmen, and more intimate associates, such as Abdulla, none were permitted to be seated in his presence. Even these could not sit within a certain distance of their sovereign. All subjects who were allowed to approach his person had to do so in the humblest manner, and with the deepest expressions of humility and subjection. His son, Kuli Beg, was still more particular in his intercourse with his subjects. Even his cousin, Hadji Torah, a man whose experience and lineage entitled him to exceptional consideration, never placed himself on an equality with this youthful despot, and always clothed his words and thoughts when in conversation with him in an outward show of humble respect and deferential obsequiousness. It will be at once surmised, and, so far as our information warrants an opinion, with correctness, that all this terrorism alienated any good feeling from the ruling family that its prowess in the field and the cabinet might have secured for it. In Kashgar we have a forcible proof of the truth of Tennyson's line, that "he who only rules by terror doeth grievous wrong;" and yet, founded as it was on a military system, and on the deepest distrust of the subject races, it could not well have been otherwise.

The most unmistakable proof of how Yakoob Beg's rule was founded, and how it was maintained, is to be seen in the fact that his *orda*, or palace, was one large barrack, the interior compartments of which were devoted to the accommodation of the royal household. His out-houses were filled with cannon of every description, from antiquated Chinese irjirs to modern Krupps and Armstrongs, and his select corps of artillerymen, clothed in a scarlet uniform, seldom left the chief cities, except for serious operations against foreign enemies. At the Yangy-Shahr of Kashgar, too, he kept his military stores, and it was said that in his workshops there he was able to construct cannon and muskets in considerable numbers in imitation of the most perfect weapons of European science. But it must be noted that we have no record of any of his home-made weapons being used in actual hostilities, while the supply of arms received from Russia, or this country, is known to have been made the most of. Besides the natural aptitude of his subjects of Chinese descent for imitation, he had in his service, particularly in his artillery, many sepoys who had deserted our service either at the time of the mutiny or since. These soldiers, valuable either as non-commissioned officers or in higher ranks still, combined with a large number of good troops from Khokand and the mountain tribes of the neighbourhood, gave a cohesion and vigour to the whole army that was simply inestimable. That army, it may be here convenient to say, was divided into two classes widely differing from each other, and called upon, except in an emergency, when all the resources of the state were summoned to take part in its defence, to perform duties as opposite as their own composition. The army of the Ameer, founded on

that confused assemblage with which he ·conquered
Kashgar, was divided into two bodies, the *jigit* or
djinghite, the horse soldier, and the *sarbaz*, or foot
soldier. The former of these was the more formidable
warrior, being selected for personal strength or skill.
The *jigits* were trained to fight on foot as well as on
horse, and were armed with a long single-barrelled gun
and a sabre. Their uniform was a serviceable coat of
leathern armour mostly buff in colour, and to all intents
and purposes they correspond with our dragoons, or,
perhaps, still more closely with the proposed corps of
mounted riflemen. The *sarbaz*, among whom are
included the artillerymen, presented greater varieties of
efficiency than his mounted comrade; still he had gone
through some regular drill and training, and resided in
barracks. He was a regular soldier, and might be trusted
in defence of his country up to a certain point. In
numbers it is impossible to state accurately how many
jigits and *sarbazes* there were in the service of the state;
some months ago they would have been placed as high
as 50,000 or 60,000 strong, possibly at a higher number
still; now we are wiser on the subject, and we have gone
to the other end of the scale. It is probable, however,
that Yakoob Beg never had 20,000 perfectly trustworthy soldiers in his army, and that after the conclusion of the Tungan wars, half that number would more
accurately represent his force of *jigits* and *sarbazes*.
But in addition to the more or less effective main body,
there was a nondescript following of Khitay, Tungani,
half-savage Kirghiz, and rude degraded savages like the
Dolans, that in numbers would have presented a very
formidable appearance. The Khitay must at once be
struck out of the estimate, for they were never permitted to go beyond the immediate vicinity of Yarkand
and Kashgar, where they kept themselves apart, and
were employed as military servants, as sentries, and as
workmen in the military shops and factories. The
Tungani, who enrolled themselves at various epochs in

the service of Kashgar, were more than dubious in their fidelity to the state ; besides they were of such questionable courage, that they were no allies of any importance. Even as compared with one another, these were of varying kinds of efficiency ; the Tungani who joined Yakoob Beg in the earlier portion of his career seeming to be the best of them. Those who joined after the fall of Aksu and Kucha, less efficient and more ambiguous in their fidelity ; and those who dwelt in the country from Korla to Turfan and Manas, were totally inefficient, and not to be trusted to any degree whatever. The Kirghiz and Kipchak nomads were rather a source of danger to their friends than of dread to their foes. Yakoob Beg had, therefore, at his orders but a very limited force to maintain his own dynasty against the machinations of Khoja and Tungan, and to defend a long and vulnerable frontier against many powerful and ambitious neighbours. It was absurd for him to think of venturing single-handed across the path of Russia, and to do him justice he never deluded himself into the idea that he could. All he seems to have aspired to was to resist to the uttermost any invasion of his territory by them, and to die sooner than surrender. Limited in numbers as his regular forces were, they seem to have had every claim to be placed high in the rank of Asiatic soldiers. They were certainly not as formidable a body as the Sikhs or Ghoorkas, probably not as the Afghans; still they were infinitely superior, except in numbers, to any forces the Ameer of Bokhara or the Khan of Khokand could place in the line of battle. To Yakoob Beg alone belongs the credit of their organization.

Yakoob Beg's system of administration was simple in the extreme. A *Dadkwah*, or governor, was appointed for each district, and in his hands was vested the supreme control in all the affairs of his province. Yet he was no irresponsible minister who could tyrannize as he pleased. Tyrannize in small ways, undoubtedly, many of them did, but, as the life of the subject could only be taken away

by order of the ruler himself, the most powerful weapon
in the hands of an unscrupulous viceroy was removed.

At stated periods, too, he had to proceed to Kashgar
to give a report of the chief occurrences in his province,
and on such occasions petitions containing charges
against the Dadkwah were formally considered in his
presence. It may be said that this proceeding was a
farce, and it is probably true that a favoured viceroy
could laugh at any ordinary accusation against his character. But that would be an exceptional case. Many
Dadkwahs were reduced in official rank, for malpractices,
and some, such as Yakoob Beg's own half-brother, were
removed for incompetence in their charges. Side by side,
too, with the Dadkwah, ruled the Kazi or Judge, who,
if of course not on a par in rank with the viceroy, was still
invested with complete authority in all legal decisions
on crime. This prominence given to the legal authorities had a good effect on the public mind, for, although
the Kazi, as a rule, might not dare to thwart the wishes
of the Dadkwah, the effect of the law being supreme
was scarcely detracted from. And what was that law? it
may naturally be asked. Precisely the same as the law of
every other Mahomedan state, with a few innovations
traceable to the influence of the Chinese. The Shariát,
the holy code of the Prophet followed in all the Sunni
states, was enforced by Yakoob Beg, with particular
severity; and in its working no sense of mercy was
permitted to temper the harshness of its regulations.
Crimes committed by women were punished with greater
inflictions than the same committed by men; and the
ordinary punishments, whipping, mutilation, and torture
could be inflicted by order of the Dadkwah. Only in
capital cases had the decision to rest with the sovereign.
Thieves, beggars, and vagrants found wandering about
the streets at prohibited hours were immediately locked
up, and brought before the Kazi, who would either
administer a caution, or a whipping, if the accused had
previously offended. Another check on the abuse of

power by the officials was to be found in the following regulation. A charge to be visited with a severer punishment than twenty heavy strokes from the *dira*—a leather strap, fixed in a wooden handle—had to be investigated by a member of each official rank ; so the Kazi passed a culprit on, with his comments, to the Mufti, the Mufti to the Alim, and the Alim to the Dadkwah. If any of these officials dissented from the remarks of his subordinate, and the matter was found impossible to arrange by mutual concessions, it was either referred to the sovereign for solution, or was permitted to fall through. The Dadkwah had also to be present at every punishment within his jurisdiction, and was directly responsible to the Ameer for any miscarriage of justice. The Kazi Rais, or head judge, had the right to decide all minor matters for himself—for instance, in his patrols through the streets, if he met a woman unveiled he could order her to be struck so many times with the *dira ;* or if he found a man selling adulterated food, or using light weights, he could confiscate his goods, or in some other manner mulct him in addition to administering a certain number of strokes. He and his attendants were particularly energetic and zealous in compelling idlers about the bazaars to repair to the mosques at prayer time, and in a very paternal and authoritative manner did the Rais exercise his petty power for the good of his people. Even on his despotism there was some check, as he had no authority to inflict more than forty blows with the *dira* for one offence. Intimately connected with the administration of justice was the police system, which in its intricate ramifications permeated all sections of society. Much as we may feel admiration for the judicial code, which, up to a certain point admirably administered, ensured a certain kind of rough justice throughout the Athalik Ghazi's dominions, the police laws and discipline have greater claims to our favourable opinion, as evidences of an astonishing capacity for government. In his legal code, Yakoob Beg simply adopted the laws enforced on all true believers by the Koran, and he had no claims to originality as a lawgiver. But as a ruler adopting all those checks on sedition which lie at the disposal of an unscrupulous sovereign, and which were brought to such a pitch of perfection under Fouché and the Second Empire, Yakoob Beg has reason to be placed in the very highest class of such potentates. In this achievement, too, he was not a plagiarist, and, as he must have been ignorant of similar regulations existing in Europe, he must be allowed the credit of having originated a system of police in which it is difficult to find a single flaw. In China, indeed, something of the same kind has at all times existed, and at periods when the Emperor grasped the sceptre firmly, and made his individuality felt in the management of affairs, the police were one of the most active tools of power. But even in that empire there is no record of their having attained so complete a control over the actions and sentiments of the people as in Kashgaria during the last decade. It appears, too, that in superiority of system lay the sole pre-eminence of the latter; for the Tungan, or police-man, of China was, individually man for man, a superior class to the Kashgarian and other constables of Yakoob Beg. In short, the whole credit of their existence belongs to that ruler.

Let us now give some account of this important body. It was divided into two chief divisions quite distinct from and irrespective of each other, secret and municipal. The *secret* was not, like ours, a perceptible class of detectives, acting in combination with the municipal, to which was entrusted the discovery of crimes and conspiracies. It may loosely be described as consisting of every member of the community, for all desired to stand well with the powers that be, and the easiest way to attain that object would be to place all confidential information at their disposal. But it is evident that even in a state of irresponsible power, like Kashgar, a clear encouragement, such as this, to invent libels of one's neighbours, could only end in unprofitable litigation and confusion. There was certainly a check on the too zealous imaginations of the subjects, and, although there is not much evidence on the subject, it appears to have been twofold. In the first place a libeller incurred the risk of receiving very severe punishment, particularly if the person libelled were of saintly lineage, or if he filled any official post. This operated as a check on too hasty accusations, especially when it became known that the reward for such service was seldom speedily forthcoming, and scarcely ever answered the expectations of the informer. But this check, which alone seems to have been adopted in the earlier years of Yakoob Beg's authority, was found to be insufficient as his power became consolidated. The secret police then became organized to a certain degree; that is to say, they so far formed a distinct corps that a member had to be approved of either by the Dadkwah or the Rais. So well, however, was the secret of their individuality maintained that few of them were generally known to the people. Suspicion was wide-spread throughout all ranks of society, and the governor in his *orda*, or the Rais in his hall of justice, or the shopkeeper in his booth, or the artisan in his hut, never felt safe that his neighbour, the man with whom he was holding the most friendly converse, was not dissecting his expressions to discover whether they contained anything treasonable. Members of this formidable body were always attached to the suite of either foreign envoys or merchants; and their presence in the rear of the *cortége*, always effectually closed the mouths of the inhabitants, or only induced them to open them to give false or contradictory replies.

. There can be no doubt that this secret organization, brought to a high pitch of perfection during the later years of his reign, gave a consistency and strength to Yakoob Beg's tenure of power that was wanting to all his predecessors. In leaving this part of the system, it is as well to point out in conclusion that this detective force was only useful in discovering what was about to occur in the state among Andijani or Tungani, and that it was powerless to attempt the repression by force of any outbreak of popular feeling. Its members were simply spies, and as a body its value vanished when its members became generally known. Constant changing, and the introduction of fresh members, were the sole effectual means of preserving the *incognito* of a large body of men, and women even, who preserved official communication only with the local governor or judge.

The municipal police were subdivided into urban and suburban, and they present a complete contrast to the vague body we have just attempted to describe. Their functions were known and recognizable. They were the functionaries who put into practice the behests of the Kazi, and they maintained order in the streets and bazaars, much as our own do. The *Corbashi* is the head of this body, and his subordinates are styled *tarzagchi*. They wore a distinct uniform, and had drilling grounds attached to barracks, in which, however, they were not all compelled to reside. They were essentially military in their rules, and presented a powerful first front to all evil-doers and would-be rebels. It was they who accompanied the Kazi Rais in his daily circuit of the streets and market-place, and it was from their weapon, the *dira*, that the ordinary punishment was received. Their principal avocation seems to have been to maintain order in the towns during the night-time, for in the day we only hear of a few of them being detailed for personal attendance on the Dadkwah and Kazi. With sunset their true importance is more visible, for not only were they stationed in all main thoroughfares, squares, and other open places of the city; but until sunrise patrols at frequent intervals throughout the night visited all the chief quarters of the town. The power vested in their hands during these hours was very great, and it was dangerous for any stranger to venture out after prohibited hours. All persons found in the streets after

sunset were arrested and incarcerated until the morning,
when, if they could give a satisfactory account of themselves, they were released, with a caution not to keep such
unseemly hours for the future. If, however, they were
unable to explain their business, a further term of
imprisonment was imposed; and it was a matter of some
difficulty for a stranger to obtain his complete liberty
for some time afterwards. The suburban police fulfilled
much the same duties, and on all the country roads
patrols passed up and down during the night, while
pickets were stationed at the cross-roads. In the same
manner as in the towns all travellers, except those
armed with a passport, were interned for a minute investigation into their affairs in the morning. And
"thieves, beggars, and wanderers" were chastised at
the discretion of the local magistrate. The vagrant laws
were as much enforced, too, as they were in this country
in the days of Queen Elizabeth, and in a general mode
of interference with the thoughts and actions of its subjects, the Kashgarian government had attained a height
of excellence that would entitle it to rank with the
Inquisition. Still there was order. No riots occurred
to distract the harmony of the public weal, and to an
external observer, especially to one belonging to a country where order is considered the greatest *desideratum*,
the government of the Athalik Ghazi seemed to be the
perfection of an Asiatic state, and that order a reason for
attributing all other virtues to its originator.

Travellers, however, who were provided with a passport,
were accorded privileges of transit, and were permitted,
if they felt so disposed, to continue their journeys during
hours interdicted to less privileged mortals. In each
chief town there were offices for the issue of these permits to travel. Not many obstacles were thrown in the
path of those, who left permanent guarantees in the
shape of property behind them for their return, in
accomplishing their desire for travel; but rarely was
permission granted to any one, not blessed with these

worldly advantages, to proceed further than the neighbouring district. Indeed in all cases leave to visit foreign states, other than Khokand or Bokhara, was a matter of difficulty to be obtained, and only in the most exceptional cases was it granted. But it appears that there were some evasions of this regulation by a simulation of religious zeal, for the Sheikh-ul-Islam had it in his power to grant permits to leave the country on pilgrimages to Bokhara the "holy," or to Mecca. In themselves the passports were simple in phraseology. They merely stated the name and address of the traveller, the nature of his business, and his destination. Having obtained the consent of the Dadkwah, and the authority of the Kazi, no difficulty was experienced in procuring the necessary slip of paper. Infractions of this permission, by too long an absence, or by proceeding in some forbidden direction, were visited on a first offence with a fine. On a repetition of it, however, the punishment became more severe. It would be interesting to know how these protectors of the public peace were paid, and by what means. But on this point there is little trustworthy information. We, however, know of one tax which was devoted to the support of the urban police, but of the funds from which the suburban were remunerated, we have no authority for any assertion. A weekly tax was levied from all the shop and booth owners, to go towards the payment of their protectors; but it is not supposed that this amounted to a sufficient sum to maintain the large force in the more important cities. The difference was probably paid out of the state coffers under the head of justice. Judging from this we cannot be far wrong in assuming that a similar tax was levied on the farmers and country residents for the support of the suburban police; and as the secret police required less outlay in the country than in the cities, it is possible that that tax more nearly defrayed the total cost, than it did in Yarkand or Kashgar. The police supervision and the military terrorism, freely resorted to on all occasions offering an excuse for such an extreme measure, have not been without their effect in leaving traces of their existence and influence in the daily life of the Kashgari, and on the countenances and sentiments of the subject peoples. Where formerly lived a light-hearted and happy race there now seemed as if a never-to-be-removed gloom had settled down on the face of the land, and neither the assurance of security nor the irregular encouragement of the ruler to commerce could remove the blight that had fallen upon the energies and happiness of the people. As one of them expressed it, in pathetic language, "During the Chinese rule there was everything; there is nothing now." The speaker of that sentence was no merchant, who might have been expected to be depressed by the falling-off in trade, but a warrior and a chieftain's son and heir. If to him the military system of Yakoob Beg seemed unsatisfactory and irksome, what must it have appeared to those more peaceful subjects to whom merchandise and barter were as the breath of their nostrils? All the advantages of a perfect police system, heavily weighted by the incumbrance of a costly addition of spies and tale-bearers, would seem as nothing compared with the loss incurred by the fetters placed on individual motion and enterprise. Considered by itself, the police organization of Kashgar was, perhaps, the most perfect design achieved by Yakoob Beg, and his community of spies will rank with anything in effectiveness that has ever been accomplished by any potentate. But as a permanent addition to his strength it is permissible to doubt whether he really secured his rule by employing the latter, or obtained much more by the formation of the former than the services of a trained body of trustworthy, courageous men. The restrictions imposed on trade by the severance of all communications with the East by the Tungan wars and by the limited amount of liberty granted the native Kashgari, proved most deterrent to all mercantile adventure, and placed in the hands of Khokandians or Russians on the north, and of Cashmerians and Punjabis on the south, most of the trade still carried on with Eastern Turkestan.

The trade carried on by the Athalik Ghazi's state, if we are to judge solely by amount, with foreign countries, was greatest with Russia and her dependencies; but if we investigate the matter more closely we find that the result is a little more satisfactory to ourselves. The direct trade that was carried on by way of Leh with Khoten and Sanju was steadily increasing, while that of Russia by Khokand had for some time remained stationary, if it had not even decreased. And then much of the Russian trade has to be scored to this country, for in the marts of Kashgar, underneath Russian exteriors, were very often to be found English interiors, and the brand of well-known Manchester and Liverpool makers was discovered beneath some gaudy and brilliant-looking cover hailing from Moscow or Nishni Novgorod. Besides, recent investigations have proved that some of the goods exported from Shikarpore, in Scinde, through the Bholan Pass find their way through the mountainous districts that intervene into the territory of his late Highness the Ameer of Kashgar. Nor had Yakoob Beg totally neglected all means for inducing merchants to enter his state; indeed, his chief objection seemed to have been, not that they should have entered his state, but that they should leave it. Serais were built in all the chief towns for the accommodation of such merchants as might take up a temporary abode within his territory, and the Andijani Serai, or hotel, specially constructed for merchants from Khokand, was one of the largest and most striking buildings in the city of Kashgar. Yakoob Beg had even detailed off to take care of the serai and its occupants a large number of the old Khitay, or Yangy Mussulmans, who were generally employed throughout the city as domestic servants. When we come to the description of

the relations of Yakoob Beg with England and with
Russia we will speak more fully of the details of those
treaties of commerce which were ratified on several
occasions, and whose ostensible object was the promotion of trade and other friendly intercourse.

We have now considered the army, the police, the administration of justice, and the court of Yakoob Beg,
and the only chief subject that remains to be discussed are
the principles of finance adopted by the Ameer. To keep
any state, even an Asiatic state, in a fit condition for preserving its independence, a settled revenue is requisite,
and Yakoob Beg, whose atmosphere was one of almost
continual warfare, was on several occasions pressed for
money in a manner difficult to be conceived by us.
His military operations languished for the want of
the sinews of war, and we are told on credible authority that many of his soldiers received only payment
out of the spoil taken at the sack of Turfan and other
places. So long as his ordinary expenditure was increased by the addition of an extraordinary war outlay, so long was he unable to make his receipts and
expenditure balance. On the cessation of hostilities against the Tungani, and the partial revival
of trade in consequence, his fiscal affairs assumed a
brighter aspect, and it is possible that during the last
few years of his reign his revenue showed a surplus.
But to obtain that success, a most joyful one to every
embarrassed potentate, Yakoob Beg had to resort to
many strange expedients, and to manifest much patience
and long-suffering; and in overcoming petty obstacles
and minor details, he proved himself to be a man of more
than average ability, no less than he had previously by
the skilful manipulation of armies and intriguers. Here
again he erected a structure distinct and separate from
that handed down to him by the Chinese. Compara-
tively speaking, the Chinese had been wealthy to the
Athalik Ghazi, and they received in moderate imposts
on merchandise alone almost a sufficient sum to defray

the total cost of their administration. Yakoob Beg had
no such certain source of revenue; he had to raise from
an impoverished and only half-conquered state a sum
almost as large as that required by the Chinese. That
he did it remains the chief proof of his skill as a finance
minister, and is another reason for our regarding this
extraordinary ruler with admiration. We may feel sure
that if we could follow closely the history of his fiscal
efforts, and the numberless plans that proved abortive,
we should have revealed one of the most instructive and
interesting narratives of modern Asia. There are no
materials out of Kashgar, if there are such there, for
such an investigation however, and we can only follow
as best we may be able, the thread of events by the light
of such authorities as are at our disposal. In court and
personal expenditure he set an example that might with
advantage be followed by other rulers in Asia even at
the present day, and in a strict economy and supervision
of the petty sums that in the aggregate make all the
difference in any state between a surplus and a deficit,
were to be found the two guiding principles of his conduct. Kashgaria might be in a very backward state of
cultivation, and years of commotion and warfare had
undoubtedly thrown it back in the ranks of prosperity
and civilization, but the Athalik Ghazi was persuaded
of the truth of the Latin philosopher's saying, that
" Parsimonia magna vectigalia est."   It must be remembered that Yakoob Beg set himself a different task
to accomplish than had the Chinese. Their idea was
not so much to extend their empire, although there has
always been a tendency with the Chinese to be aggressive
against small neighbours, as to acquire a territory that
could be made a paying thing : much as the pioneers of
Anglo-Saxon conquest have made their impression in
every quarter of the globe in search of wealth and adventure, did the Chinese by a seemingly irresistible impulse
spread over the continent of Asia. In doing so they were
actuated as much by calculation of possible profit as by

any desire for military renown. The Emperor Keen-Lung himself was flattered by the triumphs achieved beyond Gobi; but his lieutenants and viceroys aimed at more mercenary objects, and but for the golden promise held forth by a permanent conquest of Turkestan would have induced their master to direct his efforts to some more profitable undertaking. The Chinese, having acquired Kashgar, were far too sagacious to use up its resources by an organized system of pillage, and they accordingly, let it be granted chiefly with a view to their own personal aggrandizement, devoted their attention to the development of its natural wealth by means already detailed in a previous chapter. For three generations the officials grew rich on the prosperity of their dependency, and for the same period the people themselves were scarcely less flourishing. The Chinese had accepted no slight responsibility in undertaking the government of Kashgar on principles identical with those by which they held authority in Tibet; but, owing to wonderful perseverance and good management, they triumphed over every difficulty. The revenue raised for state and local purposes was very great, and it sufficed to preserve good order for many years, and to add permanent improvement to the state in every direction. The task voluntarily undertaken by the Chinese was far more onerous than that Yakoob Beg found he had to execute; but they came to it with many advantages that he wanted. They had a large and faithful army; he had only an uncertain gathering, which might flee or desert on the first symptom of disaster: they had the resources of a great and powerful empire at their back; he had nothing but his own energy and determination: and above all, they had a reputation that added to their strength and facilitated their undertakings, while he was regarded as a mere military adventurer, receiving the contempt of Tungan and Khoja alike. The very nature of things made the Chinese turn most of their attention to commerce, while for years Yakoob Beg's solo thought was to consolidate his military strength and form a large standing army. For many years, then, Yakoob Beg only spent money on the drilling of soldiers and the purchase of weapons. Now and then, when some danger seemed to threaten him, either from Russia, Afghanistan, or the Tungani, he would devote considerable sums to the construction of forts in the line of the menaced position. But his chief expenditure was confined to his army, and the maintenance of his dynasty by his police system. The administration of justice required a certain sum of money, and the Church for its support came in for a fair share of the good things that were going. It is clear that his expenditure, if not very great in our eyes, would severely tax a population of 1,000,000 people in no very high state of prosperity. The chief source of wealth in the past had always been the trade with China, and when that was broken off, the slight increase in intercourse with Russia and India was not a sufficient compensation. In fact, the country was very poor, without the ingenuity and commercial instincts of the Khitay. During the days of the war under Buzurg Khan, the only means of obtaining the necessary revenue was by despoliation and enforced levies on the occupied portion of the territory. When the western portion of Kashgaria was subdued, Yakoob Beg found himself without any money in his exchequer, and no easy means of filling it presented itself to him. In these straits he had recourse to an expedient that, if not very novel, was at all events very effective. He issued a proclamation to his faithful subjects to the effect that as conqueror he was landowner of the whole state; but that he was willing—eager would have been the more correct expression—to sell it to them at a cheap rate. He, however, exempted from this the old possessions of the Chinese Wangs and Ambans, and distributed their extensive domains among the more prominent of his followers, who in return acknowledged their liability to military service. The system was an exact copy of the old feudal régime, and Yakoob Beg was vested with all the rights and authority of the feudal lord of the Middle Ages. The parallel is still further maintained by the large reward that the Church received for its aid to the new ruler. The old revenues, devoted to the support of the temples and religious seminaries in the past, and which had miscarried during the troublous period of the war for the possession of Turkestan, were restored, and fresh possessions were added thereto, to demonstrate the generosity of the sovereign and his veneration for the religion of Mahomed. His old friend the Sheikh-ul-Islam was still more fortunate, and a large estate was set apart for his special enjoyment. Nor does it appear that the Mussulman priests abused the fresh power and advantages they thus secured; for among the toilers in Kashgaria none were more energetic than they in educating the people, and in extending their influence over their minds, both for the benefit of their religion and for the security of the power of the Athalik Ghazi. But in one respect, and it is impossible to exaggerate its importance, Yakoob Beg's endeavours to found a strong military class, bound to him by ties of past favours and others yet to come, were abortive ; for with rare exceptions his followers refused to fill their new avocation of landed proprietors. Instead of devoting their attention to the questions arising from agriculture and other rural pursuits, they sub-let all their possessions to Andijani immigrants, and, residing in their city *ordas*, gave themselves over either to lascivious pleasures or to complete indolence. Even so distinguished a warrior as Abdulla Beg, the slayer of more than 12,000 persons, as his panegyrists boasted, suffered from the pervading effeminacy on the cessation of active hostilities ; and in the lower ranks of the service such deterioration in energy was still more manifest. This change in the spirit of his earlier supporters, among other things, obliged Yakoob Beg to depend the more on the Andijani merchants and shopkeepers, and conduced to his adopting more favourable views on foreign trade in the later years of his power.

The sum of money which he immediately received by the sale of lands placed him in a condition to undertake those wars against the Tungani, which added so much to the extent of his territory and to the responsibilities of his position. Indeed, for several years after its first enforcement it continued to bring in a certain amount to the coffers of the State. But even this resource was transitory, and the sum of money received by this means and in the shape of spoil, from Yarkand, Kashgar, Khoten, and other places, was not sufficient to meet the expenditure caused by the formation of a large army. Neither of these practices could be regarded as a permanent means of obtaining a revenue, for the former would scarcely admit of a repetition, and the latter soon exhausted itself. So when his rule had become a little settled, and these modes of raising money, in addition to the still more reprehensible practice of robbing foreign merchants, had become out of date to a certain degree, the Athalik Ghazi had to place his fiscal arrangements on a more practical and honourable basis. While he laboured under some disadvantages, already enumerated, as compared with the Chinese, he had the great advantage over them that he strove for an object more easily accomplished than the restoration of Kashgar to its pristine welfare; and in his budget he had only steadily to keep in view how much he required to maintain so many *jigits*, and so many police in his pay, and to keep in his exchequer a small surplus for any untoward emergency. He left the roads to take care of themselves; the irrigation works, sadly wanted in various parts of the state, must be reserved for his successors; and all proposals for the amelioration of the people were shelved for a more opportune occasion. But so many thousand *jigits* must be in the ranks; so many fresh guns and cartridges must be placed in the arsenals; and so many adventurers must be induced by good pay to take service in the army as non-commissioned officers, in order that the rank and file should be well drilled. The very necessities of his position compelled Yakoob Beg to make all these military preparations; but the cost was great, and the sacrifices thus imposed on ruler and on people were a terrible strain. Recent events make us inclined to believe that a less active military and foreign policy, and a more peaceable and domestic one, would have tended to have added more strength to the Athalik Ghazi's rule than the somewhat ostentatious military parade to which he had recourse. Be that as it may, Yakoob Beg instituted in 1867 two taxes, which may be supposed to represent the two chief classes of receipts during his tenure of authority. The first of these was a tithe on all the cereal produce of the country; this tax was called the *Ushr*. The second, called the *Zakat*, was a customs due levied on all merchandise entering Kashgar. The *Ushr* was payable on all land except that occupied by the Church, or by those who owed military service to the crown instead of other payment; and even those who rented land from the noble classes were obliged to surrender a tithe to the ruler. It would appear, therefore, from this that it was not so much the land as its legal possessor who was exempt from liability to the usual obligations of citizenship. The danger contained in the acquisition of all the crown lands by Andijani merchants, and the gradual displacement of his more immediate followers through the energy of these people, was not imperceptible to Yakoob Beg, and he accordingly adopted measures for preventing his nobles selling their land without his sanction. The receipts from this *Ushr* were very considerable, and it was the main source of his revenue for years. We have some idea of the approximate value of land in Kashgar. The method of measuring land for sale, and consequently also for taxation, is peculiar. It is not by any given size that it is computed, or, indeed, strictly speaking by the amount of crop it produces; but at a rate in accordance with the amount of wheat with which it had been planted. The average rate was about a pound for as much land as was sown with 20 lb. of wheat. The tenant, as has been said, paid the government dues and handed over three-fourths of the net produce to the landlord as rent, receiving for his portion only the one-fourth remaining. Under this system it was only in very prosperous years that any but very large tenants made sufficient to earn a competent livelihood. In bad years it is possible that the landlord had to satisfy himself with a smaller share, if he was not induced to surrender his claim altogether for the disastrous period. But the tax-farmers, entrusted with the collection of this rate, were eager to become rich, no less than to earn a good name with the authorities for bringing in a list with no defaulters. The unfortunate people were completely at their mercy, and without any means of ascertaining the accuracy of the claim, or of opposing extortionate demands on the part of the tax-collectors. They paid without a murmur, perhaps without a suspicion of the imposition that was being practised upon them, the sum demanded of them, if they were able; and as their dues were payable without delay and on demand before anything else was taken out of the total sum of the produce, the Athalik Ghazi received his share with regularity, and his tax-collector pocketed the excess sum for his own satisfaction. In many cases it is known that the amount claimed by the official exceeded by threefold the legal demand. Such a system was no less hurtful to the ruler than it was ruinous to the people. That in one tax alone a larger sum should be extracted from the people for the benefit of the officials than was contributed for the necessities of the state, exhibited a very loose system of supervision on the part of the sovereign, and is a strong piece of evidence that in many ways Yakoob Beg was a mixture of contradictions. We can scarcely persuade ourselves that he was aware of these occurrences, and yet how could he be ignorant of them?

In addition to the *Ushr* there was another tax on home produce, viz., the *Tanabi*, or tax on land devoted to the production of vegetables or fruit. The Tanab is, by the way, a lineal measure of forty-seven yards, and a Tanabi is a piece of land forty-seven yards square. On this extent of land cultivated for vegetables, or fruit, a small tax was raised. More than any other tax did this vary according to the character of the district, and to the quality of the year's crop. It was seldom less than a shilling a Tanabi, even in the least renowned district, whereas in some parts, in good years, it was five shillings, or even more. Here again, however, the middleman interfered, and exacted as much as he saw there was any possibility of his obtaining. This tax undoubtedly ought to have produced a large sum, as a larger portion of the soil is laid out as fruit and vegetable gardens than for crops; but whether it was more difficult to raise, or there was more peculation *in transitu* from the tax-payer to the imperial exchequer, it is certain that we hear much less of this tax than we should be disposed to imagine. The two great taxes on home productions were therefore a corn due and a fruit due. The rate was not in itself excessive, and could be paid by any community without embarrassment. It is uncertain to what extent the avarice of the officials had made the conditions of these two taxes more onerous, although, on the most favourable supposition, the citizen was mulcted in no inconsiderable sum. A more serious question for the ruler was, how did it affect his own position with regard to his subjects? Did Yakoob Beg appear in the eyes of the Kashgari as an exacting and oppressive tyrant on account of these heavy impositions?

It is impossible to speak on this point with any degree of certainty, but it is only natural to expect that such was the case. No tiller of the ground can feel grateful to a sovereign who required him to hand over almost one-third of his receipts before he made use of one penny of them, even for the payment of his rent. It is scarcely probable that Yakoob Beg approved of such enormous profits going to his officials; but, that having tolerated petty exactions in his earlier days, he found himself unable to attempt the task of coping with the evil when it had assumed such alarming proportions. It is impossible to believe that he remained in ignorance of what was occurring under his very eyes, and there is some evident foundation for the accusation that he participated in the division of the profits of his tax-gatherers. We should be loth to admit the accuracy of such a charge, and yet the arguments in its favour are too plausible to admit of a very confident contradiction. It would not speak well for the efficiency of his secret police if he had remained in ignorance of a fact which was losing him the sympathy of his subjects.

The gold mines at Khoten were worked after the fall of that city in 1868, and continued productive down to the present time. There is no information on the quantities of the precious metal that are there turned out in the year, but it is probable that they are not very great. The coal mines near Aksu and Kucha are no longer made use of, except by a few individuals, and the copper mines in that district have, since the departure of the Chinese, only been very partially explored. The jade that used to come in great quantities from Aksu and Khoten, is still to be found throughout Kashgar; but although it is probable that it still nearly all comes from those cities, the Kashgari themselves tell a hesitating tale as to its place of production. A visitor to Kashgar, on going the round of the bazaars, soon found that the people's tongues were tied by the presence, in his train, of a number of the secret police, who had been specially told off to prevent the Feringhee obtaining any troublesome information on the state of the people, or the resources of the state. A striking instance was given him of the close attention paid by these guardians of order to the veriest trifles. The traveller inquired in one stall where the jade, which was the chief commodity of the merchant in question, came from, and received the reply, Aksu. Proceeding to another shop in the street, he repeated the question, when he was informed that it was imported from Khokand. But the traveller said, your neighbour told me it came from Aksu. The shopkeeper, taken aback by this abrupt remark, became confused, and admitted that it came from Aksu. Warned by a look from the official, he then repeated his original assertion that it came from Khokand. The use of all this absurd shuffling, and attempt to throw dust in strangers' eyes, is impossible to discover; for it was a matter of little moment whether jade came from Aksu, or Khokand, so long as we knew that it formed an important commodity, both in the rough and in the chiselled state, in the cities of Kashgaria.

The customs tax, or *Zakat*, is sanctioned by the Shariát, and was levied at all the border posts on the various roads leading into the state. Up to the ratification of the treaties with Great Britain and Russia, its regulations were vague and elastic in the extreme. In fact, any merchant who might have been so foolhardy as to venture into Kashgar would have had reason, before these events, to think himself fortunate if he escaped the penalty of his rashness; for assuredly his luggage would not, but would have been confiscated for the special benefit of his Highness the Ameer. So late as 1869, Russian merchants were robbed of their baggage, and personally ill-treated, and only after long years of negotiation did the Russian Government obtain any satisfaction for the injuries and loss inflicted on one of their subjects. And then how did the Athalik Ghazi send the sum of money he agreed to pay for the loss the merchant had incurred?—why in a depreciated Chinese currency, part of a large number of coins that he had found in a disused temple in Kashgar! Before this, all the external trade had been carried on with Khokand and Bokhara, Afghanistan and Badakshan, and the receipts from *Zakat* were quite insignificant, barring such treasure trove as the spoliation of a merchant from Tashkent, or from Leh.   But with the persistent efforts on the part of the Russians on the north, and of the English native merchants on the south, to pierce the gloom hiding the country of Eastern Turkestan, it became impossible for Yakoob Beg to maintain much longer the incognito he was so jealous in maintaining. Perhaps also the prospect of deriving an income from *Zakat*, that should smooth down many of his difficulties, was not without some influence on his mind when he came into direct contact with civilized empires.   His expectations were far too sanguine, and he seems to have once more, during the last twelve months of his life, become indifferent to the advantages or disadvantages of trade with his neighbours.   In fact, when he placed his customs on a fair footing, he found that it would require many years to recoup him for the excessive exactions he surrendered.   The merchants who first attempted to commence intercourse with Kashgar became speedily discouraged by the dangers of the route, and the small opening for a large remunerative trade in a country whose wealth and population had been magnified tenfold.   In a country where the richest merchant in the chief town possessed only a capital of £8,000, not much could be expected in the way of fortune; and although the legal dues on all merchandise were fixed at an *ad valorem* rate of $2\frac{1}{2}$ per cent., it was soon discovered that if the ruler happened to be in want of cash he would not scruple to take what he could from the stranger.   Both to the ruler, and to the foreign merchant, the new arrangement contained distasteful matter.   The former perceived that he had surrendered some of his imperial rights, and that he was not to be recompensed by his receiving more money, and the latter knew that the treaty stipulation would not save him from having to pay excess fees.

The *Zakat*, far from showing the expected disposition to increase, seemed rather inclined to remain stationary, if not to decrease; and the foreign merchant had obtained some promise on the part of the ruler of personal protection, and of assistance in the disposal of his wares. His discontent at the stagnation in the customs soon showed itself by his exacting excess dues, sometimes on British, sometimes on Russian, but more often on Khokandian and Afghan merchants. Instead of increasing his receipts, these strong measures only threw them back, and left him in a worse plight than he was in before. He had not the patience necessary to enable him to wait with confidence the fuller development of trade, nor had he the perseverance or tact to place fresh inducements in the path of merchants to renew their intercourse with him and his state. Many visited Kashgar with merchandise a first time; but few, indeed, repeated the visit. The ruler was off-handed in his reception of them. They were scarcely accorded any liberty in their movements, and the profit of their journey was greatly reduced by the payment of a due of 5 per cent. instead of the stipulated condition of $2\frac{1}{2}$ per cent. It is a pure fiction, therefore, to say that trade with Kashgar had increased during the rule of the Athalik Ghazi through his friendly inclination. If the amount of merchandise imported into his state had increased, it was owing only to the necessities of its inhabitants, and was a fact that must have taken place either by intercourse direct, or through native states, with the two great providers of Central Asia. The exaggerated enthusiasm that it was endeavoured to raise up in this country about this same mythical ruler of Yarkand never spread far, and there was always some scepticism, if there could be no disproof, of the reports of the formidableness of this new kingdom. Looking calmly at the real state of Yakoob Beg's position, even at the height of his power, we find him to have always been a pecuniarily embarrassed ruler, glad of the smallest windfall in the shape of the spoil of a single merchant. The *Zakat*, his advisers pointed out to him, might be made a most productive source of revenue, if foreign merchants could be induced to bring their wares into the country. The loss the people had felt in the departure of the Chinese might be amply repaired by the appearance of Russian and English merchants to supply the same place that they filled. If his aspirations were disappointed, and the *Zakat* did not show any signs of possessing that elasticity which had been predicted, it is probable that in his impatience, heightened by the perception that foreign trade might lead to foreign complications, he did not give the scheme a sufficient time for a fair trial. His other sources of revenue, *Ushr* and *Tanabi*, and the gold mines of Khoten, brought in a sum enough to meet the current expenses of the government and to maintain in his service as many soldiers as his recruiting officers were able to secure. But there was little if any surplus; and local improvements, and all outlay that might have been reproductive and for the benefit of the people, were strictly forbidden. The only works we can find constructed by him, with a view to the advancement of the interests of his subjects, were the merchants' *serais*, built in each city, and these were self-supporting. Yakoob Beg has no claim to being considered as a beneficent ruler. He was a military dictator, who had shown a rare power for inaugurating a rough system of government, and whose campaigns had always been singularly successful. As a ruler, showing a full appreciation of the wants of his people, and adopting the best possible measures to obtain them, he had no claims to consideration. Indeed, he could not be compared with the Chinese, who, however personal may have been their motives, certainly raised the state to a high pitch of material prosperity, and left many enduring marks of their past occupation. These two dominations, foisted on the Kashgari by the strong arm, while each immeasurably superior to the Khoja claimants, represented two distinct modes of governing a subject race. The Chinese endeavoured to conciliate, and to make the necessity for their presence felt by the people; the Athalik Ghazi was supremely indifferent to the prosperity of his subjects, so long as they were willing to pay him the tribute money, and to serve in his army. An exactly opposite result might have been expected, for there was far more kinship between the Khokandian adventurer and the Kashgari, than there was between the Khitay and the Andijani. Admirers of Yakoob Beg may, of course, plead that his rule had not acquired sufficient consistency to justify him in tasking his strength by great undertakings, such as the construction of roads and canals. In one respect he had not the labour at his disposal, and he was, consequently, hampered by a difficulty that the Chinese were free from. Still when we remember that all these works ought to have been remunerative, and to have strengthened Yakoob Beg's individual power, instead of taxing his resources, the excuse cannot be admitted as entitled to our consideration. Yakoob Beg has claims only to be admired for having given us something better than a repetition of the depravity of the Khoja rulers, and of course among his coevals he is entitled to far the highest place. If it is only asked for him that he should be placed above them, no one can raise the slightest objection to it; for beyond the shadow of a doubt, he was the most energetic and talented ruler that had appeared among the Khanates for several centuries. But it would be affectation to deny that a higher place than this has been claimed for him; and before according his right to occupy it, the evidence on which his claim rests must be sifted with the greatest care. Even now I do not say that his claims are unproven; but that it is open to doubt whether his work has not been exaggerated, I think must be admitted by every one who has studied the course of his life in Kashgar. It is absurd to talk of Yakoob Beg having been an equal of Genghis Khan or of Timour, in any other way than that of showing that his personal abilities were of a transcendent order.   As a legislator and public benefactor, it is fair to compare him with the Chinese, who possessed some advantages over him, but who laboured under some disadvantages in religion, and other conditions, as compared with him.   And when we do this, after impartial consideration we find that the balance is greatly in favour of the Chinese.   What can we judge from this, but that the rule of Yakoob Beg, while presenting some striking features, was inferior in degree to that of the Chinese?   It is only fair to remember that the difficulties in his path were great, and that he overcame many of them.   Before closing this chapter some description of the chief men who assisted him to conquer the country, and then to govern it, may be not without interest to the reader.

First among these, by right of his position as well as by his high abilities, comes the Seyyid Yakoob Khan, or Hadji Torah, as he has more conveniently been called, the prince who has recently visited several of the principal courts of Europe.   He is a near relative of the Athalik Ghazi, although, strange to say, there is no consanguinity between them.   He is a son of Nar Mahomed Khan, the governor of Tashkent, who married as his second wife Yakoob Beg's sister, and who was instrumental in advancing the interests of Yakoob Beg during the earlier days of his career in Khokand.   The Seyyid was almost as old as his uncle, the Ameer of Kashgar, having been born in Tashkent in 1823; but despite this near connection Hadji Torah played no part in the conquest of Kashgar.   Until Yakoob Beg achieved complete success in his enterprise in Eastern Turkestan he was considered by Khokandians of high rank a simple adventurer.   The Seyyid Yakoob Khan was of the best lineage in Turkestan, and it is very possible that until the year 1867 he regarded his uncle with a considerable amount of indifference.   Certain it is that Hadji Torah was far otherwise employed than in assisting his relative

when the latter was engaged in some of the desperate
encounters of his not uneventful career. In the civil
administration of Khokand he filled, under Alim Kuli,
high posts, such as Principal of the Madrassa of Tashkent, and then he was appointed Kazi, or Judge. It
was after the fall of Ak Musjid that he commenced
that career of activity as a traveller and a negotiator
which brought him to the shores of the Bosphorus and
to the banks of the Neva and the Thames. That was
in the year 1854, and he was appointed as a sort of
secretary to the embassy of Mirza Jan Effendi, the ambassador sent by Mollah Khan to Constantinople for
aid. On a subsequent occasion he again visited Constantinople in a similar capacity, after the death of
Mollah Khan, and during the brief tenure of power
by his successor, Mahomed Khan, the nominee of Alim
Kuli. This was in 1865, and during the troubles that
ensued in Khokand and the final success of Khudayar
Khan, the legal ruler of Khokand and antagonist of
Alim Kuli, Hadji Torah resided quietly at Constantinople, where Abdul Aziz entertained him with sump-
tuous hospitality. It would appear that he obtained
some kind of reputation among the numerous visitors
from either Turkestan who came to Turkey, and apart
from his sacrosanct character few could fail to be impressed favourably by his cheerful yet dignified manner.
His uncle in 1870 had indeed overcome all opposition
to his rule, and it might at a first glance appear strange
why he should desire to secure the services of a man of
whom he could have seen or known little for many
years. But Hadji Torah possessed abilities and experience rare among the inhabitants of Central Asia, and
to Yakoob Beg the very talents his nephew possessed
were those he was most in need of.

In 1870 the Athalik Ghazi was anxious to draw close
the bonds of alliance with the Porte ; who could assist
him better than the man who had resided in Constantinople for several years, and who had formed a friendly

intimacy with the Sultan?   In 1871 Yakoob Beg first recognized the imminence of danger to his state from Russia, then put in possession of Kuldja; who could instruct him in the most effectual way of warding off that danger, either by an alliance with England or by propitiating the Russians, than the travelled Hadji Torah?   The very qualities that the Seyyid Yakoob Khan possessed were those the Ameer Yakoob Beg stood most in need of.   He might search among all his followers, those who had shared every vicissitude of his strange fortunes, and he could not find one other with an identical capacity.   The overtures to his nephew are thus easily intelligible, and the nephew himself gladly greeted his entry into a wider career than was that of an honoured guest on the hospitality of the Porte. His subsequent embassies in the service of Kashgar to St. Petersburg, Calcutta, Constantinople, and London are too recent and too well known to require mention here.   When he settled in Kashgar he married a daughter of Mahomed Khoja, the Sheikh-ul-Islam of Kashgaria.   His weight with the people was consequently very great, and his judgment was greatly valued by the Ameer.   Even over Beg Bacha, the turbulent and ferocious heir-apparent, Hadji Torah had acquired some influence by his ready tact and *bonhomie.*

Of the two chief personages, Mahomed Khoja and Abdulla Pansad, the priest and the soldier, who assisted Yakoob Beg, it is unfortunately impossible to discover much, and that little has already been stated in the preceding pages.   There can be no doubt, however, that they were the principal instruments in promoting the aggrandizement of Yakoob Beg, and the two who enjoyed more than any other the confidence and friendship of the man they had supported so faithfully. But of another well-tried follower we know more, chiefly through the pages of Dr. Bellew.   Mahomed Yunus seems to have been the most educated and well informed among the governors of Yakoob Beg. He had the reputation of being quite the best-informed man in Kashgar, but as the *curriculum* of instruction did not include modern languages, it is difficult to guage the exact degree of that reputation. He was an old and trusted follower of the Athalik Ghazi, for when he was in the service of Khokand Mahomed Yunus officiated as his scribe. He, however, as a civilian, took no part in the expedition of Buzurg Khan, and it was not until after the death of Alim Kuli and the success of Khudayar Khan that he joined his firm friend and master in Kashgar. So high an opinion had Yakoob Beg of his talents, and so pressed was he for skilled rulers, that Mahomed Yunus was at once appointed Dadkwah of the recently conquered district of Yarkand, the richest, the most populous, and the most turbulent of all the governorships in Kashgaria. The skill with which he brought the troublesome Yarkandis into complete submission to the new ruler, and the rare ability he manifested in his administration of his province down almost to the present time, justify the selection of his whilome comrade in Khokand. At first it seems that the governor ruled with a high hand, and that the slightest symptom of insubordination was checked by an immediate arrest and a not long-delayed execution. During the last seven years, however, his government had become milder, chiefly because all evil-doers had been got rid of. Among some of the minor followers may be mentioned Alish Beg, Dadkwah of Kashgar; Ihrar Khan Torah, the first envoy despatched from Kashgar to India; and Mahomed Beg of Artosh: but we have no sufficient information of them to give an account of them that would be interesting to the general reader.

CHAPTER X.

YAKOOB BEG had in the earlier days of his career come into contact with the Russians, and although, in the long interval between the fall of Ak Musjid and his departure from Khokand, the Russians, chiefly owing to the prostration resulting from the Crimean War, did not press on with the energy that their first advance on the Syr Darya seemed to promise, there is no doubt that the possibility of its occurrence was the foremost thought in the minds of Yakoob Beg and his contemporaries. In 1865, when the Russians threatened and eventually occupied Tashkent, and brought their frontier halfway on its journey to the Oxus, Yakoob Beg was far too much occupied with his own affairs in Kashgar to attempt any interference in Khokand. With, however, the dismemberment of Khokand and the rout of the Bokhariot army in the spring of 1866, his attention was forcibly claimed by a fact that seemed in the future to involve him as the next victim of Russian aggrandizement. In that year, too, he had not only overcome all resistance in the more important districts of Kashgaria, but he had to a greater extent than before, become responsible for the political actions of the people of this state through the deposition of Buzurg Khan. As early as 1866, it may be assumed that the new ruler of Kashgar had his attention directed to the movements of his old antagonist, by their successes against the Khokandians and Bokhariots; but it is clear that the Russians were not equally interested in his doings at this period.

With the occupation of the northern portion of Khokand, the rule of Russia was brought into nearer proximity with that of the new power of Kashgar, and it
became only a question of time whether the two
governments were to attain a harmonious agreement, or
whether a series of petty disputes was to result in a
further extension of the Russian Empire, towards both
India and China. The independent portion of the
Khanate of Khokand still intervened, and the difficult
country of the Kizil Yart mountains served the useful
purpose of giving the Athalik Ghazi breathing time,
ere he should arrive at a decision about his future
relations with Russia. Indeed, up to this point the
interest of Russia in the affairs of Kashgar had been
very slight, for it does not appear that much, if any,
intercourse had been carried on between the two territories in the past. Far otherwise was it in Ili, where
the Russians had for many years been located as
merchants or as consuls. Their station at Almatie or
Vernoe, an important town and fort situated about 50
miles north of Issik Kul and 250 west of Ili itself,
had in a few years become a large and flourishing city,
instead of preserving its original character of a small
mountain fort. Russian merchants carried on a very
extensive trade by this road with Ili, Urumtsi, Hamil,
and Pekin, and their relations with the Chinese merchants had attained a very satisfactory basis. It was,
therefore, with no friendly feeling, that the Tungan
rising in Ili was regarded by a very large section of
the Russians in the neighbourhood. The disturbances
that thereupon broke out, effectually put a stop to all
trade in this quarter for some time, and the old traffic,
or such of it as continued, with China had to be conducted along the less direct route through Siberia. For
six years, the Russians tolerated the uncertain state of
affairs in Ili, where the Tungani and the Tarantchis
disputed between themselves as to which should be
the ruling party; but their dissatisfaction was scarcely

concealed at the substitution of a native government for that of China. When, therefore, Yakoob Beg, having conquered the country south of the Tian Shan, seemed to threaten the provinces north of that barrier, it is not surprising that the Russians availed themselves of excuses for forestalling him, and for placing their commercial relations on an equally good footing as they had been in the past with the inhabitants of Ili, by a forced occupation of that territory. But the Russians were resolved to give as little umbrage as possible to the Chinese. Ili was formally acknowledged to be Chinese territory, and the Czar voluntarily promised, through his representative at Pekin, to restore it as soon as the Emperor of China was able to despatch a sufficient force to preserve order therein. This tact secured the permanent goodwill of the Chinese, and Russia obtained, in several important trade concessions, a very gratifying reward for her skilful diplomacy. Her friendly action to the Celestials was also heightened in its effect by a piece of unfortunate policy on our part. The Panthays had erected in Yunnan a Mahomedan power, which seemed to have broken off completely from Pekin, and report brought such tales to our frontier of the power and goodwill of the Sultan of the Panthays ruling in Ta-li-foo, that in an ill-advised moment we entered into negotiations with this potentate. The Chinese authorities very naturally took umbrage at this tacit support of a rebellious vassal, and all our subsequent efforts have been unable to remove the suspicions produced by our vacillating attitude on that occasion. The Russians still further preserved the appearance of friendship for China by their refusal, maintained during several years, to acknowledge the government set up in Kashgar by Buzurg Khan and Yakoob Beg. This action was however the less worthy of approval, because at that period the Russians had no immediate concern in Kashgaria. Their sole interest lay in the course of events in Jungaria, with which they were intimately connected by trade and political associations, stretching back for almost a century. Undoubtedly Jungaria was much affected by commotions in Kashgaria, and we accordingly see, when the march of events in the latter province assumed an aspect menacing to the future independence of Jungaria, the Russians taking prompt measures to secure the possession of that province for themselves. When Ili passed into the hands of Russia, the old trade revived along this route to a certain degree, and some intercourse ensued with the Tungani of Urumtsi, Manas and Hamil. Measures seem to have been taken to impress on the rulers of those cities the prudence of not interfering with merchants or travellers, and matters became to a certain degree satisfactory for Russian tranquillity. The city of Ili never, however, recovered its former prosperity, for Vernoe still remains the most important town in this region. Originally a fort constructed in 1854, as a small mountain post, to defend the road from the marauding Kirghiz, it has increased from its insignificant origin into a large settlement of Cossacks and Calmucks, and is now a very thriving community. It was, therefore, it must be remembered, primarily with Jungaria that Russia was interested. So far as the internal affairs of Kashgar were concerned, she could have disregarded the dispute between the rivals, Yakoob Beg and the Chinese; it was only when a powerful Mahomedan state was erected in Eastern Turkestan, and threatened both the independence of Ili, and also to raise up disunion in Khokand, that Russia was compelled to consider what policy it would be wise to adopt towards the recently proclaimed Athalik Ghazi. Whether it was absolutely necessary or even prudent to annex Ili, may be doubted with some reason, but it is impossible to find fault with the Russians for that step. Probably it was the most excusable of all their conquests, none the less may the decision have been founded on a misapprehension of circumstances, or it may have been

premature to shut Yakoob Beg out from advancing into
a region where he would have been at the complete
mercy of the Russians. Nor is it clear even that
Yakoob Beg had the intention, so generously attributed
to him, of committing what would certainly have
resulted in political extinction, viz., an advance to the
northern side of the Tian Shan. The reader will, we
hope, perceive that as little interest was felt by the
Russians in the events transpiring in Kashgar as there
was in India, and this indifference continued down at
all events to the end of 1866. At that date Yakoob
Beg's enterprise had been crowned with complete success and the Russian Government, far more promptly
and accurately apprised of the course of events than our
Government in India, was obliged to devote some attention to this new power, whose appearance was already
beginning to raise a ferment in the Mahomedan
states lying to the west of Kashgar.

In 1866, however, some indefinite agreement was
arrived at by the commanders of forces along the Naryn
borders, to abstain from interfering with each other's
actions. The Russian forces were permitted to follow
refugees from Khokand and predatory Kirghiz within
the nominal frontier of Kashgar, and when occasion
arose a similar right was accorded to the Kashgarian
officials. By some good fortune, perhaps caused by a
feeling of mutual respect, no collisions of any consequence occurred between the representatives of the two
powers during these early and vague negotiations. Although the Russian governors of Siberia and Turkestan
refused to acknowledge either Buzurg Khan or Yakoob
Beg, they seem to have done their best to make use of
these conciliatory measures along the northern frontier as
a lever for inducing Yakoob Beg to make overtures to
them for their support. If such was their intention
the firmness of Yakoob Beg thwarted all their designs,
as will be seen in the sequel. To obtain, however, some
advantage out of the apparent apprehension of the

Kashgarian ruler for Russian power was absolutely necessary, if only to demonstrate the perfection to which Muscovite diplomacy had attained. So, while refusing to acknowledge the new state in Eastern Turkestan and deeply deploring the departure of the Chinese, orders were given to the frontier officers to obtain the sanction of the Kashgarian officials in the neighhourhood to the construction of a bridge across the Naryn and of a military road over the Tian Shan into Kashgar. This was in 1867, and it is not to be wondered at that the Kashgarian authorities replied with a categorical refusal. To have acquiesced in this demand would have been to have placed the city of Kashgar at the complete mercy of the Russians. The position of that city is most disadvantageous in a military point of view, and the only obstacle an army advancing from Issik Kul has to encounter is the difficulty of the road from the Naryn torrent, and the general impracticability of the passes through this portion of the Tian Shan range. The Russian government was much disappointed at this rebuff experienced at the hands of a native ruler, and accordingly in great haste it was resolved that a fort should be constructed on the Naryn just within their frontier. In 1868 this fort was completed, but by that time a fresh change had taken place in the state of affairs, and hopes were entertained that an agreement might yet be arranged by peaceful means with Kashgar. During these two years there had been continual disturbances and fighting in Western Turkestan. Bokhara, instigated, according to Russian assertions, by Yakoob Beg, had joined with Khokand and Khiva in a combined uprising against Russia; but in so far as that uprising was combined it never occurred, for both Bokhara and Khokand fell an easy prey in detail to the armies of the Czar. The punishment of Khiva was reserved for a future occasion, and indeed of all the confederates Khiva was the only one which obtained any successes in the field. The most palpable result of that campaign was the acquisition of Samarcand by Russia, and for a time all opposition seemed to be stamped out. No sooner, however, had the main Russian army returned to Tashkent than a large force invested the small garrison left in Samarcand, and the whole country rose in arms again. The Russian garrison held tightly on to its post, and, although in comparison to its strength its loss was most severe, the town was preserved until the arrival of General Kaufmann with reinforcements. Bokhara then sued for peace, which, after some delay, was concluded with the unfortunate Ameer Mozaffur Eddin. By that treaty the Russians obtained the right to place military cantonments at Kermina, Charjui, and Karshi. Kermina is situated about fifty miles east of the town of Bokhara, on the road from Katti Kurgan and Samarcand; Karshi about sixty miles south of Katti Kurgan, and half way to the Oxus; while Charjui is on the Oxus and some eighty miles west of Bokhara. Of all these the last is the most important, for thence a direct caravan route leads to Merv and Meshed. Once more, in 1870-71, Bokhara entered the field, but the enterprise collapsed through the unconcerted measures of the allies and the weakness of Khokand. During these five eventful years of rebellion amongst the races of Western Turkestan, Yakoob Beg preserved his neutrality. If the assertion is correct that he had played an underhand part in the formation of the league against Russia, assuredly he endeavoured to make his actions contradict his diplomacy. Not a Kashgarian soldier participated in the efforts made so repeatedly by Bokhara and Khokand to shake off the bonds of Russian vassalage. Like Shere Ali of Cabul, he devoted his attention exclusively to the affairs of his immediate province, and wars in the extreme east of his dominions against co-religionists were a preferable alternative to the risks attending a *jehad* against the most formidable enemy of Islam! Russia had indeed little to complain of in Yakoob Beg's interference in their possessions. His instigation of premature rebellions, or, if he did not instigate them, the approval extended to them by some of his chief ministers, was the very kindest act he could have conferred on the ruling power of Turkestan, for Russia never has had anything to fear from any isolated risings among the people of this part of Central Asia. Nothing less than an unanimous and concerted rising in Western Turkestan, aided with a nucleus of regular troops and officers, such as, to go no farther, either Afghanistan can supply, or Kashgar could at one time have supplied—nothing less than this will ever produce a complete catastrophe to the Russian arms, and in a short campaign of a few months send the Russian legions back to their old quarters of thirteen years ago. Whether Yakoob Beg ever was strong enough to risk the independence of his state on so important an enterprise may fairly be doubted, and he showed a commendable prudence in abstaining from hostilities when he had sufficient matters to occupy all his attention, and to task all his resources within his own borders; but assuming such to have been the case, his indifference to the suffering thereby inflicted on the Khokandians must remain a blot on his fair fame. If the part he played in these earlier plots was scarcely honourable, how much less so was his action in the last rebellion of 1875. But it may be as well to postpone considering that event until later on in this chapter. Yakoob Beg most probably took a very selfish view of the state of affairs. His own extremely uncertain tenure of power made him anxious lest any storm from beyond his frontier should wreck the frail bark in which he had asserted his claim to independence, and the whole object of his policy was simply to divert attention from himself to other quarters. The Russians above all must have their work cut out for them in repression of continual sedition in their possessions; while each day of respite witnessed Yakoob Beg in a better position for making a strenuous resistance when the time should come, according to Russian ideas, for an attempt to be made to crush his power.

Viewed from this standpoint, the conduct of Yakoob Beg towards his fellow-countrymen appears in a slightly more favourable aspect, although his policy of expediency has little in it to command admiration. Yet the result answered his expectations. In 1868 the construction of Fort Naryn was the avowed preliminary measure to an occupation of Kashgar; from that danger this policy of compromise saved him. Again, in 1870, was he pronounced an incorrigible enemy of the Czar, and an expedition was prepared which was to bring him to his senses; once more a revolt in Khokand intervened to distract Russian attention and Russian arms from the Naryn to Ferghana. The expedition against Khiva in 1873 also served the purpose of diverting to another quarter the blow which should, according to many, have descended on the offending head of the Athalik Ghazi; and lastly, in 1875 the insurrection in Khokand, the most serious and the most nearly successful of all the native wars against Russia, saved him from an invasion for which every preparation had been made.

To return to the year 1868, when the Russian government had constructed the fort on the Naryn, and had openly proclaimed its intention of punishing the slight put upon it by Yakoob Beg's refusal to permit the construction of a road over the mountains to Artosh. Up to that year the intercourse had been of a semi-official character between the officers on either side of the frontier. We have now come to a phase of the question of a slightly different import. The Russian officials endeavoured to obtain from Yakoob Beg concessions that would be advantageous to their country, at the same time that they categorically declined to recognize his official *status* as an independent prince. Their antagonist was far too astute to permit himself to be out-manœuvred by so simple a device, and his officials were quite unauthorized to enter into any arrangement without its being brought before their master in the manner consistent with his dignity. We have seen that the Russians, failing in their diplomatic chicane, had recourse to threats, although the irony of fate prevented those threats ever being put into execution.   But concurrently with these efforts on the part of the Russian government, others of a different kind were being made by individuals.   The Russian merchants of Kuldja contained in their ranks several men whose enterprise and courage had been remarkable in the manipulation of trade with the Chinese and the Tungani.   They were not easily deterred from any undertaking which promised them brilliant remuneration, even though the risk and uncertainty might be great.   The pioneers of commerce were free from the fetters that hampered official movements.   It was of little moment to them who ruled in Kashgaria so long as he extended his protection to their goods and their persons whilst they were within his territory.   The Russian government viewed with favour the efforts that were made to cross the Tian Shan, for on the individual fell the greatest portion of the risk, while the government profited much by the fruits of his experience.   The Russian merchants were, therefore, not discouraged by their authorities when they laid their proposals before General Kolpakovsky, as English merchants would have been under similar circumstances by the authorities at Calcutta—nay, it is tolerably certain that they received many inducements to persist in their intention; both their patriotism and desire for advancing their own worldly concerns were appealed to, to urge them to attempt to obtain admission into Kashgar.   When, therefore, it became evident in 1868 that nothing was to be obtained from Yakoob Beg by indirect means, and when it was also decided that a military remedy would not be convenient, the field was fairly cleared for another kind of performers to begin operations.

Early in the year 1868, a Russian merchant, named Kludof, collected at Vernoe a small caravan.   His chief commodities consisted of those gewgaws, which, prepared in Moscow, have been found, according to Russian experience, the most marketable articles in Western Turkestan; but, in addition to these trumpery packages, more useful necessaries, such as cotton goods and cutlery, were taken as specimens of some of the real advantages that would come in the wake of Russian trade. Kludof set out with the intention of crossing the Tian Shan by the Naryn, and making for the border town of Ush Turfan, whence Kashgar is easily reached by the high road. But he had not proceeded far beyond Fort Naryn, then in course of construction, when he was attacked by a band of marauders. With the loss of all his possessions he must still be considered fortunate in having escaped without any serious personal injury. Perhaps the robbers were inspired with some respect for the person of a Russian subject, or, as the indictment against Yakoob Beg affirms, by the express orders of that ruler, who wished to deter, without causing any serious complication with the government, Russian subjects of any kind whatever from entering his kingdom. As it happened, however, Kludof was a very determined fellow, one not easily balked when he had set his mind on accomplishing anything. The government viewed his case with commiseration, and he was assisted in collecting together another caravan of larger proportions than its predecessor. But before setting out on the same road he determined to make an effort to reach the ear of Yakoob Beg himself, and by a singular piece of good fortune he was able to do so through a Kashgarian subject residing in Kuldja. The presents, judiciously selected, with which he accompanied his letter complaining of the injury he had received at the hands of Kirghiz subjects of the ruler of Kashgar, yet only demanding as a reparation permission to come into that state as a peaceful subject of the Czar, fully propitiated Yakoob Beg, who sent a safe conduct to Vernoe for Kludof and his caravan. This merchant made a most favourable impression on the ruler of Kashgar, and it seemed at one moment as if he would achieve what all the diplomacy of the two previous years had failed in accomplishing. Even Yakoob Beg was induced to take a slight step towards a better agreement with his neighbour, for in the summer of 1868, he sent Shadi Mirza, one of his nephews, to Vernoe, requesting that he might be permitted to go on to Tashkent, to place before the governor of Turkestan certain proposals from his master for a complete understanding with Russia. Simultaneously with the despatch of Shadi Mirza by Yakoob Beg, a Russian officer, Captain Reinthal, was commissioned by General Kolpakovsky, the governor of Kuldja, to proceed to Kashgar and demand the surrender of some Kirghiz robbers, who, from within Yakoob Beg's dominion, had sallied forth to pillage Russian merchants. They had also seized several inhabitants of Khokand and the Naryn district; and the Russian government demanded the unconditional surrender of these individuals as her subjects. Captain Reinthal was instructed to make these two demands in a peremptory way, and to convince the new government that Russia would not permit any infraction of the spirit of the treaties concluded with the old government under the Chinese. Captain Reinthal was received in a sufficiently hospitable manner, but his movements were scrupulously restricted to the city. He did not, on this occasion, learn much of importance about the country, but he was impressed favourably by the appearance of such of the army as he saw. The Kirghiz robbers were captured by the order of Yakoob Beg, but he stoutly refused to surrender them. The Russian prisoners were also kept in honourable confinement as a guarantee for the safe return of Shadi Mirza. They were, however, permitted to return to Russian territory when it became known that Shadi Mirza was progressing favourably with his mission to Tashkent. Captain Reinthal accomplished little or nothing on this embassade, and had to report, on his return to his superior, the strange tidings that the new power was resolved to play an independent part in Asia, and to answer defiance with defiance, and threat with threat. This report must have seemed scarcely credible, but there is no doubt that Captain Reinthal advised, as the result of his experience, the adoption of a lenient and friendly policy towards the new-comer. This concession to a Central Asian despot was not agreeable at head-quarters, and the question was shelved for the time. Shadi Mirza, who had been detained at Vernoe, was at last permitted to continue his journey to Tashkent, where he found General Kaufmann absent in Europe. Instructions were then issued to send him on to St. Petersburg, where he arrived in the last days of 1868. He had several informal interviews with the governor of Turkestan, but he was not received by the Czar or any of the higher officials. In fact, he was only treated as an ordinary traveller, and not as the representative of a neighbouring state. Nothing up to this had been done by the Russian government, showing that they recognized Yakoob Beg as ruler of Kashgaria. The Chinese were still, in their eyes, the *de jure* owners of that province, whoever might be the temporary owners *de facto*. On the return of Shadi Mirza to Kashgar, in January, 1869, the relations between Russia and Yakoob Beg may be said to have returned to the exact *status quo ante*. All the Russian demands for trade had been unsuccessful, and, except the brilliant journey of Mr. Kludof, no one had broken through the mystic charm that shut out the Garden of Asia from all foreign spectators. Their envoy, Captain Reinthal, had been treated in a precisely similar manner to that in which Shadi Mirza had been received at Vernoe and St. Petersburg; and a firm and dignified attitude had effectually checked the Russian officer when he attempted to express those threats which formed the principal part of his instructions. There was something imposing in the quiet way in which Yakoob Beg asserted his equality in rank with the Czar of All the

Russias. His invariable reply, when the great power
of Russia was made use of as an argument to overcome
his refusal to accede to the trade concessions demanded,
was, " My brother, the White Czar, is a most powerful
monarch, and rules over the greater portion of the
earth, and I am only an insignificant prince in comparison to him. But none the less can I encounter the
danger like a true man, and esteem it a happiness to
die in defence of my country and my faith." To so
courageous and so honourable a reply what rejoinder
could be made by the abashed officers? It is impossible
to refuse Yakoob Beg the highest admiration for his
stanchness in his opposition to Russia. If for his own
narrow interests it may have been imprudent to throw
down the gage of battle so freely, all the more does that
attitude claim respect when we see him trampling on
purely selfish motives, and asserting his claim to leadership in that wider question of Asiatic against Muscovite, of Mahomedan against Greek. Had he only been
consistent throughout his career, had he only been as
firm in his convictions and as prompt in carrying them
into practice as he generally was, when the occasion
came for a great effort against Russia, how different
might have been his own fate and the present aspect of
affairs in Central Asia !

For some time after these abortive proceedings the
Russians abstained from any direct interference in Kashgar, but the conferring of the title of Athalik Ghazi, or
Commander of the Faithful, on Yakoob Beg by the Ameer
of Bokhara had roused the susceptibilities of Russia too
much to be allayed. It seemed, indeed, as if this acknowledgment of the orthodoxy of Yakoob Beg by the Head of
Islam in Central Asia heralded forth some understanding
between the two states, and that a menace was directed
against the Russian government. Whether there was any
agreement between Mozaffur Eddin and Yakoob Beg it
is not possible at present to say, but that such should
have been brought about by their mutual antipathy to

Russia would not have been very wonderful. However, in the disturbances of 1870 Yakoob Beg took no active part. While the Russian arms were triumphing over every opponent in their newly acquired province of Ferghana and its vicinity, Yakoob Beg was busily engaged with the Tungani, who at that time were causing trouble to him along his far eastern frontier. The revolt collapsed in Khokand, and Yakoob Beg, apparently unconcerned with the events transpiring in the West, was carrying his victorious arms to new conquests in the East. During the year 1870, when murmurs of the approaching storm were becoming audible, the Russian government endeavoured to obtain the alliance of Khudayar Khan, of Khokand, for the purpose of bringing Yakoob Beg within their influence. This Khan had, as has been already mentioned, been betrayed by Yakoob Beg, who had followed the example of the ambitious Vizier Alim Kuli, and was now mainly dependent on the Russians for support against his rebellious subjects. He could not be considered in any way, therefore, as likely to be favourably disposed towards his neighbour of Kashgar, or as lukewarm in the cause of his protectors and benefactors. The Russians felt assured of his hearty support in advocating their plan, which was as follows. From time immemorial, as has been seen in the sketch of the history of Kashgar, there have been two rival elements in Kashgaria—the Chinese and the Khokandian. The Chinese was triumphant in modern times for a little more than a century, while the Khokandian has, more or less, at all other times been paramount. But whenever a native dynasty had attained a certain degree of security therein, it was always threatened by the ambitious designs of the Khan of Khokand, who had generally contributed most towards its successful establishment. The Russian government resolved to avail themselves of this historical fact to pour into the ear of Khudayar Khan insidious counsels as to his claims as feudal lord over Eastern Turkestan. There once more, so

they argued, had a Khokandian subject formed an independent and rival administration, and all his victories
had been won by Khokandian sympathies, and by the
good right arms of Khokandian subjects. And how had
this soldier of fortune acted towards his own country
when he had received everything from her that he
needed? By offering an asylum to all those who had
participated in the plots against Khudayar Khan himself, by encouraging sedition in the state itself against
the Russians and their nominee, Khudayar, the legal
ruler of the state. As if these crimes were not sufficiently serious, he had added thereto the insult of having
refused to recognize in Khudayar his liege lord; and
Khudayar's own personal fears were worked upon to
yield that acquiescence to the Russian proposal that was
necessary to secure its success. It was pointed out to
him that a strong military power in Kashgar might give
an impetus to the plots then fermenting in the active
brain of Aftobatcha, the ambitious son of Mussulman
Kuli, the prime minister and vizier of thirty years ago.
The arguments were specious, and it cannot be doubted
that they made some impression on Khudayar Khan.
This much-to-be-pitied ruler, forced by the necessities of
his position to humour his Russian advisers, still had
the courage to refuse to assert his claims as lord over
Kashgar. With a gentle irony he pointed to the map,
and showed how Khokand's frontier should extend
farther to the west than it did, and that a conquest over
the barren regions of the Kizil Yart would be but a
sorry equivalent for the loss of Tashkent and Hodjent.
He, however, promised to make use of his best means
for inducing Yakoob Beg to make overtures to the
Russian government for the ratification of a treaty of
commerce. So Khudayar Khan indited a letter to
Yakoob Beg, at the dictation of his Russian friends, to
this effect; but he silvered the pill by a private message
giving information of the Russian intentions in the
future. The tenor of that communication was that the

Russians were less eager than might have been supposed to bring matters to a final crisis with Yakoob Beg, and that they were most desirous of settling the question without any flagrant loss of dignity by being the first to recommence negotiations. Both publicly and privately Khudayar Khan advised that the Athalik Ghazi should make some concessions in form to the Russian government. The Russians themselves, having failed to induce Khudayar Khan to put pressure on Yakoob Beg, appear to have arrived at the same conclusion as that set out in the letters of Khudayar. Yakoob Beg must make the sign, and they would meet him half way in his desire to share in the great benefits accruing from a Muscovite alliance. The authorities at Tashkent went so far as to flatter themselves that they had attained a solution of one of their chief annoyances. They had, by making use of the mediation of Khudayar, gone so far as to open the door for Yakoob Beg to abase himself. Such condescension was unheard of, and no doubt was entertained but that this proud Mahomedan ruler would gladly hasten to avail himself of the last chance accorded him by the clemency of the Czar.

But they were reckoning without their host. Yakoob Beg quickly perceived that the bold exterior of the Russian demands concealed a vacillating purpose, and that a power which would go out of its way so far to bring about an arrangement, would yield much more when the discussion became directly carried on. He had evidently impressed the few Russians who had visited him with a belief in his strength, and rumour had magnified his resources, and converted his small and heterogeneous following into a regular and trained army. He was not the man to destroy, when the game was almost in his hands too, all the favourable impressions, that stood him in such good stead during his career, which his policy for four years had succeeded in creating about his personality. After a suitable delay his formal reply to the official letter of Khudayar arrived, and its

contents must have been eminently displeasing to the
Russians.   In general terms he refused to enter into
negotiations with the Russians, because they had refused
to acknowledge his own government, and had ever supported the cause of his enemies the Chinese.   But, not
content with this blunt refusal to the offer made from
Tashkent, he went on to minor matters and dealt with
the question of Russian policy in specific. language.
The common enemy of him and all his co-religionists was
not worthy of any consideration from him or his allies,
the rulers of Khokand and Bokhara.   " The Russians
that have come here, into my state of Kashgar, look at
these localities and become acquainted with the state
of the country, and therefore it is better to forbid'their
coming, for they are a treacherous and crooked-minded
people."   In such plain terms did Yakoob Beg speak of
a power which could without any serious risk have
crushed him at any moment.   Yet in one sense his
boldness was the height of prudence, and succeeded
when perhaps a less decided attitude would have completely failed.   The Russians were fairly deluded in their
estimate of their new antagonist, and all means having
been exhausted for inducing Yakoob Beg to abandon his
indifferent attitude towards themselves, it began to be
seriously discussed at Tashkent whether, if simply for
the purpose of obtaining accurate information of his
country, it would not be prudent to acknowledge the
existence of a ruler who had for nearly six years been
established as responsible sovereign of a very large portion of Asia.   The path was smoothed, too, for the
Russian diplomatists by Yakoob Beg sending a letter to
the governor of Turkestan, stating that it was useless
for the Czar to attempt the establishment of diplomatic
relations through the good offices of Khudayar Khan ; but
that if the Russians really desired to enter into alliance
with him they could send an embassy to him, when formal
steps could be commenced for securing the trade and
other agreements that were desirable.   The letter was a

very dignified piece of writing, such as one European sovereign would have sent to another in the Middle Ages. "He did not deny," he said, "either the power or the resources of Russia, but as a brave man he placed his trust in God, and he would never shirk the contest, because all he aspired to was to die for his faith." This letter produced a great impression at Tashkent, and it was resolved to send an ambassador to Kashgar.

Before pursuing the narrative, it may be as well to sum up what had passed between Russia and Kashgar up to this period, for henceforth these two states were to stand in a completely different relationship towards each other. The Russians strove to induce Yakoob Beg to make the most favourable commercial and political concessions to them, while they refused to grant him any equivalent, except the dubious one, "advantage from the produce of Russian manufactures." They even added insult to injury by openly proclaiming that they only recognized the Chinese as the rulers of Kashgar, and refused to discuss the arguments advanced by Shadi Mirza in favour of his uncle's claim to be considered *de facto* sovereign. They adopted an attitude of bullying towards this Asiatic prince, and loudly proclaimed in their practice the truth of the aphorism, that might is right. They backed up their verbal threats on several occasions by a show of military preparations, but not once did they put those threats into execution. On the other hand, Yakoob Beg's policy was consistent throughout and dignified. While studiously avoiding any aggressive measures, even under the excuse of defensive precautions, he was always firm in his refusal to recognize any of the semi-official overtures that were repeatedly made to induce him to show his hand. Instead of appearing in the light of a suppliant, as according to all precedent he should, he assumed the position of a dictator. "Acknowledge me as legally constituted ruler of Kashgaria, or else there is an end to all negotiation. Send a properly accredited ambassador to me, and he shall be honourably received.   A representative of recognized rank shall then convey my token of friendship to your master.   Refuse to grant me these just considerations, and my kingdom is closed to your merchants and officials without exception.   Admission shall only be obtained over my own body and that of my devoted army." For the first time in the annals of Russian history an Asiatic ruler had tired out the finessing and intrigue that had become customary with that empire as the means for infinite conquest. Yakoob Beg was the only sovereign who refused to be subservient to the Czar, and eventually achieved a diplomatic triumph over his representatives.   In the spring of 1872, Yakoob Beg was at the very acme of his prosperity.   Not yet had he commenced those later campaigns against the Tungani, which more than anything else tended to weaken his power and to raise discontent against his administration ; and, fresh from his diplomatic success over the Russians, he appeared in the eyes of many Asiatics as a fit champion to redeem their fortunes in a conflict with Russia.   Excusable as their enthusiasm undoubtedly was, it is tolerably certain that the power of Yakoob Beg was exaggerated both by the adulation of his friends and by the nervous susceptibilities of the Russians.   It is noteworthy that Russia proved herself on one occasion to be quite as liable to this latter disease as England is assumed to be.

To Baron Kaulbars, the explorer of the sources of the Syr Darya, was entrusted the delicate mission of representing the Russian government for the first time at the court of the Athalik Ghazi, and to no better diplomatist could it have been consigned.   He set out from Kuldja early in May, 1872, carrying with him a large collection of presents for the ruler and his chief advisers, and arrived in Kashgar without any mishap in June of the same year.   Here he was received in the most cordial manner, and the consideration and hospitality exhibited towards him by the ruler were beyond all expectation.   In the picturesque phraseology of the East, the Athalik Ghazi, at his first audience with Baron Kaulbars, said, "Sit upon my knees, on my bosom, or where ye like ; for ye are guests sent me from heaven." The most complete freedom of action was accorded, for the first time, to all the members of the embassy, and two merchants who had accompanied it for the purpose of exploring the country received a safe-conduct to go on to Yarkand and Khoten. Yakoob Beg scarcely attempted to conceal his gratification at the presence of the Russians; possibly his pleasure chiefly arose from such an unmistakable admission of his skill as a diplomatist. But in every way facilities were afforded his visitors for seeing all objects of interest round Kashgar. Reviews were held in honour of the occasion, and as there happened to be a considerable number of troops in the vicinity, passing through to operate against the Tungani beyond Kucha, the show was imposing enough. The Russians were favourably impressed by what they saw, and Baron Kaulbars expressed himself surprised at the military exactitude with which the manœuvres were carried out. Yakoob Beg, always open to flattery, exclaimed in an enthusiastic moment, "I look upon the Russians as my dearest friends; if I had not, should I have shown you my military power? Assuredly it is not usual even with you to make known one's actual condition to an enemy." Matters were now in a fair way to a pleasant solution. Baron Kaulbars and Yakoob Beg were mutually delighted ; but, after the time for pleasant talk had expired, it was necessary that some definite arrangements should be drawn up for the political and commercial relations of the two countries in the future.

The chief objects the Russians had in view when they sent Baron Kaulbars to Kashgar were three. In the first place they wanted to acquire general information about that state, and to discover whether Yakoob Beg was as powerful as report had asserted. In the second, they wished to put their relations on such a recognized basis

with him that they might know what policy he was disposed to adopt in Turkestan and Kuldja; and in the
third they desired to secure the monopoly of the trade
of his state, so that they might forestall British enterprise, already beginning to direct its attention to this
quarter, since the journeys of Messrs. Shaw and Forsyth.
The last of these was the easiest to obtain, and the Athalik
Ghazi considered all the Russian proposals with regard
to trade in a very amicable spirit; but with regard to the
second *desideratum* nothing but the vaguest generalities
could all the tact and ingenuity of Kaulbars succeed in
obtaining from his host. The first object was amply
secured, in so far as geographical and scientific information was concerned; but the precautions taken by the
Athalik Ghazi to deceive the Russians as to his power
and hold on the country appear to have been successful.
Baron Kaulbars certainly confirmed much that had previously rested on mere hearsay; the question is rather,
did he not vouch for more than his experience justified
him in doing? The result of his mission was, that the
Athalik Ghazi was elevated to a position on a level with
the Ameer of Cabul, and there is no doubt whatever that
such a comparison was not warranted by the facts. A
treaty was signed by the Athalik Ghazi and Baron
Kaulbars, on the 2nd of June, 1872, but according to
the Old Style, still adopted by the Russians, this was
the 21st of May, St. Constantine's day. There are two
stories with respect to this coincidence, and there is as
much evidence for one version as there is for the other.

It was said at the time that Yakoob Beg was so
desirous of showing his goodwill to the Russians that he
had insisted on signing it on that day in honour of the
Grand Duke Constantine. Now there were two or three
improbabilities in this statement that struck several
observers. In the first place it was extremely improbable that Yakoob Beg knew it was St. Constantine's
day at all; and again, in the second place he was quite
as probably ignorant of the existence of a Grand Duke

Constantine. At all events, there was no valid reason why a Central Asian ruler should conceive that his politeness to that Grand Duke in particular would demonstrate his desire to be on good terms with Russians in general. The other version, which, like many other circumstances, has only leaked out in the pages of Mr. Schuyler, is altogether more probable, and is not open to the same objections.   According to this, it was Baron Kaulbars, who of course was aware of the saint's day, who demanded that the treaty should bear that date, and who, as soon as it was signed, sent off a message to General Kaufmann saying that the Athalik Ghazi, out of friendship to that general, had specially requested that the treaty should be signed on that day in honour of General Kaufmann's patron saint.   However flattered that distinguished general and governor may have felt at the delicate attention of his ambassador, he had to decline the proposed honour ; and in the despatch that was sent to St. Petersburg, describing the event, the name of the Grand Duke Constantine was substituted for his own.   There is little doubt that this is the correct statement, and it certainly suggests quite a revelation as to the system in Russian Asia of making things pleasant and agreeable to one another, always, however, assuming that there be an exceptional degree of power and pomp reserved for his Excellency General Kaufmann.

Soon after the signature of this treaty, which bears the name of its framer, Baron Kaulbars took his departure, with many expressions of friendship and goodwill from the Athalik Ghazi.   Arrangements were, however, made, before he left, for an envoy to visit Tashkent from Yakoob Beg.   This ambassador took with him the signed stipulations to be ratified, and was received at Tashkent with every demonstration of amity and respect. So certain did the Russian government appear that their relations with Kashgar would, if only for a short period, be satisfactory, that special care was taken to make a favourable impression on the Kashgarian envoy, and after a short residence in the capital of Turkestan, the nephew of Yakoob Beg, Hadji Torah, who had followed the train of the treaty on a special mission, went on to St. Petersburg, where he was entertained by the Czar, taken to the reviews, and treated in a most hospitable and princely fashion. The contrast between the reception accorded to him in 1873 and that to Shadi Mirza in 1869 clearly marks the difference that was considered in well-informed official circles to have taken place in their relations with Kashgar.

We have now to consider whether the Russian Government was justified in assuming so confidently that it had secured the permanent friendship of the Mahomedan ruler of Eastern Turkestan. On concluding his visit at St. Petersburg, Hadji Torah turned south, and after stopping for a brief delay at Moscow and Odessa, he arrived in Constantinople, where he already had many friends and connections. Without inquiring too deeply into his actions at the Imperial City—for of them the reader will be able to judge best by the sequel—we will here simply observe, that having also concluded his residence on the Golden Horn, he took passage by the Suez Canal for India, and arrived there in time to join the mission of Sir Douglas Forsyth, then on its way to Kashgar. Hadji Torah therefore brought to his uncle a vast amount of information concerning the three Powers chiefly concerned in the fortunes of Kashgar—Russia, Turkey, and England. But even before his return home, fresh disagreements had broken out between Russia and Yakoob Beg. The year 1872 had not closed, before the Athalik Ghazi concluded some secret negotiations that had been pending for some time with the Sultan, and this champion of Islam appeared in a new and holier light to Asiatics as Emir, or Ameer. He acknowledged the suzerainty of the Porte; and, not content with this formal declaration, gave an extra significance to the event by issuing a fresh coinage, bearing on one side the head of Abdul Aziz. The Russians were, it can well be imagined, displeased at this alliance between two Mahomedan states which might both be considered hostile to their interests, and a very large party in military circles clamoured for an expedition to be sent at once against the insolent Mussulman. At one moment it seemed as if this bellicose party was to gain the day, for the testimony of all the officers and merchants who had visited Kashgar showed that each day Yakoob Beg was becoming more formidable. Prompt measures were pressed on the government of Tashkent, and General Kaufmann seemed half disposed to acquiesce in the proposal to inflict summary chastisement on the Athalik Ghazi. Fortunately for Kashgar, the Khan of Khiva had been an older offender in the eyes of the Russians, and the Home Government peremptorily forbade any steps being taken in the regions bordering on the Chinese Empire. It is sufficiently clear that the moderation of the home authorities was a wiser policy than the impulsive demands of certain officers in Tashkent; but it is not so evident why Yakoob Beg abstained from appearing in the *rôle* of the liberator of Khokand, at so opportune a moment as that afforded by the great expedition against Khiva in 1873. The treaty of Baron Kaulbars had stipulated for the free admission of Russian merchants into the state on the payment of a $2\frac{1}{2}$ per cent. *ad valorem* duty. Not only was there to be no further exaction, but good treatment was guaranteed to such Russian subjects as desired to travel in Kashgar, and who came provided with a passport, and permission to travel, from a Russian governor. During Baron Kaulbars' residence in the country, nothing could be more considerate than the treatment extended towards the members of his suite, and the merchants who went on to Yarkand were afforded facilities for disposing of the small stock of merchandise which they had brought with them on this journey. This friendly reception of such merchants as came to Kashgar was maintained during the period over which these negotiations extended down to the departure of Yakoob Beg's own ambassador

from Russian territory; but with the arrival of Hadji
Torah at Constantinople, and the proclamation of the
fact that Yakoob Beg had been elevated to the dignified
position of Emir by the Sultan of Roûm, a change came
over the spirit of his policy towards Russia. Indeed,
Yakoob Beg saw himself menaced by an unforeseen danger in this treaty of commerce. He had formerly been
averse to the presence of Russian merchants in his state
because he regarded them as spies; but now that the
necessities of his position had to some extent compelled
him to enter into a formal treaty with their government,
he perceived that his little state literally ran the risk of
being invaded by the Russian merchants and traders who
flocked to Kuldja for the purpose of participating in the
spoils to be obtained by trafficking with the inhabitants
of Eastern Turkestan. He had always been averse to
trade. He was a warrior, and inclined to feel and to
express contempt at the juggling tricks of Muscovite
or Khitay.

But as the former could provide him with better
weapons for his army, and warmer clothes for his people,
in addition to trinkets for his *serai*, their presence, if only
they came in limited numbers, and at stated intervals,
could be tolerated; but when he perceived they were
about to descend on his state, like so many birds of prey
on an abandoned carcase, and when he surmised that in
all likelihood they would endeavour to mix themselves
up in the political divisions of Kashgar as they had in
Bokhara and Khokand, he determined to impose some
other check on their visits besides that insignificant $2\frac{1}{2}$
per cent. on goods that returned a profit of cent. per
cent. He had given his plighted word, however, that
merchants should receive fair treatment, and how could
he find a loophole to avoid fulfilling what he had promised, and yet at the same time escape bringing about an
open rupture with the Russian Government. The matter
required most delicate manipulation, but Yakoob Beg
proved himself equal to the occasion. It was not to be

expected, however, that Yakoob Beg could accomplish his task of discouraging Russian enterprise without giving some umbrage to the government.

Despite the friendly reception of Baron Kaulbars, there still remained some uncertainty in the minds of individuals, whether the Athalik Ghazi was as sincere in his protestations as he would have it believed. There was, consequently, some disinclination among the merchants of Kuldja to be the first to send a caravan to Kashgar. They were all willing enough to share the profits, but it was a risky experiment all the same; and each would prefer that his neighbour should inaugurate the enterprise. In commercial circles, there was much discussion on the new state, and the prospects of trade therewith, and there was much talk as to "who should bell the cat." The hesitation, if indeed so natural a sentiment deserves to be specified here, soon passed off, and Mr. Pupyshef, a merchant, who had had very large business connections with most parts of Central Asia, resolved to send the first consignment of merchandise to Kashgar. Mr. Pupyshef was, however, unable to go in person, so his caravan set out under the charge of his clerk Somof. It arrived without "let or hindrance" in Kashgar, where Mr. Somof was provided with accommodation in the Caravanserai specially set apart for foreign merchants. But a change was at once perceptible in the sentiments of the ruler, as the personal freedom of the members of the expedition was curtailed, and all their movements were watched with the most exacting surveillance; and the residence of Mr. Somof was brief in the extreme, for the Athalik Ghazi himself bought up the whole of his stock of merchandise. Viewed as a commercial speculation, this result should have been eminently satisfactory; the Russian merchant had to experience no loss from delay in finding a purchaser for his articles. There was, however, another matter to be taken into consideration, and that was the mode of payment by the purchaser. Mr. Somof received so many Chinese coins at a value fixed by the Ameer himself, and Mr. Pupyshef, on the return of his representative, estimated the loss at 15,000 roubles. The Russian government took up the case of their subject, and presented a remonstrance at Kashgar, demanding the immediate restitution of the loss incurred by the Russian merchant. Yakoob Beg's reply to this summary request was a model of courtesy and tact. He denied altogether that Mr. Somof had in any way been interfered with. That gentleman was always at perfect liberty to do what, and to go where, he pleased, and he was quite mistaken in supposing that he, the Ameer, had purchased his goods. The Badaulet had nothing whatever to do with trade, which he left entirely to his subjects. He was simply a warrior and a follower of the Prophet. He had nevertheless instituted inquiries into the matter, and he had discovered that some of his officers, who should be punished, had purchased the merchandise in his name, hoping thereby to obtain it at a cheaper rate. The Athalik Ghazi expressed his regret at the occurrence, and would be most happy to refund whatever sum the Russian government considered their subject had lost by the transaction. A commission was appointed at Tashkent, to inquire into all the circumstances of the case, and after some discussion the demand of Mr. Pupyshef was reduced from 15,000 to 12,000 roubles. The Ameer acquiesced in the decision, but many months elapsed before Mr. Pupyshef received his money, and then it was again in a depreciated Chinese coinage. We are justified in assuming that this was all planned, and that the obstacles thrown in the path of Mr. Pupyshef were part and parcel of a systematic attempt to disgust Russian merchants with Kashgar. The Russian government, too, was afforded no clear case for complaint, as Yakoob Beg expressed his regret without reserve for the occurrence, all the responsibility of which he shifted on to the shoulders of some of "his officials whom he had ordered to be punished." He paid without a murmur the fair demands of Mr. Pupyshef, and if there was some delay in the refunding of the money, it must be attributed to the poverty of his exchequer, and not to any want of goodwill. The burden of his complaint was, "I am a poor prince; my country is impoverished by the wars that have occurred since the departure of the Chinese; and you will find little therein to repay you for your trouble and expense in entering it. Why therefore will you persist in coming to it? You can do neither yourselves nor my people any good by doing so, and you only cause me anxiety and trouble in preserving your countrymen from insult and injury, which you must admit I have ever done." There was an under-current of truth in this statement of the case, although it was not credited in Kuldja, where everything that went amiss was set down to the hostility of the Ameer. Yakoob Beg had, however, succeeded in throwing cold water on the enthusiastic preparations that were being made for exploiting Eastern Turkestan, and his mode of doing so had been quite original and characteristic. Few rulers would have foreseen that the best way to get rid of a troublesome visitor was to purchase what he had brought to sell to the people; and that the simple remedy of paying in a questionable currency would suffice to deter hundreds from following the example of Mr. Somof. Yakoob Beg, however, was not satisfied with leaving well alone. Having paid the claim of Mr. Pupyshef, it might have been supposed that he would maintain a discreet silence on his intentions in the future with regard to Russian merchants. He might have let the question, indeed, find, as it would have found, its own solution; but, in a weak moment, to place his own *bona fides* beyond suspicion, he desired the Russian government to send another merchant to Kashgar, and then it could judge by his reception whether the Ameer was not amicably disposed towards his "close allies," the Russians. The Russian authorities took him at his word, and after an interval of more than twelve months, during which Kashgar had been unvisited by a Russian merchant, another, a Mr. Morozof, came to put Yakoob Beg's assertions to the test. True to his word, the reception of this gentleman was most cordial. Facilities were placed in his way for getting purchasers of his articles, and the Ameer bought for his arsenals such of them as seemed suitable. Mr. Morozof returned to Kuldja, narrating how cordially he had been welcomed by the ruler himself, and how the enterprise had commercially been a success. Others followed his example, and during the last two and a half years of his rule Russian merchandise, either through Russian or native agents, found its way in considerable quantities into Kashgar. But this trade was always liable to periods of depression through the clouds that frequently darkened the political horizon, and the Russians did not derive the advantages from trade with this state, that they had previously convinced themselves they were to do. Indeed, English manufactures, after the year 1873, entered into keen competition with theirs in the cities of Kashgar, and had driven their goods out of the market of Yarkand at all events before the close of the year 1876. But this fact only served to impress more forcibly on the Russians the necessity either for annexing Kashgaria or establishing on its throne some puppet, who would be content with the post of deputy of the Czar. Indeed, many suggested that the Chinese should be brought back ; but then they were so far off, and apparently so weak. The party advocating the absorption of Kashgaria every day became stronger and more pronounced ; and all observers agree that it was only a question of time when the imperial fiat should go forth for the extinction of the rule of Yakoob Beg. Colonel Reinthal was sent in 1874, to endeavour to place matters on a more hopeful footing, but with little success. In addition to the question of trade privileges, the Russians, in negotiating with native states, or securing treaties at the point of the sword, always demanded the right of having consular agents in the chief cities of the state. The ostensible duty of these official representatives was to look after the interests of their government, and to protect the lives and property of Russian subjects as best they might be able. So far as these very necessary functions were concerned, Russia had a perfect right in demanding these safeguards, when such were deemed to be required. But unfortunately for the reputation of that country, the experience of Asiatics had amply demonstrated that these declared duties were the least important part of their office.

Their secret instructions were to lose no opportunity of discovering the drift of public sentiment in the state where they were stationed; to learn all the ramifications of the dynastic intrigues that unfortunately form the chief incidents in the history of these states, and to promote, by every means at their disposal, the interests of the great empire into whose service they had been admitted. When such latitude was allowed in their instructions, and so many private and public inducements were offered to raise their zeal, it cannot be matter of surprise if we find the government informed promptly of the shiftings of public opinion in the independent and semi-independent Khanates of Central Asia. Yakoob Beg was keenly alive to the dangers that would arise to him personally from the introduction of such a system into Kashgar, where the discordant elements out of which he had welded a military organization were far from being completely healed. If the presence of a mirza in Khokand and Bokhara had entailed a decade of troubles and of gradual subjection, what was he to expect, a mere military adventurer and a foreigner in the land, from their presence in Eastern Turkestan? But Baron Kaulbars had demanded this concession, perhaps more than any other, and Yakoob Beg had to yield something in form, if he did not surrender much in substance, to the importunities of his visitor. As a great favour he consented to the appointment of *caravan-bashis*, or superintendents of the personal comforts of the merchants when they should arrive; but a *caravan-bashi* was an uneducated, unimportant personage, from whom nothing need be feared. This did not at all please the Russian administrators, and all their subsequent efforts were mainly devoted to the attempt to obtain an alteration of this unimportant personage into the prying and inquisitive *mirza*. To defeat their design Yakoob Beg was no less firmly resolved, and the history of the embassies, from that of Baron Kaulbars to that of Captain Kuropatkine, was one long course of fruitless efforts to force the hand of the Athalik Ghazi on this point. Colonel Reinthal was sent in 1874, after the successful journey of Mr. Morozof, to see if any better arrangement could be attained, but, although the Ameer entertained him very hospitably, he fared no better than any of his predecessors. In that year, too, Yakoob Beg's position had become firmer in his own state. The Tungani had been driven back north of the Tian Shan beyond Turfan, and into the regions east of Lake Lob; the disaffection, too, in the cities of Kucha and Korla was also, to all appearance, dying out; but, above all, the vast ægis of English protection had appeared to be thrown over the integrity of his state. However unjustified this supposition was by the treaty with Sir Douglas Forsyth, the Ameer made as much use as possible of his new-found ally; and the large section of Anglo-Indians, and authorities in this country on the affairs of Central Asia, who, either out of sympathy for the man, or from a belief in the identity of British interests with his cause, proclaimed the advisability of supporting him against Russian aggression, gave a colourable excuse to his declaration that England had extended for the first time in her Trans-Himalayan policy her protection to a native state lying north of her natural frontier. The Russian governments in Siberia and Turkestan, emphatically cautioned by their Foreign Office to give this country no cause for umbrage, were at first inclined to make that assertion an excuse for pushing their friendly relations with the Ameer; but their advances were not reciprocated, and as it became more clear that the importance of the Forsyth mission had been greatly exaggerated by the representations of the Ameer, the language of the Russian authorities became once more peremptory and menacing. In short, matters after more than two years' discussion had retrogressed to the condition they were in before the Kaulbars treaty. The Russians had not obtained their chief desire, the establishment of consular agents in Kashgar, and Yakoob Beg, as in the past, boldly met threat with threat. Relying on his increased reputation as the most orthodox and the most puissant of Mahomedans in Central Asia, and confident that England would intervene between the Russians and the collapse of his state, he even went so far as to temper his defiant, and almost bellicose, attitude with such irony as the following incident is a characteristic specimen of. Early in the year 1874 the Duke of Edinburgh married Marie Alexandrovna, the only daughter of the Czar; and Yakoob Beg seized the occasion to send a message of congratulation to the Czar of All the Russias on the auspicious event— saying, that he had heard that the son of his good ally, the Queen of England and of India, was about to wed the daughter of his friend the Czar, and that he hastened to send him his congratulations upon the event. To this effusive epistle no reply was deigned, and it is doubtful whether it ever got farther than Tashkent. There is no difficulty in arriving at the conclusion that such exhibitions as this is an instance of detracted from the otherwise great and striking characteristics of the ruler of Kashgar. His opposition to Russia was most laudable; his maintenance of his privileges as an independent ruler was prudent and worthy of our respect; but his petty insults to Russia were neither wise nor dignified. He

was clearly in the right in checking the aggressive
instincts of Russia, clothed in the specious garb of
commercial advantage; he commands not less our
admiration for the energetic and persistent manner in
which he thwarted every endeavour to introduce Russian
espionage and intrigue into Kashgaria; but why should
he have weakened the effect of these splendid achievements, why should he have risked all he had secured,
by so senseless an insult as the message to the Czar that
has been just referred to?

The authorities in Tashkent, perceiving that it was
doubtful whether English public opinion was ripe yet
for an active interference in Central Asia, reverted,
despite all orders from the home authorities to the
contrary, to their original intention of coercing the
ruler of Kashgar. In 1874, therefore, all preparations
for commencing the campaign in the approaching spring
were made ready. Provisions and munitions of war
were despatched to Naryn, and an auxiliary division
was to make a flank movement by the Terek Pass on
the west. It has been laid to the charge of the Russian
generals in Asia, that expeditions are arranged for their
mutual advantage, both in obtaining higher rank and
orders. So seriously bitten had every officer since
Perovsky become by the desire for promotion and distinction, that the disease became generally known as the
St. George or the St. Ann Cross fever. Now during
the seven years previous to the date at which we have
arrived, if there had been a fair share of distinction and
spoil for the soldiers and the lower ranks of the officers,
some of those in higher posts considered that they were
aggrieved by the monopoly of supreme credit obtained
by General Kaufmann. This, indeed, had shown itself
very clearly after the fall of Khiva, a success for which
Kaufmann obtained all the credit, and yet towards
which the division under his command contributed little
or nothing. The etiquette, too, maintained in the little
court at Tashkent, and the semi-regal state observed by

the successful general, were irksome to officers more accustomed to the licence of a camp than to the punctilio of a palace. Nor were there wanting more sinister motives still among some of the chief general officers who filled the subordinate posts in the service of the Czar's representative. Prominent among them was the youthful Scobelef, who, burning to distinguish himself, clamoured loudly for some expedition which, when accomplished successfully, would be recompensed with the Cross of St. George. Strong as General Kaufmann may really be in the good opinion of his superiors, he was unable to resist, if he were inclined, the demands pressed upon him by Scobelef and his father, and the more warlike portion of his forces. It is said, that in addition to these palpable reasons there were others touching the family rivalries of the Kaufmanns and Scobelefs, who appear to have been at feud with each other when younger men in the service of the palace, when Nicholas was Czar. To remove these differences, and to satisfy the demands of his other subordinates, General Kaufmann consented that an expedition should be arranged against Kashgar, and entrusted to the command of the younger Scobelef. Towards the end of 1874 the war-cloud was drawing ominously over the Athalik Ghazi, and to all observers it seemed as if it were about to break with destructive violence on his devoted head. Loudly was it asserted that nothing but British intervention would save him, and it was only too clear that England's policy would be guided by events. The Viceroy had certainly not advised that an active participation should be undertaken in this question. The failure, too, of the Granville-Gortschakoff negotiations to define a neutral zone had convinced this country of the inutility of solving the question between the two countries by treaty. But it was not clear that, even if Kashgar were to fall into the power of Russia, our interests would suffer so much as to justify us in adopting an extreme remedy. The path being thus left clear for Russia to strike, every precaution was taken by Generals Kaufmann and Scobelef that the blow should be sharp and decisive. Not fewer than 20,000 Russian troops in all were to be directed against Yakoob Beg, who too late now attempted some concessions to his neighbours. Such troops as he could raise were massed in the neighbourhood of Kashgar, while another force under his son was stationed at Aksu. But of the result there could not be two opinions. Very few weeks' respite remained to the intended victim, when an event occurred which changed the whole current of Russian thought into a different channel. Yakoob Beg was saved by the outbreak of disturbances in Khokand, and, although the Russians never acknowledged that they were so serious as to prevent them persisting in their Kashgarian enterprise, still gradually the troops who had been despatched to the frontier were recalled, and those who had been ordered to set out for Naryn were retained in Tashkent and Hodjent, the two towns chiefly threatened. Although this event is not part of Kashgarian history, yet it performed so useful a function to that state, which indeed it may be said to have saved, that some brief account of it here may not be unwelcome.

Khudayar Khan, after the death of Alim Kuli, his hostile minister, in 1865, had been reinstated in his possession of Khokand, partly by the efforts of his own faction, and partly by Russian assistance. From that year to the year 1875 he was *de facto* as he was *de jure* Khan of Khokand, and, although imbroiled on several occasions with Russia and with his own subjects in those ten years, he still maintained a nominal independence in the western half of Khokand, with his capital at the city of the same name. For some reason, however, this Khan never was popular. So far as we know concerning him, he does not appear to have been any way worse than his neighbours; but one party in the state accused him of being a tool of the Russians, while another, urged on by the agents employed by that government, declared that he was gradually drifting the country into a hopeless contest with that Power. Widespread throughout the state there was dissatisfaction at his rule, and the occasion afforded by a commotion among the Kirghiz was eagerly seized by his subjects to rise for the purpose of subverting his power. At first this movement seemed to possess no importance for the Russians, and was regarded as one of those dynastic squabbles that had become too ordinary an occurrence to occasion any surprise. The insurrectionary party, too, had put on the throne Nasruddin, the eldest son of the Khan, a youth who was supposed to be friendly to Russia, and who was not likely to prove in any way formidable, having become passionately addicted to *vodka* drinking. But behind this ostensible ruler there were others who aspired to greater eminence than the king-makers of a petty state like Khokand. Chief among these was Khudayar's brother-in-law, Abderrahman Aftobatcha, who was entrusted with the chief control of the military arrangements. This chief was the son of Mussulman Kuli, the Kipchak minister of Khudayar's earlier days. Either incredulous of the maintenance of a neutral attitude by Russia, or urged on by a patriotic impulse to free the enslaved portion of Khokand, these confederates issued a proclamation of war against General Kaufmann. The border districts rose in response to the proclamation, the communications between Tashkent and Hodjent were severed, and confusion for a time reigned supreme within the Russian possessions. The Khokandian forces hesitated to make any serious attack and wasted their time in useless depredations in the mountains. Had a prompt move been made on Tashkent, or even on Hodjent, the insurrection might have been successful. Bokhara might have struck in at the critical moment, and Yakoob Beg awoke from the lethargy into which his warlike spirit was sinking. Such was not to be, however; and gradually the Russian scare wore off. Colonel Scobelef scoured the country with his Cossacks; telegraphic communication was restored between Hodjent and Tashkent; and the country was rapidly cleared of the rebels. The fugitives who had accompanied Khudayar in his flight were sent to the rear, and reinforcements were hastily summoned to take part in the necessary offensive measures against Khokand. It will-be sufficient here to say that, having been defeated in the fight at Makhram and several other small engagements, the party of Nasruddin and Aftobatcha sued for peace. This was granted, but Khokand became the Russian province of Ferghana, Colonel Scobelef was raised to a major-general, and obtained his Cross of St. George by the battle of Makhram. This event, generally known as the revolt of the Khokandians against Russia of 1875, marks an important era, for it convinced the Khokandians and other Asiatics that any attempt to obtain their liberty, short of a concerted and organized movement, would be fruitless. There has been no renewal of the attempt that then failed, but which ought to have achieved more success.

To the discord unhappily existent among its victims has Russia been chiefly indebted for the facility with which her Asiatic conquests have been acquired, and to the same ally it seems probable that she will be chiefly indebted for their preservation. There is no clearer evidence of this than the history of this last war with Khokand. But when we endeavour to divide the share of culpability for this dissension, we are on this occasion bound to admit that the chief blame attaches to Yakoob Beg. More than any other Asiatic ruler had he assumed to himself the title of general protector of his religion and his order, against the conquering strides of Russia; more than any other had he fostered, by his bold and defiant attitude towards that state, the belief that there still remained some hope of coping with the danger by a united league of Central Asian states; more than any other had he seemed to justify this aspiration; and more than any other must he be held culpable when he permitted the moment that seemed most auspicious to slip by unutilized. Moreover, when this insurrection broke out in Khokand, he had made every preparation to defend himself against a Russian invasion. He saw the Rsusians compelled, by the very necessities of their position, to call off their forces to other quarters, and yet he abstained from striking a blow in defence of those interests which he had ever declared were most sacred to him. It is impossible to explain such apathy on so important an occasion as this was; and his refusal to strike in on the side of Aftobatcha must remain the greatest blot on an otherwise brilliant reputation. With the collapse of that effort, and the subsequent occupation of Ferghana, Russian attention seemed to become more occupied with the state of affairs on the Oxus and in Cabul, than with the fortunes or misfortunes of Kashgar. During the few months that intervened between the annexation of Khokand and the appearance of the Chinese north of the Tian Shan, Yakoob Beg adopted a more conciliatory policy towards Russia, and might in a short time have sunk into the position of a somewhat more important Khudayar or Mozaffur Eddin. Other events intervened, however, and gave a complete change to the question, as will be considered in a later chapter. We take our leave of this narrative of his dealings with Russia with an admiration that would be perfect but for the weakness he exhibited in 1875. Even that vacillation will scarcely destroy all the claim that his bold defiance and consistent opposition to all Russian pretensions to supremacy over Eastern Turkestan gives him to our respectful and admiring consideration.

CHAPTER XI.

YAKOOB BEG'S RELATIONS WITH ENGLAND.

In describing the relations that subsisted between England and Kashgar, while under the rule of Yakoob Beg, there will be no necessity for us to enter so deeply into the under-currents that guided those relations, as was necessary in the preceding chapter, where we detailed the rivalry of Russia and Kashgar. While England could hold out a hand of friendship to the Athalik Ghazi, because he sought to please us by making commercial concessions, Russia felt doubly piqued with the man who for long refused her a similar foothold, and who, for a brief space, went still farther in his defiance, secure—as he thought—under British protection. Our government could not fail to see, in the bold conduct of this ruler, the result of a mistaken notion of what it would do in the event of a war in Central Asia, and it strove to bring home to the mind of Yakoob Beg and his emissaries a sense of our determination not to interfere beyond the Karakoram. Looking back now on the old legends that successive travellers brought us from Eastern Turkestan, where such strange things had been wrought, where the Chinese had been expelled, and a new king from Khokand enthroned, and regarding them in the light of our greatly extended information, even since Mr. Shaw penned his interesting volume on High Tartary, it will not be without some interest to trace back the story of how Yakoob Beg's name first became known to us, and how, for eight or nine years, a large section of Englishmen wove a romance round his name, and converted "the land of the six cities" into a fertile and populous region, which might serve as a barrier to Russian progress, and which, like Cabul elsewhere, should extend as another " cushion " from the mountains of Hindostan to the Celestial range of the Chinese. Those dreams have vanished now, and in their place has risen up the very unromantic and matter-of-fact spectacle of a Chinese triumph.

Whoever has chanced to reside in the valleys of the Himalaya—Mr. Shaw is the authority—must experience a desire to know of the countries beyond that range. The desire is natural, but the obstacles of nature are stupendous. To enter Tibet has been the object of numerous Englishmen, from the time of Warren Hastings, yet that object has been only attained by three of our countrymen, the latest sixty-six years ago. There are forty or fifty passes of various degrees of practicability leading into Tibet from Nepaul, Sikhim, and Bhutan; and to act as a spur to the explorer there is a highly civilized and peaceable race just beyond our border of whom we know scarcely anything. Yet the vision of Warren Hastings and of Thomas Manning remains unfulfilled.

North of the Karakoram there were no similar incentives. Mr. Moorcroft who, fifty years ago, resided in Ladakh, does not appear to have manifested any desire to pierce the iron barrier to the north, although towards Ruduk and Tibet he turned as if irresistibly fascinated. The character which the brothers Michell gave Little Bokhara, or Eastern Turkestan, expressed a fact, which long deterred any traveller from attempt- . ing to explore it. " Little Bokhara," they said, " was a country where every man carried his life in his hand, and there were indubitable excuses for each successive traveller who recoiled before the hardships and dangers of a journey through that country." But although no Englishman traversed the dizzy passes of the Karakoram and the Kuen Lun, now and then the people from Sanju, Khoten, and the neighbourhood came to Ladakh, where they brought intelligence of the political events that were taking place further north. Their intelligence was often completely false, it was always vague and exaggerated, but it, at all events, told us whether peace or war, satisfaction or dissatisfaction, was the existing circumstance in Eastern Turkestan. It was known in a general sense that China was the nominal ruler of this vast region; but the exact relations China held there, how she conquered the country and when, and by what means she retained her conquest, all these were unascertained. There had, indeed, been one break in this state of darkness when the learned traveller, Adolph Schlagintweit, in 1857, penetrated, with a few native followers, into Kashgar. The initial difficulties were successfully overcome, and fortune seemed at first disposed to smile upon his enterprise. Herr Schlagintweit had come, however, at a singularly inopportune moment. The Khoja Wali Khan had just invaded Kashgar, and his forces had spread as far south as Yarkand, when the traveller approached that city. He appears to have been able to report himself to the Aksakal, representing Cashmere at Yarkand, who, in turn, communicated with the Chinese Amban, for permission for him to enter the city; but while detained outside the walls he was captured by a roving party of Wali Khan's army. He was at once hurried off to Wali Khan's head-quarters at Kashgar, where that despot, in a fit of fury, brought about by excess in " bang," ordered him to be executed. His followers escaped, and brought back the tale of his death to Ladakh.

Such was the untoward fate of the first explorer of Kashgar. In the course of the early summer of 1868, it became generally known that the Chinese had been driven out of Kashgar, and that Yakoob Beg was ruling the country, under the title, conferred upon him by the Ameer of Bokhara, of Athalik Ghazi. He had sent a sort of semi-official messenger, Mahomed Nazzar, in that year into the Punjab, to take notes, as it were, of our dominions. Mr. Shaw, in Ladakh, had heard of the recent changes in Eastern Turkestan, and mentioned to this envoy on his return the desire he had to visit Kashgar, and see the widely famed Athalik Ghazi. The envoy received the proposition with enthusiastic approval, but it was considered more prudent to await the formal assent of the ruler himself. After overcoming the difficulties that beset his task, with prompt resolution Mr. Shaw entered the dominions of the Athalik Ghazi in December, 1868, being the first Englishman who had ever entered Little Bokhara. His reception was singularly cordial, and everything that the officials could do to make his sojourn in the country pleasant to him was done. One and all of the Khokandian dignitaries received him as a friend and a brother ; and even Mahomed Yunus, Dadkwah of Yarkand, the second man in the kingdom, treated him in a spirit of marked cordiality. It should be remembered that Mr. Shaw went there without any official *status* whatever, and simply as an English traveller. Of course, it was the best policy for the Kashgarian rulers to greet him hospitably, and prove that they had completely pacified Eastern Turkestan ; but in pointing out the hospitable reception that was given to Mr. Shaw, it is impossible to detract from its merit by referring to such latent political motives as these. Yakoob Beg received the English traveller in special audience at Kashgar, and treated him in the most cordial manner. On Mr. Shaw offering him a few presents that he had brought from India, such as rifles, &c., the ruler laughed, and said, " What need is there of presents between you and me ? We are already friends, and your safe arrival has been sufficient satisfaction to me." During Mr. Shaw's residence in Kashgar, which extended over a period of three months, he had three interviews with the Athalik Ghazi, who on each occasion became, if possible, more friendly than on the previous one. Mr. Shaw was fairly treated on the whole, and has of all writers on Kashgar given us the most graphic description of the people and the country. Mr. Shaw's position was to a certain extent compromised by the arrival of another Englishman, the lamented Mr. Hayward, who was murdered in a somewhat mysterious manner, three or four years afterwards, in the neighbourhood of the Cashmerian fortress of Gilgit. Both travellers were for a time detained in a sort of honourable confinement in Kashgar, but all ended happily, and the first two English explorers of Eastern Turkestan returned in perfect safety to Ladakh. The result of Mr. Shaw's interesting journey was not made known in England until 1871, after he had set out and returned from Kashgar a second time, in the first embassy of Mr., now Sir, Douglas Forsyth. The result of this visit to Yarkand and Kashgar was almost magnetic. Not only did the Indian Government promptly take into its consideration the question of what our political relations were to be with the Athalik Ghazi, but the whole Anglo-Indian community turned an attentive ear to the stories told of the new country. A new avenue for commerce had been opened up, and Eastern Turkestan might, after all, prove the true gateway to the marts of Bokhara and Kuldja. In our more immediate vicinity there was the jade trade of Khoten to be revived, and the wool of Tartary, of ancient fame, should alone form a staple article of commerce. For Manchester goods and Indian wares there was also a very inviting prospect in the thickly populated districts of Yarkand and Kashgar, which were at first supposed to contain a much larger population than as a matter of fact they did. At first it is probable that the main sentiment was one of satisfaction on commercial grounds alone; later on, the progress' of events in Khokand and Kuldja made the political motives appear more prominently before English minds. A trading company was formed in conception, but it did not begin operations until several years later on, after the signature of the Forsyth treaty, for which, and the official regulations concerning the working of that company, the reader may be referred to the Appendix of this volume.

Mr. Shaw himself formed a very roseate estimate of the future of the trade between India and Kashgar, and participated with all his wonted activity in promoting the fortunes of the Yarkand Trading Company from his advantageous post at Lêh. Although the more sanguine expectations were never realized, the company itself was successful, and performed a very useful work under no easy circumstances. Its functions are suspended during the uncertainty that always follows a change in the ruling power of a state, until it is seen what steps are taken by the Chinese, or this country, to perpetuate, under the Chinese sway, those good feelings which first arose under Yakoob Beg. Many are sceptical of the possibility of living on terms of good neighbourship with the Chinese, and of carrying on an intercourse, which certainly does not exist anywhere along the whole extent of the Anglo-Chinese frontier. But these persons will scarcely admit that the Chinese are to blame in this respect if we neglect the subject, for Russia by right of several treaties, and by right also of diplomatic tact, has a commercial *status* in every northern mart of the Chinese Empire, from Ourga to Urumtsi, Manas, Chuguchak, Kuldja and Kashgar. If the Chinese were reinstalled in every one of their old possessions, yet Russia would have a legal foothold in all those outlying dependencies. English commerce must not by any means despair of success in opening up the interior of China from the direction of India and Cashmere. In most cases, political action generally follows upon commercial enterprise; but in our dealings with the Chinese the order is reversed, and political overtures and diplomatic arrangements must clear the way for the commerce that must infallibly spring up between Hindostan and not only Tartary and Tibet, but also the home provinces of Yunnan and Szchuen. The root of the difficulty is no doubt to be found in the fact that the Mantchoo caste is in many respects as much a race apart from the mass of Chinamen as the Norman was in England during the twelfth century. The Mantchoo mandarin believes that in some undefined manner the introduction of European science and civilization into China would tend to lower his influence and political power. But if we are wise, we shall ignore this sentiment, and endeavour to reach the people through their legitimate authorities, the Tartar conquering race of two centuries and a half ago, and not by attempting to influence the rulers by a propagandist crusade among the people, as some advise.

Some months after the return of Mr. Shaw to Lêh, the Athalik Ghazi, who had doubtless considered very attentively that gentleman's suggestion to maintain a representative at Lahore, despatched an envoy to India for the purpose of expressing his desire for the establishment of friendly relations with the British Government, for the development of trade between the countries, and for the visit of a British officer to his capital. He had fully realized by this time what Mr. Shaw meant by saying that he came in no official capacity. If he intended, therefore, to reap any reward for the manifestation of his friendship towards England, or to be able to play England's alliance off against Russia's hostility, he discovered that he must take the initiative. In consequence of that discovery, Ihrar Khan came to India, and was entertained by our Government in a very friendly manner. It was in response to Ihrar Khan's visit that Mr. Forsyth was sent as our first envoy to Kashgar, in the following year.

Mr. Forsyth was accompanied by Mr. Shaw, who had volunteered for the service, and by Dr. Henderson. He reached Yarkand, by the same route as that followed by Mr. Shaw, in safety, and without suffering any great amount of inconvenience. But the mission had reached the scene of its labours at a very inopportune moment. The Athalik Ghazi had just been summoned away to the far eastern frontier to repress hostile movements on the part of the Tungan cities of Turfan and Urumtsi, and it was very uncertain for how long a time he might be detained there. Mr. Forsyth accordingly left Yarkand in the month of September on his return journey, without having had an opportunity of settling the future of the relations between India and Kashgar. Dr. Henderson, in his "Lahore to Yarkand," chronicled the events of this journey to the region north of the Himalaya.

The very next year, 1871, Yakoob Beg sent Ihrar Khan once more to India to renew his protestations of friendship, entrusting him with letters, not only for the Viceroy but also for Her Majesty the Queen. But there was no immediate result from this later overture.

In the meanwhile Russia had broken ground more firmly in Eastern Turkestan. The treaty of commerce between Russia and her neighbour, which had been for several years on the carpet, had at last been signed at Kashgar on the 8th of June, 1872. That treaty conceded no inconsiderable trade privileges to Russia, for, as will be seen from a perusal of its clauses, Russian goods entering the country could not be subjected to a higher tax than $2\frac{1}{2}$ per cent. *ad valorem*. In fact, but for Yakoob Beg's prudence in restricting the appointment of Russian commercial agents in the cities to the inferior *caravan-bashi*, a far different personage to the Aksakal, that treaty would have placed Kashgar virtually in the possession of General Kaufmann. Even as it was, Russia, regarded as a foe, had out-distanced England, who was held to be a friend; and for a considerable time afterwards, English commerce, which had no status there, hesitated to seek admission into the dominions of the Athalik Ghazi.

But the treaty of Baron Kaulbars was in its essence a sham, for no good feeling sprang up between the countries; and where there was distrust on either side, trade languished, as was to be expected. Two months

after this treaty, Yakoob Beg sent his nephew, the Seyyid
Yakoob Khan, on a special embassy to Russia, whence
he went on to Constantinople, and returned *viá* India.
He then had several long discussions with our authorities relative to the measures that should be adopted
to place everything on a friendly footing between
Kashgar and ourselves. The Sultan had conferred
upon the ruler of Kashgar the high title of Emir ul
Moomineen, and shortly afterwards Yakoob Beg proclaimed himself in consequence of that decree Emir or
Ameer of Kashgar, under the title of Yakoob Khan. It
is appropriate here to say something of these two titles,
Khan and Beg.   In this work the ruler of Kashgar has
been consistently called Beg or prince, and not Khan or
lord ; and for the following reasons.   The title of Khan
is much higher than that of Beg ; it is, moreover,
hereditary.   Gibbon, whose authority in these Central
Asian matters stands higher than many modern
scholars will admit, defines it as the distinguishing
mark of the descendants of Genghis Khan.   His
heirs and their children became the Khans of Western Asia.   The Mongol who grafted himself on the
Turk and the Usbeg, brought with him the unique
authority that was vested by public voice in the house
of Genghis, the Khan of Khans.   Now, although in his
later days Yakoob Beg, or his admirers, invented a
lineage for himself back to Timour, consequently making
him of Mongol descent, it is highly improbable that this
mythical descent was based on any reliable *data*, nor
can we admit any other claim to according Yakoob Beg
that higher title than one that will stand the criticism of
history.   Yakoob Beg was not free from some of that
craving that haunts the minds of rulers "born out of
the purple" to claim cousinship with the select caste
of former sovereigns ; and the visible embodiment of
temporal sovereignty in Turkestan was this very title of
Khan, which has been so much abused in its application.
 It is wrong, in a strict sense, to apply the title of

Khan to Yakoob Beg, although he undoubtedly made use of it during the last three years of his reign; but as a matter of mere convenience, it is also misleading. On the stage of Asiatic politics there is another Yakoob Khan, who is, by descent, a Khan, and possesses qualities not less eminent than did his namesake in Eastern Turkestan. Confusion was often caused by the confounding of one of these personages with the other, whereas if each had been defined by his legitimate title, there would have been no misunderstanding. Towards the close of the year 1873, the Seyyid Yakoob Khan, who, by descent, could claim the title which was not his uncle's, returned to India, where he found that the English mission was a few days ahead of him on its journey to Kashgar.

The Indian government had, in the meanwhile, appointed Mr. T. Douglas Forsyth as their envoy to Kashgar once more, and, during the summer of 1873, preparations were busily in progress for the important embassy that was to counteract the adverse effects of Baron Kaulbars' treaty. As this is the turning-point in Anglo-Kashgarian relations, it is necessary to follow it in considerable detail. Upon Mr. Forsyth's embassy depends the whole fabric of our policy in, and intercourse with, Eastern Turkestan during the past four years. In fact, but for Sir Douglas Forsyth's Report and Treaty, even Mr. Shaw's interesting volume and intrepid journey would have failed to have preserved the vitality of our interest in Kashgar and its ruler.

By the month of July, everything was in readiness for a forward movement, but owing to the delay in the arrival of Seyyid Yakoob Khan, or Hadji Torah as he was more usually termed, Mr. Forsyth still lingered at Murree. Captains Biddulph and Trotter, and Dr. Stoliczka, in the meanwhile set out for Lêh to explore the routes between that town and Shahidoola. These three gentlemen explored the country beyond Ladakh very carefully, although it had already been described by Messrs. Shaw and Hayward, and Dr. Cayley. Mr. Forsyth and the headquarters, after a short stay at Srinagar in Cashmere, arrived at Lêh on the 20th of September. It may be useful to give here the names of those who comprised this important embassy. In the first place there was the envoy himself, Mr., now Sir, T. Douglas Forsyth, C.B., and now K.C.S.I. His second in command was Lieut.-Colonel T. E. Gordon, C.S.I., who, after the prime object of the mission had been accomplished, explored a very considerable portion of the Pamir, the result of whose investigations is to be found in his work "The Roof of the World." Then came Dr. Bellew, C.S.I., Surgeon-Major, entrusted with the medical control of the expedition. The three military men—Captains Chapman, Trotter, and Biddulph—held various functions; the first as secretary, the latter two in scientific capacities. In addition to these there were the learned Dr. Stoliczka, who died from the effects of the rarefaction of the atmosphere; an English corporal of a Highland regiment, and six native officers and skilled assistants. There was also an escort of ten sowars, one naick, and ten sepoys furnished by the Corps of Guides.

The appointments of the embassy were also most carefully selected, and with special regard to the difficulties that lay before it in the obstacles of nature, and the inconveniences attending complete dependence on natives for the means of transporting the large quantity of *impedimenta*. One hundred mules "of a fair stamp" were accordingly purchased in India by Tara Sing, a merchant, and the treasurer to the embassy. And these were equipped with saddles and trunks of a special pattern, made in the government workshops at Cawnpoor. Altogether, then, this English embassy to Kashgar was a very formidable undertaking, and in its proportions assumed something of the appearance of a small army; in camp there were " 300 souls and 400 animals." The day had gone by when English travellers entertained doubts of entering Kashgar in company at the same time, lest they should arouse the apprehensions of the people. Mr. Forsyth came vested with all the authority of his Sovereign and the Viceroy, to negotiate a treaty of amity with the ruler of Kashgar, and the people generally saw in that fact a guarantee of the preservation of their liberties and independence.

So far as Shahidoola, the journey was in a well known region, and outside the frontier of Yakoob Beg. At that place the first sign of that ruler's power was encountered in the same way as Mr. Shaw, five years before, had witnessed the advanced limit of the power of the Athalik Ghazi in a southerly direction. A captain of the Kashgarian army, Yuzbashi Mahomed Zareef Khan, had been deputed to receive our envoy at the frontier, and to give him a hearty welcome. After a rest of four days, the whole expedition, advancing in two bodies over the Grim Pass, Sanju Devan, entered the inhabited territory of Sanju. Here Hadji Torah, who had been travelling "post" after them from India, caught them up, and by his tact and real friendship for this country, contributed greatly to the complete success of the mission. The passage of the Grim Pass, although accomplished with success, was no easy task. Dr. Bellew, in his book "Kashmir and Kashgar," gives the following graphic description of it, which may be quoted with advantage as showing some of the "obstacles of nature" to the advance either of an army or a caravan in this quarter :—

"The scene which now burst upon our view is one not easy to describe, still less to forget. Immediately on either hand, like the portals of a gate, stood bare banks of silver grey slate, which gently spread away on each side into the slopes that, inclining together, formed the theatre of the spectacle they limited. And immediately in front commenced that gentle rise over slabs of slate *débris*—the natural dark hue of which was lost in the bright sparkle of its abundant mica—which led at once on to the field of our vision. Here, at the foot of the ascent, one step took us from the tiresome monotony of the bare rocks behind, with all their dulness of hue, on to the snow, which overspread all before with a white sheet of the most dazzling brilliance.   On the left and on the right it spread with uniform regularity to the crests of the bounding ridges in those directions; whilst in front, it rose up as a vast wall, whose top cut the sky in a succession of sharp peaks with a clearness of outline rarely witnessed. And above all, stretched the wide expanse of heaven, with a depth unsearchable, in the speckless purity of its azure, and with a calm such as often precedes the storm.   Wonderful was the scene!"   .

Such is the description of an eye-witness of this striking scene, which in its solemnity approached the sublime, in its grandeur the terrible.   The last hundred feet of the ascent was a sheer wall of ice, like the Matterhorn, and up this the troopers' horses, and the baggage mules and ponies, had to be lifted by human force.   More than a whole day was occupied in surmounting this obstacle alone, but it was surmounted with the small loss of eight mules and three ponies.   With the crossing of the Grim Pass, the difficulties of nature disappeared, and henceforth the course of the mission lay in the more sheltered plains of Kashgaria.

After leaving Sanju, the country had, for some days' journey, an appearance of barrenness, that was only relieved by the avidity with which patches of more promising soil had been cultivated, a fact which testified alike to the beneficence of the ruler and to the assiduity of his people.   There is good reason for believing that in the Yarkand and Khoten districts, Yakoob Beg's administration was most successful.   This may have been caused by the superior qualities of the people over the Tungani, and mixed populations farther east; but it must also be attributed to the absence of those desolating wars which went on without any long intervals down to the year 1874, in the country held by the Tungani. The treachery of Yakoob Beg in murdering the Khan Habitulla of Khoten had aroused suspicions as to his good faith that only lay dormant during the days of his power ; but the people of Khoten, Sanju, Karghalik, and Kilia were far too thrifty and too prudent to sit down supinely and dwell upon their wrongs. They neither forgot nor forgave, but they suppressed all trace of seditious opinions against the new ruler.

The next city which Mr. Forsyth reached, Karghalik, showed still further signs of prosperity and civilization. "An eating-house, with its clean table, and forms, and piles of china plates and bowls, at once took us back across the seas to the recollection of many a country restaurant in France." Special preparations had in every way been made for the reception of the representatives of England, and Mr. Forsyth expressed his surprise at finding fire-places, like our own, ventilators, and rich carpets from Khoten, famous in days of yore for its manufacture of those articles, in the quarters that had been set apart as his residence. Similar preparations had been made at every stopping place, and the people not less than the sovereign did their best, and spared no exertion, to make the stay of the Feringhees as pleasant as possible for them. More than that, even at the resting places during the daily march, the headman or local magnate, without exception, always entertained them at a "dastarkhwan," that is to say, at a course of refreshments. The "dastarkhwan" literally means table-cloth, and consists of any number of distinct dishes, sometimes as many as a hundred, held by as many attendants. This is a national custom, from which there is never any deviation. It is incumbent upon the guest to break bread first, and then present it to his host. One of their customs is refreshing to any one who has come fresh from India, with all its troublesome caste distinctions. "Be the host Turk or

British, he and his guests eat alike from the same dish, and hand food to the surrounding attendants, who are troubled with no scruples of caste to interfere with their hearty appetite."

The mission was now drawing close to Yarkand, politically and commercially the most important city in the state, and accordingly preparations were made for a formal entry. At a village called Zilchak a chamberlain, or Yasawal-Bashi, came out with a party of the royal body-guard, Yakoob Beg's favourite *jigits*, in their buff leather uniform, to act as an escort, and the party was swollen *en route* by numerous influential citizens and merchants, who advanced to give an early welcome to the new arrivals. By these additions quite an imposing cavalcade drew nigh to the walls of Yarkand. The quarters set apart for the Englishmen were in the fort, which lies to the north of the city, so that Yarkand had to be ridden through before their halting place was reached. The people who thronged to witness the sight seemed very well disposed, and altogether there was every reason to feel well satisfied with these mutual first impressions, which, some had asserted, would be far from pleasant.

The following day there was an interview of ceremony with the Dadkhwah of Yarkand, Mahomed Yunus Jan, for whose history the reader is referred to Chapter IX., and then the visitors were permitted to go wherever they liked. On Mr. Forsyth's former visit a similar freedom had not been accorded him. Their first appearance in the streets was the occasion for a great deal of bustling on the part of the curious, but of friendly goodwill also. All the principal streets and bazaars were visited in turn, such as the butchers' street, or market, where the varieties of meat were clearly to be seen, and their quality tested by their tails or heads being left untouched. It appears to be the fashion in Yarkand to purchase the necessaries of life during the morning, and the luxuries in the evening. There is a special evening bazaar, called Shám, where hats and other clothes, in addition to various other articles, are put up for sale in the afternoon. This, when lit up with Chinese lamps, must have presented a stirring sight, very similar to a country fair in our country. Sir Douglas Forsyth does not tell us whether under Yakoob Beg it was customary to illuminate this bazaar with the gaudy lamps of the Chinese, or whether our imagination of such a scene must be referred back to the days of the old domination.

Nor were these harmonious relations confined to the lower people and ourselves alone. Their rulers set an example that all strove to imitate. Between the officers of the mission and the Dadkhwah something more cordial than a chivalrous sentiment of guest towards host sprang up, and was heartily reciprocated ; while Hadji Torah smoothed down all difficulties by his ready tact and never-failing resource. The latter did not remain the whole time of the three weeks that the mission remained at Yarkand, but set out for the capital, in order to put the Ameer *au courant* with English affairs, and the exact objects our authorities' had before them with regard to his country.

MahomedYunus had placed at the disposal of the mission a considerable number of the carts of the country, which proved very serviceable. These carts are strongly built, with two wheels, six feet in diameter, and are drawn by four or six ponies, as the case may be. They are not permitted to carry a greater weight than ten hundredweight, but with that load it is quite customary for them to perform journeys of twenty and twenty-five miles a day. In carts of this kind the heavier baggage was carried from Yarkand to Kashgar, while the members of the mission with a lighter camp followed on some days afterwards. While mentioning these carts, so superior to the Indian modes of conveyance, we will remark that they also are used as omnibuses and stage coaches. They ply frequently between the fort and city of Kashgar, a distance of five miles, and they are also used as a stage coach doing the whole distance from Yarkand to Kashgar in five stages. But no company with its regulations and bye-laws has a monopoly of this branch of locomotion, and there is a tariff fixed by law which cannot be departed from.

On the 28th of November the mission set out from Yarkand, and for a certain distance high officials, by order of the Dadkwah, bore it company to speed it on its journey. From Yarkand to Yangy Hissar the country was equally prosperous-looking, but there was much desert land as well. The villages of Kok Robat and Ak Robat (names meaning Blue and White Post-house respectively) wore a flourishing look, and the appearance of Yakoob Beg's soldiery, still *jigits*, who looked prim on parade, and yet could play the part of waiter, carpenter, or what not, with equal facility, added a sense of order and cohesion to the whole display. The appearance of Yangy Hissar was made more imposing to the view by the proximity of the formidable fort Yakoob Beg had erected there ; but in itself, owing to the houses being surrounded by mud walls, with crenellated tops, it closely resembled a fortification. There was only a brief stay here, and the mission then commenced its last stage of all. The 4th of December, 1873, was the eventful day which first saw an English envoy enter that capital, which Mr. Shaw had visited four years before in a non-official capacity. Special quarters had been prepared, at a short distance from the fort, where is also the royal palace, for the envoy, and these Elchi Khana had been fitted up in a very comfortable, if not luxurious style. Ihrar Khan Torah, who had visited India as envoy twice before, was the first to pay a visit to the new arrivals, and to request that they would come at once to see the Athalik Ghazi. The following description is Sir Douglas Forsyth's own account of his first interview with the Ameer :—

" According to etiquette we dismounted at about forty paces from the gateway, and walked slowly along with

Ihrar Khan, the Yasawal-Bashi, or head chamberlain,
with white wand in hand going ahead. In the outer
gateway soldiers were seated on a dais with their fire-
arms laid on the ground before them, their arms folded,
and their eyes on the ground. We then crossed obliquely
an empty court-yard, and passing through a second gateway filled with soldiers, crossed another court, on all
sides of which soldiers in gay costumes were ranged
seated. From this court we passed into the penetralia, a
small court, in which not a soul was visible, and everywhere a deathlike stillness prevailed. At the further
end of this court was a long hall, with several window
doors.   Ihrar Khan then led us in single file, with
measured tread, to some steps at the side of the hall,
and, entering almost on tiptoe, looked in, and, returning,
beckoned with his hand to me to advance alone. As I
approached the door he made a sign for me to enter, and
immediately withdrew. I found myself standing at the
threshold of a very common-looking room, perfectly
bare of all ornament, and with a not very good carpet on
the floor : looking about I saw enter at a doorway on
the opposite side a tall stout man, plainly dressed. He
beckoned with his hand, and I advanced, thinking that
it must be a chamberlain who was to conduct me to
'the presence.' Instinctively, however, I made a bow
as I advanced, and soon found myself taken by both
hands, and saluted with the usual form of politeness,
and I knew that I was standing before the far-famed
ruler of Eastern Turkestan. After a few words of welcome the Athalik led me across the room and seated me
near him, by the side of a window. At this moment a
salute of fifteen guns was fired. His Highness asked
in an eager tone after the health of Her Majesty, and
of the Viceroy, and soon afterwards called, in a low voice,
to Ihrar Khan to bring in the other officers. They
came in one by one, and each was shaken by the hand,
and made to sit down by my side. Then there was a
long and somewhat trying pause, during which the

Athalik eyed each one of us with intent scrutiny. I had
been told that etiquette forbade the guest to speak much
on the first interview, and that it was a point of good
manners to sit perfectly still with downcast eyes . . . .
After this silent ordeal had been undergone for some
time, at a sign from the Athalik, sixteen soldiers came
in with the dastarkhwan, and the Athalik breaking a
loaf of bread shared it with us. After the cloth was
removed, we, remembering our lesson in manners, rose
up, and stroking our beards, said, 'Allah o Akbar;' soon
after which the Athalik said, ' Khush, amadeed ' (' You
are welcome ')."

Thus ended this imposing interview, imposing not for
any magnificence or barbaric splendour that appertained
either to the court or person of the ruler, but by reason
of the mysterious character of the Ameer himself, of his
vague power and influence, and of the hold he had acquired over such of his subjects as comprised his court
and his body guard. All his Khokandian friends and
relations, whose fortunes, indeed, depended on his power,
were stanchly attached to his person. It could not be
given to envoys to possess such complete prescience as
to foresee that the jarring elements, that still existed
beneath the surface would suffice to overthrow his rule
still more irretrievably when it received its first shock
from external foes. To the observer, the appearance of
Yakoob Beg and his military following was the highest
evidence of latent power. Order was supreme, and discipline was as apparent in the palace of the Ameer as in
the barrack yards of his fortresses.

The formal interview took place on the 11th of
December, when the presents from our government to
the Ameer, carried by over 100 men, were delivered to
His Highness. There were guns of all kinds, including
two small cannon, vases, &c., &c.; but the token of
friendship at which the ruler showed most symptoms
of pleasure was the autograph letter of Her Majesty.
This letter was enclosed in a " magnificent casket of

pale yellow quartz, clamped with gilt bands and handles, and bossed with onyx stones." The Ameer received this with unconcealed satisfaction, several times repeating, "God be praised." And then he made those declarations of friendship which, taken in conjunction with our admiration for the man, were the means of riveting England and Kashgar into a closer alliance than any that has as yet subsisted between ourselves and any other Central Asian ruler. "Your Queen is a great sovereign. Her government is a powerful and a beneficent one. Her friendship is to be desired, as it always proves a source of advantage to those who possess it. The Queen is as the sun, in whose genial rays such poor people as I flourish. I particularly desire the friendship of the English. It is essential to me. Your rule is just. The road is open to every one, and from here to London any one can come and go with perfect freedom."

On the 13th of December our representatives paid their first visit to the city of Kashgar. The country round Kashgar is very fertile, highly cultivated, and thickly populated, and the mission was not less struck by the air of prosperity prevalent here than it had been at Yarkand. In addition, the people had a healthier appearance, mainly through the absence of goitre. The Dadkhwah of Kashgar, Alish Beg, who was a Kashgari and not a Khokandian, was not less friendly than the Governor of Yarkand had been, and a very pleasant day was passed in his company. On the 18th a grand review was held, but for some reason, far from clear, only of the old Chinese troops who had taken service under the new ruler when Kashgar citadel fell. The description of the manœuvres which this force performed reads more like the display of an itinerant circus than of a disciplined army, but, nevertheless, these Khitay troops were excellent material for an army. Their practice with the *tyfu*, an awkward weapon, being a sort of gun-cannon, carried by two men and served by three, was pronounced very good up to 250 yards.

It is proper to state here, very clearly, that while the English mission was on Kashgarian soil it lived and travelled free of all expense, and as the Ameer paid his subjects in hard cash for whatever service they rendered, it is obvious that for a small state such as his was this was no trivial expense. It is only fair that this fact should be as widely known as possible, for some discontent was aroused by a similar hospitality being extended to the Seyyid Yakoob Khan last year. That discontent arose from ignorance; for it is hardly to be imagined that any Englishman would grumble at reciprocating the courteousness of a Central Asian potentate. The mission remained at the capital almost four months, and altogether the time passed very pleasantly. The weather was certainly rigorous; but then there was much to be done in the way of business, sight-seeing and amusement.

On the 2nd of February Yakoob Beg placed his seal to the treaty of commerce, and this act concluded the business portion of the English mission. On the 16th of March formal leave was taken of the Athalik Ghazi, and the mission returned to India. It had accomplished its task with pre-eminent success, and the Forsyth Embassy deserves long to be remembered as the most ably conducted and practically useful embassy that ever set out from India.

Since the signature of that treaty the Turkestan Trading Company has been very actively engaged in despatching several caravans annually into Kashgaria; but now, whether temporarily or permanently remains to be seen, its operations have come to a standstill. In these later years, Mr. Shaw, in his old post as Commissioner in Ladakh, had been as quietly performing his useful work as ever before; and there were rumours that he was to receive his reward in being sent as

another envoy, or rather as a resident agent, into Kashgaria, last year. If the appointment were made, it has
at this date (October 1st) been for the time suspended;
and such entirely new considerations have come into
play that it may be postponed for an indefinite period.
Hadji Torah's visit to this country, in June and July,
1877, when the Turko-Russian war had rendered the
Eastern Question once more acute, revived our interest,
which had been flagging, in Eastern Turkestan. But
he came at an unfortunate moment, for June brought
us tidings of reverses round Turfan, and July did not
pass away without the intelligence of the death of the
Athalik Ghazi himself.

There had, before the receipt of this definite intelligence, been absurd rumours of the part Yakoob Beg
was resolved to play in Central Asia as the ally of the
Porte, while he, poor man, was opposing with despair,
and at the cost of his life, a relentless and irresistible
foe. Such is the irony of circumstance! The van-
quished in Asia was by some freak of imagination converted in Europe into the arbiter of a great question,
and the guide of all those peoples of either Turkestan
who chafe at the bit because of Russian rule. But in
reality, with the return of Sir Douglas Forsyth, our
relations with Kashgar, which at one time promised
to have been most cordial, languished for want of a
motive. No amount of admiration would suffice to
make us permanently guarantee Kashgar against Russia,
for the bare facts concerning the intervening country
at once chilled the sympathy at our hearts. The Grim
Pass, and the road lined with desiccated travellers and
animals, effaced the bright picture of the orchards of
Kashgar and the busy streets of Yarkand. There was
a sigh of profound relief, that would not be suppressed,
when Sir Douglas Forsyth's report made the fact clear,
that wherever else India might be menaced she was safe,
at least, from attack north of Cashmere. It is true that
there is a feasible route from Khoten to Ruduk, and

thence to India; but Yakoob Beg did not hold it, and its consideration was considered to be beside the question. In fact, after 1874, we entertained much the same opinion towards Kashgar and Yakoob Beg that we did towards Poland and Kosciusko; and we were beginning to reconcile ourselves to a Russian installation in that state, when the returning Chinese made us reflect more deeply on Central Asian matters, and discover that after all has been said against the assertion there exists a third, and hitherto neglected, great Power in Central Asia. There was never anything save a kindly feeling between the two countries, and all who could admire bravery and justice and hospitality and frank courtesy were attached to the individual who had proved that he possessed all these attributes in no mean degree. But there was no deeper sympathy than this, or rather there was no stronger connecting link. The Indian government felt that it would be championing an unrecognized cause in supporting Yakoob Beg against all comers, and in the press of more urgent matters our relations with the Athalik Ghazi became lost sight of.

The effect of this treatment upon the Ameer was not unapparent, and during the last twelve months of his rule he had become more Russian and less English in his policy. But we preserved "the even tenor of our way." Yakoob Beg had no hold over us such as must always be possessed by the ruler of Afghanistan. Practically speaking, his state was more inaccessible to us than Tibet, and the Russians at Yarkand would be a source of far less danger to us than warlike and hostile Chinese might become at Lhasa. To sum up, England and Kashgar were friends because they had no reason to be foes; but they were indifferent friends. The tear might be shed for mutual misfortunes, and condolences might be uttered when cause for grief arose; but that was all. There was no alliance in the true sense, nor was there firm and unswerving friendship. There was a brief space occupied by sympathy and goodwill; then ensued an unbroken period of unvarying indifference. Before 1877, the spark that had been kindled by Mr. Shaw, and fanned to the dimensions of a flame by Sir Douglas Forsyth, had gone out, and with its extinction passed away the solid fabric that many had hoped to rear upon the base which the enterprise of a few intrepid men had diligently prepared. Whether we were prudent or imprudent, true or false, kind or unkind, Yakoob Beg leaned on a broken reed when he bade defiance to Russia, trusting on our support. This chapter of our policy in Central Asia may be closed as speedily as possible; if we do not come out of it with much glory, it is to be hoped that a lenient posterity may judge our demerits with a merciful consideration for the preservation of a strict and irresponsible neutrality.

CHAPTER XII.

YAKOOB BEG'S LAST WAR WITH CHINA, AND DEATH.

UNTIL the close of the autumn of 1876 Yakoob Beg had not devoted much personal attention to his eastern frontier. After the first Tungan war and the capture of Kucha he had confided to his son and his lieutenants, the charge of maintaining order in the annexed districts, and of protecting his dominions against any hostile attempt on the part of the Chinese. About the month of September in that year couriers arrived with strange tidings in Kashgar. The message, we can well imagine, was terrible in its brevity. The Chinese had appeared north of the Tian Shan. They had sacked Urumtsi, and were laying close siege to Manas. Their numbers rumour had magnified to almost a hundred thousand combatants, and they came armed with all the auxiliaries Western science could supply.

Before following the movements of the ruler of Kashgar upon the receipt of this intelligence, it will be necessary to consider what had been the history of this Chinese army which had so suddenly appeared in Jungaria. When in the natural course of events the Chinese government, having solved the Taeping and Panthay difficulties, having restored order where disorder had been supreme, and having created an army where there had been only a disorganized rabble, turned its attention to the question, which it had never lost sight of, of chastising the Tungan rebels beyond Kansuh, the victorious soldiers of Yunnan, instead of being disbanded, were invited to participate in a fresh cam-

paign in the regions beyond Gobi. It requires no great
stretch of imagination to realize the scene when the
imperial edict came before these veterans, calling on
all true soldiers to vindicate their country's honour and
their outraged religion against the Tungan outcasts;
how the generals, such as Chang Yao, set an example of
enthusiasm which the main body of their soldiers
speedily followed. In the presence of such military
enthusiasm we are transported back to the days of
imperial Rome, when the subjection of one province
was only the prelude to some fresh triumph, and when
every campaign found in the ranks of the army the
veterans of the last. So it was that the victors of
Talifoo, by long marches through Szchuen and Shensi,
reached Lanchefoo, the capital of Kansuh, where the
viceroy of that province was gathering together the
munitions of war, and the recruits who were to swell
the nucleus of trained soldiers to the proportions
suitable to an invading army. Some have considered,
and we are far from denying that there is much to
support such a view, that there was a political motive
at the root of this enterprise, the motive being a desire
on the part of the ruling family to give employment to
a large disciplined body of men, who if retained in
China proper would be at the service of any powerful conspirator or presumptuous aspirant to imperial
honours. Whether there is any foundation or not for
this supposition, it is certain that those troops who
were not required for garrison work in Yunnan were
taken by a round-about route at a great distance from
the capital to the north-west frontier town of Lanchefoo, there to prepare for the most arduous military
enterprise China had undertaken since her conquest of
Eastern Turkestan in the last century.

It is not certain when these movements began to be
carried out, but there appears to be no reason to doubt
that the advanced portion of the Chinese army had commenced its march westward before the end of the year

1874.   In the barren region between Lanchefoo and Hamil, a tract of country some 900 miles as the crow flies, but probably nearer 1,200 by the road followed by the Chinese, such difficulties were encountered that one if not two winters were occupied in overcoming these preliminary obstacles to the advance of the main force. The interval was not passed in complete idleness at headquarters, where magazines of arms and stores were being collected, recruits enlisted and drilled, and the plan of campaign that was to astonish Asia, if not Europe also, was being drawn up by the Viceroy of Kansuh in person and his able lieutenants.   At last, with the break of spring upon the desert plains of Gobi, the Chinese army, which numbered in its entirety some 50,000 men, set out on the long road across the desert to the more fertile regions lying north and south of the Celestial Mountains.   Of the details of this portion of the enterprise the *Pekin Gazette* is strangely reticent. The most profound secrecy was observed, and, although it was known that military events were in progress in the north-west, their object and their extent were mysteries.   After the delay experienced by the advanced guard, which had to form fixed encampments, or rather settlements, in the desert, and plant the corn that was to enable it to advance in the following spring, no serious check was experienced by the Chinese until they appeared before the walls of Urumtsi, which the Tungan leaders had resolved to defend.

Although several officers in the service of Yakoob Beg happened to be in the city, and several of the leading Tungani resided there, the defence was not prolonged, and after a few days Urumtsi surrendered to the Chinese. Many of the inhabitants had fled to the neighbouring city of Manas, but the garrison was massacred by order of the Chinese generals.   There is no mention in this case of what fate befell those of the inhabitants who remained.

Urumtsi surrendered towards the close of August,

1876, and on the 2nd of September the Chinese sat
down before the fortifications of Manas, a much more
strongly situated city, and defended with the whole force
of the Tungan people. The first panic at the appearance
of the Chinese had passed off, and the defenders of
Manas recognized that they were not only fighting for
their cause and independence, but also for their lives
and the honour of their families. The terrible lesson
of Urumtsi was not without its effect upon the resolute
but despairing garrison of Manas. The capture of
Urumtsi was a creditable performance in a military sense,
but the campaign had to be decided before the ramparts
of Manas. On the 2nd of September the Chinese bat-
teries commenced to play on the north-east portion of
the wall, and for two months the bombardment was
carried on on all sides with more or less vigour. Several
assaults were repulsed, and the Tungani, in face of
superior odds and weapons, had behaved like brave men.
But the Chinese were as persistent in their attack after
an eight weeks' siege as they had been on the first day
of their arrival, and the provisions of the Tungani were
almost exhausted. With their supplies ebbed also their
courage, and, after an unsuccessful sortie, the Tungan
general, Hai-Yen, presented himself to the Chinese outposts begging to be accorded an honourable capitulation.
Ostensibly, terms were granted—or, rather, to put the
matter as it is expressed in the official Chinese report,
everything was left vague—and on the 6th of November
Hai-Yen and the main body of his fighting men came
forth from the city towards the Chinese camp. The subsequent events are not clear, but it seems that the attitude of this body was suspicious. The men were armed,
they were in a well-ordered phalanx, and to the Chinese
on the hills around it looked as if they were about to
attempt to cut their way through. Once the Chinese
generals entertained the suspicion, they proceeded to
act promptly upon it, as if it were an incontestable fact,
and the Tungani, attacked from all sides, by artillery,

horse, and foot, were in a short time annihilated. Such of their chiefs as were not slain were brought before the Chinese generals, and forthwith executed "with the extreme of torture." Every able-bodied man found in the city or its vicinity was massacred; but the report distinctly states that the women, children, and old men were spared, and there is no reason to doubt the veracity of the Chinese. There would, in their eyes, be no need to palliate such strictly just acts of retribution as these.

Not content with having chastised the living Tungani, by annihilating them, as a race capable of self-defence for a generation to come, the bodies of some of the prime movers in the Tungan movement in its infancy, such as To-tch-lin, Heh-tsun, and Han-Hing-Nung, were exhumed and quartered, as an example to all traitors to the Chinese Empire. The fall of Manas struck a blow that resounded throughout Central Asia, and at the intelligence a panic spread among all the peoples of Chinese Turkestan and Jungaria. The enterprise had been conducted with such astonishing secrecy, and the blow had been struck with such rapidity and skill, that the effect was enhanced by these causes, new alike in the annals of China and Central Asia. Not only had the Khitay returned for revenge, but they had brought with them all the auxiliaries that make England and Russia the dominant powers in that continent. The Khitay no longer advanced in the clumsy formation of a long-forgotten age, but in obedience to orders based on the models of France and Germany. Their artillery was not a source of danger to the artillerists alone, but as effective as the workshops of Herr Krupp can supply. But, above all, their generals had made still more astonishing progress. In the sieges of Urumtsi and Manas they had proved themselves to be no mean tacticians; in their next and more extended enterprise they were to show that they must be ranked still higher as strategists.

Before the end of 1876 the Tungani had ceased to be

an independent people. The great majority of them had fallen either in the field or by the hand of the executioner; and with their disappearance the first portion of the task of the Chinese army was completed. The blood of the Khitay massacred in 1862 and 1863 was atoned for, and Chinese prestige restored to as great a height as at any time it had been in the present century. More remained to be accomplished, in its danger as in its result more important, which we have now to consider, before their full task should be consummated; but the Chinese army and its generals had done, even up to this point, a feat of which any country might be proud.

These events appear sudden and strange to us who are far removed from their influence, and who only entertain a languid kind of supercilious interest in matters in which the Chinese are the guiding spirit. But what must they have appeared to Yakoob Beg in his palace at Kashgar, although that palace was 1,000 miles removed from the spot where his victorious enemies lay encamped?   It is impossible for us to gauge the feeling of apprehension with which these first triumphs of the Chinese were viewed throughout Eastern Turkestan; and if the bold heart of the Athalik Ghazi did not misgive him, it was not through any light spirit as to the gravity of the danger.

Intelligence of the fall of Manas reached Yakoob Beg, probably, before the end of November, and in consequence of the lateness of the season he had the whole of the winter before him to make his preparations for defence. The surrender of these cities was not generally known in this country until April, 1877, when we also heard of Yakoob Beg's march eastward to protect his menaced frontier.   There is very little to be learnt of the internal affairs of Kashgar between March, 1876, and March, 1877; that is to say, between the close of the revolt in Khokand, with the surrender of Abderrahman Aftobatcha, and the mustering of

Yakoob Beg's army round the city of Turfan, or
Tarfur. There can be no doubt that in that period
some important changes had taken place in the sentiment of the Kashgarian people; these changes may
not have been very perceptible to a casual observer,
yet in their consequences they were as important as
manifest sedition. It is not difficult to suggest what
some of these modifications may have been; of what
they resulted in there can be no doubt—the weakening
of the power of the Athalik Ghazi.

Yakoob Beg's over-caution in November, 1875, when
the last rising broke out in Khokand, damaged his
prestige more than a lost battle. It damped the
ardour of the Khokandian element among his followers,
and when we remember that these were his ablest and
most devoted partisans, this alone was a serious blow.
But there are many tokens that the disaffection was
not confined to any special party among his people,
but was spread amongst them all. The Tungan wars
had never been popular, and had been costly and
sanguinary operations. The old trade with Russian
territory, that once had been so lucrative, languished
for want of a fostering hand, and the difficulties of
that northern range of mountains, which the patience
and care of the Chinese had for a time pierced through,
were made the most of to prevent intercourse with
Kuldja and Vernoe. More than all, too, all Yakoob
Beg's skill as a "manipulator of phrases" could not
conceal the fact that his treaty with England was a
failure. It did not give him that British protection
which alone he cared for, and it did not provide, through
the greater obstacles of nature, his people with that
new trade outlet which was the sole object worth
securing in their eyes. The Forsyth treaty seemed to
bring the relations of England and Kashgar to a
sudden termination; and the Kashgari were quite
shrewd enough to perceive that the Athalik Ghazi
would not be buttressed by English bayonets against

Russian aggression, if that instrument was to be held, as in their eyes it could not be otherwise than held, the only connecting link between the countries. The consequence of this belief was a resignation to a Russian subjection at no distant date.

Yakoob Beg's tenure of power would be morally weakened by the existence of these causes for discontent among his people, and it was at such a moment, when they had perhaps only slightly become clear to his eyes, that the return of the Chinese was heralded. In the face of a great and common danger a well-affected people would have rallied round their head, and in the crisis have found a joint necessity to produce a better understanding than existed before among their component parts. The country east of Kucha, where it was inhabited at all, was inhabited by the few survivors of the massacres ordered by Yakoob Beg's representatives. Amongst these there could be no great amount of affection towards his cause. The garrison of the city of Kashgar consisted in the main of the pardoned Khitay soldiers—Yangy Mussulmans, as they were called—and from them no stanch support could be expected against their Buddhist countrymen (see Appendix). The Tungani of Kucha and Aksu and the neighbourhood were the most numerous recruits in the army, and from them at least it might have been supposed that the Athalik Ghazi would obtain faithful service. Even among them, however, there was discontent. They had everything to dread at the hands of the Chinese. It was they who had massacred the helpless Khitay, a deed from the stain of which Yakoob Beg at least was free; and it was they against whom the wrath of China would in the first place be directed. But they had also their grudges against the ruler. He had beaten them in the field of battle, and had compelled more than he had induced them to join his army. They hated the Mahomedan Andijani only one degree less than the Buddhist Chinaman, and their ambitious game had been foiled by the military talents of their present ruler. They had run, in the years 1862-65, all the risk attaching to a revolt against China, and when they had accomplished their task they found themselves defrauded of their reward. Therefore, in the face of a Chinese invasion there was disunion in the ranks of the very Mahomedan rebels who had originated all these troubles. The nucleus of Yakoob Beg's army, when these have been struck out as non-efficient, was small indeed; but it was only on that nucleus he could depend in fighting for his crown and his religion.

During the winter of 1876, when he was busy in collecting arms, ammunition, and stores at Yarkand and Kashgar, he must have discovered many of these discordant elements; yet he pushed his preparations resolutely on. He conceived that under the circumstances the boldest policy would be the most prudent, and that if he could but beat the Chinese in the field by superior tactics he might ride triumphant over all his difficulties and dangers. With these views uppermost in his mind he concentrated all his forces, Tungan included, along the southern slopes of the Tian Shan, with his headquarters at Turfan. The Russian officer, Captain Kuropatkine, who had been sent to Kashgar on a mission, and who had journeyed through the whole extent of Kashgaria to meet the Ameer at Turfan, computed Yakoob Beg's army at the following strength, and supplied the accompanying information concerning its disposition along the frontier.

The fort of Devanchi, guarding the principal defile through the mountain range, was garrisoned by 900 *jigits*, armed with muskets and two guns—one a breech-loader. At Turfan there were with the Ameer 3,500 *jigits* and 5,000 *sarbazes*, with 20 guns, mostly of ancient make. Toksoun, a fortified place, some miles nearer Korla, on the main road, was occupied by 4,000 *jigits* and 2,000 *sarbazes* with five guns. Hacc

Kuli Beg had command here. At Korla there were also about 1,500 men, who were brought up to the front shortly after Captain Kuropatkine's departure. With these 17,000 men, scattered over a widely extended area, Yakoob Beg had to defend himself against an enemy superior in numbers, and, as the result showed, in generalship as well.

The Russian officer gave, on his return, a very gloomy account of Yakoob Beg's affairs, predicting the speedy disintegration of his state. He also asserted that the Tungani were deserting in great numbers, and that everywhere east of Kucha there was discontent and distrust of the Kashgarian rulers. This disparaging account was confirmed by Colonel Prjevalsky, some months afterwards, upon his return from his adventurous journey to Lob Nor. In a letter, dated from Little Yuldus, May 28, 1877, he said he had been very kindly received, but also suspiciously watched by Yakoob Beg. " All the way from Hoidu Got to Lob Nor he was escorted by a guard of honour, who officiously endeavoured to satisfy his smallest wishes, but would not allow him, or any of his people, to come in contact with the inhabitants. Yakoob Beg somewhat peremptorily asked Colonel Prjevalsky to explain why the Russians had provisioned the Chinese forces arrayed against him ; but, in an interview at Korla, he again and again assured the Russian traveller that he was a friend and well-wisher to Russia. Notwithstanding these precautions, Colonel Prjevalsky and the other members of the expedition succeeded in making the natives tell them that they were disgusted with the military despotism of Yakoob Beg, and that they hoped the Russians would soon be coming."

The information contained in this letter refers to the end of April, 1877, or to a time after the first defeat of Yakoob Beg by the Chinese, and his withdrawal to Korla; but it is *à propos* in this place as confirming Captain Kuropatkine's remarks.

In addition to the 17,000, more or less, disciplined soldiers whom Yakoob Beg had mustered at the frontier, Captain Kuropatkine mentioned 10,000 Doungans —that is, the Tungani inhabitants of this eastern region. Not only were these notoriously untrustworthy, but they were also badly armed, and were, on the whole, a source of weakness rather than of strength. Before the close of the month of February the Athalik Ghazi was at Turfan, constructing forts at Toksoun and towards the Tian Shan, and endeavouring to inspire his followers with his own indomitable spirit.

In the meanwhile the Chinese had not been idle. They had, after their triumph over the Tungani, established their headquarters at Guchen, near Urumtsi, and had so far secured their communications with Kansuh that a regular service of couriers was organized, and a continual supply of arms, military stores, and men flowed across Gobi to the invading army. For instance, a large arsenal for the storage of arms was erected at Lanchefoo, and on one occasion as many as 10,000 rifles of the Berdan pattern were sent in a single convoy. While Tso Tsung Tang, the Viceroy of Kansuh and Commander-in-Chief, was making these preparations north of the Tian Shan, for forcing the range with the melting of the snow, another Chinese general, Chang Yao, was stationed at Hamil for the purpose of seconding the main attack by a diversion south of the range. In estimating the total number of the Chinese army at 60,000 men—that is, 50,000 round Guchen and 10,000 at Hamil—we would express only what is probable. The total number may have been more or less, but in estimating it at 60,000 men we believe we are as close to exactitude as is possible under the circumstances. In the month of March the Chinese generals had made all their preparations for attacking Yakoob Beg. So far as our geographical information goes there is no direct road from Guchen to Turfan, and consequently the chief Chinese attack was made from Urumtsi against Devanchi, where Yakoob Beg had constructed a fort. But, although the larger army was manœuvring north of the Tian Shan, the decisive blow was in reality struck by the smaller force advancing from Hamil. If we are to judge from the disposition of the Kashgarian army, the movements of this brigade had not obtained that attention from the Athalik Ghazi which they merited.

General Chang Yao captured the small towns of Chightam and Pidjam in the middle of April without encountering any serious opposition. And from the latter of these places, some fifty miles east of Turfan, commenced that concerted movement with his superior, Tso Tsung Tang, which was to overcome all Kashgarian resistance. A glance at the map will show that Yakoob Beg at Turfan was caught fairly between two fires by armies advancing from Urumtsi and Pidjam, and if defeated his line of retreat was greatly exposed to an enterprising enemy. Upon the Chinese becoming aware of the success of their preliminary movements a general advance was ordered in all directions. It is evident that the Chinese were met at first with a strenuous resistance at Devanchi, and that the forcing of the Tian Shan defiles had not been accomplished when news reached the garrison that their ruler had been expelled from Turfan by a fresh Chinese army. It was then that confusion spread fast through all ranks of the followers of Yakoob Beg ; in that hour of doubt and unreasoning panic the majority of his soldiers either went over to the enemy or fled in headlong flight to Karashar. In this moment of desperation the Athalik Ghazi still bore himself like a good soldier. Outside Turfan he gave battle to the invader, and though driven from the field by overwhelming odds he yet once more made a stand at Toksoun, forty miles west of Turfan, and when a second time defeated withdrew to Karashar to make fresh efforts to withstand the invading army. Yakoob Beg probably lost in these engagements not less than 20,000 men, including Tungani, by desertion and at the hands of the enemy. He consequently conceived that it would be prudent to withdraw still farther into his territory, and accordingly left Karashar, after a few days' residence, for Korla.

Some weeks before the occurrence of these striking events Yakoob Beg had sent an envoy to Tashkent to solicit the aid of the Russians against the advancing Chinese. But the Russians only gave his messenger fair words, and did not interfere with Mr. Kamensky's commercial transactions with the Chinese army. At the moment, too, Russia was so busily occupied in Europe that she had no leisure to devote to the Kashgarian question.

The Chinese had for many years been good friends with Russia, and Yakoob Beg had all his life been a scarcely concealed enemy. Between two such combatants the sympathies of the Russian government must at first have certainly gone with the former; nor had Yakoob Beg's attitude towards Russia of late been as discreet as it might have been. His nephew, the Seyyid Yakoob Khan, was notoriously an agent for some indefinite purpose at Constantinople. His protection of the Bokharan prince, Abdul Melik, or Katti Torah, the most bitter enemy of Russia in Central Asia, was also ill calculated to attract Russian sympathy to his side.

Moreover there was little or nothing to arouse Russian susceptibilities in Chinese victories so far distant as Urumtsi or Turfan. In many respects, too, this Chinese invasion was a relief for Russia. It freed her hands in Central Asia in a manner that perhaps will never be sufficiently appreciated. Buddhist victories in Eastern Turkestan struck a severe blow at Mahomedan vigour throughout the Khanates, and the waning prestige of the Badaulet, or the "fortunate one," acted as a warning of strange significance to all the neighbouring princes.

It is not difficult, therefore, to discover valid reasons

why the Russians declined to negotiate between the combatants, and although Yakoob Beg endeavoured to come to terms with the Chinese, on the understanding that his personal safety should be guaranteed, all his diplomatic overtures were met by categorical refusals.

The Chinese after entering Toksoun came to a sudden halt, for which the causes are not evident. But the terror of their name had gone before them, and the country east of Karashar was hurriedly abandoned by its inhabitants. The Chinese delay may have been caused by the necessity for collecting provisions to enable them to advance further, or perhaps it may have arisen from the outbreak of some epidemic, as asserted by one of the Indian journals. On this point the *Pekin Gazette* is profoundly silent. The number for the 23rd of June contained a narrative of the operations round Turfan, and also a list of the honours and rewards given to the successful generals ; but it and its subsequent issues are silent as to the causes for the Chinese inactivity that then for many months ensued. The most striking sentence in this report is that which says that " the Mahomedans who submitted themselves were permitted to revert to their peaceful avocations ;" and if this be true, this is one instance, at all events, of the Chinese exercising moderation. Strange as it may seem, with this preliminary success the vigour of the Chinese invasion appeared to die away, and for five months nothing more was heard of the whereabouts of the Chinese army. In that interval the most important events occurred in Kashgaria, but with these, the Chinese, although the originators of them, had nothing to do. In the closing scene of all of the eventful life we have been in these pages considering the invading Khitay had no part. They were probably not aware of what was taking place some 300 miles from their camp until many weeks after it had happened ; and then conceived that their best policy would be to give time for the disintegrating causes at work within the state to

have their full effect before they advanced westward
When Colonel Prjevalsky saw Yakoob Beg it must have
been within a very short period of his death. The
shadow of approaching events may have been upon the
defeated conqueror, who from recent disaster could
only presage worse yet to come.

Of the exact manner of Yakoob Beg's death there
are various accounts. The most probable is that he was
murdered by a party of conspirators, who were led by
Hakim Khan Torah. The date given is the 1st of
May. That Yakoob Beg should meet with a violent
death, considering that he was surrounded by such
doubtful followers as the Tungan chiefs, is not to be
marvelled at, and that the first reverse in his career
should be the signal for fresh disturbances is only what
we should expect from a consideration of his country and
its peoples in the light of past history. So far, then, as
the assertion goes, that Yakoob Beg was murdered, there
is nothing improbable about it. But there are many
discrepancies in the accompanying narrative. The first
intelligence of the death of the Ameer of Kashgar was
contained in a telegram published in the *Times* of
July 16 last year. It stated that his death occurred
at Korla, after a short illness, and that he had
nominated as his successor Hakim Khan Torah, to the
express disregard of his own sons. The telegram went
on to say that Hakim Khan had declined to accept the
gift, and that the Ameer's eldest son, Beg Kuli Beg, had
succeeded to the throne. A few days after this telegram Hakim Khan Torah was identified with the
ancient dynasty of Kashgar, which Yakoob Beg had
first seated on the throne, and then displaced in the
person of Buzurg Khan. All this intelligence came
from Tashkent. On the 23rd of July we learnt in this
country, from the same source, that Beg Kuli Beg had
notified his father's death and his own accession to the
throne to General Kaufmann. There no longer
remained any doubt that Yakoob Beg was really dead.

For some reason or other Beg Kuli Beg does not appear to have been a favourite with the Russians; but this aversion to him was based on some mistake, for Beg Kuli Beg was certainly unfriendly to England, and was scarcely civil to our envoy, Sir Douglas Forsyth. Moreover, he at once placed himself in communication with the Russian government, asking for advice as to the course he should pursue with regard to the Chinese invasion, and renewing his father's request that Russia should stop the supplies sent to Urumtsi and Turfan from Kuldja. It was reported, but not confirmed, that his latter demand was complied with.

Nothing more was heard of the history of these events until the end of August, when news reached India through Ladakh and Cashmere that Yakoob Beg " had been assassinated by Hakim Khan Torah, the son of Buzurg Khan." This was the first hint that Yakoob Beg had fallen by the hands of discontented partisans. In itself so natural, it threw fresh light on the strange deed he was reported to have done of disinheriting his own family, and it speedily became the accepted version. The question then was, who was Hakim Khan Torah? Two versions were put forward; one was that he was the son of Buzurg Khan, the other that he was a Khoja chief of Kucha. The former was the more plausible, but as his name does not occur in Sir Douglas Forsyth's exhaustive report, it is open to some objection, more particularly when we are told that he bore a principal part in the conquest of Kashgar by Yakoob Beg. The latter suggestion was much more difficult to prove, but was not open to the same objection. Grant that Hakim, or Aali, Khan Torah was a pardoned Kucha chief when that city fell into the hands of the Athalik Ghazi, and there was nothing extraordinary in his having proved a traitor. Assume that he still conceived he had claims upon the governorship of that city, of which the *Turkestan Gazette* asserts he had been Dadkwah, and there is nothing inconsistent in his having sought to realize his own ambitious schemes the moment fortune frowned upon his conqueror. That Hakim Khan, if son to Buzurg Khan, should seek to revenge his father's deposition and life of exile is not in itself strange we admit; but if he were a subjected ruler, who regarded Yakoob Beg as an adventurer from Khokand with no claims to his fealty, his plot against and murder of the Kashgarian prince at once appears not only possible, but the true story. As a leading Khoja of Kucha he would also have claims to represent one branch of the old reigning family of Kashgar. In the face, too, of a great and pressing danger from the Chinese, his hereditary enemies, a son of Buzurg Khan would scarcely make confusion worse confounded by murdering the *de facto* sovereign; whereas a Kucha leader might aspire to play in such a crisis the same part that Amursana did in the last century. It was said that Hakim Khan entered into some negotiations with the Chinese, who gave him little encouragement.

The *Turkestan Gazette* still adhered to its original statement that Yakoob Beg had died of fever on the 1st of May, after an illness of seven days' duration, and that on the 13th of May the body was brought in state from Korla to Kashgar for the purpose of being deposited in the mausoleum of Appak Khoja. Then, according to the *Turkestan Gazette*, there ensued one of those atrocious deeds which have so often marked the history of Central Asian states. The second son of the dead Ameer, Hacc Kuli Beg, who had been with him during his last moments, escorted the funeral cortége, and was met at a short distance from the city by his elder brother, Kuli Beg. The elder son at once knelt before his father's coffin, and then rising, without a moment's delay fired a pistol at his brother, who dropped down dead. Not content with this fratricide, Kuli Beg had the whole of the escort put to the sword, and returned to Kashgar with his own followers escorting the coffin. We know nothing whatever of the reasons for this atrocious act, but the fact of Kuli Beg being in Kashgar, and not in the east, shows how Hakim Khan was able to establish his authority in Kucha and Korla. It will be more convenient to consider in another chapter the further course of these internal troubles, and also the final triumph of the Chinese.

There are, therefore, two versions of how Yakoob Beg met his death, and in support of each view there is a certain amount of evidence. All the information on the subject has been recorded, and it is conflicting. The Chinese reports in the *Pekin Gazette* ignore the subject altogether. Their personal hatred was directed more against Bayen Hu, a Tungan leader who had fled from Hamil some years before, than against the Athalik Ghazi. Of the main fact that Yakoob Beg died at Korla in May, 1877, there is no doubt, and that the most eventful career that has marked its track in the history of Central Asia for several generations was then brought to a close.

Whatever opinion may be formed of the man from his varied fortunes, there will be few who will deny that he possessed great mental qualities ; some will be found, no doubt, to question his action in deposing Buzurg Khan, and with more justice may his earlier life be blamed for his repeated desertion of his friend and patron Khudayar. Others will call to mind his vacillating conduct in 1875, and deny that he possessed that decision of character which is the salient feature in all truly great men. His unnecessary wars with the Tungani, and the short-sighted policy he pursued of extending his empire up to the vicinity of China, were also calculated to lower his claims to be considered a general or a statesman. In extenuation of these acts, which decidedly undermined the fabric of his rule, it may be mentioned that there is one side of Yakoob Beg's character that has never received sufficient attention. It is what was the secret to his foreign policy.　He certainly did not aspire, as many thought, to contest unaided the palm of superiority with Russia in Central Asia.　He was far too well informed to dream of that.　Nor could he expect to be able to extend his power to the south, where both Afghanistan and Cashmere would resent his presence. The only option left to him as a conqueror was to continue aggrandizing himself at the expense of China. We know not what dreams may have entered the mind of the stanch Mussulman in his palace at Kashgar of uniting in one crusade against China all the followers of the Prophet in Central Asia and of emulating the deeds of some of his predecessors who had carried fire and sword into the border provinces of China, and whom even the Great Wall could not withstand.　Over these bright imaginings, arising from tales told of the decadence of China, we know not how much Yakoob Beg may have brooded as he saw his power spread eastward through fifteen degrees of longitude, through Aksu to Kucha, Kucha to Korla, Korla to Karashar, and Karashar to Turfan, until from his far outpost at Chightam he could almost see the rich cities of Hamil and Barkul, cities which are the key to Western China and Northern Tibet, and imagine them to be within his grasp.　But the policy of Yakoob Beg will not be clearly appreciated, unless we bear in mind that these ambitious longings were held in check by fear of Russia, and by the hostility of the Tungani, who continued to plot even when subdued.　His keen spirit must have chafed greatly under the inability to accomplish that which he conceived to be possible, and despite his numerous triumphs he was at heart a disappointed man.

Moreover, during these later years, when the task he had set before him had been nearly accomplished, and he had leisure to look around, he was no longer young or as energetic as he had been.　He was entering, for an Asiatic, upon the evening of life, and had no longer the physical power to essay any protracted and desperate enterprise.

For a " forlorn hope " he was as eager and as effective as ever, but for those undertakings which require not only desperate courage but also forethought and patience he was no longer fit.   But the Chinese invasion dispelled all these, and many other illusions.   In their eyes and before their power, he was only another Sultan of Talifoo.   His great qualities, which attracted sympathy and a certain amount of respect, in India and England were vain in the eyes of a people whose " empire has," in their own tongue, " been planted by heaven."   Before Chinese viceroys and Mantchoo chivalry Khokandian soldiers and Mussulman pride must be held vain.   So thought the Chinese, if they thought upon the subject at all.   And so must we think who view past history by the aid of Yakoob Beg's overthrow.   Yakoob Beg's rule in Kashgar was for twelve years a visible fact; it was recognized by England and by Russia. The Central Asian Khans gladly acknowledged the admission of another to their fast dwindling ranks.   Even Shere Ali, an ostensibly powerful ruler, honoured Yakoob Beg not so much with his friendship as with his jealousy.   Yet it was all fleeting fast away.

In comparison with Chinese power his was as nothing; in comparison with Chinese perseverance his was weakness; in comparison with Chinese tactics, his tactics were those of a school-boy; and even in comparison with Chinese courage his courage had to confess an equal. There was not only the dead weight of numbers against him, but there was also the quick weight of superior intellect.   There were superior strategy and superior weapons; greater force and greater determination; no hesitation in action, and perfect unaminity in council ; all combined to crush one poor forlorn man, fighting with all the desperation of despair for life, if not for liberty. Worthier of a better fate, and meeting destiny with the calm that is natural to brave men, Yakoob Beg's defeat and death may serve to " point a moral and adorn a tale." The tale has been told in these pages with as close a

regard for fact as the meagre records will supply, and
for the personage whose name is the pivot round which
the main facts concentrate, it may be claimed that he
deserved attention even from Englishmen. It may well
be that some future generation may recur to this career
with interest as marking the only real break in the
Chinese domination in Eastern Turkestan. When the
massacres and other atrocities that marked the Khoja
invasions and the Tungan outbreak on both sides shall
have been forgotten or condoned, then it will be
admitted that, despite the great benefits conferred by
China on the people in the way of trade-fostering and
good government, there was some merit in the administration which a Khokandian soldier had unaided created
in this region. High credit, then, let us, who view the
subject from an impartial stand-point, pay this departed
warrior, who as a soldier met few equals, as a governor
none in his long career. Much as we may marvel at,
and perhaps impugn, Chinese strength, let us not judge
Yakoob Beg harshly, because Chinamen out-manœuvred
him, and overthrew him in fair fight. It is an easy
gauge to apply, and one which would dispel all the
reputation the Athalik Ghazi had secured, if we deny the
Chinese the great qualities those who know them best
will accord them without hesitation. But in applying
so shallow a test to the case before us we should be
wronging our own understanding quite as much as its
victim. However much we may blame Yakoob Beg for
going out to encounter an enemy whom he ought to
have awaited either at Kucha or Aksu, his valour, and
also his mistaken contempt for the Chinese, are made
all the more clear. We may fairly claim for him that he
was the most remarkable man Central Asia in its fullest
extent has produced since Nadir Shah; and that he
accomplished with insignificant means a task which
ordinary men, though born in the purple and ruling a
prosperous and thickly populated state, might have

failed to do. What better epitaph could be placed over a courageous and just ruler?

The moral of his career is a short one, but for us full of significance. Those independent rulers who establish themselves for a space on the confines of China are mere ephemeral excrescences; birds of passage who must betake themselves away, if they can, when their little hour has struck. English governments have never understood the vitality of Chinese institutions. They should appreciate it better in the future.

CHAPTER XIII.

THE CHINESE RECONQUEST OF KASHGAR.

WHEN Yakoob Beg died at Korla the task of reconquering Kashgar had barely commenced. The Chinese army, victorious at Turfan, was lingering in idleness round that city, exhausted, as some believed, by the greatness of the effort. It was not clear even that the Chinese aspired to achieve any greater triumph than that they had already won, viz., the subjection of the Tungani, a subjection which could not be considered accomplished so long as Yakoob Beg remained in the neighbourhood at the head of a large army; and that with the withdrawal of the Kashgarian army to Karashar the Chinese generals might call a halt of an indefinite duration. Nor did it follow as a matter of necessity that because the Chinese had aken Turfan they could capture Kashgar or Yarkand. Distance alone was no slight obstacle, and when added to the barrenness of the country, which would be made more desolate by the retreating army of the Mussulmans, an impartial observer might have hesitated to predict any very speedy triumph for the Chinese. But besides these, there were other impediments, of which a prudent general had to take careful cognizance. To seize Karashar or Korla only needed a bold attack; but to subject Kucha might have been a more arduous undertaking than was even the siege of Manas. A delay of two months in the heart of Eastern Turkestan must have strained the resources of the Chinese very much, and might have ruined their whole enterprise. And even if Kucha fell there still remained

Aksu, and afterwards Ush Turfan in the north, and Maralbashi in the south, barring the way to the vital portion of the state round Kashgar and Yarkand. Now the death of Yakoob Beg did not remove any one of these defences, and for a time it was believed that his son, who had always the repute of being a good soldier, would make the best of the very strong line of defence that he undoubtedly possessed. As a matter of fact, the death of Yakoob Beg was an irretrievable disaster, for it destroyed whatever cohesion and unity there were in the country. He himself might have been unable to avert a final overthrow, but the contest would have been made more protracted. Therefore in the months of May and June, 1877, immediately after the death of the Athalik Ghazi, it is strictly true to say that the Chinese reconquest of the country had barely commenced.

The hesitation shown by the invading generals after the victory of Turfan was at first caused by a belief in the formidableness of their antagonist, and, when that antagonist died, by a prudent resolve to permit the disintegrating causes that speedily manifested themselves in Kashgaria to have full time to work in their favour. Meanwhile they formed their plans in secret, laid in large stores of supplies from Russian territory, and explored the little-known passes of Tekes and Yuldus. A large number of fresh troops was received from the Calmucks north of Chuguchak, who during the worst period of the Tungan revolt had preserved that city for the Chinese.

But before following the forward movement of the Chinese it is necessary to say something of the internal disturbances in Eastern Turkestan, more especially of the rivalry of Beg Bacha and Hakim Khan for supremacy. In the first place, it is necessary that it should be distinctly understood that of the events that occurred in Kashgaria between the death of the Athalik Ghazi and the final advance of the Chinese army we are really without any definite intelligence at all, and it is not probable that we shall ever be accurately informed of the course of events during those five months. In the absence of exact *data*, we must assume the events to have taken place which are most in accordance with probability. On Yakoob Beg's death, his eldest son, Beg Kuli Beg, was either in the city of Kashgar or somewhere on the road thither. It is probable that he had been despatched to the rear, to bring up reinforcements after the defeat at Turfan, and in his absence Hacc Kuli Beg, the Ameer's second son, assumed the command of the army when his father died. It is certain that he accompanied the funeral cortége of Yakoob Beg back to Kashgar, and that he was murdered outside the walls by his brother. It was during this time that Hakim Khan Torah appeared upon the scene. It should be remembered that tidings of the death of Yakoob Beg travelled very slowly to this country, and that almost immediately after it arrived we received intelligence of events that had occurred many weeks after the death of the Ameer. We were therefore hearing at the same time the particulars of the circumstances of Yakoob Beg's death, and of those commotions which broke out some weeks after that event.

When Hacc Kuli Beg left Korla no personal representative remained there of the dynasty of the Athalik Ghazi, and during that interval the occasion arose for the intriguing elements that a mixed court, such as that of Yakoob Beg, could never be free from. Hakim Khan seized that opportunity, and established his authority in Karashar, Korla, and, probably, Kucha also; and during a short time Kashgaria was accordingly divided into three hostile camps. It appears that Beg Bacha, lulled into a false sense of security by the inactivity of the Chinese, resolved to chastise the insolence of his rebellious governor, a task which he should have left for the Chinese. A war then broke out between Beg Bacha and Hakim Khan, which exhausted the few resources that still remained to a ruler of Kashgar. The contest appears to have been of a desultory nature, and although the final result was in favour of Beg Bacha, he never appears to have recovered possession of Karashar and Korla. In the neighbourhood of Aksu the battle of this war took place, and Hakim Khan was defeated, "by the overwhelming numbers of his enemy." Beg Bacha's chief loss was the death of Mahomed Yunus, the Dadkhwah of Yarkand, his ablest and most faithful adviser. Hakim then fled to Russian territory, with 1,000 *sarbazes*, who were promptly interned by order of General Kolpakovsky, and there he sought to restore his shattered fortunes by carrying on intrigues with the Russian government. It is scarcely necessary to say that these came to nothing, and that Hakim Khan has sunk into that insignificance which, to judge from his acts when called into public life, is his most befitting atmosphere.

While engaged on this successful campaign east of Aksu, an event occurred of singular significance, as illustrating the condition of Kashgar under Beg Bacha. The Kirghiz chief Sadic Beg, who had disappeared from the scene since his old rivalry with Yakoob Beg thirteen years before, seized the opportunity afforded by Beg Bacha's embarrassment to attack the city of Kashgar, denuded of the greater portion of its garrison. He plundered the suburbs, and only withdrew when the young Ameer hastened back from Aksu to defend his capital. The Kirghiz, true to their nature, at once sought the desolate regions of Kizil Yart. They had, however, made the confusion arising from the death of the Ameer and the disaffection of Hakim Khan worse confounded, and completed those elements of weakness and discord which had always proved an invaluable ally to the Chinese. By themselves both Hakim Khan and the Kirghiz depredator were beneath contempt; but with an enemy established on the soil of the country, they assumed a too clear and mischievous importance. The minor seditions that manifested themselves in

Sirikul and at Khoten completed the round of dissension that, combined with external force, shattered the fair show of Yakoob Beg's empire. We are completely ignorant of the details of the disturbances that were reported to have taken place round Tashkurgan or Sirikul; but it is plausible to suppose that these were caused either by inroads on the part of the Wakhis or Badakshis, or by some fresh Kirghiz attack. The inhabitants of Tashkurgan being Yarkandi settlers, it is not probable that the rising, or whatever form the commotion assumed, originated with them; at Khoten the rising was more tangible, and more easily understood. The people of that city never forgave Yakoob Beg his treachery towards their ruler, and the instant he disappeared they hastened to take their revenge. When the Kashgarian garrison was withdrawn the towns-people simply deposed their *dadkwah*, and nominated a ruler of their own, who retained authority until the triumph of the Chinese made it politic for them and him to bow to the rising sun. The example of Khoten had been followed by Sanju and the vicinity; and thus the whole southern portion of the state acquiesced in the Chinese conquest, after the fall of Kashgar, without the necessity for a single Chinese soldier to be advanced south of Yarkand. It seems probable that at this very moment the Chinese troops have remained content with the submission of these districts, and have not garrisoned those important towns which skirt the Kuen Lun range with their own soldiers.

When Beg Bacha returned post haste to Kashgar, to encounter the Kirghiz, we said that Sadic Beg fled to the Kizil Yart; but he did not remain there long, for soon we find him back again at the capital in high favour with the Ameer, with whom he had come to terms. His Kirghiz followers were taken into the pay of the state, and just as this alliance had been struck up, tidings came of events that made that alliance, however futile and insignificant, a matter of the first necessity, both to Kirghiz and Kashgar. The Chinese army was at last advancing. The danger that had for five months been hanging in suspense over the devoted heads of a Mussulman people was close upon them. The long-feared and long-expected Khitay were drawing nigh to the capital, in irresistible strength ; and the apprehensions of a cowed people made them know, too surely, that their end was at hand. The dissensions among the people themselves, the discord in the ruling house, and the dissentient elements in every effort towards unity, had all operated in favour of the invader. While the Chinese had plotted and prepared in the deliberate manner of a great nation, the people of Kashgar had entered into cabals and schemes of party tactics that were well nigh ludicrous. And all the time that the sap of their vigour was being expended, the Chinese generals were drawing the noose more closely together that was to strangle the newly erected state beyond all chance of recovery. It would almost seem as if the Kashgari and their rulers had recovered from their first shock at the Chinese invasion, and were becoming reconciled to their presence east of Korla, when they experienced a second, more severe, and more lasting shock, in the announcement that the Chinese were again advancing. Their brief contentment passed away, and all their old terror revived in tenfold force. Hope died within their bosoms, and the resignation of despair only nerved them to bear a fate which their own valour should have striven to avert. It is time for us now to return to the Chinese army, and to follow its decisive operations.

North of the Tian Shan the supreme command was vested in the hands of Tso Tsung Tang, generalissimo of the army operating against Kashgar, and Viceroy of the province of Kansuh. South of it the commanders were Generals Kin Shun and Chang Yao, the former the hero of the siege of Manas, the latter of the diversion against Turfan from Hamil. The base of the former was Manas, of the latter Turfan. Their sources of supply were Hamil, Barkul, and Chuguchak, within the Chinese frontier, and Kuldja, Semiretchinsk, and Semipalatinsk, without. Their weapons and ammunition were transported across the desert from Lanchefoo, and their ranks were swollen by recruits from the Calmuck and other tribes. It does not appear that the Chinese were very eager to enlarge their army in size; they rather aimed at increasing its efficiency by the distribution of Berdan rifles and Krupp's cannon; and during the heat of the summer months they remained at rest in their recently acquired possessions. Nor is it probable that those epidemics broke out in their ranks which it was asserted had appeared amongst them. A sensational paragraph was published in the *Tashkent Gazette*, which was copied by some of the London newspapers, asserting that a species of cholera, known in Kashgar by the name of *vuoba*, had decimated the Chinese army, and that in consequence of that calamity its advance was permanently checked. Certainly, this was a piece of gross exaggeration, even if there were a substratum of fact for the assertion. Then, again, we were apprised, on high authority, that the Russian government had put a stop to the despatch of provisions to the country occupied by the Chinese army, at the request of its new-found friend, Beg Bacha. Yet there is no question that the caravans of Mr. Kamensky continued to pass between Kuldja and Manas, and that the chief caterers for the Chinese army were the Russian merchants of Central Asia. In the course of their intercourse the best feelings do not appear to have prevailed between the Russians and Chinese. The latter, flushed with their triumph, had become arrogant, and were too fond of referring to the question of Kuldja to be agreeable to the actual possessors of that province. On one or two occasions these verbal disputes assumed a more dangerous aspect, and from words the disputants proceeded to blows. Whether this collision was magnified or not, the Russian government took no diplomatic steps to secure reparation for injury to their subjects, and continued to wink at, if they did not actually approve of, their merchants supplying the Chinese. The clearest proof of this is that the moment Aksu fell a large caravan was despatched there by Mr. Kamensky. Still there was no little bad blood between the two people, and for a long time it was doubtful whether Russia would preserve her attitude of neutrality until Kashgar had been finally subdued. Beneath all this doubt, and the uncertainty of the strength and of the ultimate intentions of China, there existed a sentiment of dissatisfaction in the minds of the Russians at the renown China was acquiring, as well as at the prospect of having to restore a rich and paying province.

In short, beneath the Tungan and the Kashgarian questions there smouldered the Kuldjaquestion. Having now shown how well prepared the Chinese were at every point, how well armed, and how well fed was the tactical unit, and how Russia, although far from indifferent as to the results, was really abetting the side of China, we may pass on to those more active movements which proved that the Chinese generals possessed the ability and military knowledge necessary to make full use of the very powerful weapon which they had created, and which was capable of accomplishing the most arduous of enterprises.

The first move was made south of the Tian Shan. So far as we know, Tso Tsung Tang did not break up from Manas until many weeks afterwards. A brigadier-general, by name Tang Jen-Ho, left Toksoun on the 25th of August, 1877, with the advanced guard, to occupy the outlying villages of Subashi and Agha Bula. He does not appear to have had under him more than a few hundred men. A fortnight later, on the 7th of September, Generals Tung Fuh-siang and Chang Tsun followed after him with 1,500 troops, all infantry. They advanced through Agha Bula, Kumush, and Usha Tal to Kuhwei. At this place the troops were concentrated.

The chief duty of these detachments was to prepare the road for the advance of the main body, to lay in at stated places stores of fuel and water, and to erect temporary fortifications. So thoroughly was this portion of the task performed, that General Kin Shun, now known as Liu Kin-Tang, gave the order for a general forward movement on the 27th of September.

The infantry followed the main road, while the cavalry, under the immediate orders of the general, proceeded by by-paths in the same direction. On the 2nd of October the Chinese army south of the Tian Shan was assembled at Kuhwei. Its numbers were probably about fifteen thousand men all told. On the 24th of September a small force of Kashgarian troops threatened General Tang Jen-Ho's communications, but on the appearance of the Chinese they " turned tail and dashed away." The very next day after his arrival at Kuhwei General Kin Shun continued his forward movement. Two brigadier-generals, whose names it is not necessary to mention, were entrusted with one division, 6,000 strong, with which to perform a flanking movement against Korla. The commander in person led his main body against Korla, arriving at the River Kaidu, which flows into Lake Bostang, half-way between Karashar and Korla. But his advance was here checked, as Bayen Hu, the rebel leader, had flooded the country by damming up the course of the river. The depth of the inundation was said to be in the deepest parts over a man's head, and in the shallowest it came up to the horses' cruppers. The Chinese march was then changed to a northerly direction, in order to strike the river higher up, where the obstruction raised by the enemy would be more easily overcome. A cart-road was carefully constructed along these alkaline plains, and the Kaidu was dammed to stop the flow from the upper course, and a bridge was erected over it. This détour had caused some delay, yet Karashar was reached on the 7th of October, four days after Kin Shun had set out in person from Kuhwei. The inundation from the Kaidu had spread as far as here, and the town was several feet under water.   All the official and private residences had been destroyed alike, and the Turki-Mussulman, as the *Pekin Gazette* styles them, population had been compelled by Bayen Hu to follow him in his retreat. It would be interesting to know whom the Chinese meant by Bayen Hu, but it is almost impossible to say. As it was not Hakim Khan, the most probable personage would be one of the Tungan leaders, either of Urumtsi or Hamil, who had been mediatized by Yakoob Beg and placed in command of the Turfan region. He appears to have been the commander of that portion of the Kashgarian army which was left round Korla.

Not only was Karashar deserted by its inhabitants, but so was the whole country round about. Some, indeed, had fled to the mountains, but these were afraid to return when they saw the Chinese established in their homes. And then the conquerors followed out their usual plan by settling fresh colonists in the town. The Mongol noble, Cha-hi-telkh, was directed to move up some hundreds of the members of his tribe to occupy this important post, to restore the homes and to retill the fields; and while this work of restoration was proceeding on territory conquered by the Chinese, that through which they passed in hostile guise was subjected to far other treatment. On the 9th of October the Chinese marched against Korla from two sides, and on that day a cavalry skirmish took place, in which fifteen of Bayen Hu's horsemen were slain, and two taken prisoners. From the evidence of these, who were dressed in the Khokandian garb, but were Mussulman subjects of China, being natives of Shensi, it was learnt that Bayen Hu had withdrawn with all his forces to Kucha, taking with him the produce of the country and the majority of the people. They affirmed that the small detachment to which they belonged was only a scouting party, sent out to learn what the Chinese army was doing.

When the Chinese had exhausted their stock of information they beheaded them. The same day they entered
Korla, which they found to be completely deserted,
although not flooded. The walls remained, but many
of the houses had been thrown down. Here the general
was nearly reduced to a desperate plight, as the provision
train, which was transported by cart and camel, did not
come up, and there was the prospect of starvation compelling the victorious army to retreat. But happily the
thought struck the able general, or perhaps some one
gave him a hint, that there might be some stores concealed in the city which the Kashgari had been unable
to carry away with them. Accordingly the whole army
set to work to search the houses, and to dig into the
ground in all likely places for hidden stores. Their toil
was soon rewarded, and "several tens of thousand
catties' weight of food" were discovered. As a catty
weighs $1\frac{3}{4}$ lb., this was no slight supply for an army of
men which was probably under 10,000 strong. These
concerted movements of the army south of the Tian
Shan placed the country as far west as Karashar in the
possession of the invader. Their next advance, which
they could not expect to be as unopposed as their late
one, would bring them into the plain of Kashgar. No
sooner had Karashar and Korla fallen into their possession than an edict was issued inviting the Mahomedan
population to return to their homes, and many of them
accepted the invitation. In this quarter the arms of
China were not disgraced by any excesses, and moderation towards the unarmed population extenuated their
severity towards armed foes.

While halting some days at Korla, Kin Shun heard
that Bayen Hu was coercing the people east of Kucha
at Tsedayar and other places, and compelling them to
withdraw to Kucha and to destroy their crops. He at
once resolved to frustrate the plan, and set out in person
at the head of 1,500 light infantry and 1,000 cavalry to
protect the inhabitants. By forced marches, sometimes

carried on through the better part of the night, he reached Tsedayar on the 17th of October, when he learnt that Bayen Hu had driven off the whole of the population, and was already at Bugur, on the road to Kucha. At the next village to Tsedayar, a fortified post known as Yangy Shahr, he found that Bayen Hu was still ahead of him, and that he was setting fire to the villages on his line of march.   Kin Shun left a portion of his infantry behind to put out the conflagration, and resolutely pressed on with the remainder of his force to Bugur.   This small town had also been set on fire, but here the rapidity of the Chinese general's advance was rewarded with the news that the enemy's army, with a large number of the inhabitants, was only a short distance ahead.   The rear-guard, composed of 1,000 cavalry, was soon touched, and the Kashgari, emboldened by the small numbers of the Chinese, came on to the attack in gallant fashion.   Their charge was broken, however, by the steadiness of the Chinese infantry, armed with excellent rifles, and the cavalry performed the rest.   The Kashgari left 100 slain on the field of battle and twelve prisoners.   From these latter it was discovered that the main body of 2,000 soldiers was some distance on the road to Kucha, with the family of Bayen Hu and the villagers under its charge.   It was too late to advance further that day, but on the next the forward movement was resumed.   A large multitude—" some tens of thousands of people "—was speedily sighted by the advanced guard, but on examining these through glasses it was discovered that scarcely more than a thousand carried arms. All the troops were then brought to the front, and Kin Shun issued instructions that all those found with arms in their hands should be slain, but the others spared.

The armed portion of the Kashgarian army drew off from the unarmed, leaving in the midst the large assemblage of Mussulman villagers who were being carried off to Kucha.   These were sent to the rear by order of Kin Shun, and distributed in such of the villages as were most convenient. In the meanwhile a sharp fight took place a few miles in the rear of the old position, near a village called Arpa Tai. The action appears to have been well contested, but the superior tactics and weapons of Kin Shun's small army prevailed; and the Mussulman army retreated with considerable loss and in great disorder. Kin Shun followed up his success with marvellous rapidity and restless energy, while the Kashgarian troops fled incontinently to Kucha, abandoning the people and the country to the invader. The unfortunate inhabitants implored with piteous entreaties the mercy of the conqueror, and it is with genuine satisfaction we record the fact that Kin Shun informed them of their safety, and bade them have no further alarm.

By this time it is probable that the Chinese army had been largely reinforced from the rear, for we have now come to a more arduous portion of the enterprise, the attack against Kucha. When the Chinese appeared before its walls they found that a battle was proceeding there between the Kashgarian soldiers and the towns-people, who refused to accompany them in a further retreat westward. On the appearance of the Chinese army, the Kashgarian force evacuated the city, and joined battle with it on the western side of Kucha. The Chinese at once attacked them, at first with little success; and a charge of the cavalry, numbering some four or five thousand men, was only repulsed with some difficulty. But the cannon of the Chinese were playing with remarkable effect upon the Mahomedans, and the Chinese reserves were every moment coming upon the ground. The infantry were at last ordered to advance, under cover of a heavy artillery fire, and the cavalry made a charge at a most opportune moment. The whole army then broke and fled in irretrievable confusion, leaving more than a thousand of their number on the ground. Their general, Ma-yeo-pu the Chinese called him, was wounded early in the day, but, although stated to be a noted man, it is impossible to recognize his identity under the Chinese appellation.   This was certainly the most sanguinary and the best-contested action of the whole war. The numbers on each side were probably about 10,000 men, and it was won as much by superior tactics and skill as by brute force and courage.   All the movements of the Chinese were characterized by remarkable forethought, and evinced the greatest ability on the part of the general and his lieutenants, as well as obedience, valour, and patience on the part of his soldiers.   The rapid advance from Kuhwei to Karashar, the forced march thence to Bugur, the capture of Kucha, the forbearance of the conqueror towards the inhabitants, all combine to make this portion of the war most creditable to China and her generals, to Kin Shun in particular. The reason given in the Official Report for the Kashgarian authorities attempting to carry off the population was that the rebels wished in the first place to deprive the invading force of all assistance, thus making further pursuit a work of difficulty, and in the second place, to ingratiate themselves with the new Pahia (probably Bacha) of Kashgar, Kuli Beg, by delivering this large mass of Turki-Mussulmans into his hands.   Bayen Hu was, therefore, certainly not Hakim Khan.   It is tolerably clear that he must have been either a Tungan refugee or a subordinate of Beg Bacha's.

A depôt was formed at Kucha, and a large body of troops remained there as a garrison; but the principal administrative measures were directed to the task of improving the position of the Turki-Mussulman population.   A board of administration was instituted for the purpose of providing means of subsistence for the destitute, and for the distribution of seed-corn for the benefit of the whole community.   It had also to supervise the construction of roads, and the establishment of ferry boats, and of post-houses, in order to facilitate the movements of trade and travel, and to expedite the transmission of mails.   Magistrates and prefects were appointed to all the cities, and special precautions were taken against the outbreak of epidemic or of famine. All these wise provisions were carried out promptly, and in the most matter-of-fact manner, just as if the legislation. and administration of alien states were the daily avocations of Chinamen. There is no reason to believe that in the vast region from Turfan to Kucha the Chinese have departed from the statesmanlike and beneficent schemes which marked their re-installation as rulers; and whatever harshness or cruelty they manifested towards the Tungani rebels and the Kashgarian soldiers was more than atoned for by the mildness of their treatment of the people.

On the 19th, or more probably the 22nd of October, Kin Shun resumed his forward movement, encountering no serious opposition. His first halt was at a village called Hoser, where he halted for one night, which he employed in inditing the report to Pekin, which described the successes and movements of the previous three weeks. At the next town, known as Bai, Kin Shun halted to await the arrival of the rear-guard, under General Chang Yao. This force came up before the close of October, and the advance against Aksu was resumed. Up to this point the chief interest centred in the army south of the Tian Shan, and in the achievements of Kin Shun. Our principal, in fact our only, authority for this portion of the campaign is the *Pekin Gazette*.

We have now to describe the movements of the Northern Army, which was under the immediate command of Tso Tsung Tang, and which was operating in the north of the state, in complete secrecy. That general had under him, at the most moderate computation, an army of 28,000 men. By some it was placed at a higher figure; but a St. Petersburg paper, on the authority of a Russian merchant, who had been to Manas, computed it to be of that strength. It was concentrated in the neighbourhood of Manas, and along the northern skirts of the Tian Shan; and also on the frontier of the Russian dominions in Kuldja.   To all appearance this army was consigned to a part of enforced inactivity, since it was impossible to enter Kuldja, and thus proceed by their old routes through the passes of Bedal or Muzart.   But it was not so; the travels of Colonel Prjevalsky in the commencement of 1877 had not been unobserved by the Chinese, and it was assumed that where a Russian officer with his Cossack following could go, there also could go a Chinese army.   By those little-known passes, which are made by the Tekes and Great Yuldus rivers, the Chinese army, under Tso Tsung Tang, crossed over into Kashgaria; and it is probable that the two armies joined in the neighbourhood of Bai. It was by this stroke of strategy on the part of Tso Tsung Tang that the Chinese found themselves before the walls of Aksu, with an overwhelming army, at the very sight of which all thought of resistance died away from the hearts of the Mussulman peoples and garrisons.   Tso Tsung Tang appeared before the walls of Aksu, the bulwark of Kashgar on the east, and its commandant, panic stricken, abandoned his post at the first onset.   He was subsequently taken prisoner by an officer of Kuli Beg, and executed. The Chinese then advanced on Ush Turfan, which also surrendered without a blow.   As we said, the Chinese have not published any detailed description of this portion of the war, and we are consequently unable to say what their version is of those reported atrocities at Aksu and Ush Turfan, of which the Russian papers have made so much.   There is no doubt that a very large number of refugees fled to Russian territory, perhaps 10,000 in all, and these brought with them the tales of fear and exaggerated alarm.   We may feel little hesitation in accepting the assertion as true, that the armed garrisons were slaughtered without exception; but that the unarmed population and the women and children shared the same fate we distinctly refuse to credit.   There is every precedent in favour of the assumption that a more moderate policy was pursued, and there is no valid reason

why the Chinese should have dealt with Aksu and Ush
Turfan differently to Kucha or Turfan. The case of
Manas has been greatly insisted upon by the agitators
on this "atrocity" question; but there is the highest
authority for asserting that only armed men were massacred there. This the Chinese have always done; it is
a national custom, and they certainly did not depart from
it in the case of the Tungani and Kashgar. But there
is no solid ground for convicting them of any more
heinous crime, even in the instances of Manas and Aksu,
which are put so prominently forward.

Early in December the last move of all began against
the capital, and on the 17th of that month the Chinese
took it by a *coup de main*. Beg Kuli Beg, according to
one account, fought a battle outside the town, in which
he was defeated; according to another report, he had
withdrawn to Yarkand, whence he fled to Russian territory, when he heard of the fall of Kashgar. It is more
probable that he resisted the Chinese attack on Kashgar,
for he certainly reached Tashkent, in company with the
Kirghiz Chief, Sadic Beg, who was wounded in that
battle. With the fall of Kashgar the Chinese reconquest of Eastern Turkestan was completed, and the
other cities, Yangy Hissar and Yarkand, speedily shared
the same fate. Khoten and Sirikul also sent in formal
promises of subjection. But the capture of Kashgar
virtually closed the campaign. No further resistance
was encountered, and the new rulers had only to begin
the task of reorganization. When Kashgar fell the
greater portion of the army, knowing that they could
expect no mercy at the hands of the Chinese, fled to
Russian territory, and then spread reports of fresh
Chinese massacres, which probably only existed in their
own imagination. There can be no doubt that the
Chinese triumph has been thorough, and that it will be
many years before the people of Eastern Turkestan will
have again the heart to rebel against their authority.
The strength of China has been thoroughly demon-

strated, and the vindication of her prestige is complete. Whatever danger there may be to the permanence of China's triumph lies rather from Russia than from the conquered peoples of Tian Shan Nan Lu; nor is there much danger that the Chinese laurels will become faded even before an European foe. Tso Tsung Tang and his lieutenants, Kin Shun, who has since fallen into disgrace,—perhaps he had excited the envy of his superior—and Chang Yao, accomplished a task which would reflect credit on any army and any country. They have given a lustre to the present Chinese administration which must stand it in good stead, and they have acquired a personal renown that will not easily depart. The Chinese reconquest of Eastern Turkestan is beyond doubt the most remarkable event that has occurred in Asia during the last fifty years, and it is quite the most brilliant achievement of a Chinese army, led by Chinamen, that has taken place since Keen-Lung subdued the country more than a century ago. It also proves, in a manner that is more than unpalatable to us, that the Chinese possess an adaptive faculty that must be held to be a very important fact in every-day politics in Central Asia. They conquered Kashgar with European weapons, and by careful study of Western science and skill. Their soldiers marched in obedience to instructors trained on the Prussian principle; and their generals manœuvred their troops in accordance with the teachings of Moltke and Manteuffel. Even in such minor matters as the use of telescopes and field glasses we find this Chinese army well supplied. Nothing was more absurd than the picture drawn by some over-wise observer of this army, as consisting of soldiers fantastically garbed in the guise of dragons and other hideous appearances. All that belonged to an old-world theory. The army of Eastern Turkestan was as widely different from all previous Chinese armies in Central Asia as it well could be; and in all essentials closely resembled that of an European power. Its remarkable triumphs were chiefly attributable to the thoroughness with which China had in this instance adapted herself to Western notions.

With the flight of Beg Kuli Beg to Tashkent closed the career of the house of the Athalik Ghazi in Kashgar. Whatever turn events may take in this portion of Central Asia, whatever schemes there may be formed in Khokand, or elsewhere, of challenging anew the Chinese domination, it will not be round the banner of Kuli Beg that the ousted Khokandian officials will rally. By his flight in the hour of danger, by the hesitation which marked all his movements, and by the murder of his brother in cold blood, this prince, of whom much at one time was expected, has irretrievably ruined both his career and his reputation. If on any future occasion Russia should seek to play the part played of old by Khans of Khokand in the internal history of Kashgar, it will not be Kuli Beg whom they will put forward as their puppet. His old rival, Hakim Khan, stands a much better chance than he, more especially if it be true that he is the representative of the Khojas, being the son of Buzurg Khan, as many have asserted. But the fact remains clear, that all the dreams of Yakoob Beg of founding a personal dynasty in Eastern Turkestan are now dispelled beyond all prospect of realization.

CHAPTER XIV.

THE CHINESE FACTOR IN THE CENTRAL ASIAN QUESTION.

THE overthrow of the Tungani, and the reconquest of Kashgaria, have not completed the task that lay before Chinese generals and soldiers in Central Asia. Great and remarkable as those triumphs were, the Chinese are not satisfied with them, because there yet remains more work to be done. They have restored to the Emperor Tian Shan Nan Lu, but so long as the Russians hold Kuldja, Tian Shan Pe Lu is only half won back. Moreover, so long as a great military power is domiciled in Kuldja, China's hold on the country west of Aksu must be only on sufferance. As of old, the Chinese so often reconquered Kashgar, when it had shaken off the Chinese rule, from Ili, so might the Russians at their good pleasure play the same part against the Chinese. In short, the Russians remaining in Ili would neutralize all the advantages that China had secured by her recent military success. But, although there is a foundation of well grounded apprehension at the strategical advantages of Russia, at the root of China's demand for the surrender of Kuldja, that is not the only cause, or even the principal one, for the Chinese making it. Of all their Central Asian possessions, Ili was the most cherished, and it was to recover that region more especially that Tso Tsung Tang undertook those arduous campaigns which have so far ended in triumph, and which were designed for, among other purposes, the purpose of giving that Viceroy a prestige and influence that would enable him to play the rival to Li Hung Chang. Ili was their metropolis in Central Asia, and its fall marked the wide difference that there was between the Tungan-Khoja rising of 1862–63 and all its predecessors. The fall of Ili meant the fall of Chinese power, and Chinese power cannot be held to be completely restored so long as Ili remains in alien hands. On this point the Chinese are very keen.

Russia, on the other hand, hesitates to hand over Ili for various reasons. In the first place, it is not certain that China has *permanently* reconquered Eastern Turkestan, nor is it clear that the Imperial exchequer will be able to bear a continual strain upon it for Central Asian expenditure. Moreover there is the unknown quantity of the rivalry of Li Hung Chang and Tso Tsung Tang, and whatever influence the latter may have with the army and the ruling caste on account of his Mantchoo blood, the former holds the purse in his hands, and can at any momet paralyse Chinese activity and strength in Central Asia. The Russians also, whatever rash promises they may have given at Pekin—and they certainly did promise to retrocede Kuldja to China, whenever the Chinese should be strong enough to return to Central Asia—formally (*teste* General Kolpakovsky's proclamation) annexed Kuldja "in perpetuity." In the eyes of the people of Central Asia, that proclamation defines Russia s tenure of Kuldja, and not the vague promise that was uttered in the ears of the authorities at Pekin. Now Russia knows this as well as we do; and she is aware that no strict adherence to her word of honour will induce the people of. Western, as well as of Eastern, Turkestan to believe that she retrocedes Kuldja for any other cause than fear of the Chinese. The Khokandians, the Bokhariots, as well as the Kirghiz, the Calmucks, and the Kashgari, will all argue that Russia restores Kuldja not through any desire to fulfil her engagements, but simply because she cannot decline to fulfil them without engaging in a war with China, and her compliance with the demand would then be construed as an admission of her disinclination to encounter China in the field. In fact, even if Russia had promptly restored Kuldja, she would not have secured the credit she might have claimed for her good faith, and she would have had no guarantee that the Chinese would have rested content with the cession of Ili proper and not gone on to claim, in a moment of military arrogance, the restoration of the Naryn district, which China at a period of weakness had herself ceded to Russia more than twenty years ago. Then, besides these objections to the surrender of Kuldja on political grounds, there are commercial and fiscal reasons why Russia should be loth to restore this province. Not only has it become highly prosperous and thickly populated under Russian rule, but it has also been raised into one of the most fiscally remunerative portions of the Russian possessions in Central Asia, and then there is its admirable frontier in the Tian Shan, which places the future trade with the western parts of China more at its disposal, than it is through the Semipalatinsk and Chuguchak route, and, above all, it effectually dispels all sense of real danger from attack. The Chinese would find that to force the Tian Shan range into Kuldja would be a task almost impossible for them, and they would be compelled to enter the province from the north by Karkaru. By so doing, they would leave the whole of their flank and line of communication exposed to an attack with telling effect both at Manas and in Kashgar, and with a scientific foe such as Russia, no sane Chinaman could dream of attacking Kuldja except in the most overwhelming force. It may be as well to sketch here the history of Russia's rule in Kuldja from 1871 to the present time, before proceeding with the consideration of the questions aroused by the difficulty between Russia and China.

When an independent government had been founded in Kuldja in 1866, a ruler of the name of Abul Oghlan was placed upon the throne. He appears to have been a Tungan, and he certainly was a truculent and self-confident potentate. He refused to abide by the stipulations of the Treaties of Kuldja and Pekin, and in petty matters as in great, set himself in direct opposition to Russia. For five years he pursued his career undisturbed by exterior influences, and during that period he tolerated the inroads of his subjects into Russian territory, urged the Kirghiz tribes beyond his frontier to revolt, and forbade Russian merchants to enter his dominions. On a small scale, he aped the manners subsequently adopted by Yakoob Beg. But he was only a minor and insignificant despot. His people groaned under his tyranny, and the 75,000 slaves within his dominions were only too anxious to be relieved from their bondage by any deliverer whatsoever. The state of Kuldja, as administered by Abul Oghlan, was pre-eminently one that would fall to pieces at the first rude shock from outside. For five years, or thereabouts, the Russian authorities at Vernoe, Naryn, and in Semiretchinsk put up with his veiled hostility; but when it became evident that his state was on the eve of falling into divers fragments, of which Yakoob Beg would, probably, come in for the lion's share, the Russians, whose patience had become well-nigh exhausted, resolved not to be forestalled in Kuldja, either by the Athalik Ghazi, or the Tungani Confederation. A kind of *ultimatum* was presented to Kuldja, in which Abul Oghlan was given a last chance of retaining power, if he consented to ratify the terms of the past treaties with China. He does not appear to have distinctly refused to do so, when he was required to enter into this agreement with Russia. But he prevaricated and delayed, until at last the patience of the Muscovite authorities was quite exhausted. They resolved to destroy the government of Abul Oghlan, to annex Kuldja, and to bring their frontier down to the Tian Shan.

In May, 1871, Major Balitsky crossed the river Borodshudsir, which formed the boundary between the two countries, and, at the head of a small detachment, advanced some distance into the dominions of Abul Oghlan. His force, however, was small, and, after a brief reconnaissance, he retired within Russian territory. Six weeks afterwards the main body under General Kolpakovsky crossed the frontier into Kuldja and marched on the capital. That invading army consisted of only 1,785 men and sixty-five officers. At first the forces of Abul Oghlan offered a brave resistance, but the Russian cannon and rifles carried everything before them; and on the 4th of July the ruler presented himself at the Russian outposts. When taken before General Kolpakovsky, he said, " I trusted to the righteousness of my cause, and to the help of God. Conquered, I submit to the will of the Almighty. If any crime has been committed, punish the sovereign, but spare his innocent subjects." The next day the Russian general entered the capital after a campaign that had only lasted eight or nine days. Protection was promised to all who would lay down their arms, and the army of Abul Oghlan was disbanded. Abul Oghlan was pensioned, and Orel was appointed as his place of residence. Kuldja or "Dzungaria," as it is called in the proclamation, was annexed "in perpetuity," and became the Russian sub-governorship of Priilinsk. There can be no doubt but that the Russian occupation of Kuldja was an unqualified benefit to the inhabitants of that region. The declaration of the abolition of slavery alone released seventy-five thousand human beings from a life of hardship and hopelessness. The return of trade, which had become stagnant, ensured the prosperity and advancement of the active portion of the community, and during the seven years Russia has ruled in Kuldja, the people have steadily progressed in moral and material welfare. The population has during the same period remarkably increased, and the valleys of the Ili teem with a population at once contented and prosperous. The rule of Russia in Kuldja is the brightest spot in her Central Asian administration. The Chinese in demanding the retrocession of Kuldja labour under the one disadvantage that they come to oust a beneficent rule. This disadvantage is made the greater by the bad name the Chinese have earned in Kashgar and the Tungan country, by the atrocities they are said to have committed. Those who will take the trouble to scan the matter carefully, and to consult the *Pekin Gazette*, as much as they do the *Tashkent*, will find that these atrocities are for the most part the creation of panic, and of malicious observers, and in the few cases where Chinese vindictiveness overcame military discipline, as at Manas and Aksu, we have clear evidence that women and children were spared. The *Tashkent Gazette* has laboured strenuously, and not in vain, to disseminate the report of Chinese atrocities; and one London paper has so far assisted the object of the Russian press in raising a feeling of indignation against China, on account of these reported massacres in Eastern Turkestan, that it has placed translations of these charges before the English reader, and, on the authority of the *Tashkent Gazette*, has indicted and summarily convicted the Chinese of the grossest acts of inhumanity. We would venture to suggest, that in common fairness to the Chinese this journal should place before its readers the temperately worded and dignified reports that have appeared in the *Pekin Gazette* of those events upon which the *Tashkent Gazette* has commented so indignantly.

As we said, the Chinese are fully resolved to regain Ili. They may not be able to induce Russia easily to surrender it, yet they will not despair. In all probability they will fail altogether to re-acquire it by diplomatic means, yet they will not omit to employ all the artifices that are sanctioned by modern diplomacy. There have been rumours that China intended handing over to Russia a strip of territory in Manchuria, which would give to the Russian harbour of Vladivostock a land communication with the forts on the Amoor. But this rumour had no solid foundation, and the latest intelligence goes to show that China's successes beyond Gobi, instead of making her moderate in the north, have given her confidence sufficient to arouse her into a state of opposition to further encroachments on the part of Russia in that direction. It is now said that Russia demands pecuniary indemnification for the money she has expended in raising Kuldja to its present highly prosperous condition; and at a first glance nothing could seem fairer, nor do we think that the Chinese would have raised objections to the payment of a moderate sum. But the sum demanded by the Russians is far from moderate. The exact amount has not been mentioned, but the Chinese declare that it exceeds the total cost of the campaign in the north-west, and that certainly was not less than two millions sterling. This is, of course, too exorbitant, and is only put forward as a reason for declining to abide by her former agreement, and to give her diplomatists a *locus standi* in their discussions with the Chinese representatives. A Chinese Embassy has been authorized to proceed to St. Petersburg, and to endeavour to effect an understanding with Russia upon the Kuldja question; but it does not appear to have started, and the real settlement lies in the hands of Tso Tsung Tang and General Kaufmann. The latest report is that the former has demanded afresh the restoration of Kuldja; the Russian reply is awaited with eagerness and some anxiety. In the meanwhile the Chinese have suffered a local reverse of no significance at the hands of a chief of Khoten, and their power does not seem to extend south of Yarkand. But they are hurrying up reinforcements, and 20,000 fresh troops had reached Manas some weeks ago. They have also an extensive recruiting ground amongst the Calmucks, and their position of Chuguchak might be of great

strategical importance. If the Kuldja question give
rise to a Russo-Chinese war, the Chinese are sufficiently
numerous and sufficiently prepared to task the capacity
of an army of 20,000 Russians; and it is quite certain
there are not 5,000 in Kuldja at present. But the
Kuldja question, despite the prominence it has attained,
is only one, if the most important and pressing, of
those questions that are raised and suggested by the
appearance of the Chinese in Central Asia. More
especially is this the case if, as can scarcely be doubted,
the Russians refuse to restore Kuldja; yet the Chinese,
knowing the strength of their adversary, shall hesitate
to attack where they cannot but recognize that the
penalties of failure must be immense. In that event
the Kuldja question will long remain unsolved, and for
a time perhaps it will be forgotten. But the Chinese
will not forget, nor will they condone the offence. But
whatever may be the interval, and however great the
delay, the Kuldja question will continue to remain a
most important portion of Central Asian politics, and
must, so long as it is unsettled, operate in a manner
adverse to the interests of Russia. The Chinese need
only maintain their camps at Chuguchak, Karakaru,
Manas, Aksu, Ush Turfan and Kashgar, and slowly
bring up reinforcements from Kansuh and from the
Calmuck country, to render Russia's hold on Kuldja
dangerously insecure. In fact, in this matter the Chinese have the game in their own hands, and can play a
waiting game; whereas Russia can only hope to profit
by precipitation on the part of Tso Tsung Tang. If
the Chinese refuse to hold any intercourse with the
faithless Russians, and simply content themselves with
the declaration that they cannot re-enter into political
or commercial relations with them until Kuldja is re-
troceded, Russia can never rest tranquil either in Kuldja,
Naryn, or Khokand. Above all, so long as she is occupied in Western Asia as she is at present, she could
never dare to cross the path of China, and enter upon a

war which would rage from Vladivostock and the Amoor
to Kuldja and Kashgar. Therefore the settlement of
the Kuldja question is not such an easy matter as might
be supposed; nor does it find Russia so strong or China
so weak as might have been expected. But after all,
as we have just said, the Kuldja question is not the
only one suggested by the appearance of the Chinese in
Eastern Turkestan. There is the far wider one raised
by the appearance of the Chinese as a factor in the great
Central Asian question. The three great Asiatic Powers
have now converged upon a point; what is to be the
result?

The only way to be in a position to venture upon a
surmise as to the future, is to realize in its full significance the lessons of the past. What have been the
mutual relations between England, Russia, and China?
We have assumed throughout this volume, and we
shall assume here, the irreconcilable hostility of England and Russia, in Asia at all events, veneered over
as it is by a lacquer of politeness and civilization. We
have only to consider the relations between England
and China, and between Russia and China. To take
the latter first, they have always been united by ties of
friendship and reciprocity in commercial and political
rights. Their intercourse has been on the whole singularly harmonious, and while we have been compelled to
wage three wars to obtain a standing for our merchants
in the seaports, Russia, without being compelled to
resort to anything like the same extreme measures,
has been able to secure all she, or her merchants,
wanted in Middle and Western China. She has made
the Amoor a Russian river; she dominates the Yellow
and Japanese seas from Vladivostock; and she has
acquired in her position among the Khalkas, and in
Kuldja, two portals to various weak points in the
Chinese Empire. Yet all the time she has been on
terms of the closest amity with China. She has several
commercial treaties of the most favourable character,

and she has always been on the footing of "the most favoured nation." But she has been more than that; she has been the most favoured nation. But the Chinese have not failed to observe that this good understanding with Russia has, so far as advantages arising from it go, been a very one-sided affair. For all Russia's protestations of friendship and good-will, what advantages has China reaped from those high-flown promises? Whereas, the patriotic Chinaman has but to look to the Amoor, and to the attenuated province of Manchuria, to see what Russian friendship means. He can go farther still. He has only to enquire into the relations Russia has managed to conclude with the Taranath Lama; he has only to hear what the people of Ourga think of Russia's position in the vicinity of that important city; and he cannot fail to form a very clear and decided opinion as to what Russia's friendship signifies. The Chinese have, in the full extent of their northern frontier, a great question in discussion with Russia. So long as China was weak, and consequently unable to resent the patronage of her friend, so long was Russia able to play "my lady bountiful" with a good grace and perfect success. But the moment China became strong, and in a position to resent the condescension of her whilome ally, the Chinese took a different tone, and already we hear of the Chinese assuming a semi-hostile attitude in the Amoor region. But whereas China's apprehension—for it is apprehension that is at the root of her hostility to Russia, at Russia's designs in Manchuria and among the Khalkas is vague at present—her indignation is clear and easily defined at Russia retaining possession of Kuldja after she has demanded its restoration. In short, all her apprehension along the northern frontier, which has slumbered, but never died out, since the Russians seized the Amoor posts during the Crimean War, is reduced to a focus in Central Asia, where Russia appears inclined to throw herself in the path of, or at least to retard, their victorious career. It is not so much the Kuldja question, which is of local importance, that is of pressing moment, as the rupture between Russia and China, that a crisis in the Issik Kul region will make complete. That rupture has already taken place, and no concession on the part of Russia will restore her good name with the Chinese. She may hand Kuldja over now, or she may keep it by the strong arm if she can; but she has forfeited all claim to consideration by the Chinese, through delaying to accede to that which those people consider in every sense their right and due. Had Russia at once said to China, "We will abandon Kuldja, and only require you to guarantee the safety of the population," there would have been not only the preservation of the good understanding between the countries, but there might have been, for fresh purposes, a Russo-Chinese alliance in Central Asia. That alliance must have been fraught with danger to this country, and for reasons that will best be described under the head of Anglo-Chinese relations.

But the Russian authorities failed to grasp the situation in its full extent. They treated the Kuldja question as a mere local affair, and they trifled with the Chinese as if the latter had no very strong interest in the matter. They altogether ignored the terrible earnestness of the Chinese character, and they treated the demands of Tso Tsung Tang in a spirit of levity that must have roused the ire of that general. Their policy, regarded from any point of view, was shallow and unwise, but, bearing in mind the past tact and diplomatic skill shown by Russia in her dealings with China, it must appear more shallow and foolish. Of course this Kuldja question differs from all previous questions in the essential point of all, that here for the first time Russia had to go back instead of advancing, as always had been the case heretofore. The Russian authorities simply regarded the matter from the point of view of

what effect it would have upon the peoples of Central
Asia. They persuaded themselves that to hand over
Kuldja would be to give an impetus to every hostile
element in Western Turkestan, as well as to lower their
prestige generally throughout Asia. As a leading
Russian paper expressed it, " the retrocession of Kuldja
would be an act of political suicide, for not only would
it raise the prestige of China to a higher point than
ever before, but it would also undermine our position in
Eastern Asia, by giving the Chinese a strong military
position within our natural frontier. For these reasons
Kuldja cannot be restored." That paragraph sums up
the arguments the Russians will employ in defence of
their continuing to retain possession of Kuldja. They
add something to their effect in the popular mind by
diatribes against the Chinese for rumoured barbarities,
by drawing comparisons, flattering to themselves and
to their administrative capacity, between the present
condition of Kuldja, and what it would become under a
restored Chinese rule. In depicting what this would
be, they entirely ignore the prosperous condition of
Kuldja before the Tungan revolt, and they appear to
assume that the anarchy existing there, when they
entered it in 1871, was due to the Chinese, instead of
being caused by the ingratitude and fickleness of its
own people. And they shut their eyes to the great
benefits China conferred upon Central Asia during the
century that she was paramount therein. They would
like us, and every other observer of the crisis, to do the
same. That is impossible, for the teaching of history
is clear, and points to a diametrically opposite conclusion. We do not dispute the beneficence of Russia's
government of Kuldja. We freely admit it. That is
no reason for maligning the Chinese, and asserting that
they are utter barbarians ; nor is it a reason, in the eyes
of Chinamen, for a refusal to restore Kuldja. By
refusing to entertain the overtures of Tso Tsung Tang,
which were made, there is reason to believe, before the

attack on Yakoob Beg, the Russians huffed the Chinese;
and by procrastinating ever since, when questioned upon
the subject, they have still further displeased them.
The Russians are aware of this, and feel convinced that,
no matter how obliging they might be disposed to be,
the Chinese will now no longer appreciate their moderation. If we admit this, as can scarcely be gainsaid,
what becomes of the Kuldja question, and of its
peaceful solution that many claim to see? How can it
be peacefully solved, if Russia will not accede to the
terms from which China is resolved not to budge?
Surely not by a fresh commotion on the part of the
Mussulman population, which some persons have pre-
tended to forecast by magnifying a petty success that
has been obtained by the insignificant ruler of Khoten
over a Chinese detachment. Surely not by such trivial
circumstances as the hostility of an outlying dependency, will China be either expelled from Kashgar, or
induced to forego her claims on Kuldja. The success of
the Khoten chief is but a minor incident in the campaign, and for that district and its people it must be
pronounced a great misfortune. The Chinese will exact
a terrible revenge. The Kuldja question will not be
solved by such means, English readers can feel assured;
and the hostility of Russia and China towards each other
will become more pronounced every day. Already petty
disturbances are reported to have taken place along the
border. Russian merchants have been molested by parties
of brigands, among whom the assailed assert there were
Chinese soldiers; and no satisfaction could be obtained
from their generals. Representations have been made
to Tso Tsung 'Tang upon the subject, and his reply
has not been very amicable. Russian caravans, which
were always welcome during the progress of the war at
Manas, Karakaru, and Urumtsi, are now no longer
greeted with the same cordiality, and the Chinese are
evincing an intention to close their frontier to Russians.
Few caravans, the *Tashkent Gazette* informs us, now care

to leave Kuldja for the territory occupied by the Chinese army; and slowly, but none the less surely, is the old alliance between Russia and China departing to join the things that were, but are not. But, although so much is clear, it is almost impossible to predicate the future course of the Kuldja question. It is not probable that Tso Tsung Tang will openly attack the Russians, yet his hand may be forced by the home authorities, and he may be left no alternative between that and the abandonment of his enterprise. It must be always remembered that Russia's best weapon is intrigue at Pekin, and a skilful envoy might so far manipulate the rivalry between Tso and Li Hung Chang as to induce the latter to paralyze the ambition of the former by withholding supplies and reinforcements from the army of Central Asia. So unpatriotic a course would, we believe, be hateful to Li Hung Chang, and it, certainly, would be attended with great danger, sure to recoil upon his guilty head, if for a personal rivalry he debased himself so far as to become the tool of his country's foe. But yet it is in vain to deny that there is danger to the preservation of China's most cherished interests in the rivalry of some of her chief statesmen. The Kuldja question, which scarcely admits of peaceful solution in Central Asia, might be solved in the palace at Pekin more easily and more effectually than by a campaign on a large scale in Jungaria and Turkestan; and there is a possibility that Russia may by this means seek to nullify the danger from Tso Tsung Tang, and to stultify the recent Chinese successes. It is very doubtful whether they would succeed, for Chinese opinion runs high upon the topic, and the Mantchoo caste is united in its support of its member Tso Tsung Tang. Even if they did, it would only be shelving the Kuldja question, for so long as the Chinese remain in Kashgaria, and at Manas and Karakaru, they must regard the presence of Russia in Kuldja as a slight to themselves, as well as a menace to their line of communications.

But every probability is against their succeeding. Li Hung Chang's position is not so secure that he can dare to put himself in face of those who champion a national cause, as is the re-absorption of Chinese Turkestan. The return of Tso Tsung Tang with his veterans would be the least danger that the adoption of an unpatriotic policy would entail. If this home danger, then, does not arise, the Kuldja question will be settled between Tso and the Russian authorities in Khokand and Kuldja. The result of that discussion cannot be doubtful. The advocates on either side are soldiers, each equally confident in their own abilities and power, and each flushed by a long tide of success. They will come to the discussion of the question with heated blood and excited nerves; reason will not be the presiding goddess at the council board. There will be accusations and recriminations bandied from one side to the other. If such be the case, the Kuldja question will not be long in discussion, and before the close of the present year perhaps, but more probably early next spring, there will be war between Russia and China along the Tian Shan range. Even if Tso is content to permit his arguments to be clothed in diplomatic language, there will be no solution of the difficulty, so long as Russia remains where she is; and consequently the difference will be as great between Russia and China as if there were open hostilities between the countries. And this, after all, is the main point, for the destruction of all friendly sentiment between Russia and China means the addition of another element to " the great game in Central Asia," and that element, as an adverse one to Russia, is a beneficial circumstance for this country. The difference over the Kuldja question magnifies the previously existing discordant points between the countries, and irretrievably wrecks whatever prospect there once was of Russia and China pursuing an identical policy towards Baroghil and Cashmere. We have now to consider the past relations between England and China, in order that

we may be in a position to appreciate the full significance of China's reappearance in Central Asia, and
also what is to be the probable outcome of the gradual
approximation of the three Great Powers, and the slow
extinction of the once innumerable petty states of
Asia.

What, then, have been the mutual relations between
England and China in the past? There is no necessity
to enter into the question of the footing we are on along
the sea-coast, for that is really beside the question ; nor
need we recapitulate the wars which we have at various
times been compelled to wage in Eastern China. The
result of those wars, those treaties, and that constant
inter-communication has been, that Englishmen have
secured a foothold in many of the principal cities, and
that English trade is supreme there. But the relations
along the land frontier are quite the opposite of those
obtained on the sea-board, and they are influenced by
entirely different considerations. During the last century, and for a considerable portion of the present, we
were not, strictly speaking, neighbours of the Chinese ;
for between the two empires there intervened a belt of
semi-independent states, who nominally owned allegiance to China. Some of these were Nepaul, Sikhim,
Bhutan and Birmà, with its dependency of Assam. It
was in the days of Lord Cornwallis that we first realized
the significance of the fact that Chinese prestige had
penetrated south of the Himalaya. The Ghoorka rulers
of Nepaul had, on several occasions, molested the peaceable Tibetans, and at last had grown so bold, that on
one expedition they advanced as far as Lhasa, which
they plundered. At that moment the aged Keen-Lung
was meditating the retirement from public life, which a
few years afterwards, like the Asiatic Charles the Fifth
that he was, he adopted ; but, on the news of this insult
to his authority, his warlike spirit fired up, and he vowed
that the marauders of Khatmandoo should dearly pay
for their audacity. A large army, of the reputed strength

of 70,000 men, was collected, and the Chinese generals advanced by the Kirong Pass upon the Nepaulese capital. A desperate battle was fought along this elevated road, resulting in victory to the Chinese. Several other encounters took place with the same result, and the Ghoorkas were compelled to sue for terms. The Chinese showed no disposition to stay their advance, until Lord Cornwallis mediated between the foes, and peace ensued. Nepaul acknowledged its suzerainty to China, and agreed to send tribute every five years to Pekin. For more than half a century this was regularly sent, but during the last thirty years it has been either discontinued, or has grown irregular. But for us the main point is, after all, that the Chinese, although yielding to the remonstrance of Lord Cornwallis, really did so with a bad grace. We had stood between them and their prey.

But this was not the full extent of the mistake we had actually committed. We had annoyed the Chinese; but we had absolutely offended the people and the ruling Lamas of Tibet. Warren Hastings had sent two missions—one under Mr. George Bogle, the other under Captain Turner—to the Teshu Lama, and by means of these embassies had broken ground very happily in Tibet. He had also conferred an obligation upon him by dealing leniently with the intractable Bhutanese or Bhuteas; and he had followed up that sense of obligation by the despatch of two successful missions. When Lord Cornwallis threw the *ægis* of British protection over Nepaul, it is true that we had no diplomatic relationship with Tibet, but we were on a good footing with the people generally, having a native representative at Lhasa named Purungir Gosain, and being in high repute at Shigatze, the chief city of the southern portion of Tibet. The Tibetans, the instant the Ghoorkas raided their country, notified the same to our government, and requested its good offices to prevent the Ghoorkas invading their country. The Chinese, their lawful protectors, were so far away that much damage could be inflicted upon them before the Chinese could have time to despatch a vindicating army; therefore they appealed to their friends the English, whom they had always found so just, for assistance in their extremity. Their appeal was evidently made with the impression that it would be granted. Therefore it was with double regret they saw the English remain indifferent while the Ghoorkas were pressing on against Lhasa, and ravaging the fertile districts watered by the Sanpu. But their regret and surprise at our government remaining indifferent were as nothing compared with their indignation when they learnt that we were actually interfering on behalf of the marauding Ghoorkas. We saved the Ghoorkas from condign chastisement, and we of course prevented the establishment of a Chinese garrison at Khatmandoo, which we could whenever we chose have easily expelled; but we offended the Tibetans and the Chinese, and induced them to unite in a policy of hostility against ourselves. After that war (1792) the Himalayan passes were closed against us, and the Chinese block-houses have effectually barred the way to Tibet and Northern Asia ever since. Mr. Thomas Manning, one of the most intrepid and highly gifted of English travellers, penetrated into Tibet in 1812, and resided there some time. But that is the only instance in which an English traveller overcame Bhutea and Ghoorka indifference and Chinese hostility. Tibet remains a sealed book, and, despite treaty rights to enter it, no Englishman goes thither, although the attraction is great, and the prize to be secured far from vague or trivial. The assumed reason is the covert hostility of the Chinese.

If we turn farther to the east, to Assam—which we have absorbed—to Birmà, and even to Siam, we find the same causes in operation. We recognized in Yunnan the Panthay Sultan of Talifoo; we have always striven to treat the kings of Birmà and Siam as independent princes, whereas they are only Chinese vassals; and we are believed to have carried on intrigues with the Shans and other tribes beyond the Assamese frontier. These steps may be prudent or they may not for other reasons; but they certainly are imprudent for the reason that they offend the Chinese. As a policy intended to conciliate the Chinese, our frontier policy on the north and the east has been the worst possible, and a tissue of blunders from beginning to end; and the result is that for the last half-century we have lived on the very worst terms with the Chinese. We should have conciliated them, but we aroused instead all their latent suspicion and dislike. We should have become friendly neighbours, and, on the contrary, we are neighbours who, if not decidedly hostile to each other, shun each other's presence. And the real base of our sentiment towards the Chinese is to be seen in the fact that one of the first articles in the creed of Indian state policy is "to keep China as far off as possible." That precept, which may have been very useful, has served its turn, and it is time that our Indo-Chinese policy should be set upon a new basis. With China once more supreme upon our whole northern frontier, and with her presenting ultimatums at Bangkok, and coercing the ruler of Mandalay as she esteems fit, it is high time for us, apart from the Central Asian question altogether, to set our house in order with the Chinese. The mistakes we made in championing the Ghoorkas, in acknowledging the Panthays, and in a general policy of indifference to Chinese opinion, have all tended to bring about the present deadlock in our relations with China. Our acknowledgment of the Athalik Ghazi cannot have conduced to the creation of any very friendly sentiment among the Chinese towards us, and, therefore, at the present moment we must assume that the state of feeling existing among the Chinese in Tibet and Yunnan towards us exists in Kashgaria also; and that feeling is a veiled hostility. Therefore, while the Chinese are beginning to regard Russia with the hostile feelings that once were reserved for England, they have by no means altered their old sentiments towards us. We have done nothing whatever to induce them to do so. We have not helped them in any way to regain Kashgar, and on the whole English opinion may be said to have been more adverse to, than in favour of, their claims. They have found in the arsenals of Kashgar and Yarkand many proofs of England's alliance with, and friendship for, Yakoob Beg; and, on the other hand, they certainly owe much to the assistance of Russian merchants, and the forbearance of the Russian government. Nor should we for an instant delude ourselves with the fallacy that the Chinese will look to us for aid against Russia, as Yakoob Beg did. They have conquered Eastern Turkestan without us—in fact, despite of our moral opposition; and they will retain it if they can by their own right arms. It will not enter their head for an instant to play the old game of Yakoob Beg, of setting England off against Russia. But, although they will play a perfectly independent game, it by no means follows that they will be hostile to this country, if by some fortunate stroke of diplomacy we could bring home to their minds the fact that England is glad at the result of the war in Central Asia, however much she may have failed during its progress to recognize which was the rightful cause. But what is that fortunate stroke of diplomacy to be? and how is it to be brought to pass? To each of these questions it would be rash to give any confident reply. In dealing with the Chinese we are not only treating with a people whom we very imperfectly understand, but also with a government the secret springs of whose policy we neither know nor appreciate. The action we might therefore adopt, founded though it should be on the experience of some Englishman versed in the mysteries of China, might fail to accomplish what it seemed calculated to secure. It might be crowned with success, it might be condemned with failure. Of course the first thing to decide is, how are we to take official cognizance of China's reconquest of Kashgaria, and how are we to bring home to the minds of Tso Tsung Tang and his lieutenants the knowledge that we have repented of our shortsighted policy towards Yakoob Beg, and are willing to atone for it in so far as we are able by an ample recognition of the change in affairs north of the Karakoram?

The Che-foo Convention gave us the right to send an embassy to Tibet, on the condition that it should be acted upon within a given space. We did not avail ourselves of that concession, and the Chinese, we are informed, consider that the right has lapsed. We may have been wise or we may have been foolish—in my opinion we have been foolish—in declining to enforce the only real concession China made, in reparation for the murder of Mr. Margary. Does this concession, which we never made use of, entitle us to send a mission to the Chinese in Kashgar? Acting upon this precedent, are we justified in supposing that the Chinese would hold out a hand of friendship to an English envoy coming from Leh to Yarkand? It is much to be feared that it would not. At the present moment, too, the country must be in such a disturbed state, that the Chinese would have a ready excuse if any accident befel our envoy. Moreover, at the present moment an envoy would have no definite object before him. A few years hence, when the Chinese rule shall be completely restored throughout Eastern Turkestan, it may be reasonable to expect a revival of trade in this direction; but at present it would be premature to agitate for it. Nor would a simple embassy of congratulation look well. We have too recently befriended the Athalik Ghazi to make our congratulations to his conqueror anything but a mockery. The Chinese would be puffed up with vanity, and think that we were only worshipping their rising sun. Whatever action we do take in Central Asia, to effect an understanding with the

Chinese, we must be very careful that it has been well considered, and that it is as cautious as it must be clearly defined. Any mistake would be simply fatal to the preservation of good relations with China. Therefore, we must do nothing. *Quieta non movere* must be our motto, and we must only look forward to some auspicious occasion when it may be possible to enter into cordial relations with China.

But, although our hands are tied in Central Asia, they are not fettered at Pekin, and we certainly should congratulate, if we have not done so already, the Chinese on their remarkable successes in the Tian Shan regions. That step might be pregnant with beneficent results, and our desire to be on good terms with our new, yet our old, neighbour might be met in a cordial manner by the Chinese. The Chinese will not stoop to propitiate us in order to preserve their rule in Eastern Turkestan ; but it is against common sense to suppose that they will be eager to embroil themselves with us at the same moment that they are quarrelling with the Russians. The Kuldja question must throw China into our alliance, if we are not precipitate, and do not offer her any slight by meddling with this semi-independent chief of Khoten, who is said to have overthrown a Chinese detachment. And, in negotiating with the rulers of Kashgaria, we must remember that commercial advantages are all very well, but that political are infinitely more important. It has been tersely said that we patronized Yakoob Beg in order to make a market for Kangra tea ; but the very trivial advantages we secured in a commercial sense were far more than counterbalanced by the political disadvantages we derived from a recognition of the Athalik Ghazi. In dealing with the Chinese we must not set before us, as our guiding star, the privilege of supplying the good people of Kashgar and Yarkand with tea and other necessaries. What we aspire to is to be on terms of amity with China, as a power in Central Asia, which will possess everything it desires when Ili has been restored, and which must accordingly be inclined to resent with us the undue aggrandizement of Russia. These are the future advantages that may accrue from an understanding between England and China. But at the present juncture there are others similar in kind, but immediate in effect. The Afghan question, which now clamours for solution, and which will scarcely pass through this crisis without finding our hold on Cabul made more assured, is in many respects connected with the Kuldja.

In each case the ambition of Russia is the motive power, and in each she seeks to play her game with as little risk, and as much gain, as possible. In neither will she fight, if she can avoid the necessity, yet in each there is a point beyond which her honour and her interests alike refuse to permit her to remain concealed and neutral. The solution of the two questions is being worked out simultaneously, and the progress of the Afghan question will at least very seriously affect the later stages of the Kuldja. If Russia has to fight to defend Shere Ali, then we may be sure that Tso Tsung Tang's legions will not remain inactive, and that General Kolpakovsky will either have to beat a retreat to Vernoe, or engage in a war out of which, on his own resources alone, it will be impossible for him to issue victorious. If Russia interfere openly in defence of Shere Ali, Kuldja must be restored to the Chinese, otherwise Russia's flank would be exposed to a crushing blow, which the Chinese would not be slow to take advantage of. Present events on the Ili and on the Cabul have, therefore, this much in common, that they both aim, directly or indirectly, at the fabric of Russian supremacy in Central Asia. The occupation of Afghanistan by England, or even a partial occupation of it as is very probable, would seriously weaken Russian prestige in Western Turkestan. A Chinese occupation of Kuldja would undermine her position in Vernoe and Naryn and

among the Kirghiz. Admitting these, is it not natural
to suppose that in each case Russia will fight, or that,
even if she does not fight in each case, she will fight
in the one that she may deem of the most importance?
But we need not pursue the subject farther. The
Chinese are face to face with Russia in the heart of
Central Asia, just as a few short months ago they were
opposed to Yakoob Beg and the power of the Tungani.
Their army is drawn up in hostile array; it is each
day becoming more numerous and more perfectly prepared. Its generals are the same who have led it to
constant victory; its main body is the veterans of
three campaigns. The Chinese are persuaded, and it is
impossible to say not justly persuaded, of the righteousness of their cause. The Russians can have no equal
confidence either in their strength, or in their moral
position. They are not exactly championing a bad
cause, or a lost one, but, in comparison to the Chinese,
they have no legal position. It remains to be seen
whether by force of arms, or by diplomatic superiority,
they can make up for the flaw in their tenure of Kuldja.
Farther on, in the vista of the events yet to come, there
looms the prospect of an Anglo-Chinese alliance, that
must be most beneficial to the peoples of Asia generally.
But, before it will be possible for Englishmen to count
upon the presence of the Chinese as a favourable "factor
in the Central Asian question," our relations with China
must be placed upon a firmer and a more friendly basis
than any which has yet existed. We have it in our
power to do this, and the ever-widening breach between
Russia and China simplifies our task in no slight degree.
The day will come when Russia will discover that the
Kuldja question was no trivial matter at all, and that
to it can be traced many important events in Central
Asia. England may also recognize in it one of the most
useful circumstances that have ever operated in her
favour in her long rivalry with Russia. At the very
crisis of our border history, when we are on the eve of

dealing out well merited chastisement to an Ameer of Cabul, Russia finds herself weakened by being compelled to discuss a question with China, when her attention is required elsewhere. She will not yield what the Chinese demand, yet she dare not refuse; and the latter will simply bide their time until she is hampered elsewhere. It is no rash prophecy to say that China will be re-installed, either by peaceful means or by force, in Kuldja before the close of next year, probably long before. An alliance between any two of the three great Asiatic Powers must then be conclusive in all Central Asian matters, and, before that alliance, the third will have the prudence to submit. It behoves us to learn our lesson, when that day comes, thoroughly and in good time.

APPENDIX.

THE POSITION OF LOB-NOR.

LAKE LOB-NOR is placed in the map accompanying this volume in accordance with the explorations of Colonel Prjevalsky in 1876-77 ; the result of which was published in Dr. Petermann's *Mittheilungen* as an extra number during the spring of the present year. The accuracy of the gallant explorer in identifying Lob-Nor with his lake of Kara Koshun had not been challenged when this map was drawn, and when the following good reasons for doubting its accuracy were published on the 14th of September, it was too late to make the necessary alteration.

The quotation of Baron Ferdinand von Richthofen's strictures on Colonel Prjevalsky's lakes is taken from the *Athenæum* of the 14th of September, 1878 :—

"It would appear that the Russian traveller Prejevalsky, in his last remarkable journey in the heart of Central Asia, did not explore Lob-Nor at all, as he claims to have done. Baron Ferdinand von Richthofen, one of the first comparative geographers of the day, has examined the account of the journey, more especially by the light of Chinese literature, and proves, almost incontestably to our thinking, that the true Lob-Nor must lie somewhere north-east of the so-called Kara Kotchun Lake discovered by Prejevalsky, and that, in all probability, it is fed by an eastern arm of the Tarim river. This, at all events, would account for the remarkable diminution in bulk undergone by the waters of that stream as they proceed southward, which could not but strike an attentive reader of the Russian explorer's narrative. We have not space to reproduce all the arguments which Von Richthofen adduces, but the more important are these:—Prejevalsky's lake was fresh, whereas Lob-Nor has been called *The* Salt Lake, *par excellence*, in all ages; Shaw, Forsyth, and other authorities, report that the name Lob-Nor was known in those regions, whereas Prejevalsky found no such name applied to his lake; the Chinese maps, of the accuracy of which Von Richthofen has had repeated proofs, represent Lob-Nor as lying more to the north-east, and call two lakes lying nearly in the position of those discovered by Prejevalsky, Khasomo, Khas being the Mongolian for jade, a famous product of Khotan of which mediæval traders from China went in quest, passing by these very lakes *en route.* Another important argument is, as we have mentioned, based on the bulk of water discharged by the Tarim at its mouth. Von Richthofen's theory presupposes that the Tarim River has altered its course, and that the main rush of water is now south-east instead of due east as formerly. The whole question is well worthy of further investigation, and it is possible that Prejevalsky, whom a recent telegram from St. Petersburg reports about to return to Central Asia, may be enabled to elucidate it. He will return to Zaissan, the Russian frontier post, and thence endeavour to make his way into Tibet by way of Barkul and Hami.

" It is, however, certain that he will encounter great, if not insuperable, obstruction, for we learn from private advices from India, that the ill-advised publication in the Chefoo Convention of the then proposed mission to Tibet has resulted in the issue of the most stringent orders to the Tibetan officials at all the various routes and passes to allow no European traveller to enter into the country on any pretext whatever."

Having stated the view of Baron Ferdinand von Richthofen, which is endorsed by the high authority of the *Athenæum*, and which bears, moreover, conviction upon its face, it is but fair to give the vital portion of Colonel Prjevalsky's own description. The *Geographical Magazine*, for May, 1878, contains *in extenso* the report, and the sentences here quoted are from that translation.

"At a distance of fifteen versts from the smaller lake, Kara Buran, the party diverged southward to the village of Charchalyk, built about thirty years ago by outlaws from Khotan, of which there are at present 114 engaged in tilling fields for the state. . . . . Where Charchalyk now stands, and also at the distance of two days' journey from it, are the ruins of two towns, called Ottogush-Shari (from Ottogush, a former ruler) and Gas-Shari respectively. Close to Lob-Nor (Kara Koshun) are the ruins of a third and pretty extensive town called Kune-Shari. From inquiries, Prejevalsky ascertained that about 1861 or 1862 a colony of Russians numbering about 160 or 170 people, including women and children, with their pack-horses and armed with flint-lock muskets, settled on the Lower Tarim and at Charchalyk, but that they made no long stay, and soon returned to Urumchi, via Turfan. . . . . Turning to the Lob-Nor Lake (Kara Koshun), which the travellers reached in the early days of February, it should be observed that the Tarim discharges itself first into a smaller lake (from thirty to thirty-five versts in length, and between ten and twelve versts in breadth) called Kara Buran (*i.e.* black storms) into which the Cherchen-daria flows as well. A great part of the Kara Buran, as well as of Lob-Nor, is overgrown with reeds, the river flowing in its bed in the centre. The name Lob-Nor is applied by the natives to the whole lower course of the Tarim, the larger lake being called Chok-kul or Kara Koshun. This lake, or rather morass, is in the shape of an irregular ellipse running south-west and north-east.

"Its major axis is about 90 or 100 versts in length, its minor axis not more than twenty versts. This information is derived from the natives, as Prejevalsky himself explored only the southern and western end, and proceeded by boat down the river for about half the length of the lake, further progress being rendered impossible by the increasing shallowness of the water and the masses of reeds in every direction. The water itself is clear and sweet, though there are salt marshes all round the lake, and beyond them a strip of ground parallel with the present borders of the lake and overgrown with tamarisks. It is probable that this strip was formerly the periphery of the lake, and this conclusion is corroborated by the natives, who say that thirty years ago the lake was deeper."

It is clear that the true position of Lob-Nor has yet to be defined by modern exploration, but we may safely assume with the *Athenæum* that Colonel Prjevalsky's Kara Koshun is *not* Lob-Nor. The accompanying map then, in this particular, is unfortunately erroneous.

There is every reason for believing that Lob-Nor will be found in the position assigned to it on the Chinese chart, the accurracy of which has been so strikingly proved by the correct position given to the two lakes Khas-omo, which are identical with the Kara Koshun and Kara Bunar of Prjevalsky.

It would be most interesting to obtain a diary or other account of those Russian settlers mentioned by Prjevalsky, who entered the *terra incognita* of Central Asia during the halcyon days after the signature of the Treaty of Kuldja, and just before the outbreak of the Tungan revolt. It is possible that they may have solved during their return journey to Urumtsi the enigma of Lob-Nor without knowing what they had achieved. The reader will, therefore, have the kindness to bear in mind that Lob-Nor is really (probably about three-quarters of a degree) north-east of where it is placed on the map, and that the lake represented there is only the Kara Koshun, or Chok Kul of Colonel Prjevalsky.

The most recent information is, that Colonel Prjevalsky adheres to his view as to the position of Lob-Nor, and is preparing a reply which will be published in a few weeks from this date (October 1st).

TREATY BETWEEN RUSSIA AND CHINA.

Treaty of Commerce concluded between Russia and China, at Kuldja, on the 25th Day of July, 1851, and ratified on the 13th Day of November, 1851.

The plenipotentiary of His Majesty the Emperor of All the Russias, and the plenipotentiaries of His Majesty the Bogdokhan of Tatsing, hereby declare; the Governor General of Ili, and its dependent provinces, as well as his deputy, have, after consulting together, concluded in the city of Ili (Kuldja), in favour of the subjects of both empires, a Treaty of Commerce, which establishes a traffic in the cities of Ili (Kuldja), and of Tarbagatai (Chuguchak). This treaty is composed of the following articles :—

Article I.

The present Treaty of Commerce, concluded in the interests of both powers, by demonstrating their mutual solicitude for the maintenance of peace between, as well as for the well-being of, their respective subjects, ought to draw still closer together those links of friendship which at the present moment unite the two Powers.

Article II.

The merchants of the two Empires will regulate between themselves the interchange of commerce, and arrange the various charges at their own will, and without any extraneous pressure. On the part of Russia a consul will be appointed to superintend the affairs of all Russian subjects; and on the part of China, a functionary of the superior administration of Ili. In the event of any collision between the subjects of either Power, each of these agents will decide, in accordance with justice, the affairs of his own countrymen.

Article III.

This commerce being opened in consideration of the mutual friendship of the two Powers, it will not be in contravention of existing rights on either side.

Article IV.

Russian merchants going either to Ili (Kuldja) or to Tarbagatai (Chuguchak) will be accompanied by a syndic (caravanbashi). When a caravan going to Ili (Kuldja) shall arrive at the Chinese picket of Boro-khondjir, and when that destined for Tarbagatai (Chuguchak) shall reach the first Chinese picket, the syndic shall present to the officer of the guard the certificate of his government. The said officer, after having noted the number of men, of beasts, and of loads of merchandise, shall permit the caravan to pass, and shall furthermore cause it to be escorted from picket to picket by an officer and soldiers. During the march, all disturbance, or cause for such, shall be interdicted to soldiers and merchants alike.

Article V.

In order to facilitate the task of officers and soldiers, Russian merchants shall be obliged, in virtue of the present treaty, to follow the route chosen by their body guard, both going and returning.

Article VI.

If, whilst Russian caravans follow their route outside the limit of the guard of Chinese soldiers, bands of brigands from the outer clans (Kirghiz) shall commit acts of pillage, of assault, or other crimes, the Chinese government shall not be required to interfere in the matter. When the caravan shall have arrived on Chinese territory, similarly also during its residence in the factories where merchandise is stored, Russian merchants must themselves guard and defend their property. They will be expected still more carefully to look after their animals when out at pasturage. If, despite all precaution, something should happen to go astray, notice of such loss must be promptly given to the Chinese official; who conjointly with the Russian consul shall trace out with all possible diligence the lost article. If traces of it are discovered, and those in a village held by Chinese subjects, and the thief be captured, the punishment shall be prompt and severe. If the thing lost be recovered, or any portion of it, it shall be restored to the person to whom it belonged.

Article VII.

In the event of disputes, litigations, or other trivial incidents, between the respective subjects, the Russian consul and the Chinese official, of whom mention has previously been made, shall use all their efforts to settle the affair satisfactorily. But if, despite every effort to avoid such, a criminal case or one of general importance should arise, it shall be decided conformably with the regulations actually in force on the Kiachta frontier.

Article VIII.

Russian merchants shall arrive each year with their merchandise between the 25th day of March and the 10th day of December (of our style, or according to the Chinese calendar between the day Tchin-ming and the day Tong-tchi); after the latter of these dates, the arrival of caravans shall cease. If the merchandise imported during that period ($8\frac{1}{2}$ months) should not be sold, it shall be permissible to the merchants to remain a longer space in China, in order to complete their sale; after which the consul shall take charge of their departure. It is moreover understood that Russian merchants shall not obtain an escort of officers and soldiers, neither for going nor for returning, if they have not at the least twenty camels laden with merchandise. If a merchant or the Russian consul has need for some special matter to send an express message, every facility shall be accorded him for doing so. But in order that the service of officers and soldiers should not become too onerous, there shall only be twice in the same month these extraordinary expeditions outside the line of the advanced guards.

Article IX.

Russian and Chinese merchants can see each other without restriction about matters of business; but Russian subjects, finding themselves in the factory under the care of the Russian consul, may not walk about in the suburbs and the streets, unless provided with a " permit " from the consul; without such permit, they must not go out of their enclosure. Whoever shall go out without permission shall be led back to the consul, who will proceed against him according to law.

Article X.

If a criminal belonging to either of the two Empires should flee to the other, he shall not be afforded sanctuary; but, on the part of each Power, the local authorities shall take the most severe measures, and make the most searching enquiries to arrest him. There shall be reciprocal extradition of fugitives of this class.

Article XI.

As it is to be foreseen that the Russian merchants, who shall come to China on commercial matters, will have with them carriages and beasts of burden, there shall be assigned for their use, near the city of Ili, certain places on the banks of the river Ili, and also near the city of Tarbagatai other places where there is both water and pasturage. In these encampments the Russian merchants shall confide their animals to the charge of their own people, who shall take care that neither cultivated lands nor cemeteries shall be in any case injured or desecrated. Those who may contravene this enactment shall be brought before the consul to be punished.

Article XII.

In the exchange of articles of merchandise between the merchants of the two Empires, nothing shall be left on credit on either side. If, notwithstanding this clause, some one should purchase his merchandise on credit, the Russian and Chinese officials shall on no account interfere, and shall admit of no complaint, even if cause for such might exist.

Article XIII.

As Russian merchants arriving in China for commercial reasons should necessarily have special places for their warehouses, the Chinese government shall assign them, in the two commercial cities of Ili and Tarbagatai, plots of land near the bazaar, so that the Russian subjects may be able to construct there, at their own expense, dwelling-houses and factories for their wares.

Article XIV.

The Chinese government shall not interpose obstacles in any case where Russian subjects celebrate, within their own buildings, divine service according to the rite of their religion. In case a Russian subject in China should happen to die either at Ili or at Tarbagatai, the Chinese government shall set apart an empty space outside the walls of those cities, to serve as a cemetery.

Article XV.

If Russian merchants should take to Ili or Tarbagatai sheep for the purpose of exchanging them, the local authorities shall take, on account of the government, two sheep out of every ten, and shall give in exchange for each sheep a piece of linen cloth (*da-ba*, of the legal measure); the remainder of the animals and every other kind of merchandise shall be exchanged between the merchants of the two Empires at a price mutually agreed upon, and the Chinese government shall not intermeddle in any manner whatsoever.

Article XVI.

The ordinary official correspondence between the two Empires shall be made, on the part of the Russian government, through the medium of the superior administration of Western Siberia, and under the seal of that administration ; and on the part of the Chinese government through the medium, and under the seal, of the superior administration of Ili.

Article XVII.

The present Treaty shall be authenticated by the signatures and seals of the respective plenipotentiaries. On the part of Russia there will be prepared four copies in the Russian language, signed by the plenipotentiary of Russia; on the part of China, four copies in the Mantchoo language, signed by the Chinese plenipotentiary and his adjunct. The respective plenipotentiaries will each keep a copy in the Russian language, and a copy in the Mantchoo, for the purpose of putting the treaty into execution, and to serve for constant reference. A Russian copy and a Mantchoo copy shall be sent to the directing Senate of Russia; and a copy in each language to the Chinese Tribunal for Foreign Affairs, to be there sealed and preserved after the ratification of the Treaty.

All the above articles of the present Treaty concluded by the respective plenipotentiaries of Russia and China are hereby signed and sealed. The twenty-fifth day of July, in the year 1851, in the 26th year of the reign of His Imperial Majesty the Emperor and Autocrat of All the Russias.

(Signed) Colonel in the corps of Engineers.

KOVALEVSKI.
1 Chan,
Bovyantai.

TREATY BETWEEN ENGLAND AND CASHMERE.

TREATY BETWEEN THE BRITISH GOVERNMENT AND HIS HIGHNESS MAHARAJA RUNBEER SINGH, G.C.S.I., MAHARAJA OF JUMMOO AND CASHMERE, HIS HEIRS AND SUCCESSORS, EXECUTED ON THE ONE PART BY THOMAS DOUGLAS FORSYTH, C.B., IN VIRTUE OF THE FULL POWERS VESTED IN HIM BY HIS EXCELLENCY THE RIGHT HONOURABLE RICHARD SOUTHWELL BOURKE, EARL OF MAYO, VISCOUNT MAYO OF MONYCROWER, BARON NAAS OF NAAS, K.P., G.M.S.I., P.C., &c., &c., &c., VICEROY AND GOVERNOR-GENERAL OF INDIA, AND ON THE OTHER PART BY HIS HIGHNESS MAHARAJA RUNBEER SINGH AFORESAID, IN PERSON.

WHEREAS in the interest of the high contracting parties and their respective subjects it is deemed desirable to afford greater facilities than at present exist for the development and security of trade with Eastern Turkestan, the following Articles have with this object been agreed upon :—

ARTICLE I.

With the consent of the Maharaja, officers of the British Government will be appointed to survey the trade routes through the Maharaja's territories from the British frontier of Lahoul to the territories of the Ruler of Yarkand, including the route *via* the Chang Chemoo Valley. The Maharaja will depute an officer of his Government to accompany the surveyors, and will render them all the assistance in his power. A map of the routes surveyed will be made, an attested copy of which will be given to the Maharaja.

Article II.

Whichever route towards the Chang Chemoo Valley shall, after examination and survey as above, be declared by the British Government to be the best suited for the development of trade with Eastern Turkestan shall be declared by the Maharaja to be a free highway in perpetuity, and at all times for all travellers and traders.

Article III.

For the supervision and maintenance of the road in its entire length through the Maharaja's territories, the regulation of traffic on the free highway described in Article II., the enforcement of regulations that may be hereafter agreed upon, and the settlement of disputes between carriers, traders, travellers, or others using that road, in which either of the parties or both of them are subjects of the British Government or of any foreign State, two Commissioners shall be annually appointed, one by the British Government, and the other by the Maharaja. In the discharge of their duties, and as regards the period of their residence, the Commissioners shall be guided by such rules as are now separately framed, and may, from time to time, hereafter be laid down by the joint authority of the British Government and the Maharaja.

ARTICLE IV.

The jurisdiction of the Commissioners shall be defined by a line on each side of the road, at a maximum width of two statute *koss*, except where it may be deemed by the Commissioners necessary to include a wider extent for grazing grounds. Within this maximum width the surveyors appointed under Article I. shall demarcate and map the limits of jurisdiction which may be decided on by the Commissioners as most suitable, including grazing grounds; and the jurisdiction of the Commissioners shall not extend beyond the limits so demarcated. The land included within these limits shall remain in the Maharaja's independent possession, and, subject to the stipulations contained in this Treaty, the Maharaja shall continue to possess the same rights of full sovereignty therein as in any other part of his territories, which rights shall not be interfered with in any way by the Joint Commissioners.

ARTICLE V.

The Maharaja agrees to give all possible assistance in enforcing the decisions of the Commissioners, and in preventing the breach or evasion of the regulations established under Article III.

ARTICLE VI.

The Maharaja agrees that any person, whether a subject of the British Government, or of the Maharaja, or of the Ruler of Yarkand, or of any foreign State, may settle at any place within the jurisdiction of the Commissioners, and may provide, keep, maintain, and let for hire at different stages the means of carriage and transport for the purposes of trade.

Article VII.

The two Commissioners shall be empowered to establish supply depôts, and to authorize other persons to establish supply depôts, at such places on the road as may appear to them suitable; to fix the rates at which provisions shall be sold to traders, carriers, settlers, and others, and to fix the rent to be charged for the use of any rest-houses or serais that may be established on the road. The officers of the British Government in Kullu, &c., and the officers of the Maharaja in Ladakh shall be instructed to use their best endeavours to supply provisions on the indent of the Commissioners at market rates.

Article VIII.

The Maharaja agrees to levy no transit duty whatever on the aforesaid free highway, and the Maharaja further agrees to abolish all transit duties levied within his territories on goods transmitted in bond through His Highness's territories from Eastern Turkestan to India and *vice versá*, on which bulk may not be broken within the territories of His Highness. On goods imported into or exported from His Highness's territory, whether by the aforesaid free highway or any other route, the Maharaja may levy such import or export duties as he may think fit.

Article IX.

The British Government agree to levy no duty on goods transmitted in bond through British India to Eastern Turkestan or to the territories of His Highness the Maharaja. The British Government further agree to abolish the export duties now levied on shawls and other textile fabrics manufactured in the territories of the Maharaja, and exported to countries beyond the limits of British India.

Article X.

This Treaty, consisting of ten Articles, has this day been concluded by Thomas Douglas Forsyth, C.B., in virtue of the full powers vested in him by His Excellency the Right Honourable Richard Southwell Bourke, Earl of Mayo, Viscount Mayo, of Monycrower, Baron Naas of Naas, K.P., G.M.S.I., P.C., &c., &c., Viceroy and Governor-General of India, on the part of the British Government, and by the Maharaja Runbeer Singh aforesaid; and it is agreed that a copy of this Treaty, duly ratified by His Excellency the Viceroy and Governor-General of India, shall be delivered to the Maharaja on or before the 7th of September, 1870. Signed, sealed, and exchanged at Sealkote on the second day of April, in the year of our Lord one thousand eight hundred and seventy, corresponding with the 22nd day of Bysack Sumbut, 1927.

Signature of the Maharaja of Cashmere.

(Signed) T. D. Forsyth,

Mayo.

This Treaty was ratified by His Excellency the Viceroy and Governor-General of India at Sealkote on the 2nd day of May, 1870.

(Signed) C. U. Aitchison,

Officiating Secretary to the Government of India, Foreign Department.

TREATY BETWEEN RUSSIA AND KASHGAR.

THE FOLLOWING CONDITIONS OF FREE TRADE WERE
PROPOSED AND AGREED UPON BETWEEN GENERAL
AIDE-DE-CAMP VON KAUFMANN AND YAKOOB BEG,
CHIEF OF DJETY-SHAHR.

ARTICLE I.

ALL Russian subjects, of whatsoever religion, shall have
the right to proceed for purposes of trade to Djety-Shahr,
and to all the localities and towns subjected to the Chief
of Djety-Shahr, which they may desire to visit in the
same way as the inhabitants of Djety-Shahr have hitherto
been, and shall be in the future, entitled to prosecute
trade throughout the entire extent of the Russian Empire.
The honourable chief of Djety-Shahr undertakes to keep
a vigilant guard over the complete safety of Russian
subjects, within the limits of his territorial possessions,
and also over that of their caravans, and in general over
everything that may belong to them.

ARTICLE II.

Russian merchants shall be entitled to have caravanserais, in which they alone shall be able to store their
merchandise, in all the towns of Djety-Shahr in which
they may desire to have them. The merchants of Djety-
Shahr shall enjoy the same privilege in the Russian
villages.

Article III.

Russian merchants shall, if they desire it, have the right to have commercial agents (caravanbashis) in all the towns of Djety-Shahr, whose business it is to watch over the regular courts of trade, and over the legal imposition of customs dues. The merchants of Djety-Shahr shall enjoy the same privilege in the towns of Turkestan.

Article IV.

All merchandise transported from Russia to Djety-Shahr, or from that province into Russia, shall be liable to a tax of $2\frac{1}{2}$ per cent. *ad valorem.* In every case this tax shall not exceed the rate of the tax taken from Mussulmans being subject to Djety-Shahr.

Article V.

Russian merchants and their caravans shall be at liberty, with all freedom and security, to traverse the territories of Djety-Shahr in proceeding to countries conterminous with that province. Caravans from Djety-Shahr shall enjoy the same advantages for passing through territories belonging to Russia.

These conditions were sent from Tashkent on the 9th of April, 1872.

General Von Kaufmann I., Governor-General of Turkestan, signed the treaty and attached his seal to it.

In proof of his assent to these conditions, Mahomed Yakoob, Chief of Djety-Shahr, attached his seal to them at Yangy-Shahr, on the 8th of June, 1872.

This treaty was negotiated by Baron Kaulbars.

TREATY BETWEEN ENGLAND AND KASHGAR.

TREATY BETWEEN THE BRITISH GOVERNMENT AND HIS HIGHNESS THE AMEER MAHOMED YAKOOB KHAN, RULER OF THE TERRITORY OF KASHGAR AND YARKAND, HIS HEIRS AND SUCCESSORS, EXECUTED ON THE ONE PART BY THOMAS DOUGLAS FORSYTH, C.B., IN VIRTUE OF FULL POWERS CONFERRED ON HIM IN THAT BEHALF BY HIS EXCELLENCY THE RIGHT HON. THOMAS GEORGE BARING, BARON NORTHBROOK OF STRATTON, AND A BARONET, MEMBER OF THE PRIVY COUNCIL OF HER MOST GRACIOUS MAJESTY THE QUEEN OF GREAT BRITAIN AND IRELAND, GRAND MASTER OF THE MOST EXALTED ORDER OF THE STAR OF INDIA, VICEROY AND GOVERNOR-GENERAL OF INDIA, IN COUNCIL, AND ON THE OTHER PART BY SYUD MAHOMED KHAN TOORAH, MEMBER OF THE 1ST CLASS OF THE ORDER OF MEDJIDIE, &c., IN VIRTUE OF FULL POWERS CONFERRED ON HIM BY HIS HIGHNESS.

WHEREAS it is deemed desirable to confirm and strengthen the good understanding which now subsists between the high contracting parties, and to promote commercial intercourse between their respective subjects, the following Articles have been agreed upon :—

Article I.

The high contracting parties engage that the subjects of each shall be at liberty to enter, reside in, trade with, and pass with their merchandise and property into and through all parts of the dominions of the other; and shall enjoy in such dominions all the privileges and advantages with respect to commerce, protection or otherwise, which are, or may be, accorded to the subjects of such dominions, or to the subjects or citizens of the most favoured nation.

Article II.

Merchants of whatever nationality shall be at liberty to pass from the territories of the one contracting party to the territories of the other, with their merchandise and property at all times, and by any route they please; no restriction shall be placed by either contracting party upon such freedom of transit, unless for urgent political reasons to be previously communicated to the other; and such restriction shall be withdrawn as soon as the necessity for it is over.

Article III.

European British subjects entering the dominions of His Highness the Ameer, for purposes of trade, or otherwise, must be provided with passports certifying to their nationality. Unless provided with such passports they shall not be deemed entitled to the benefit of this treaty.

Article IV.

On goods imported into British India from territories of His Highness the Ameer, by any route over the Himalayan passes, which lie to the south of His Highness's dominions, the British Government engages to levy no import duties. On goods imported from India into the territories of His Highness the Ameer, no import duty exceeding $2\frac{1}{2}$ per cent., *ad valorem*, shall be levied. Goods imported, as above, into the dominions of the contracting parties may, subject only to such excise regulations and duties, and to such municipal or town regulations and duties, as may be applicable to such classes of goods generally, be freely sold by wholesale or retail, and transported from one place to another within British India, and within the dominions of His Highness the Ameer respectively.

Article V.

Merchandise imported from India into the territories of His Highness the Ameer will not be opened for examination, till arrival at the place of consignment. If any disputes should arise as to the value of such goods, the customs officer, or other officer acting on the part of His Highness the Ameer, shall be entitled to demand part of the goods, at the rate of one in forty, in lieu of the payment of duty. If the aforesaid officer should object to levy the duty by taking a portion of the goods, or if the goods should not admit of being so divided, then the point in dispute shall be referred to two competent persons, one chosen by the aforesaid officer, and the other by the importer, and a valuation of the goods shall be made, and if the referees shall differ in opinion, they shall appoint an arbitrator whose decision shall be final, and the duty shall be levied according to the value thus established.

Article VI.

The British Government shall be at liberty to appoint a Representative at the Court of His Highness the

Ameer, and to appoint a Commercial Agent, subordinate to him in any town or place considered suitable within His Highness's territories. His Highness the Ameer shall be at liberty to appoint a Representative with the Viceroy and Governor-General of India, and to station Commercial Agents at any places in British India considered suitable. Such Representatives shall be entitled to the rank and privileges accorded to ambassadors by the law of nations, and the Agents shall be entitled to the privileges of Consuls of the most favoured nation.

Article VII.

British subjects shall be at liberty to purchase, sell, or hire land, or houses, or depôts for merchandise, in the dominions of His Highness the Ameer, and the houses, depôts, or other premises of British subjects, shall not be forcibly entered or searched without the consent of the occupier, unless with the cognizance of the British Representative or Agent, and in presence of a person deputed by him.

Article VIII.

The following arrangements are agreed to for the decision of Civil Suits and Criminal Cases within the territories of His Highness the Ameer, in which British subjects are concerned :—

(*a*.) Civil suits in which both plaintiff and defendant are British subjects, and Criminal Cases in which both prosecutor and accused are British subjects, or in which the accused is a European British subject, mentioned in the Third Article of this Treaty, shall be tried by the British Representative or one of his Agents, in the presence of an Agent appointed by His Highness the Ameer;

(*b.*) Civil suits in which one party is a subject of His Highness the Ameer, and the other party a British subject, shall be tried by the Courts of His Highness, in the presence of the British Representative or one of his Agents, or of a person appointed in that behalf by such Representative or Agent;

(*c.*) Criminal cases in which either prosecutor or accused is a subject of His Highness the Ameer shall, except as above otherwise provided, be tried by the Courts of His Highness in presence of the British Representative, or of one of his Agents, or of a person deputed by the British Representative, or by one of his Agents;

(*d.*) Except as above otherwise provided, Civil and Criminal Cases in which one party is a British subject, and the other the subject of a foreign power, shall, if either of the parties be a Mahomedan, be tried in the Courts of His Highness; if neither party is a Mahomedan, the case may, with consent of the parties, be tried by the British Representative or one of his Agents; in the absence of such consent, by the Courts of His Highness;

(*e.*) In any case disposed of by the Courts of His Highness the Ameer to which a British subject is party, it shall be competent to the British Representative, if he considers that justice has not been done, to represent the matter to His Highness the Ameer, who may cause the case to be re-tried in some other Court, in the presence of the British Representative, or of one of his Agents, or of a person appointed in that behalf by such Representative or Agent.

ARTICLE IX.

The rights and privileges enjoyed within the dominions of His Highness the Ameer by British subjects under the Treaty, shall extend to the subjects of all Princes and States in India in alliance with Her Majesty the Queen; and if, with respect to any such Prince or State, any other provisions relating to this Treaty or to other matters should be considered desirable, they shall be negotiated through the British Government.

ARTICLE X.

Every affidavit and other legal document filed or deposited in any Court established in the respective dominions of the high contracting parties, or in the Court of the Joint Commissioners in Ladakh, may be proved by an authenticated copy, purporting either to be sealed with the seal of the Court to which the original document belongs, or, in the event of such Court having no seal, to be signed by the Judge, or by one of the Judges of the said Court.

ARTICLE XI.

When a British subject dies in the territory of His Highness the Ameer his movable and immovable property situate therein shall be vested in his heir, executor, administrator, or other representative on interest or (in the absence of such representative) in the Representative of the British Government in the aforesaid territory. The person in whom such charge shall be so vested shall satisfy the claims outstanding against the deceased, and shall hold the surplus (if any) for distribution among those interested. The above provisions, *mutatis mutandis*, shall apply to the subjects of His Highness the Ameer, who may die in British India.

Article XII.

If a British subject residing in the territories of His Highness the Ameer becomes unable to pay his debts or fails to pay any debt within a reasonable time after being ordered to do so by any Court of Justice, the creditors of such insolvent shall be paid out of his goods and effects ; but the British Representative shall not refuse his good offices, if needs be, to ascertain if the insolvent has not left in India disposable property which might serve to satisfy the said creditors. The friendly stipulations in the present Article shall be reciprocally observed with regard to His Highness's subjects who trade in India under the protection of the laws.

This treaty having this day been executed in duplicate and confirmed by His Highness the Ameer, one copy shall, for the present, be left in the possession of His Highness, and the other, after confirmation by the Viceroy and Governor-General of India, shall be delivered to His Highness within twelve months in exchange for the copy now retained by His Highness.

Signed and sealed at Kashgar on the second day of February, in the year of our Lord one thousand eight hundred and seventy-four, corresponding with the fifteenth day of Zilhijj, one thousand two hundred and ninety Hijree.

(Signed)   T. Douglas Forsyth,

Envoy and Plenipotentiary.

Whereas a Treaty for strengthening the good understanding that now exists between the British Government and the Ruler of the territory of Kashgar and Yarkand, and for promoting commercial intercourse between the two countries, was agreed to and concluded at Kashgar, on the second day of February, in the year of our Lord eighteen hundred and seventy-four, corresponding with the fifteenth day of Zilhijj, twelve hundred and ninety Hijree, by the respective Plenipotentiaries of the Government of India and of His Highness the Ameer of Kashgar and Yarkand, duly accredited and empowered for that purpose: I, the Right Hon. Thomas George Baring, Baron Northbrook of Stratton, &c., &c., Viceroy and Governor-General of India, do hereby ratify and confirm the Treaty aforesaid.

Given under my hand and seal at Government House, in Calcutta, this thirteenth day of April, in the year of our Lord one thousand eight hundred and seventy-four.

(Signed)   NORTHBROOK.

Seal.

RULES FOR THE GUIDANCE OF THE JOINT COMMISSIONERS APPOINTED FOR THE NEW ROUTE TO EASTERN TURKESTAN.

1. As it is impossible, owing to the character of the climate, to retain the Commissioners throughout the year, the period during which they shall exercise their authority shall be taken to commence on 15th May, and to end on 1st December.

2. During the absence of either Commissioner, cases may be heard and decided by the other Commissioner, subject to appeal to the Joint Commissioners.

3. In the months when the Joint Commissioners are absent, *i.e.* between 1st December and 15th May, all cases which may arise shall be decided by the Wuzeer of Ladakh, subject to appeal to the Joint Commissioners.

4. The Joint Commissioners shall not interfere in cases other than those which affect the development, freedom, and safety of the trade, and the objects for which the Treaty is concluded, and in which one of the parties, or both, are either British subjects, or subjects of a foreign state.

5. In civil disputes the Commissioners shall have power to dispose of all cases, whatever be the value of the property in litigation.

6. When the Commissioners agree, their decision shall be final in all cases. When they are unable to agree, the parties shall have the right of nominating a single arbitrator, and shall bind themselves in writing

to abide by his award. Should the parties not be able to agree upon a single arbitrator, each party shall name one, and the two Commissioners shall name a third, and the decision of the majority of the arbitrators shall be final.

7. In criminal cases the powers of the Commissioners shall be limited to offences such as in British territory would be tried by a subordinate Magistrate of the First Class, and as far as possible the procedure of the Criminal Procedure Code shall be followed. Cases of a more heinous kind should be made over to the Maharaja for trial, if the accused be not a European British subject; in the latter case he should be forwarded to the nearest British Court of competent jurisdiction for trial.

8. All fines levied in criminal cases, and all stamp receipts levied according to the rates in force for civil suits in the Maharaja's dominions, shall be credited to the Cashmere Treasury. Persons sentenced to imprisonment shall, if British subjects, be sent to the nearest British jail. If not British subjects, offenders shall be made over for imprisonment in the Maharaja's jails.

9. The practice of cow-killing is strictly prohibited throughout the jurisdiction of the Maharaja.

10. If any places come within the line of road from which the towns of Leh, &c., are supplied with fuel or wood for building purpose, the Joint Commissioners shall so arrange with the Wuzeer of Ladakh that those supplies are not interfered with.

11. Whatever transactions take place within the limits of the road shall be considered to refer to goods in bond. If a trader opens his load, and disposes of a portion, he shall not be subject to any duty so long as the goods are not taken for consumption into the Maharaja's territory across the line of road. And goods left for any length of time in the line of road subject to the jurisdiction of the Commissioners shall be free.

12. Where a village lies within the jurisdiction of

the Joint Commissioners, then, as regards the collection of revenue, or in any case where there is necessity for the interference of the usual Revenue authorities on matters having no connection with the trade, the Joint Commissioners have no power whatever to interfere; but, to prevent misunderstanding, it is advisable that the Revenue officials should first communicate with the Joint Commissioners before proceeding to take action against any person within their jurisdiction. The Joint Commissioners can then exercise their discretion to deliver up the person sought, or to make a summary inquiry to ascertain whether their interference is necessary or not.

13. The Maharaja agrees to give rupees 5,000 this year for the construction of the road and bridges, and in future years His Highness agrees to give rupees 2,000 per annum for the maintenance of the road and bridges. Similarly for the repairs of serais a sum of rupees 100 per annum for each serai will be given. Should further expenditure be necessary, the Joint Commissioners will submit a special report to the Maharaja, and ask for a special grant. This money will be expended by the Joint Commissioners, who will employ free labour at market rates for this purpose. The officers in Ladakh and in British territory shall be instructed to use their best endeavours to supply labourers on the indent of the Commissioners at market rates. No tolls shall be levied on the bridges on this line of road.

14. As a temporary arrangement, and until the line of road has been demarcated, or till the end of this year, the Joint Commissioners shall exercise the powers described in these rules over the several roads taken by the traders through Ladakh from Lahoul and Spiti.

(Signed)   Maharaja Runbeer Singh.

,,   T. D. Forsyth.

(These rules were agreed upon in 1872, between the Indian Government and Cashmere, for the purpose of promoting trade with Eastern Turkestan and Central Asia, which had been sanctioned by the Treaty of Commerce of 1870.)

A STORY FROM KASHGAR.

MIRZA MULLA RAHMAT, of Kashgar, who arrived at Peshawur lately, on his way to Mecca, has told what he knows about events in Kashgar. The following is his story:—In the month of Jamadi-us-sani 1294 (June-July, 1877), that Mahomed Yakoob Khan, the Badshah of Kashgar, collected a large army to fight the Chinese. He died near the town of Balisan (? Bai), and his army then recognized Hakim Khan Torah as his successor. The mullahs in Kashgar in the meantime appointed Beg Kuli Beg, Yakoob's eldest son, as their Badshah, according to Yakoob's will. Hakim Khan and the army which joined him then came to Aksu, where Beg Kuli Beg also arrived, meaning to capture the place and the person of the usurper. A battle was fought between Kuli Beg and Hakim Khan on the 26th and 27th of Rajab (27th and 28th July, 1877), and Hakim Khan was defeated. Many of the soldiers belonging to Hakim Khan's force fell in the battle, and many others were starved, and some were drowned crossing a river. Hakim Khan then went into Russian territory with 1,000 chosen soldiers. Beg Kuli Beg now seized several towns and returned to Kashgar. In the meantime Naiz Hakim Beg, the Governor of Khoten, re-belled, and Kuli Beg met him in the field, and captured Khoten. The Beg was scarcely a week at that place when he heard that the Chinese had arrived at Aksu and had taken it. An officer (Kho Dalay ?) of the Chinese army who had turned Mahomedan (but subsequently recanted) attacked Yangy Shahr, the capital, and, capturing it, shut himself up there. The town was then besieged by the Governor of Kashgar, and the siege continued for fifty days. Then Kuli Beg came up, and, forcing his entry into the town, took possession of it, and destroyed the fort. But on the 10th of Zillhij (16th of December) a strong Chinese force entered the country, and rapidly reconquered the possessions of the late Yakoob Khan. Beg Kuli Beg then fled with his men to Tashkent, which he reached by Mingyol Osh and Marghilan, and put himself under the protection of the Russian Governor there. Mulla Yunus Jan, the Governor of Yarkand, and his son and brother fell into the hands of Hasan Jan Bai, Ikskal (? Aksakal).

The above is taken from the columns of an Indian journal, and is inserted here for the purpose of showing that the converted Chinese, or Yangy Mussulmans, did revolt from their allegiance to Yakoob Beg the instant a Khitay force appeared in Altyshahr.

INDEX OF SUBJECTS.